HELLCAT

A Joe Sterner Mystery

J. Alan Hostetter

HELLCAT

For Christy

1.

THREE WEEKS BEFORE OPENING DAY

Cat True was bowhunting whitetail high up Rattlesnake Ridge, though the property was posted and she was trespassing. There was a big buck moving back and forth along the steep slope two hundred yards below the crest, between the Pennsylvania state forest where she was allowed and the neighboring private land where she wasn't, and she found the temptation to go after him irresistible.

Sign was everywhere. Among the laurel and loblolly pine were handfuls of raisin-like scat. Scrapes on the forest floor, hoof-dug craters with the pungent odor of doe urine on bare dirt, aroused and alerted him that a hot doe was nearby. He left fresh bark rubs on saplings and small trees to show off his virility. He'd rubbed raw an eight-inch maple trunk next to the trail, scratching off the summer's itchy felt to smooth his bone-hard tines.

He must be a monster. Even fully gutted, it would be hell dragging him back through the public land to her pickup along the road, but it was mostly downhill, and she figured it would be well worth it to help feed her and her mother through the winter. And her mother Sally, a half-blooded Catoosa from Tulsa, coveted the big racks as much as the local white men.

Cat climbed a tractor trailer-sized granite outcropping above the deer trail and crouched to study the terrain, a serene slope of oak and maple skeletons and wild brush swallowing severed limbs and lichen-covered rocks, everything blanketed in dead leaves. She listened intently to the chatter of the squirrels objecting to her presence, the "caw, caw, caw" of an equally perturbed passing crow, the screech of a suspicious circling hawk, the "knock, knock, knock" of an oblivious far-off woodpecker.

As she did at the start of every hunt, she had begun her day before dawn with a leaf bath upon entering the woods, a ritual as sacred for her as a devout Catholic dabbing holy water and making the sign of the cross before entering the sanctuary. She rolled back and forth on the forest floor, rubbing the fragrant brittle leaves into the fabric of her clothes and hair and under her arms. It was an old Indian trick her mother had taught her, imparted generation to generation from those whose very survival depended on their hunting expertise, camouflaging her scent from the deer whose sight and hearing were no better than human, but whose sense of smell was extraordinary. Every advantage counted, but for Cat it was something more. It was a way to formally turn her back on the grim world of men and machines and quiet her mind before approaching nature's holy altar.

She wore faded Levis, worn high-top Keds and a tree bark camouflaged vest over a tight-fitting, pine-colored, hooded sweatshirt. The insulated vest had long sleeves that detached with zippers. She'd removed them when the morning frost first melted and she could no longer see her breath. They were stuffed in an inside pocket in the lining at the small of her back along with her rarely-used bow counterweight. Her clothes were old and torn, repaired with duct tape and sewing thread, but clean, washed with odorless detergent, air-dried on a clothesline deep in the woods far from the human smells of home.

She traveled light and carried only what she needed. A recycled water bottle filled from a mountain stream, a USMC Ka-Bar Fighting Knife sheathed on her leather belt, a zipper-lock freezer bag, a ten-foot length of number eight sash cord and her Pennsylvania resident hunting license. She didn't need a compass or a watch. She could read the sun.

Careful to make no noise, she was a good hunter--patient, quiet and able to keep still for long periods--though her mother's ancestors back in Oklahoma would surely have laughed at her fancy bow, an Oneida Strike Eagle, once the Cadillac of compounds, an extravagant gift from an old boyfriend. She'd stripped it down, eliminating the gaudy sight and onboard quiver to lighten the weight, but there was no denying the distinctive modern design, wicked in its lethal beauty. When she wasn't hunting, she liked showing it off, hanging it face down on the rifle rack behind the seat of her beat-up pickup, where some hunters showed off their guns.

She didn't like guns. They were heavy and noisy. The gunpowder stank, as did the men who carried them, more often than not. They could shoot further, but not always more accurately. She liked the stealth of her bow. She once made a heart shot on a six-point not fifty yards behind the back of a muzzle-loader in his tree stand, dressed it and dragged it off under his very nose and the fool was never the wiser. She was happy to take this prize buck now, three weeks before rifle season opened and the real shooting started, when local hunters took off work, schools shut down for the day and out-of-staters invaded. Up from Virginia, Maryland and D.C., in from Ohio, down from New York, over from Jersey. They'd fill the local

motels and lodges and taverns. The countryside would crackle and echo
with high-powered rifle shot. Deer carcasses became automotive hood and
roof ornaments. And gun shop owners, hardware store clerks, butchers and
taxidermists would keep busy through Christmas.

She carried mail-order aluminum arrows in a traditional buckskin
quiver slung over her shoulder, a clearance item from a closing hardware
store. The plastic tail of each arrow was specially marked with Native
American glyphs to distinguish it from the others. She liked to think that
they each had a unique personality. They were like her children. She loved
them all, but treated each differently, since some invariably flew farther and
straighter than others. Only the favored ones were awarded expensive steel
razor tips. The others merited mere lead practice tips.

Suddenly she heard dry leaves rustle in a thicket of grape vines forty
yards down the trail to her left. It could have been a gray squirrel or a wild
turkey, but it could have been him, too. Her favorite arrow was ready to fly,
poised astride the rest, nock snapped onto the bowstring, glove trigger
release locked beneath the nock. Despite the quickening of her pulse, the
only movement she made was an imperceptibly slow turn of the head.

It was cagey, whatever it was, and it would not leave the tangled
thicket before pausing for long periods to scan for danger. That's what's
kept him alive this long.

She waited, listening for fifteen minutes without moving. She didn't
raise the bow when he, with his ten-point rack, eased cautiously from the
knotted brambles, taking a few timid steps, swiveling his head in every
direction, turning his muzzle up into the breeze. He was mature, at least
five years old, his coat a grayish brown, with darker markings, allowing him
to blend in easily with his surroundings. His rack was dark, too, thick and
magnificent, nourished by a steady diet of acorns. There had been no late
frosts last spring, and the oak trees had covered the floor with their bounty,
providing a hearty diet. It was hard to distinguish him from the landscape at
all, except when he moved. He eased into the clear, his neck swollen with
pride, displaying a good hundred and eighty pounds of muscled
magnificence and regal countenance.

It was a shame to kill him, but she would apologize later, as she
always did, just after cutting his jugular and before dressing him. As she
waited for him to bleed out, she would say a prayer and explain to him in
hushed tones how sorry she was. She'd promise to remember him at every
meal and honor his antlers by displaying them proudly in her home. She
would then thank him and tell him what a blessing his meat was to her and

her family, and wish him well in his journey to the next world. And then she would turn him up and gut him.

It was customary among her ancestors to cut out the beating heart first and eat it whole, believing as they did that you could absorb the soul and strength of the animal, taking into you its spirit to be a part of your own forever. She did not follow this tradition exactly, but brought along the plastic bag to salvage the stilled heart and boil it later for the evening meal. Still, sometimes she could not resist slicing off a small sliver of the red raw muscle and placing it on her tongue like a communion wafer.

Adrenaline accelerated her heart, triggered by the excited anticipation of the kill and memories of ancestral hunts eons before she was born, memories lying dormant deep in every hunter's primitive brain until the time came to kill again. The elation was difficult to contain, but still she did not raise her bow.

She salivated over the cuts of meat he would provide. Succulent roasts from his thick neck, basted twice a day in maple syrup in the fridge for three days, then slow-baked in their wood oven. Juicy steaks from his loin, grilled with a little salt and pepper. Tasty chops, marinated in wine and fried up with soy sauce. The rest cut into cubes and thrown into a vegetable stew or ground up and mixed with fatty pork for burgers and meatballs or baked in a meatloaf with eggs, onions and bread crumbs.

The wind shifted. She noticed a strand of her long black hair blowing in his direction. She watched him turn his nose up again to sniff and knew she had only this one chance before he detected her.

He moved. She followed, and in one smooth motion, drew up and pulled back, touched the kisser button to the side of her lips, aimed and trigger-released. The soft twang of the bowstring was muffled by splaying cattail silencers, deer hide threads tied above and below, to absorb the vibration and quiet the shot. A sapling she hadn't noticed eight feet in front of him shivered as the razor tip was deflected from its path through his heart and instead punctured his lung and stopped short at a rib bone on the far side, not passing through as it should have. He fell over backwards, wide-eyed with surprise, as if sucker-punched from a barstool, then jumped to his feet, tearing off down through the woods without so much as a snort.

Motherfucker. Her facial expression contorted in disappointment. A fatal shot, to be sure, but hardly the perfect kill. His meat would not be quite so tender or sweet, and now she would have to earn her reward by tracking him across the private land at the risk of arrest and a fine. At least he ran in the general direction of her pickup, making the drag back through the woods a mite shorter.

Fifteen minutes later, she set out on his blood trail. She'd given him plenty of time to run and stop, feel safe, lie down to rest, and then slide into unconsciousness and die. He had sprinted at first. There was only a single drop every twenty yards or so. But his hooves had stirred the leaves in his wake and the crimson wetness from the lung shot shone like a bright signpost against the dull brown oak leaf carpet.

As the steep incline angled to a tamer downward slant, she noticed the clearing on a plateau below and stopped to scan the woods for trouble. She knew there was a hunter's hut there, a small old chicken coop with four walls, a tin roof, no door and two open portals where a window and a hatch had been knocked out. There might well be a hunter inside bow-hunting or readying himself for the muzzle-loading season, which was to start next week. Bad enough she'd had to track her prize, but getting busted for poaching would really ruin the day. She'd claim the shot was made on the public land--which wasn't far from the truth--and she just might get away with it. But it depended on who caught her. As was their legal right, property owners sometimes seized deer killed by trespassers. Fortunately, it was a Monday, and odds were the fools were all at work.

She continued to track him, turning now northeast, moving parallel to the ridge back towards the state forest. The blood trail was more evident here, drops every four yards, which meant the buck had slowed to a trot. Then he turned downhill again. She followed. He must be headed to water. He couldn't be far now. There would be a spring sprouting up from underground somewhere below down in the hollow. She paused and looked up again, scanning the woods and the clearing.

The chicken coop stood in the middle of a gently sloping vacant field of thigh-high grass. There were a few dying apple trees planted long ago to attract the deer and the ruined stone foundations of a long-gone farmhouse. It was a small unpainted structure, crudely-milled, knotty one-by-six planks overlapping a two-by-four frame, abandoned decades ago, a monument to a failed human effort to live off the land and, as such, now ignored and unappreciated. Until a torrential wind or a chance lightning strike destroyed it, it served no other purpose than to shield the seasonal hunter from the elements.

That's when she noticed it, distinct in the morning sunshine. Something red lay on the south-facing doorstep of the hut. Dark red, like blood. Not blood from a lung shot, but darker, from the heart. She squinted harder. More like the plastic red tail of a green-stemmed aluminum arrow not unlike her own. It was no arrow, though. It was something else laid upon the shed step. Something even more incongruous out here in the middle of nowhere, so far from the conventions of modern civilization. It was a freshly-cut, long-stemmed red rose.

Cat could contrive no purpose, reason or accident why such a flower should be where it didn't belong. Curious, she moved closer to investigate. She scanned the clearing and the woods around the perimeter again and again. No trucks. No ATV three- or four-wheelers. No dirt bikes. No tire tracks of any kind. Weird. Why would anyone bring a lovely long-stemmed rose deep into the woods during bowhunting season? It was hardly a place for romance.

Even as she moved into the clearing and made her approach, she felt something was wrong. But curiosity got the better of her. The curiosity of a cat. She remembered how an old lover teased her about her name, in his own infantile--though quite charming--way. In his case, satisfaction had not brought *him* back.

She stepped warily and stopped short of the rose, half-expecting some fool to leap out of the hut to yell, *Surprise!* But everywhere was quiet and still but for the gentle breezes rustling through the pines and grasses. Above her, billowing white clouds floated across the deep blue heavens. She knew with all her highly-tuned senses that she was alone out here. And yet--

She had never dared to venture this far into the clearing before and now noticed an old dirt road winding up from the woods below and circling around the hut, leading nowhere. Wild grasses between the tracks nearly erased them.

She made a cautious approach toward the doorstep to examine the rose close-up. It was indeed a magnificent specimen, beads of dew glistening on the vein-branched, red-velvety petals blossoming in the sunlight.

And then she looked inside, peering into the dark, into the shadows. A chill ran through her soul. Her eyes widened at the horror of it. Goose bumps leapt up and down her arms and across the back of her neck. Suddenly the sweet solitude of her morning's hunt turned to absolute terror at being totally alone in the wilderness in the season of death. If this was somebody's idea of a scarecrow to keep poachers away, it was a good one, she thought.

And ran.

2.

SIXTEEN DAYS BEFORE OPENING DAY

Sheriff Vernon Guise's five-year-old Explorer heaved and bucked like a rodeo bull as it climbed a deep stretch of rugged logging road in low gear, four-wheel drive refusing to surrender to the deep ruts made by years of flood erosion and poor maintenance. Inside, the Sheriff, a heavyset man of sixty, with a pink complexion, the waning testosterone of a teenage star athlete in middle age and a bad comb-over, wiped his runny nose with a red handkerchief. His passenger had a hard time seeing the man past the cliché, with the typical ego of a lifelong bourgeois bureaucrat who called everybody by their first name but was addressed only by his title, who never bothered to look both ways crossing busy intersections in his hometown, relying instead on his status for protection and faith that no one possessed the effrontery to run him over, an attitude that had proven justified, so far.

The Sheriff, in turn, grunted amusement at his passenger, a skinny, somber, some kind of wannabe artiste twenty years his junior, clutching a silver camera case to absorb the shock. The passenger's head bounced off the ceiling, his elbow smashed against the side door, his knees banged against the dash, but that sacred camera case of his remained well-protected. Since when did Pennsylvania State Police detectives start wearing black berets turned backwards and sweatshirts celebrating the Negro Leagues of baseball under a brown leather bomber jacket? If he wasn't going to wear a uniform, the least he could do was wear a proper white shirt and tie, as the Sheriff did himself, Saturday or not. And at least he could come to work clean-shaven. And what was up with that brown mop of hair? Didn't he know what a comb was for?

"I hope your deputy knows how to preserve the scene," Joe Sterner said soberly to his host without looking at him, annoyed to be the object of amusement. The detective sensed the Sheriff saw him as a city-slicker, which for someone who once lived and studied in New York City was accurate enough.

 The truth was, the Sheriff thought Sterner showed about as much personality as a dime-store mannequin, par for the course when it came to the impersonal Smokeys who routinely looked down on local lawmen. The Sheriff had narrowed his eyes, too, at all the gear Sterner transferred from the trunk of his issue Crown Victoria to the Sheriff's SUV a half-hour before. A fingerprint kit, a body bag, evidence processing equipment, a notebook computer, a haz/mat body suit, for crying out loud.

 "I don't think there'll be too many civilian gawkers, if that's what you're worried about," Sheriff Guise replied. "It's a pretty remote area."

 "I mean, I hope he doesn't contaminate the evidence himself." Sterner looked over at him with piercing gray eyes that suggested he'd seen too much and slept too little. A permanent cleft in Sterner's brow made him look worried for losing faith in human nature.

 Annoyed by the implied criticism of his department, the Sheriff said through gritted teeth, "Deputy Kendalhart knows his job, detective. He may be a dumb little shit, but I trained him not to mess with anything till those smarter than him can have a go at evidence, and that includes just about everybody else in law enforcement," and snorted back a raspy bovine sinus-full, gargled up one juicy pumpkin ball of phlegm and let fly the disgusting discharge out most of his half-wound-down window, no country bumpkin, he. "Hockadooner," he exclaimed. In his rearview, he spied Trooper Hollings following in his own SUV and wondered why in hell the damned Smokeys didn't ride together, for all the lack of conversation.

 "Well, he did the right thing calling us in," Sterner said.

 "Not if this is just some prank, he didn't. Halloween was just two weeks back. Warren wouldn't know what was real or wasn't. You fellers would sure be wasting your time if all this is just the work of some teenager with a twisted sense of humor."

 "Look, I don't want to step on anybody's toes here, Sheriff, but strictly speaking, this is our jurisdiction."

 "Except you boys didn't know the way, did you? We're the one's got the call. This is my county. Folks elected me to know what's going on." And then he muttered under his breath, "If I hadn't had my annual physical this a.m. with Doc Johnson sticking his greasy finger up my A-hole, I'd've already been up here and gone already."

 "So if it turns out to be a prank, that's one thing. If it's something else, you just saved yourself a round trip down the mountain to fetch me. Anyway, we're all on the same team, aren't we?"

They were on level terrain now, the ride almost smooth. Guise didn't care much for the word *fetch* and displayed his irritation by grinding his gearshift from four-wheel low to high and floored the gas pedal, accelerating over the potholed path, grinding leaves, rocks and fallen branches under his Firestones, Trooper Hollings tight on his tail.

Sterner's cell rang, the ring tone an old-fashioned telephone. He pulled it out of his jacket pocket to check caller ID, and an unexpected smile blossomed across his face.

"Hey, Pookie, how are you?" His expression and tender tone seemed so completely different--that is to say, human--the Sheriff imagined for a moment a new passenger had climbed into the cab when he wasn't looking.

"What are you doing, Daddy?" she said.

"Daddy's working."

"Putting away the bad guys?" Sterner laughed. This was his explanation to her of his job, but it sounded funny coming from a toddler.

"That's right."

*"Are you--*crackle, crackle--*morrow?"*

"Say that again. You're breaking up." Sterner heard only static. "I'll see you tomorrow. Listen, Daddy's working, honey." There was a garbled response amid more crackling static. "Daddy's in a bad cell phone area. What did you say? Can you put Mommy on? Hello? Hello?"

Sterner frowned, checking the reception bars on his Nokia. It switched between one and none. He sighed and put it back in his inside jacket pocket.

"Boy or girl?" the Sheriff said in a softer tone with a slight smile.

"Girl, three and a half, actually my ex-stepdaughter. Her real father's out of the picture. Her mother and I divorced last year," Sterner said.

"Sorry to hear that," the Sheriff said. "Pitfalls of the job. Must be tough."

"We all get along a lot better since I moved out." Sterner wanted to change the subject. "What do you know about this property?" he said.

Finally.

"Hunted up here once. It's owned by a local hunt club, I know them all. Roy Fries is a member, he's the one called it in. Went to high school together back in the Stone Age. There was a farm up here some eighty years back but there was a fire and the family pulled up stakes. Land ain't worth much. Lumber company harvested some tracts ten, twenty years back. It's next to the Mary Jenison State Forest which is public, and anybody could've come onto the property. Game warden nails poachers out here every now and then. Property line ends at the top of the ridge where the county line runs. Not to point fingers, but over there in Burnside County they got all kinds of weirdoes and troublemakers. You got your backwoods hermit pervs and your hippie pot farmers and a biker gang that runs methamphetamine up and down the valley in three states. I even hear they got a witch's coven over there, I shit you not. I wouldn't put a stunt like this past any of em."

"If it is a stunt," Sterner said.

"Yeah. If."

———————

Doolittle County Deputy Warren Kendalhart's Explorer and Roy Fries' green Wagoneer were parked in the grass off to the side of the hut. Warren was casually gossiping with Fries but stiffened when Sheriff Guise and Sterner pulled up. He had put up crime scene tape and the Sheriff now frowned as he wound down his window.

"Warren, why in hell would you waste good crime scene tape like that?"

"Looks like a crime scene to me, Sheriff."

"Have you got a body? A murder scene? No. All you've got is a bunch of bones, son. If that."

The deputy chewed his lip. He was younger than Sterner and handsome in his immaculate deputy uniform, creased to perfection, though his drooping posture made him look all of sixteen years old. Hollings, by contrast, stepped out of his SUV and approached, nodding gravely at the deputy and the civilian. He was twenty-six years old and two hundred pounds of Olympian determination, more robot than human, as he coolly circled around behind to the passenger side of the Sheriff's vehicle to attend to his superior.

"Afternoon, Sheriff," said Fries with a cordial salute.

"Roy," the Sheriff nodded, threw his shift into park and then pointed his thumb at the Smokeys. "Detective Joe Sterner from Harrisburg, Trooper Hollings from the local barracks." Hollings tipped his hat but offered nothing more.

Ignoring the lot of them, Sterner was rapidly assembling his Cyber-shot from the aluminum case, screwing in the extender with the flash attachment, plugging in the connecting cable and hanging the strap around his neck. As the three local men and the trooper looked on in silence, he donned white plastic gloves, booties over his black Van sneakers and, in place of the beret, a hair cover that made him look like a food service worker. He climbed out and approached the crime scene tape, scrutinizing the ground for trace evidence, Hollings in his wake like a respectful manservant awaiting instruction. *Click!* Sterner captured a shot of the hut and made his way to the dried flower stem at the doorstep with a single wilted dark rose petal. *Click!* It wasn't the sound of an actual shutter, but a digital recording generated by the camera to simulate one. High above them, a turkey buzzard circled the scene. *Click!*

Sheriff Guise heaved a sigh, locked his brake and turned off his engine. He climbed out of his vehicle, hesitated and grimaced to break wind, and then followed Sterner's path to the doorway, stuffing his hands into his oversized Carhartt jacket to keep them warm. The deputy followed, sharing smirks with Fries.

The hut interior was an unfinished shell of a room with a sturdy tin roof, but cracks between the open door and windows on either side allowed the wind to blow through freely. It was empty but for its occupant, a human skeleton, the bones meticulously arranged as if attached and intact. The bones looked like they'd been recently excavated and washed clean. The ivory-colored foot, leg and hip bones were laid out neatly on the floor, the ribcage and upper arm bones leaning against the back wall. The skull rested atop the long stack of vertebra and ribcage held together by mummified tendons, the lower jaw hanging crookedly beneath. It grinned a twisted, awful eternal grin, and strewn across the tibia leg bones lay a bouquet of wilted long-stemmed roses.

A cold breeze suddenly blew through the doorway, whipping up the dried rose petals scattered across the floor and funneling them into the air, depositing several on the rib cage.

Human remains were one thing, but there was something positively chilling about the way these bones had been displayed. There was a calculated effort to shock, and it did. It was a macabre image from a nightmare, as if the skeleton was lounging casually on the floor awaiting her suitor's imminent return for a little post-prom hanky panky. The pelvis bone and the smooth contours of the skull indicated it was female.

More rattled than he should be, Sterner swallowed hard, hoping the others did not notice. *Click!* He captured the image before realizing he hadn't switched on his flash, erased it and quickly made the correction. *Flash-Click!*

Sheriff Guise came up behind him and wiped his runny nose with his handkerchief.

"You got a cold, Sheriff?" Fries said.

"Allergies," the Sheriff said quietly, snorted up another lugey and spat it out behind him. "Hockadooner," he exclaimed. "This how you found it?"

"Why, yeah, well, uh, I come up here this morning to check on the hut like I do every year," Fries explained. "Muzzle-loading starts Monday. I hike up before sun-up and spend the day. I don't like surprises, like if some skunk's moved in or a bear's taken a big old crap. So, like today, I always drive up Saturday before to clean it out. I almost shit my pants when I got a gander inside."

"Anybody you know might want to play a practical joke on you, Roy?"

"No. Positively not. You know our members. We take the hunt serious."

"How about trouble with neighbors?" Sheriff Guise said.

"We get along good with everybody."

"What about poachers?" Kendalhart interjected.

"Warren," the Sheriff said, sighed, irritated by the interruption, "why don't you go survey the perimeter, see what you can find. I don't like that buzzard overhead. Means something meaty's dead someplace."

"Yessir." The deputy moved off with a sigh.

"Got problems with poachers, do you?" the Sheriff said.

"Well, yeah, like I told Warren, we've had our run-ins. State forest is just a few hundred yards off," Fries nodded to the northeast. "Property line's well marked between us and them. Truth is, I count on their pressure to drive them bucks up my way. But we give trespassers what-for when they stray over this far. Nobody ever got so pissed off they'd do something like this to get back at us, though, I don't think."

Sterner was alone inside shooting closer shots of the bones now. *Flash-Click! Flash-Click!* They watched him work.

"You use special film in that camera?" Fries asked finally.

"Digital, no film," Sterner said without breaking concentration. He then added, "Ten-point-three mega-pixels with a two-gig memory stick. Eighty shots RAW before I have to download to the laptop." He spotted a small black fiber wedged in a floorboard splinter and pulled a six-inch plastic ruler from an inside jacket pocket and laid it down next to it. *Flash-Click!*

Fries grunted, amused. "Everything's digital nowadays, huh, Sheriff? My daughter's got herself a digital TV. Looks the same as the old one. Just costs more."

Sterner set his camera aside on the open window sill and tweezered the fiber into a tiny plastic baggie. He spotted a tiny hair close by--a short rust-colored hair--it, too, wedged under a splinter. He repeated the procedure with the ruler--*Flash-Click!*--and bagged it, as well.

"Detective Sterner says he can *e-mail* his pictures directly to the crime lab in Harrisburg on his laptop computer."

"All the way to Harrisburg, ain't that something." Fries shook his head.

"That's if I can get a cell signal," Sterner said and pulled out his Nokia to check. AT&T showed him no bars. "Which I can't here."

"I must be living in the wrong century. My son-in-law offered to give me a computer but I don't want one. The girl who does our billing said she'd show me how to use it, but I said, 'no thank you.' Life's complicated enough."

Sterner could not fathom such an attitude and paused to take a good look at Rip Van Winkel. Fries was trim, with white temples and bushy eyebrows to match, dressed in hunting clothes that fit him well and looked like they came straight out of the Cabela's catalogue. Sterner took him to be a doctor or a lawyer.

"What do you do for a living, Roy?" Sterner said.

"I have a dental practice in Samaritan."

The Sheriff yawned, already bored with the case. "Gets me, Roy, is they used to sell station wagons. Then they changed the back doors and became hatch-backs. Then they added a foot to the roof and made mini-vans. Then they beefed up the engines and jacked up the suspension, and that gets you a *sports utility vehicle.* When you get right down to it, though, it ain't nothing but a station wagon. Just costs more."

Fries chuckled. "Ain't that the truth!"

Distracted, Sterner glanced over trying to figure out if the Sheriff was somehow impugning his methods, implying that recent strides in forensic science were so much bullshit. They were staring at him. He checked their hands for a Mason jar of hooch, then their feet for the proverbial sleeping hound dog under the wood stove, sighed, and turned back, concentrating on the scene.

The vertebra should not logically support the weight of the skull, he decided. He lightly took hold of the sides of the cranium with the tips of his middle fingers and lifted it away from the wall. It caught on something and then wriggled free, the tenuously hanging jaw bone crookedly counter-swaying against his movements. The skull had been hung on a bent, rusted four-penny nail protruding from the wall, the head of which caught the top edge of one of two small but decidedly *unnatural* holes in the occipital bone.

"Hello," Sterner said.

His change in tone immediately piqued Sheriff Guise's interest. He withdrew his hands from his pockets. "What?"

Sterner furrowed his brow. "Any homicides around here twenty, thirty years ago, the victim a woman approximately five feet tall, shot twice in the back of the head?"

The Sheriff scanned his memory and said carefully, "Not that I know of."

"I suggest you check the local cemeteries for any disturbed graves. Sheriff, I think we're looking at a homicide here."

"Shit."

"*Sheriff! I got something here you should see.*"

It was Deputy Kendalhart.

By the time Sterner caught up to them a few minutes later, they were all standing over the emaciated carcass of a ten-point buck, dead several days, ravaged by maggots and worked over by any number of carnivorous forest creatures.

"That's a hell of a buck," Sterner said.

"That's exactly what I just said," Fries said. "Goddamn poachers. Bad enough they trespass our land and shoot the nicest buck of the season but to leave it here to rot is a fucking sin. Get a load of that rack."

"It could've been wounded on the public land and come here to die," Kendalhart said.

"Or whoever shot it tracked it here and saw something scared them off," Sheriff Guise said looking over his shoulder back at the hut.

"Would you be able to trace that arrow, detective?" Fries said to Sterner.

"I don't know. I could try to dust it for prints but..." Sterner said shrugging.

There were three plastic feather guides on the tail. Two were green. The third was yellow. Sterner noted two parallel squiggles marked on the yellow guide with a felt tip pen.

"Don't have to," Sheriff Guise said. "Belongs to Cat True."

———————

Sally Dancing Feather True watched her daughter primp in front of the bathroom mirror, amused, somewhat envious of her beauty, but proud, too, and said, "When are you going to bring him home so I can meet him?"

"Who?" Cat said, not really listening as she quickly brushed her silky, straight hair and applied a natural color lipstick, wary of smudges.

"Whoever you're seeing," Sally said.

"What are you talking about? I'm not seeing anyone." Cat frowned at her mother. Sally tilted her head and arched an eyebrow in response. Cat tossed her lipstick into her green cloth handbag perched on the toilet tank with more force than was necessary to telegraph her irritation, and checked her teeth. "Seriously. I'm not. I always put on makeup for my night job, you know that. I'm the first person the customers see when they walk through the door. I have to look halfway presentable, don't I?" Cat stepped back to review her appearance from various angles, deeming it acceptable. She wore tight black jeans, a long-sleeved oversized black tee, black work boots and a dab of gift perfume on either side of her neck. No jewelry, just attitude.

"You can't tell me Rosita's is open till four in the morning."

"I hung out with Delbert's band last night at the bar after closing, I told you. They all have girlfriends and wives. You know Shirley and Rita. It doesn't mean I'm shacking up."

"Okay," Sally said, appearing to buy her daughter's explanation, but not really. She wandered back to the kitchen.

Cat rolled her eyes and sighed, ill prepared for a fight. No matter how old she got, her mother always made her feel like she was sixteen. It was infuriating. "I'm late. Don't wait up," she said, grabbed her bag, swiped the furry underbelly of Mister Jeepers, her mother's sleeping gray tabby, sprawled out upside down across the kitchen table like a rack of meat on a platter. He jerked awake, then lay back, oblivious.

"Drive carefully," Sally called out, watching Cat grab her leather jacket off the hook in the mud room without even slowing down on her way outside to her pickup. But as usual, Cat ignored her.

Sally adjusted her moth-eaten woolen shawl as she sat down at the kitchen table to scrutinize discount coupons from competing supermarket periodicals, cutting out the good ones with a pair of sewing scissors. She was a heavyset woman with high cheek bones and long gray hair pulled back in a pony tail. She wore a jogging suit of mismatched colors, a pastel maroon sweatshirt with green sweatpants, thick socks and bedroom slippers. As a young woman barely out of her teens, she had been swept off her feet by a dashing, honorably-discharged Green Beret, rescued from an exhausting, dead-end job behind the cash register at a Tulsa diner and transplanted to the backwoods of Pennsylvania. A decade later, she was a single parent raising an eight-year-old, time robbing her of her bathing beauty figure, and today, unemployed and disinterested in the outside world, she looked and acted older than her fifty-eight years.

She knew Cat was a grown woman and needed her privacy, but she also knew her daughter still sometimes lied to her about her activities. She worried Cat might be drawn into some abusive affair--or worse, prostitution--by some of the lowlifes who frequented Rosita's, or become an alcoholic like Sally's father, who drank himself to death when she was twelve, or a drug addict like her cousin Kenny, who ODed two weeks shy of his nineteenth birthday. Cat *did* drink too much. There were nights when her daughter did not return home until well after daylight. Sally could only hope no harm would come to her, since efforts to discuss the problem fell on deaf ears. Things were not always peaceful living under the same roof, but the truth was, she truly loved her daughter and welcomed her company after her divorce forced her back home. Cat brought in needed income and made Sally feel less lonely. She knew it could not last. Sally wanted grandchildren, and the only way she'd get some was to give her daughter some space.

When the phone rang, it surprised her. It wasn't often anyone called after dark. Those who knew her were well aware Sally was an early riser, often in bed by seven, up at four.

"Hello?" Sally answered.

"*Sally, it's Vern,*" the Sheriff said gruffly. "*Let me talk to Cat.*"

"She left for work. You just missed her."

He sighed. "*All right, look, when she gets home you tell her I want her in my office Monday morning nine a.m. sharp, no excuses. Got that?*" It wasn't like him to be brusque with her. It must be serious.

"What's this about?"

"*Never you mind. You just tell her the State Police want her to answer some questions. I pulled some strings and she'll be talking to me, not them, but they'll be listening. Just you make sure she's here.*"

"Okay. I will."

"*Thank you.*" He hung up the phone. Not even a "Goodbye."

As Sally lowered the receiver into the cradle, her knees went weak. She opened the fire door on the woodstove with a rag and poked the embers, then sat back down in her chair, allowing her imagination to run wild. She listed the scenarios that might prompt such a strange call. The State Police? Had Cat actually succumbed to prostitution, as Sally feared? Had she beaten someone, robbed them? Or was it something else? Stealing from her employer? Money? Drugs? She'd once stolen drugs from Helen Dietz. Could she be dealing at Rosita's? Maybe she side-swiped somebody with her truck. A hit and run? Or did this have something to do with the thing Sally vowed never to think about? She grew uneasy.

It was difficult to concentrate on the coupons. The wind picked up outside, and she heard the cabin roof creak and moan and whistle as the gusts ebbed and flowed.

And then came the voices again. Whispering at first. At times, soft-spoken words, almost intelligible. Almost. Up in the attic. Below the floorboards. Out in the mud room. Back in Cat's room. Back in her own.

"Don't think I can't hear you," she offered loudly. "Don't think I don't know you're there." And she got up a few times to investigate, but there was never anyone there.

Oh, they were always good at hiding from her, spying on her from the trees when she chopped firewood in the backyard, listening in on all her phone calls, following her to the store, passing her car when she slowed down to get a better look at them, scaring her by jumping out of doorways as she walked down the sidewalks in town, laughing in her face. She'd confronted them on occasion, but they pretended she was mistaken or crazy or just shrugged, as if not understanding or not caring. They were clever, yes, they were. She'd asked them who they were and what they wanted, other than to harass her, and they never, ever gave her a straight answer.

But she knew. Secretly, she had always known. Of course she did. They were working for Cat's father, who was mixed up with the Mob, involved in CIA conspiracies, government corruption, corporate world domination, international assassinations and all manner of political intrigues. They hid miniature microphones and cameras all over the property, inside and outside the house, in her car. They transmitted to satellites in space. They were keeping track of her every movement, where she went, who she saw, making sure she didn't spill the beans about what she knew. Because she knew way too much. Because she was a liability.

"Why are you doing this to me?" she said. The voices quieted for a time, as they always did when she challenged them, no doubt waiting for instructions from their supervisors, but then continued, whispering quietly again, then louder, reporting on her movements, cataloguing everything she did and said for review later by the higher-ups, moment after moment, on and on, for minutes, hours, days, weeks, months, years.

She went through the motions of going to bed, undressing and putting on long underwear and a nightgown, pretending not to hear them, pretending it didn't matter, anymore, because she was so used to it by now. What were they saying exactly? Why couldn't she understand their exact words? Who were they talking to, exactly? How many of them were there? How much were they being paid? Why would anyone spend so much money on little, old Sally? If they paid her a tenth of what this surveillance must be costing, she'd be rich. They grew quiet for a time as she climbed under the blankets and comforter, and lay perfectly still, Mister Jeepers curled up between her feet. But then they grew loud again, more intense, more insistent. They were outside her window now arguing. Grunting, growling at each other, digging in the ground, probably planting another transmitter or replacing one that went bad. In the backyard. Right now!

She jumped out of bed, sending Mister Jeepers out of the room, and reached for the .32 Winchester Special she kept fully loaded in the back corner of the closet. A nice, loud warning shot over their heads might shut them up and scare them off. For awhile, at least. So she could get some sleep. She went to the window, pushed aside the curtains and peered out, but saw nothing. She set down the rifle and pushed up the lower window glass panel and stuck her bare head out into the cold darkness, shivering. There was nothing anywhere.

And then there was something! A silhouette. She squinted hard into the dappled moonlight of prancing shadows. And saw it! A dark, squat figure, caught out in the open at the compost pile, hoping stillness would render him invisible. She grabbed her rifle and stuck the barrel out the window to sight in the mysterious figure. She fired high, the blast deafening as the retort crackled around the wooden walls of her room and echoed around the hollow outside. She quickly reloaded, cocking the handle that ejected a smoking shell and breached a fresh round. She would show them who they were dealing with. He had ducked after the round passed over his head by inches, but now took off running on all fours with everything he had, into the dark scrub of the canopied forest, away and gone, a three-hundred pound black bear.

3.

FIFTEEN DAYS BEFORE OPENING DAY

A complete stranger opened Emily's front door the next morning, and for a second Sterner thought he'd pulled up to the wrong house. He quickly checked his bearings. He was indeed on Prendergast Drive near the intersection of Tyler in a suburban development west of Linglestown. Emily's unmistakable black BMW Z-4 was parked in the driveway, with vanity plates reading "MLE-1." There was the familiar pastel Neapolitan flagstone pattern in the stone walkway to the front porch, the cracked glass in the hooded sconce light beside the front door. He should know where he was. This was his home for sixteen months. He had the right house, just the wrong occupant. Who was this guy?

"You must be Joe," the man said. Suddenly a riptide of nausea swirled up Sterner's throat from his stomach and must have registered on his face, because the man then said, "I know how you must feel, but I hope you can keep an open mind about me. Name's Teddy." He offered a charming grin and held out his hand.

Sterner took Teddy's hand, shaking it automatically, but fought the urge to twist his arm out of its socket. Teddy was in his stocking feet wearing faded red sweatpants and a sleeveless white tee-shirt that advertised his small athletic physique. He looked like a medium weight boxer, but Sterner believed he could take him. Sterner must've interrupted his work-out because he was perspiring and there was a white hand towel draped around his neck.

"C'mon in," Teddy said. "Becca's been askin' bout you all morning," with an accent that betrayed him as a native New Yorker. Brooklyn or Queens, Sterner suspected.

"Is it Daddy? Daddy!" An impossibly beautiful cherub with a helmet of corn silk clumped at the temple with a smear of oatmeal appeared in the hallway, dressed in a pale blue nightgown with a pattern of daisies and a milk stain. Her expression lit up like it was Christmas and Sterner was

Santa. She dropped her coveted pink teddy bear and ran for him, arms outstretched.

"Hey, Pookie," Sterner said and lifted her high over his head then into a tight embrace. "How's my little petunia? You ready for the playground?"

"Emily's in the kitchen," Teddy said. "You want a cup a coffee or something?"

"Sure."

"Mommy's in the kitchen," Becca said as he put her down. She took his hand and led him through the passage, retrieving her bear along the way.

"I'm very sorry our call got interrupted yesterday. Daddy was in a bad cell phone area."

"That's what Mommy said. Did you put away the bad guys, Daddy?" Like the bad guys were scattered toys in Daddy's playroom that had to be picked up and put away. As an attorney, Mommy's job was to free the good guys. The truth was, of course, somewhat fuzzier.

"I'm working on it," his standard reply.

Emily was in her gray quilted designer housecoat at the kitchen table, her back to the wall, coffee mug in one hand, the other flattening a fold in The New York Times Op/Ed section as she skimmed it. The remains of a continental breakfast and other sections of the Sunday edition were strewn about the room. A flat screen hi-def TV mounted on the wall nearby was tuned to a muted CNN Headline News.

She looked ravishing, as always. She didn't have to work at it. Her skin, like porcelain from the Orient, smooth and creamy, her dark blue eyes shining, her golden hair tumbling over her shoulders, hooked over one ear and nearly concealing the eye on her opposite side. At thirty-three, even without make-up and fresh out of bed, the woman was more attractive than any ten Charlize Therons, Sterner thought. Looks *and* smarts, was how Sterner always described her. She had a magnetic self-possession, a kind of charismatic awareness that said she knew exactly who she was and what she wanted and you'd better steer clear or you'll get run over. It turned him on. If only her heart were less capricious!

She smiled but barely moved. "Hey, Joe," she said.

"Becca's not dressed?" he said. "It's after ten."

"Is that an admonishment or a question? We had a late night, okay? And Moira's off today," she said. Moira Ferguson was the Irish au pair, barely out of her teens and in need of her own supervision.

"You want I should dress her?" Teddy said bringing up the rear.

"Sure. That would be sweet of you, Teddy," Emily said. "Thanks."

"I want Daddy," Becca said.

"Daddy and Mommy need to have a chat, Pookie," Emily said. "Let Uncle Teddy dress you just this once, okay?"

Becca heaved a sigh. "Oh, alright," she said rolling her eyes in a comic, dead-on impersonation of her mother on the rare occasions she caved in at the end of an argument. She turned back through the hallway toward the stairs, reaching for Teddy's hand.

"Teddy's really great with her," Emily said taking a sip of her coffee.

"*Uncle* Teddy?" Sterner said, whispering so as not to be overheard. Sterner moved closer to her. "How do you know he isn't some pedophile or something?"

"Teddy's no pedophile, I can assure you," Emily said, adding an unnecessary wicked grin that suggested intimate and thorough familiarity with the man's sexuality.

Sterner chose to ignore it. "They don't come with labels on their foreheads, you know. So who is he?"

"He's a dancer who moonlights as a bartender," Emily said.

"A dancer?" Sterner said.

"He's on sabbatical from the Capital City Dance Company in D.C. He teaches a class in toddler ballet at the community center."

"You must be kidding," Sterner said. "How long have you known him?"

"Seven weeks." She sipped her coffee. "Really, he's great with her."

"So you've said. Twice."

"I *knew* this was going to happen." Her ire up, she ran her fingers through her hair, a pre-battle ritual. You always knew in a courtroom when she was about to score against the opposition, because she always ran her fingers through her hair just before. "You just want to pick a fight."

"You're telling me you're letting a complete stranger into your home and, as we speak, are allowing him to dress our daughter in her bedroom without supervision?"

"He's hardly a complete stranger. He's funny, candid, emotional, everything you're not."

"You've known him less than two months."

"How much caffeine did you have this morning?"

"Don't change the subject," he said, took off his jacket and sat down. She uncapped a bottle of Tylenol sitting next to the TV remote. "Did he get you hammered last night? Were you even sober enough to keep track of him when you got home?"

Emily threw two large tabs into her mouth and washed them down with a gulp of coffee. "Look, Teddy's been a really great friend. Becca's been really rambunctious lately, okay? The terrible twos are a complete myth. It's the terrible threes you have to worry about. Her shrieking episodes are becoming more frequent. Our therapist says she's upset about the divorce, which is understandable. But she's still having accidents, even though she's been potty-trained for three months now, and if she doesn't get with the program, they're gonna kick her out of pre-K. I just can't take it anymore."

"*Our* therapist?"

"Becca and I see him together. Separately and then together. He's helping us work through issues."

"Issues?"

"You might benefit from therapy, too, you know. You have issues. Trust. Abandonment. Sharing. We could discuss them all at our next joint session, if you'd care to come. Or you could speak to Dr. Cross privately. I think you'd really get a lot out of it. Tomorrow afternoon, five-thirty?" She pushed a business card she'd readied for him across the table. It read: *Dr. Nathaniel Cross, MD, Psychiatrist.* Sterner recognized the office address as one of the townhouses a block from the river downtown near the hospital.

"I'm not seeing your shrink," he said. "Forget it."

"It isn't my idea. It's Dr. Cross's. And this isn't about you. It's about Becca."

"Forget it," he said, and pushed the card back across the table. "And stop changing the subject. What's Teddy's last name?"

"Don't make trouble."

"He's alone upstairs in our daughter's bedroom undressing her, and before I go up, I want to know his full name. Unless you want me to ask *him*."

"She's not even *your* daughter."

"Tell *her* that."

"Oh, alright," she finally said, rolling her eyes exactly the way Becca had. "Lamotti. Theodore Lamotti."

"Middle name?"

Emily sighed. "Balzac."

Sterner raised an eyebrow.

She shrugged. "Mutt Western European."

"Aren't we all!" he said.

———————

Sterner stepped quietly up the stairs and watched Teddy and Becca in her room from the shadows of the hallway. Still in her pajamas, they were sifting through her blouse drawer. Teddy would pull out one top and show it to her and say, "How 'bout *this* one?" And Becca would say, "No, not *that* one." And then Teddy would fold it neatly and put it back and pull out another and the whole routine repeated. When she finally settled on a white cotton pullover sweater she resisted Teddy's help putting it on.

"I can do it myself," she insisted. And did.

As he watched them, he concluded Emily was right about one thing. Teddy was great with her. He was patient, tender, kind--qualities he knew were missing in his ex-wife. It occurred to him that were he not emotionally involved, he might've mistaken them for father and daughter. But he was, and so wrestled with the little green monster inside his head.

Still stricken with low-grade rage, Sterner stopped at his car on their walk down the street to the playground to retrieve his Glock from the glove compartment and clip the leather holster onto his belt over his left hip. He didn't know why he did it. He had no intention of shooting anyone. It just made him feel better.

It was Sunday morning and the righteous were in church. So by eleven o'clock, only a few of the local heathens had brought children to the unfenced acre at the end of Prendergast Drive at the edge of the wood that stretched up Third Mountain to the ridge and beyond. There were fewer mothers than children, and only one other father, whom Sterner did not recognize.

When she was younger, Sterner felt obliged to follow Becca around to ensure she did not hurt herself on the sliding board or ladders or platforms or ramps or swings, or trip over her own feet for that matter. But as she grew into her two-year-old body and learned to run he held back, partly because it was harder to keep up and partly so as not to intrude as she developed into a more independent person and forged friendships on her own. Now that she was three he was content to sit at one of the benches at the perimeter and watch, intervening only when he felt she needed a spotter, a coach or a referee.

At first she only wanted to play with him, of course, since she only got the chance once a week but when she recognized another frequent playmate she ran off to play without him. He watched her run back and forth with a little boy her age along the alphabet road, the stretch of blacktop at the center of the playground colorfully painted with giant letters large enough to arc rainbow-like twenty yards from A to Z. They then took turns chasing each other around a waste can until they both fell down laughing.

Sterner smiled. He loved the playground. It was the only environment he'd ever encountered past his own puberty where gender was not an issue, including his experience at the Academy, where a mandate required that everyone treat the odd female recruit like anybody else. There was no flirting with the opposite sex among the caregivers here that he was able to detect. It was all about the kids. Adults here forgot their own petty problems and enjoyed themselves vicariously through the children. The kids themselves were asexual innocents, totally open with their feelings, able to relate to the opposite sex as easily as their own. Tempers flared, greed reared its ugly head, jealousy ran abundant, but by and large the kids were full of love and trust and curiosity and wonder. And Sterner loved that about the playground almost as much as he loved hearing Becca laugh.

He noticed the other father watching him. He was a white bread version of himself, someone he might've gone to high school with, but prematurely gray, with a receding hairline and a bit of a paunch. They made eye contact and the man nodded, then approached and sat next to him.

"You must be Becca's dad," he said and held out his hand. "I'm Sid, Marty's dad. That's him playing with Becca." There was an unwritten rule that within the boundaries of the playground, last names were irrelevant.

"Joe," he offered with a smile. "Nice to meet you."

"I usually see Becca with Moira and I've met Emily once or twice, but I don't believe I've ever seen you here before. Then again, we usually come Sunday afternoons, if at all. We're playing hooky from church today, since the wife's doing her girls-gone-wild thing in Fort Lauderdale this weekend with her bridge club."

"Sounds like fun."

"I hope so. She needed a break."

"I only have Becca Sundays."

"Oh. Yes. Divorced, right?"

"Yeah."

Sid nodded and was silent for a moment. "I can see the resemblance, though," he said, an awkward non sequitur.

Sterner had heard this before and didn't feel the need to correct him, though it was of course a biological impossibility. "Say, I don't suppose you happen to know anything about this toddler ballet class at the community center," Sterner said.

"Yeah, Marty goes every week with Becca. He loves it. It's pretty chaotic. It's not really a dance class per se. More like an introduction to stretching and movement."

"What do you know about the teacher?"

"Teddy? Oh, he's great with the kids."

"So I hear."

"We actually saw him perform in *The Nutcracker* last Christmas at the Kennedy Center."

"Really!"

"Wonderful production, although Marty found the Rat King a little scary," he said, his glance lingering too long on Sterner. "I guess I know why you asked."

Sterner looked him in the eye.

Sid winced. "I'm sorry. It's none of my business but it's no secret. Scuttlebutt on the playground is he's moved in with them."

An electrical shock compelled Sterner to sit up.

"But I guess you knew that. Which is why you asked." He saw Sterner's expression and shook his head. "I do apologize. I talk too much. My wife is always on my case for sticking my foot in my damn mouth."

"It's okay," Sterner said, as much to himself as Sid. "I've moved on. Say what you were going to say."

Sid shrugged. "Nothing, really. For what it's worth the general consensus is it's the best thing that could happen to Becca. He really is a wonderful guy."

"Daddy, we want to play *Ring Around the Rosey*," Becca said to Sterner.

"So? Go ahead."

"We don't have enough people. Will you play with us?"

"Okay."

"I'll play, too," Sid said.

Becca took Sterner's hand, always a welcome and surprising sensation. Marty took Sid's hand. The kids took each other's hand, leaving Sterner and Sid to hold hands to complete the circle. They all sang the merry nursery rhyme about the Black Death dancing clockwise like pagans around a fire. Then, on cue, they all dropped onto their rear ends, rolling onto their backs with their feet kicking in the air and laughing. Marty and

Becca were in hysterics. Sterner chuckled, too, but more at the silliness of his and Sid's unreserved collusion.

Then Sid's expression turned to horror. He sat straight up and stared at the ground next to Sterner. His Glock. The weapon in its holster had tumbled from his belt and now sat inert but very much out of place in the center of the playground. *Inappropriate?* Duh.

"Daddy!" Becca said scolding him.

"Is that a real gun?" Marty said, eyes wide with delight.

"I'm a cop," Sterner said to Sid with a shrug and quickly clipped it back onto his belt beneath his jacket.

When Sterner got back to the house an hour later, having returned the Glock safely to the glove compartment and securing a promise from Becca not to tell Mommy, they found Teddy preparing a mushroom and tomato omelet with soy sausages and English muffins with orange marmalade.

Sterner might have enjoyed himself under other circumstances, but he had no appetite and sat sullenly through most of the meal, trying in vain to size up Teddy and fathom Emily's attraction to him. It was a mystery to him what attracted most women. He always thought Mel Gibson and Brad Pitt were attractive men. Emily called them *pretty boys*, preferring instead Tommy Lee Jones and David Strathairn, actors Sterner found unremarkable in their sex appeal. Then again, she had found him attractive, so how could he complain?

Emily, too, sat in silence, which left it to Teddy and Becca to make conversation. Teddy was solicitous of Becca's opinions and Becca was forthcoming in return, all of which depressed Sterner even more. Becca seemed genuinely happy to be with people she loved and who loved her all together at the same table. In fact, she would have been perfectly happy if Sterner married the nineteen-year-old Moira and moved back in, so they could all live happily ever after--and said so.

Becca's mood changed when it was time for her nap. She threw a temper tantrum, flailed, cried and screamed. Instead of bringing out her motherly instincts to console her daughter, Emily just looked out the window, leaving it to Sterner to carry Becca up the stairs to her bed, where he rocked her for a few minutes until she calmed down. Then he read her several bedtime stories from her many books and laid next to her on the floor. When she was finally asleep around two o'clock, he closed the door and found Emily in the study downstairs, checking e-mail on her notebook computer. Teddy was doing dishes on the other side of the house, giving Sterner another chance to speak freely.

"Rumor has it Teddy's moved in," he said.

"Who've you been talking to?"

"Scuttlebutt on the playground. I was told it was no secret. So imagine my surprise to be the last to know."

"He has a room over his sister's garage in Lemoyne but he doesn't have much stuff so, yes, he's spending a lot of time here. But I wouldn't say he's moved in, exactly." She turned around to face him. "Could we just be civil about this? And I think your behavior at lunch was atrocious, by the way. Teddy was very hurt. You owe him an apology."

"I want you to know my concerns. First, I think it's ridiculous to talk about medicating a three-year-old because she's behaving like a three-year-old. Second, I don't think you're creating the stable environment she needs. I thought I could bring something permanent to her upbringing by staying in the picture, but you're going to have to consider the effect you have on her as a role model with a revolving bedroom door."

"Are you calling me a whore, you son of a bitch?"

Sterner took a deep breath. "Fine. I've made my point. I have some work to do at the lab. See you later." He walked away.

"That's it, just walk away like you always do," she said. "Digging up Teddy's past doesn't serve Becca's sense of stability, either, you know. Think about that, detective!"

He didn't respond, just exited the front door, but had to wonder what skeletons in Teddy's closet she was referring to.

———————

4.

TWO WEEKS BEFORE OPENING DAY

On Monday morning at nine a.m., Cat True arrived as summoned to the low-ceilinged Sheriff's Office beneath the historic Doolittle County Court House a block off the square in historic downtown Samaritan. As she was shown into the Sheriff's private sanctum for the interview, with its shabby wood paneling and county maps, floor to ceiling American flag, politician's portraits, high, squat windows facing the alley and noisy, exposed plumbing from the restrooms upstairs which made disturbing noises, Sterner took stock of her.

She was an attractive woman in her late thirties, tall and athletic. She had a proud, straight posture, but the corners of her mouth seemed naturally down-turned. She wore tight black jeans and black leather work boots with an oversized long-sleeved black tee, which tried but could not conceal a curvaceous figure. She wore no make-up and no jewelry. She carried a plain, dark green cloth bag with a long thick strap, like a messenger bag, for a pocketbook. Her look seemed out of place for a small town in the Appalachian foothills. Sterner wondered if she was an artist of some kind.

The Sheriff introduced Sterner as head of a homicide investigation for the State Police. She shook Sterner's hand without enthusiasm, not meeting his eyes. He wasn't sure she understood what the Sheriff had said, since the word "homicide," which normally got people's attention, did not register on her face in any way. Then again, maybe she was unsurprised that there *was* a homicide investigation. In which case, Sterner found her even more interesting.

She sat in the hard-backed metal chair opposite the Sheriff's clunky bureaucrat's desk, as instructed, and crossed her legs while Sheriff Guise eased into his swivel chair behind it and shuffled some papers. Sterner dropped back to a neutral position, leaning against a Shaker table across the room, observing them both in profile for the interview.

"Honey, do you know why I asked you in here this morning?" Sheriff Guise said, peering at her over his half-moon reading glasses.

Cat shrugged.

The Sheriff opened a drawer and produced the arrow found in the ten-point, minus the arrowhead which had permanently lodged in the ribs of the carcass and would not be easily extracted. He set it down on his desk and waited for a response. He got none. "This belong to you?"

Cat shrugged again and gazed blankly at him, eyes dull.

"You shoot a ten-point buck in the state forest sometime in the past week?"

"Yes," she said flatly.

"I'm not interested in busting you for poaching or trespassing. We're investigating a homicide. What day did you shoot that buck?"

"Last Monday," she said in a low voice.

"Morning or afternoon."

"Morning."

"Did you track him outside the public land?"

"No."

Sheriff Guise paused, glanced at Sterner, shifted his weight uncomfortably, and then tossed his glasses on the desk and leaned forward. "Now, honey, I've known you all your life. Your daddy was one of my best friends, and I've always felt terrible about what happened and what happened later, too. I've always supported you and defended you, you know that. I also know what a good hunter you are with that bow of yours. So don't you sit there and tell me you didn't track that buck outside the public land, because I know you did."

She looked at the ceiling. "It scared me," she said.

"What did?"

"That skeleton."

The Sheriff exchanged raised eyebrows with Sterner, who pulled up a straight-back chair and sat straddling it.

"Then you *did* see it," the Sheriff said leaning in.

"Yes."

"Scared you so bad you gave up the buck, is that right?"

"Yes."

"You should've called me right away, you know that."

"I was trespassing."

"Hell, that wouldn't've mattered! Did you see anybody else while you were out there in the woods?"

"No."

"In the state forest or the private land?"

"No."

"Did you see any vehicles?"

"No."

"Four-by-fours? Dirt bikes?"

"No."

"Did you see any tire tracks of any kind?"

"No."

The Sheriff sighed. "Take us through the morning, through your own eyes, exactly what you saw and did."

She told them quickly and succinctly, if not quite truthfully, ignoring Sterner's stares.

"How fresh did the roses look?" Sterner said finally.

"*Very* fresh," she said, turning to look directly at him, her eyes no longer glazed, and scrutinized his clean-shaven face and enigmatic expression for the first time. Her green eyes were striking. "That's what scared me the most." She examined his cleft brow, combed hair, broad shoulders, blue turtle-neck sweater and brown slacks and was amused by his black Van sneakers.

"Did you go inside the shack?" Sheriff Guise said.

"No," turning back to the Sheriff.

"Did you see anyone else that day in the woods?"

"No."

"What time did you leave?"

"Around ten o'clock. I had to be at work at noon."

"Did you tell anyone about what you saw?"

"No."

"Keep it that way," Sheriff Guise said and dismissed her. She hesitated, expecting more, was not disappointed, and withdrew from the room without another word, but looked over the detective with curiosity on her way out. He smiled and nodded.

After she left, Sterner slipped into her vacated chair. "Okay," he said. "If she found it Monday morning, Sunday was the likely day he put it there."

"Agreed," Sheriff Guise said, closing his eyes to think out loud. "That makes sense. There wouldn't be any hunters in the woods. Hunting's illegal on Sundays and it's not like it's a popular hiking area. Unfortunately, it didn't rain for two weeks before last Tuesday, when we had a downpour and another thunderstorm on Thursday, which may account for the fact that there were no tire tracks. But he could've hiked in, too. I checked the cemeteries and there're no reports of grave-robbing that anyone knows of."

Sterner's gaze fell on the Sheriff's dirty fingernails, which showed oil paint of different colors. "How long have you been painting?"

The Sheriff looked up, surprised, and then remembered. He examined his fingernails, then self-consciously hid them under the desk. He coughed, pulled at his belt, and quietly fessed up, "About six months. Still life's mostly. Doc Johnson tells me I need a hobby to ease my transition into retirement, so I don't have a coronary if I lose my next election."

"You knew her father?"

The Sheriff heaved a sigh, leaned back in his chair, and clasped his fat hands behind his head. "He was a year ahead of me in high school, played varsity basketball when I was JV. Aggressive as hell, even a little scary. Went into Army Special Forces and off to Nam. I joined the Navy. Never knew him that well until later when we were deputies together." He grinned at the memory. "Used to call me *Swabby*, tease me about the Viet Cong Navy. He was a rising star, showed me the ropes, then up and abandoned us." He dropped his hands and shook his head, lowered his voice and leaned in. "The job, the family, everything. Ran off with another woman. She's been through a lot of heartache, that one. I look in on them now and again. Mother's a little wacky."

"And what happened later?" Sterner said and watched Sheriff Guise shift uncomfortably in his chair. "You mentioned something happened?"

The Sheriff looked irritated. "That you don't need to hear about. It's got nothing to do with this case. Now, do you want me to look into getting a chopper? Because I have a contact with the DEA."

"No, let me make some calls first. We used an infra-red scanner on a state chopper in a kidnap/murder case last year. I'll see if I can get it for a fly-over." Sterner opened his leather brief case and handed over a copy of his preliminary report. Guise put on his reading glasses and studied it with interest. Sterner referred to his own copy.

"Crime Lab takes at least a week to process evidence and file an official report, but I've concluded the holes in the back of the skull are likely from a .38 or 9 millimeter firearm," Sterner said. "The powder charge was likely doctored for low velocity impact, since the bullets didn't pass through. Yet no fragments were found in the skull cavity. The shooter was probably a professional, or certainly someone who knew his way around cartridge load manufacture and manipulation. The bullet fragments were removed from the skull bone before being displayed. There were no fingerprints on the surface of the bones.

"The victim was a woman, five feet-four inches tall, thirty to forty years old, and had likely never given birth. She had broken her right leg in childhood. She had good teeth and a proper diet. I believe the bones had been in the ground no less than twenty nor more than thirty years, then wholly unearthed. Had erosion bared part of the skeleton, the exposed bones would have been discernibly bleached and dried by the elements, and that was not the case. They were likely exhumed, washed down, then transferred to the hut, there being no grave dirt or other chemical signatures, like lime, which might have helped identify a grave location.

"Computer Imaging should have a reasonably accurate facial reconstruction by the end of the week. It will go up on our website with the nine other open cases of unidentified remains, none of which, as it happens, seem related to this one. The Crime Scene techs will work the black cotton fiber and the short strand of reddish hair found at the scene, though how much help they will be is debatable, since the hut was likely not the scene of the murder."

Sheriff Guise nodded.

Sterner handed him another page. "I made a carbon impression of the teeth before sending them to be X-rayed and molded by the forensic odontologist. You might make copies for area dentists. Roy Fries should be at the top of your list, since he seems to have been the intended recipient. The roses were generic American Beauty. Nothing helpful, I'm afraid."

"I'll have my girls assemble a list of area florists, nurseries and greenhouses," Sheriff Guise said. "If your guy didn't grow them, he bought them somewhere." He shook his head. "A woman in her thirties, five foot-four, who broke her leg as a child," Sheriff Guise said, frowning. "I went over all the missing persons reports twenty to thirty years back--mostly runaway teenagers. I'm drawing a blank. I keep going back to this biker gang in Burnside County, the Berzerkers. Five'll get you ten it's them or the pot farmers. My gut says she ain't local or she'd've been missed and a report filed. D.C. is only an hour and change from here. Always been a lot of drugs down there, prostitution, maybe she's some intern had an affair with a congressman. CIA. Mafia. Who knows?" The Sheriff put his hands behind his head and leaned back. "How's your little girl?"

"Oh," Sterner smiled. "She's fine. Rebecca is her name. Becca, for short. She's starting to talk like an adult, which is scary. They grow up so fast. You have kids?"

"Nope. Never found the time or the right woman."

Louella interrupted with a knock on the door. She was a tall, severe-looking office manager, about fifty, with a perfect Dutch bob haircut and a pair of Lilly Tomlin glasses. Sterner had arrived at the Sheriff's Office that morning in time to witness Sheriff Guise barking at his uniformed civil servants in a most uncivil way. Arriving before dawn to review the missing persons reports from twenty years ago, the Sheriff found the files in disarray. Louella had given Sterner a friendly wink to let him know the boss's guff and bluster was all part of a job she didn't take home with her. By contrast, Suzy Bream, her assistant, who bore the brunt of the tirade, seemed on the edge of tears. She was short, about thirty and heavily overweight, stretching the seams of her ill-fitting deputy uniform and wearing her hair up in an unflattering bun.

"Suzy's got a reporter from the *Harrisburg Tribune* on the line, asking questions about that skeleton," Louella said now. "What do you want her to tell him?"

"Here comes the shit storm," Sheriff Guise grumbled.

"Tell him we can't comment on an ongoing investigation," Sterner said. "And refer all calls to the office of Chief of Detectives Benjamin Taylor at State Police Headquarters." Louella nodded and disappeared behind the closing door. Sterner checked his watch. "Which reminds me, I've got to get back and brief the Chief in person. With a case as unusual as this one, he may want to make a statement for the five o'clock news. And I'll be spending the afternoon figuring out what he should and shouldn't say."

"Public Relations," the Sheriff scoffed, "my least favorite part of the job. Roy Fries gave me a list of all the members of the hunt club. There's about a dozen names. Louella'll make you a copy. I told him they'd have to postpone their muzzleloader plans until later in the week. He's called an emergency meeting at their lodge tonight. He asked me to brief them on the case, since he didn't know what he was supposed to say. They know the property better than anybody. They can be a big help finding the grave, not to mention having some ideas about who Jane Doe is, who killed her and who dug her up. You want to speak to them tonight?"

Sterner thought for a moment. "ID-ing the victim and finding the grave are paramount. Speculation about who did it or who dug her up invites gossip, which is distracting and unhelpful. I suppose it wouldn't hurt to meet them, though. What time?"

"Seven o'clock."

Sterner pursed his lips. "I'd be fighting rush hour," he said. Then finally, "You go tonight. Tell them everything we know about the woman but as little as possible about the scene or the investigation. Oh, and ask them not to talk to anybody about it."

"It's a small town. That might be a tall order." Guise chewed his lip for a moment. "Maybe I could deputize them or something. You know, make them all swear an oath. It wouldn't mean anything but I bet it would bring them into the fold."

"Good idea," Sterner said and shook the Sheriff's hand. "We'll speak tomorrow."

"There's a grave out there somewhere," the Sheriff said. "It's the perfect place to hide a body."

Sterner was glad to escape the Sheriff's claustrophobic dungeon. But outside in the alley, a press photographer snapped his picture. As he drove out of the parking lot, a TV news truck with a satellite tower folded on its roof drove in. What had the Sheriff said? *Here comes the shit storm.*

Sterner drove around the Court House and made the left onto Middle Street and into the town square a block away. The streets were littered with traffic signs and route numbers, directions to Samaritan College, Nussbaum Foods and the interstate. The buildings lining the cracked cement sidewalks were mostly three-story nineteenth century brick, stone and clapboard townhouses, commercial buildings and small factories that had been renovated and converted into apartments, offices, boutiques and restaurants, a poor protestant church every third block. It looked like a hundred other small towns in the state, power and telephone lines strung up above the streets like black cobwebs, a looming gray water tower stenciled with the town name like some giant spider with its legs stretched. He wasn't romantic or sentimental about such places. Tourists may have found it quaint, but it looked and felt ugly to him. There was a closed five-and-dime in mid-reconstruction with a sign announcing a new chain drug store, a mom-and-pop shoe store, a clothing store with jogging clothes on headless mannequins in the windows, two or three restaurants with posted menus. It was one part Norman Rockwell, one part Depression Era detritus and one part mall sprawl. Sterner found it depressing.

He tried to remember what he had read last night when he went online to see what the Chamber of Commerce website had to say about the town. Samaritan was a quiet burg of six thousand friendly residents or something like that, nestled between the Tunney and Wilder mountain ranges that ran northeast to southwest through several states in the eastern quarter of the Appalachians. Samaritan's name derived from a famous stage coach stop called the Good Samaritan Inn, whose motto was "No one turned away." Established at the end of the eighteenth century, it had been located on the town square until a fire claimed it in the 1890s but was then rebuilt in the 1920s. It offered hospitality for travelers between Washington or Philadelphia and Pittsburgh. The era of train travel that followed did not diminish its popularity, but as commercial interest in nearby timber and limestone deposits and rustic early American and faux colonial furniture manufacturing dwarfed its importance as an economic force, the inn became a symbol of the growing town's identity.

He glanced over now at the new Good Samaritan Inn, a convincing replica of eighteenth century design. It looked hospitable and inviting, like the food might be edible, and he made a note to check it out. As he drove the quarter circle around the square, a pine tree was being trimmed with Christmas lights by two civil servants dressed in red plaid and green camouflage hunting clothes. It made Sterner wonder if they meant to lure Santa close enough to shoot his reindeer out of the sky like wild geese.

At the edge of town, he passed the fenced entrance to a collection of factory buildings behind a sign identifying it as the Nussbaum Foods Company and remembered reading about lush orchards and a wide variety of apples which thrived in the foothills surrounding the county seat. The Nussbaum Apple Company was founded by an enterprising German Mennonite named Karl Nussbaum in 1922 and grew to include scores of orchards, several packing plants and the famous factory that supplied the popular brand of apple sauce around the world. As the Chamber of Commerce detailed Nussbaum's invention of a patented machine which simultaneously drilled out the apple core and peeled its skin in the first stage of sauce-making, Sterner had logged off.

But the phrase now echoed in Sterner's mind as he headed out to the interstate. *No one turned away.* Maybe shot twice in the back of the head, buried thirty years until mysteriously exhumed, but not turned away. Praise the Lord and pass the doctored .38 caliber ammunition, honey.

———————

"Do you know what happens when a bomb goes off next to another bomb?" Chief of Detectives Benjamin Taylor said. Sterner had a hunch it was a rhetorical question.

Taylor was an effective bureaucrat but a demanding taskmaster, capricious but brilliant in his way. He was tall, humorless, with dyed-black hair. He had a law degree from the University of Pennsylvania, making him an excellent Chief of Detectives but slippery in the eyes of his investigators, since he kept company with the lawyers they distrusted. His law-speak particularly made Sterner uncomfortable, since his own ex-wife was just such a lawyer. Taylor was also a skilled political animal with ambitions to run for Governor. He had proved willing on numerous occasions to sacrifice subordinates for the sake of his own career. He was not well-liked by anyone, including his wife, an aging Philadelphia debutante.

Taylor's office was spacious and impeccably decorated and paid for by his wife, with thick gray carpet and healthy ivy and fern plants, daily fussed over by his diligent secretary, cascading from antique European earthenware. There were original works of modern art on the walls and small Roman busts among the law books on built-in shelves.

When Taylor glared at him, Sterner realized he was expected to answer.

"Two bombs go off?" he said.

"That's exactly right," the Chief said. He turned back to the window again. "And what you get is a really, really big explosion. Which means not just those in the immediate vicinity get hit with shrapnel but also those standing behind them and those behind them and maybe even those like me standing way far away watching from what they think is a perfectly safe distance."

Sterner raised his eyebrows. He was waiting for the punch line but it was all too cryptic for him to decipher. "I'm sorry, sir, you lost me," he said flatly. "Are you saying this is somehow an APE case?" An *Actual Political Emergency* was something all members of law enforcement feared and loathed--a case where the media and politicians got involved, adding unwelcome pressure to hasten investigations. Where hearsay and speculation led to rumors. Where hurried methodology led to mistakes. Where insufficient evidence led to premature arrests. Where ambitious state's attorneys led to overzealous prosecutions. And--worst of all--where over-priced appeals led to overturned convictions.

The Chief turned again and sat down at his cherry wood Chippendale desk. "Does the name *Hellcat* ring a bell with you?"

"Hellcat?" Sterner said. "You mean the airplane? Like *Hellcats of the Navy*?"

"The Hellcat *case*, detective," he said. "Samaritan, Pennsylvania?"

The Hellcat case? That seemed out of left field, he thought. He searched his memory. "I was at John Jay when that happened. Twenty years ago? High school girl, was it? I think she was retarded or something. Three football jocks raped her and she castrated one of them. Is that the case you mean?"

"She wasn't retarded. Just unwilling to talk. And she didn't castrate him completely. She shot him up with Special K, gagged and hogtied him, and then surgically removed one testicle, warning him if he ever raped again she'd come after the other one. The whole time the boy's family was asleep upstairs, oblivious. He was only discovered the next morning after she was long gone. Seventeen years old! She could've taught the Delta Force a course in stealth at Fort Bragg. It happened the week Oliver North testified before Congress about Iran/Contra, so it fell to the back pages in the national press. But it was a *huge* story in *this* state, let me tell you. Everybody was talking about it. Every columnist, commentator and cab driver had an opinion. Stirred all kinds of debate about the prohibition of *cruel and unusual punishment*. Constitutional lawyers had a field day. Some shyster representing a serial rapist in New Mexico actually argued in court his client's testicles were responsible for his sex crimes and that he should be castrated, not imprisoned. They called it *The Hellcat Defense*. He was convicted, anyway. Then some joker introduced a bill in the California legislature offering reduced sentences to convicted sex offenders who agreed to a partial castration. They called that *The Hellcat Law*. But it never passed."

Realization dawned over Sterner's face. "No, wait, you're telling me that was Cat True?"

"She was a minor then. Her name was withheld. Some tabloid dubbed her *Hellcat* and it stuck. The other two boys were minors, as well, and confessed to the rape in front of a grand jury in exchange for leniency so she was only charged with burglary and assault with a deadly weapon. The ACLU represented her. Radical feminists rallied eager to canonize her as a martyr. She never went to trial, though. I think the court recommended psychiatric counseling or some shit. Then the boy's family lost their civil suit against her the following summer since everybody felt he got what he deserved. Her name was out by then, too, because she was eighteen, but the story was stale. To answer your question, detective, yes, her name was Catherine True from Samaritan, Pennsylvania."

"The Sheriff mentioned something had happened to her but when I asked him about it he clammed up, told me it was irrelevant."

"Everything is relevant while conducting a homicide investigation," the Chief said. He held up a copy of the day's *Harrisburg Tribune* and tapped his index finger on a headline below the fold which read: *Skeleton Found in Woods Near Samaritan*.

"Somehow word's already leaked out. Do you know what tomorrow's headline will be? *Hellcat Implicated in Skeleton Horror*! Or how about *Hellcat Returns--Did She Go Too Far This Time*? This office has been barraged with calls all day. I don't know where they're getting their information but word has spread like wildfire--AP, UPI, Reuters, CNN, *Time, Newsweek*. We've scheduled a press conference. Now do you understand my two-bomb analogy?"

"These things are out of my control."

"Yes, they are, and that's precisely my point. Your cold case will have an elevated profile now, and, yes, runs the risk of becoming an APE case. Just keep your mouth shut to the press and do your job."

"Understood," Sterner said.

"What other cases are you working on?"

"The Elizabethtown College drowning, the Indiantown Gap shooting, the hanging suicide at Caledonia...."

"Put em all on the back burner." Then he leaned into Sterner's face. "I'll be watching you very closely on this one. I want daily reports. Screw up just once and--well, you know when *I* cut them off, detective, I get them *both* the very *first* time."

Taylor had Sterner wait at reception while he went upstairs for a brief private meeting with the Commissioner, and then all three entered the press room precisely at 5:01 p.m., timed to give the local five o'clock news anchors a lead-in to open their newscast and introduce the story.

In his opening statement, Chief Taylor presented the bare facts of the case with an appeal to the public for information in helping to identify the mystery woman. He then took questions from individual reporters.

"Catherine True was the first to discover the skeleton last Monday and provided certain details which have helped investigators establish a timeline."

"Is she a suspect in the murder?"

"She is not a suspect at this time, no."

"If she discovered the skeleton last Monday, did she report it to the authorities?"

"No, she did not."

"Why not?"

"You'd have to ask her, but I know she showed concern she was trespassing. Next question?"

"Given her history, why are you ruling her out as a suspect?"

"We don't rule anybody out as a suspect. As the investigation proceeds, the evidence will speak for itself."

"Then she *is* a suspect."

"Next question."

And that was pretty much the end, since nobody wanted to ask about anything after that except Cat True. And the Chief's response to each question was, "No comment."

It was already dark when Sterner walked out of the elevator in the parking garage adjacent to State Police Headquarters. He reached into his pocket and felt a business card. Dr. Nathaniel Cross, M.D. Psychiatrist was only a few blocks away. He checked the time on his cell phone. It was 5:45 p.m. He took a deep breath and then did an about-face back to the elevator.

Ten minutes later he knocked on the office door and was greeted by a scholarly-looking gentleman in his early sixties, with long white hair pulled back into a pony-tail. He was wearing a blue blazer over an open-collared dress shirt, faded blue jeans and flip-flops.

"Daddy!" Becca said with a wide, bright smile, looking up from the carpet with blocks in her hands, in capris and a long-sleeved striped tee. She giggled, jumping to her feet and ran to embrace his knee.

"Sorry I'm late. Held up at work," Sterner said to Dr. Cross. "Joe Sterner."

"Hey, Joe," Emily called behind him.

"Why, yes, welcome," Cross said. "Glad you could make it." Cross sat down behind his desk and motioned for Sterner to pull up a chair beside Emily, immaculately gussied in a blue designer suit and patent leather heels.

"I don't want to waste your time," Sterner said as he sat down, scanning a side wall of awards and degrees, "but I wanted to voice my concern over the use of medication."

"I really don't think he has a say in this," Emily said.

"You're not the child's father?" Cross said, looking at Emily.

"Ask her," Sterner said pointing to Becca.

"That's my daddy," Becca said.

"Not biologically," Emily said.

"But emotionally," Cross said. "I understand. In today's world of broken, new and extended families, familial ties are sometimes complicated."

"And you, not he, are uniquely qualified to prescribe drug therapies, Doctor," Emily said. "He's a policeman and often encounters criminals using drugs, and is therefore unusually prejudiced against psychiatric pharmacology."

"Becca's behavior," Sterner said and took a breath to quell his fury, "as I've observed it, is perfectly normal for her age."

"How many three-year-olds do you know?" Emily interjected. "Dr. Cross is preeminent in the field of child psychiatry."

"You know as well as I do, doctor, there's a conflict of interest among those in the medical profession who receive bribes from drug companies to prescribe new pharmaceuticals, creating a kind of medical industrial complex funded by the insurance industry and the federal government and bilking the taxpayer out of billions every year."

Cross held a finger in the air.

"Tom Cruise with a badge," Emily said to Cross.

"You are a terrific lawyer, Emily, but true to your stripes, you seize upon a position prematurely and then bolster your arguments as evidence presents itself, remaining entrenched to the bitter end, regardless of the truth."

"He's hostile. There. See that?" Emily said to Cross.

Any hope of a reasonable discussion flew out the window when a bloodcurdling shriek pierced their eardrums, prompting three sets of hands to cover three sets of ears. Sterner imagined the glass in the windows might crack. Emily shivered. Becca ran to Sterner, burying her head in his lap. Sterner rubbed her back to calm her. Emily drew a trembling hand to her mouth and began to cry.

"One could jump to conclusions that these shrieking episodes are psychologically based," Cross said finally. "But before we consider a diagnosis and treatment, we ought to eliminate the possibility of any physical cause for this anomalous behavior. I'd like you to ask your family doctor to conduct a thorough physical examination to include an MRI brain scan."

Sterner had trouble sleeping again. He fidgeted, trying different positions that might encourage sleep. The mattress was salvaged from a dumpster behind the building the day he moved in. It was lumpy and he needed a new one. He needed a whole new bed. In fact, one of these days he really had to buy some new furniture.

He got up to find his ToughBook and stubbed his toe in the dark on a box in the hallway filled with photography art books. Robert Frank, W. Eugene Smith, Walker Evans, Weegee.

It had only been thirteen months since he'd moved here after splitting up with Emily and he still hadn't gotten around to unpacking. But then why should he if he meant to move out sooner rather than later?

After going online on the living room floor he Googled "hellcat samaritan castration." Dozens of sites referenced it. An AP photo of a seventeen-year-old with a stripe over her eyes barely concealed Cat's identity. She was in handcuffs, escorted into the Doolittle County Court House by none other than Deputy Vernon Guise himself. Another AP photo showed a group of protesting feminists outside the Doolittle County Court House.

He scanned an editorial arguing in favor of reduced sentences for sex criminals willing to undergo partial castration procedures, putting the blame for criminal behavior on an over-production of testosterone. How many convicts were serving sentences, not just for sex offenses but violence or reckless endangerment, because their bodies produced too much male hormone? Why else was there such a discrepancy between the number of men and women in prison? How many women were serving sentences merely for their association with such men? Other redundant human organs were routinely removed, allowing the patient to live a healthier, happier life. Why not over-active testes? A single testicle removal would not prevent sex or the fathering of children, but might allow for a more normal life. And what was, after all, more cruel and unusual? Partial castration or decades of hard time in a violent maximum security facility strained from overpopulation?

Another editorial was against the idea, arguing that America's founders would turn over in their graves if punitive mutilation of the human body was ever approved under U.S. law. Severing testicles was no different than cutting off a thief's hand or a liar's tongue, exactly the kind of medieval torture in the Old World that the Founders wanted banned in the New. The problem was not in any one human body part but rather in the mind and soul of the criminal. With the exception of the death penalty, this democracy held that humane incarceration was adequate and appropriate, giving the offender time to contemplate the consequences of his actions and rehabilitate himself while removing him from society where he clearly posed a threat to the citizenry.

He also read a disturbing article called "Rape Is Cruel, Too, But Hardly Unusual!" It said that every year one percent of all women were victims of assault, that sexual or physical abuse was *the* leading health problem among women aged 15 to 44 and that more than fifty percent of women who were murdered were victims of so-called *loved ones*. About halfway through this article, he grew depressed and checked his e-mail.

He found two responses from his FBI contact, Roger Dooley, at the Behavioral Science Unit in Quantico, Virginia. Sterner had met him at a joint conference on national security after 9/11 at the J. Edgar Hoover Building in Washington D.C. They'd had a couple of drinks after hours and he'd told Sterner if he ever needed help in profiling a suspect to feel free to forward his report. The first e-mail read: "RE: Skeleton

"Perps are likely two people. The Killer seems dispassionate and professional whereas the Ghoul seems passionate, even reckless, probably Caucasian male between 20 and 40, a practical joker interested in the occult, horror films, heavy rock music and/or death imagery. He may look and/or dress unconventionally. Probably immature or an outcast, but also a showoff. Probably single, may live at home or alone and may be sexually immature. He may have worked for a mortuary or morgue or in a cemetery and is used to dead bodies, especially skeletons, and may have been dismissed for inappropriate behavior. He may have had medical or anatomical schooling and flunked out because of a conflict with authority. He's probably been in trouble with the law and/or has a bad reputation in the community.

"Keep me up to date, if only for curiosity sake. --Dooley"

Sterner plugged in his printer and made a hard copy. The follow-up e-mail from Dooley read: "RE: Ghoul.

"Is it possible Ghoul obsessed with Cat True? If so, likely from afar, i.e. roses may have been meant for her. Saw photo emerging from Sheriff's Office and she's a looker. --Dooley.

"P.S. If Killer not also Ghoul and still alive, find Ghoul before Killer does."

Clay Whipple adjusted his red paisley ascot in his reflection in the jukebox glass and punched the number for Guns'N Roses' "Welcome to the Jungle," siren howling along with Axl Rose. He then slither danced to a booth in back under the TV, mouthing out the lyrics, using his Bud Lite bottle as a make-believe microphone to ape the singer. *Welcome to the jungle, we got fun and games.* It made his cousin Peter chuckle. But it also got the attention of the bartender and a large-bellied regular at the far end of the bar. So Peter sobered quickly and motioned for Clay to settle down.

"So?" Peter said sucking on his Heineken. Clay liked making entrances, he knew. He'd always been dramatic, always looking for attention.

"So." Clay echoed, teasing him.

"C'mon, what's the story?"

Clay shrugged casually. "Oh, he agreed."

Peter leaned forward. "No shit."

"No shit," Clay said.

"Just like that."

"Just. Like. That." Clay broke into a grin and slammed his hand on the table. Then the two cackled, their composure broken, and traded a ghetto handshake.

"Holy shit," Peter said, "I never really thought he'd go for it."

"I guess all the publicity got his attention. Good strategy."

"Precious sure did her job there. One hundred fuckin' grand, cuz,"

"Chump change for that motherfucker, you said so yourself," Clay said. "You know, just like before, as soon as he agreed I thought, fuck, we could've doubled that and he'd still've agreed."

"Don't get greedy, cuz. This is it, okay? Right? We take this and that's the end of it. We don't watch out, we're gonna get caught. I just want to get out from under, jump ahead on the mortgage, whittle down the debt and be done with it."

"Absolutely. The end. Me, I'm gonna disappear after this. Next time you see me it'll be up there," Clay said pointing to the TV above their heads, now showing a rerun of *Frasier.* "California, here I come. Fuck Samaritan and fuck you."

"Very funny. So how long will it take him to raise the money?"

"He said he needed a few days. I was very understanding but warned him not to screw around or another skeleton was bound to fall out of his closet."

"You didn't say that."

"I did."

"And what did he say?"

"He told me he'd kill me." Clay said casually and then slammed his hand down on the table again and screamed silently, feigning horror, eyes bulging wide in mock terror.

Peter arched an eyebrow. He was not so cavalier about a death threat.

"If you wanna know the truth, it sounded like he was relieved I called. Letting him stew all this time was good strategy," Clay said.

"I'm happy to relieve him--of his *money!* And if he decides to change his mind, we have insurance, right?"

Clay clinked the neck of Peter's bottle with the lip his own and winked. "What do you think about all this Hellcat stuff?"

They knew Cat only by her notoriety. They'd been in the third grade when Hellcat made their town infamous. The adults around them thought they were too young to know any details, but they understood that Cat had done something very naughty that had put their community in a bad light. Only later would they learn why she was considered such a pariah, why their parents whispered and pointed her out when they spotted her in town and then crossed the street to avoid her.

"Couldn't be better," Peter said. "Sends the police and our favorite senior citizen in a whole different direction."

But Axl was pronouncing: "You're in the jungle, baby. You're gonna die."

———————

Cat shivered under her covers. The temperature had dropped below freezing, but she was too cold to get up and stoke the fire in the woodstove in the kitchen on the opposite side of the wall behind her pillow.

From the time she had gotten home from work Sunday morning until she went off to work again Sunday night, her mother had pestered her with questions. "What do they want? What do you think it's about?"

"I don't know."

"Are you stealing drugs from Helen Dietz again?"

"No."

"Are you selling your body?"

"Heavens, no."

"Did you hit someone with your truck?"

"No, Mom."

"Well, why do you think the State Police want to talk to you?"

"I don't know, Mom."

Sally would not buy it, nor would she leave it alone. When finally she arrived home that morning from the Sheriff's Office, Sally was returning to the kitchen from the woodpile in the backyard with an armful of kindling. She stacked it in the wooden crate next to the woodstove and adjusted her shawl. She opened the fire door with a rag and tossed in a wedge of tinder. "I saw that black bear nosing around the compost pile again," she said. "I brought out the trap, but I need help setting it."

"Okay."

"What did Vern want? Did you hurt somebody again?"

"No!" Cat went to the sink and petted Mister Jeepers, who'd perched himself on the windowsill next to the stove. He came to life, swishing his tail, and purred.

"Then what did they want you for?"

Cat ignored her, turned on the cold water and splashed her face. She poured herself a mug of coffee, looking around the room at the trophy antlers mounted on every wood-paneled wall of the living room. Sally reached up into the cupboard for a jar of generic peanut butter.

"Come on, help me set this trap. It'll take two seconds."

"Can I drink my coffee first? I'm still a little hungover."

"You drink too much," Sally said and headed out the back door.

"Maybe you don't drink enough," Cat said under her breath.

"Bring your mug with you," Sally called from outside.

Cat groaned, but obediently followed her mother outside and past the woodpile, where Sally extracted her ax from a rotting stump and carried it past the stone smokehouse to the compost pile at the far end of the yard.

"You don't have to tell me, you don't want to," her mother said.

"I'm not supposed to talk about it."

Sally swung the flat end of the ax to hammer a stake further into the ground that was chained to the bear trap on the far side of the earthen hump where they buried their biodegradable garbage. As Cat sipped her coffee, she watched her mother roll a heavy rock the size of a cement block over the stake. "Who'm I gonna tell?" her mother said good-naturedly, knowing full well *they* were listening.

"Remember I said I shot that buck?"

Sally then opened the peanut butter jar and smeared the trigger, and said, "No shame in losing the blood trail." Sally set down the jar and wiped her fingers on her sweats. Cat set her mug on the ground. The two women took hold of either side of the rusty steel jaws. "On three. Ready? One, two, three."

Together, they heaved both sides downward. The trap jaws opened and locked into place, the trigger clicking upward into position. Sally sprinkled leaves over the jaws to camouflage them, but left the trigger with the peanut butter smear exposed.

Cat returned to her coffee. "I stopped looking."

"You were late to work, you said." Sally wiped her brow with her sleeve, out of breath from her labor.

"I found a skeleton in the woods. A human skeleton holding a bouquet of roses. I don't know what it meant. A scarecrow, maybe. I was kind of trespassing."

Sally gasped, thinking out loud. "Unburied dead. Troubled spirits." She shivered, then added quietly, "What is he up to now?"

This upset Cat. "Mom, it's got nothing to do with Daddy," she said.

"He's a killer. You have no idea what he's capable of."

"He was a soldier. He did his job."

"You believe what you want. Why you won't accept what I tell you, I'll never know," Sally said, abruptly marching back to the house.

Cat closed her eyes and sighed. She'd had no choice moving back home after her divorce. She couldn't afford the apartment she was living in. But if this was any indication of things to come, she'd rather live in the street.

When she got home from work later in the day, she found her mother on the phone with a reporter from Reuters explaining her theory that Cat's estranged father was somehow connected to the skeleton Cat found, just as he was responsible for the people who followed Sally and eavesdropped on her telephone conversations. Cat grabbed the receiver and slammed it into the cradle, reminding her Sheriff Guise had warned her there would be consequences to talking to the media. The phone continued to ring. Eventually they stopped answering and had to unplug it to get any sleep.

Now Cat was still awake. She tossed and turned and wondered if it would ever cease haunting her, this mistake that had ruined her life like a crippling accident in her youth. It had poisoned all her relationships and caused her to mourn the life she might have had. She was not a whole person and had not been for over half her life. She did not cry. She could not. Sometimes she wondered if she would ever feel anything real again.

Even now, all these years later, she could not remember anything of that night. She'd blocked it out, a gory horror so traumatizing she could not endure it. But she remembered everything that led up to it with perfect clarity. She replayed it over and over in her head, obsessing night after night, year after year, decade after decade.

———————

She stayed late shooting stick at the pool hall that Friday night with her high school friends, drinking cokes and smoking Marlboro's. One of them, a boy named Denny Louba, had an old beat-up Volkswagen Beetle. He usually gave her a ride home, since it was on his way back to his house near Pineville, but he'd been getting serious with her friend Mary Snyder. They decided to go to the Bijou downtown, see a movie and make out in the balcony, which left Cat without a ride.

About ten o'clock Cat walked to the northern outskirts of town near the high school and stuck out her thumb at the oncoming headlights. It was cold and she had on only a sweater.

When Billy Morrison's mini-bus, spray-painted in various shades of gray urban camouflage, pulled into the emergency lane, she groaned. Billy's dad owned a small fleet of school buses and had given his son a mini for personal use. She didn't like Billy and his jock buddies, who routinely ridiculed her and her friends at school, calling them "losers," making an "L" sign on their foreheads with their right thumb and forefinger. They even made fun of her heritage, holding one hand up to the back of their heads like a feather in a headband and tapping their open mouths with the other. And in the hallways Billy would sometimes claw the air in front of her face when he crossed her path, squint his beady little eyes at her and go, *Meow, meow, pussycat.*

But at least Billy wasn't by himself. Jonathan Sachtler was in the passenger seat and she didn't mind him too much, having known him since the first grade. When Jonathan smiled sweetly at her from the seat next to the doorway, she thought it would probably be okay to get in.

"Where you headed?" Billy said through the levered doors from his perch on the driver's seat.

"Hoover Road," she said.

"Hop in." He adjusted the rounded rim of his ball cap and checked his rearview. She found her choice of seats limited to sharing Jonathan's shotgun position or falling into a dull red beanbag chair on the blue shag carpet behind Billy. She chose the beanbag, but was barely in it before Billy gunned the engine and they sped back out onto the highway. Only then did she turn and see Claude Van Aiken grinning at her as he lounged in another red beanbag chair in back between stereo speakers beneath a mirrored disco ball swaying from the ceiling. Cat hated him. He was a bully who'd been Billy Morrison's best friend since junior high, and had a reputation as a braggart and a liar. All three boys had been on the high school football team. Billy was a senior with only a month left of school. Jonathan and Claude were juniors and shared classes with her. She could only hope Jonathan was a moderating influence.

"Don't worry," Claude said, "we won't bite." He showed her a toothy grin under his trucker's cap as he stared at her through his knees.

"We're headed up to the reservoir to smoke some hash," Billy said, "Wanna come?"

"No, I have to get home."

"Ah, come on. It's early. Let's party," Claude said.

"I've gotta get up early to go to work," she said. Billy turned up the cassette-player as the Billy Idol song "Rebel Yell" came on. In front Jonathan and Billy started punching the air in time to the music and singing along.

"She cried more, more, more," Claude yelled along shaking a power fist and playing air drums. "More, more, more." Van Halen's "Panama" came on after that, so they kept the volume high, making conversation impossible.

She eventually looked up to see they had passed Hoover Road a couple miles back and said, "Hey, you missed my stop. I have to get out. Pull over."

"Oh, shit, I'm sorry," Billy said and glanced over at Jonathan.

"Relax. We'll get you there, eventually," Jonathan said and then looked back at Claude and grinned. The oblivious Claude just nodded in time to the music with his eyes shut.

"Sure, I'll take you up and drop you off at your front door, you want me to," Billy said. He seemed sincere. "Twenty minutes, tops."

They drove to a remote turnaround along the Doolittle Reservoir Road. Billy stopped the van and shut off the engine, cutting off Bon Jovi's "Shot Through the Heart" in mid-lyric. It was suddenly very quiet but for the distant din of crickets.

"You want to smoke a bowl with us?" Billy said.

"No," Cat said. "I want to go home."

"Jesus Christ, loosen up a little. You're so uptight." Billy reached into the glove compartment and retrieved a small ball of tin foil, a pipe and a butane lighter. "We'll be out of here in ten minutes, tops. You gotta learn to smell the roses, girl. Look at all those stars, chrissakes. God, what a beautiful night!" Billy looked up into the heavens.

He was right about that. It was a cloudless, moonless night and you could make out thousands of stars. Claude took a blanket from the back of the bus with him and threw it down over the wild grass. The boys all sat down and looked up at the sky and into the water of the reservoir which reflected it. After Billy got the pipe going, they passed it around.

"Sure you don't want some?" Jonathan said smiling over at her in his former seat upfront.

Cat began to feel self-conscious. "Why not?" she said, figuring it wiser to be sociable than a party-pooper. She got out and went over and sat down and took a toke. She'd smoked before. It was no big deal.

They gossiped about what an asshole the history teacher was, what a dope the principal was, what a *hotty* the art teacher was. They told a dirty joke or two and she laughed along with them. She was thinking to herself that maybe she had misjudged them. They didn't seem like such bad guys after all. Just immature.

"Speaking of nookie," Billy said out of the blue, "I am so fuckin' horny right now." He fell against her and at first she thought it was a joke, until he threw his entire weight onto her. She opened her mouth to object and instead found his tongue halfway down her throat. She pushed him away with both hands only to feel Claude grab her by the shoulders and pin her while Jonathan threw himself on her feet. When Billy came up for air, he said, "And when I'm horny, there ain't but one fuckin' cure and that's fuckin', for sure."

Claude snickered. "Fuckin' A."

Billy undid her belt buckle and zipper and started pulling at her jeans. She tried to knee him but Claude then flipped her over onto her stomach as Billy pulled her underpants down as far as her knees and pushed her sweater and bra up as far as her shoulders.

"It feels better when you squirm," Billy blurted and spit saliva down there for lubrication.

After Billy, there was Claude, and then Jonathan. There was no resisting them. Two always held her down. She stopped struggling. No words were spoken beyond a grunted curse as they ground into her, kneading her breasts and buttocks. After Jonathan finished they released her and casually smoked another bowl.

Cat laid face down where they left her. A light wind purred against her flesh and she listened to the crickets chirp in the field nearby. She wasn't crying anymore.

"I'm freezing," Billy said finally. He slapped her bare buttocks and stood up. "Let's get out of here." The three boys climbed back onto the bus and Billy turned over the engine. The cassette player went on and "Shot Through the Heart" picked up where it left off.

"Hey, you comin', or what?" Billy said, impatient. They ignored her as she slowly got to her feet, pulled up her jeans, adjusted her bra and sweater and staggered toward the open door.

"Hey, don't forget the fuckin' blanket," Claude said.

Like an automaton she turned and went back to retrieve the blanket. She climbed onto the bus and huddled on the floor.

They drove in silence listening to Bon Jovi and then George Thorogood and then Led Zeppelin. Billy slowed at the intersection of Hoover Road. "This is you," he said.

She walked along the paved road until it curved and then walked the final quarter mile up the dirt road to the cabin. Something was disconnected between her brain and her feet. She stepped carefully and occasionally stumbled as if she were learning to walk again.

She did not wake her mother, who had already gone to bed. She did not call the police. She did not call for an ambulance to take her to the hospital. She dropped her clothes into the laundry hamper and climbed into the bathtub and washed herself with soap and hot water and a washcloth. Then she crawled into bed and lay there staring into the darkness for several hours until her eyes finally closed.

The next morning her mother cooked her breakfast. If Cat was a bit quieter than usual, Sally didn't comment. Cat might have told her then what had happened the night before, but she didn't. Sally drove her to work, as usual, dropping her off at Doc Deitz's. It was a weekend job Cat had started the previous summer. She had a good rapport with the veterinarian, not to mention the animals in her care. Helen Deitz was one of the few women vets in the state and, like her own mother, a single parent raising a four-year-old daughter.

Cat might have confided in the older woman, who went out of her way to be nurturing and supportive, but she didn't. She cleaned out the cages and fed and watered all the patients by lunchtime, paying special attention to her two favorites, a small farm mutt named Joker, who'd lost both hind legs to a combine, and a tiny Maine Coon kitten with a singed coat the Doc named Smokey, left orphaned after a fire claimed its siblings and mother before it was weaned. She then drove Helen in her *Docmobile*, a Sixties-era station wagon full of drugs and tools and medical instruments, to a farm eight miles south of Samaritan near the Mason Dixon Line. There she helped the Doc castrate adolescent swine to increase their muscle mass and market value.

While the farmer clutched a pig upside down by its hind legs, Helen slit the skin of the scrotum with a mat knife and pushed out the testicles with her fingers. After snipping them off with a pair of garden shears it was Cat's job to spray disinfectant onto the wound. The squealing critter was then released into the population and the next was selected, cornered and captured. In all, they castrated twelve pigs in under a half hour, treated a sick cow with a suppository, the doc doping it with a shot of liquid ketamine hydrochloride to calm it before fisting her entire forearm up to the elbow into its butt hole, and then drove to another farm to help deliver a colt.

On Sunday she worked a half day feeding and watering the animals and cleaning their cages. When she was done and Sally picked her up, she said she was tired and went straight to bed. But she barely slept.

On Monday at school she overheard two girls in the locker room at the end of gym class whispering about a sophomore girl who had claimed she was raped by Billy Morrison and his friends over the winter. One of the girls called them *pigs*. Cat could have spoken up then and told them the same thing had happened to her. She could have gone to the principal's office or the nurse's office and reported what she'd overheard and what had happened to her. But she didn't.

She saw Jonathan and Claude in several classes and they ignored her. She saw Billy and Claude together at lunch in the cafeteria at their usual table and they glanced at her and then away as she passed with her food tray. She began to wonder how many girls they had violated, and why they had not been caught and punished. She began to wonder how many more lives they would ruin if somebody didn't do something to stop them.

She could not later remember when exactly the idea came to her. It was as if a black mass of poisonous bile backed up in her soul like a flooded septic tank. She could not eat. She could not sleep. She could not concentrate on school work. She was chastised by more than one teacher for not paying attention in class. Sally caught her staring into space at the supper table Tuesday evening and asked her what the matter was. She just shrugged. Sally concluded it must be spring fever, which Cat didn't contradict.

She knew where Jonathan lived. She'd gone to a party there on his tenth birthday. She found Billy's address in the phone book because she knew he was William Morrison III. Everyone called him Billy Three. Claude's address was tougher because there were six Van Aiken's in the phone book. She called the first and asked for Claude. The woman was very helpful. She said Claude was her nephew and gave her the number.

There was a first aid kit with a bottle of disinfectant in the medicine cabinet at home, a roll of duct tape in a drawer of a tool cabinet. Sally had a hank of sash cord hanging in the breezeway next to a hunting knife for general use. Her father had shown her how to tie different knots before he'd left them. A slip knot, a clove hitch, a square knot, a trucker's hitch. Her mother had taught her how to tie a large animal to a stick and carry it through the woods. She'd seen a war movie where men were tied like that. The expression was *hog-tied*. It all seemed to fit.

On Wednesday night after her mother went to bed she dressed in a black long-sleeved tee, black jeans, socks and sneakers, darkened her face and hands with charcoal from the woodstove, took the car keys out of Sally's purse and the hunting knife from the breezeway. Claude and Jonathan both lived in a suburban development on the edge of town called Blocher Park, just six houses from each other, while Billy lived a mile west of town in an older wood frame farmhouse built before World War I.

Claude's house was a brick ranch, the patio door in back unlocked. Quaking with nerves, she eased inside, allowing a full minute to open and then close the squeaky glass storm door in one-inch increments. She allowed her eyes to adjust to the darkness, found herself in a small dining room, and nearly jumped out of her skin when the refrigerator compressor rattled on. When she recovered, she found her footfalls muffled by wall-to-wall carpet as she made her way down the hallway. Finding her prey was easier than she thought, his bedroom door decorated with a football poster and a large *Keep Out!* sign. She heard him before she saw him. He was the lump along the far wall, heaving up and down, softly snoring as he lay on his side, his face to the wall, in a single bed under the curtained window, a polyester blanket pulled up to his neck, the floor littered with clothing, comic books and pornographic magazines.

Jonathan lived in a split level whose first floor was wainscoted on the outside in bleached brick, white aluminum siding above. Again, the back patio door was unlocked, but without a squeaky screen or storm door to compromise her. With more confidence this time, she again allowed her eyes to adjust and finally set out in silence, again on wall-to-wall carpeting.

At the top of the half-staircase she found a half-opened door where his little sister, a six-year-old, she guessed, lay in pale green pajamas, splayed unconscious on an island of blankets and pillows in a sea of teddy bears. Behind the door across the hall, she found her prey breathing deeply, inert in a single bunk, swaddled in Green Mutant Ninja Turtle pajamas, a modest aquarium by the window nearby lighting up the room, an electric water pump gurgling bubbles out of a treasure chest half-buried in pebbles with a bobbing lid for the benefit of a few oblivious tropical fish.

Billy's mini-bus was parked in a field next to a half-dozen yellow school buses lined up like soldiers facing the paved road beside a rundown barn, a lone, high, blue-green sodium vapor light attached to its far side illuminating the gravel driveway in front of the house. She drove past and parked over the next hill beside a fenced pasture gate and hiked back, keeping to the shadows. The wooden porch steps to the back door, the door itself and the floor inside were all weathered and creaky. She took her time. She could not afford to be caught. She made her way at a snail's pace through the kitchen, past the stairs to the basement, into the dining room, the living room, a den where the father snored loudly, fully clothed, face-up on an overstuffed leather couch, an empty bottle of scotch on its side an arm's length away. There was a dark forty-eight inch television in one corner and a wet bar in another, between them a mural showing various breeds of inebriated canines sidled on barstools nursing cocktails. There were three bedrooms upstairs, two unoccupied, the third where the mother slept. The room was chilly, a window open. There was a bottle of prescription drugs on the bedside table next to a princess phone. The mother had on a frilly nightgown with a pink satin face mask under a comforter in a luxurious canopy bed surrounded by soft fabrics and fluffy pillows and pink wallpaper. The vanity in the corner featured a mind-boggling array of medicine bottles, perfumes, powders, lotions and creams, its arched mirror angled to mock Cat in the doorway. She was about to explore the attic when she remembered the stairway to the basement.

She moved slowly back downstairs, across the dining room again, into the kitchen and down to the basement, one careful step at a time, keeping her hands on the stair rails, her feet to the sides to minimize noise, until finally she found him, asleep in his white briefs, his cotton sheets and bedspread kicked to the floor on his single army cot in the corner of the warm, dank, refinished room with linoleum tiles covering a cement floor. The room was lit by a glowing light switch at the bottom of the stairs and a nightlight in a wall outlet near his cot. Surrounding him seemed an

improbable warehouse of Nautilus body-building equipment until she
realized opposing floor-to-ceiling mirrors made the room look bigger than it
was. It was hot down there and smelled of sweat, the hum of a gas furnace
blazing somewhere behind a wall.

Her reconnaissance had proven a success, in and out, without any
problems. All three boys slept alone in their own rooms. She wouldn't have
to worry about younger siblings waking up in the next bed. And none had a
family pet that might announce an intruder.

She stopped at the Dr. Dietz's on the way home. She knew where the
spare key was hidden under a rock next to the side door. She stole three
hermetically-sealed hypodermic needle packs and a bottle of liquid
ketamine. She was ready.

The next day in school, her last, she felt as if she were moving in a
fog. She spoke to no one at all. Her every thought was wrapped up in
detailing the specifics of her operation, factoring contingencies, mindful of
the tight time table. It was during lunch period that she began to have
doubts. She realized how lucky she had been not to have gotten caught the
previous night. Getting all three in one night, she realized, would be next to
impossible. She worried about Claude's strength and heft and Jonathan's
younger sister. The walls of those new houses were thin, too. It would be a
miracle if the parents slept through her attacks. She focused on Billy. Billy
was the initial perpetrator, the instigator, the facilitator. Billy slept in
isolation. The father drank. The mother took pills. Billy was easier prey.
He alone would suffer the swath of her revenge.

She went to bed early that evening just after supper, with a stomach
ache, she told Sally, and jerked awake just before midnight. She was home
before dawn, cooked herself breakfast and went back to bed. Her mother
never knew she had been gone. Cat told her she was too sick to go to
school, and Sally left for work. Cat slept soundly, only waking up around
noon when Sheriff Hetrick came to the door to arrest her on charges of
breaking and entering, assault with a deadly weapon and attempted murder.

5.

THIRTEEN DAYS BEFORE OPENING DAY

Sterner got out of the shower and turned on the local news. It was an otherwise slow news day, so the local morning newscasts all covered the story about the Hellcat case, mentioned in connection to a bizarre discovery in Samaritan involving a skeleton found in the woods holding a bouquet of dead roses. The front page of the _Tribune_ read above the fold: "Hellcat First to Find Mystery Skeleton." In the article, an unnamed source speculated that the victim may have been Cat's rival in a love triangle, though Cat was likely in grade school when Jane Doe was killed. Sterner tossed the newspaper in the trash can.

He drove to Samaritan through rush hour traffic on I-81 South, bumper-to-bumper in Carlisle, and then forty miles per hour across the Pennsylvania Turnpike West to I-20 South. Including a stop for gas at this last freeway intersection, at a truck stop called "Blocher's Truckers Paradise," a low-rent version of Breezewood's highway bazaar, it took him a full two hours to get from his apartment north of Hershey to the Doolittle Station State Police Barracks two miles south of town. That would mean a four-hour commute every day, twenty hours a week minimum wasted in his car going to and from work. That was unworkable. He'd need a local motel and knew Taylor would approve the expense.

Captain Ethan Hand stood up from behind his desk, reached over and gave Sterner a firm handshake of welcome, offering him a seat for the requisite update.

"I was visiting my sister and new nephew in Richmond this weekend," he said. "I'm sorry to have missed you. I'm sure Trooper Hollings took good care of you. He's a Marine combat vet. You order those square heads to take the hill, they don't hesitate."

"I like the hardcore rookies," Sterner said. "They're not jaded." Sterner asked him how the search for the grave was going, since he'd summoned several troopers from the station to help Hollings survey the property both Sunday and Monday. Hand told him there was no news, even though they'd brought in Donald and Valerie Fripp's bloodhounds, Bonnie and Beatrice, who were trained as cadaver dogs and on retainer by the PSP, down from Millersburg to join in the search. Their skill at finding makeshift graves, however dated, was nothing short of remarkable. All the hounds did, though, was stir up a den of foxes and scare the wild turkey and deer. Today they were widening the search area from the initial parameters and would continue to sweep until told to stop. It was looking like the hut was an intentional showcase. Sterner told him he would request a helicopter fly-over with an infra-red scanner.

Sterner then brought him up to speed on everything he had on the skeleton, as well as the red hair and black cotton fiber.

"Cold cases are the worst," Hand said. "After twenty years, there's no telling if the killer is even still alive."

"We have to assume he is," Sterner said. "And the victim's ID is the key to finding him."

In addition to requisitioning an office to work out of, he wanted to ask Captain Hand about Sheriff Guise's reluctance to disclose the link to the Hellcat Case.

"I was in high school in Monongahela when Hellcat happened. It was the talk of the town for a couple of weeks. But since being assigned to the Doolittle Station, I've only ever heard the case mentioned once by my predecessor when he said it had eclipsed the Doolittle County Depositors Trust scandal in the 1960's. Hellcat was not something anyone much liked to talk about since everything that could be said about it had been and everybody in Doolittle County was sick of the subject.

"And if you lived in a community like Samaritan most your life," Hand added, "as the Sheriff has, would you want it known to the outside world as a place where some rapist got a gonad cut off by his victim? That's not exactly an image the local Chamber of Commerce wants to promote. They want Samaritan seen as the apple sauce capital, with folks as friendly as apple pie. And remember, Sheriff of Doolittle County is an elected position, and he's as much a politician as a lawman. The territory doesn't come without an ego."

Sterner thought about his boss Benjamin Taylor, an egomaniacal politician in his own right. "As I remember my Bible," Sterner said, "the parable of the Good Samaritan was poignant only because Samaritans were not generally thought to be caring and generous to strangers."

"Well, those were the days before Chambers of Commerce," Hand said. "Philadelphia is the City of Brotherly Love, but it seems like half the murders in the state are committed there. I've always known the Sheriff to be an honest and thorough lawman."

It was a long-standing policy of the Pennsylvania State Police Department that troopers were never assigned a station in the same county where they grew up. It was intended to prevent the kind of nepotism and cronyism that led to, at the very least, a lack of objectivity in investigating and prosecuting crimes, and at the very worst, corruption. Sterner knew he could absolutely trust the troopers because they had no history or ties to the community. Troopers like Hollings were taught to have total loyalty to the force, with the highest standards of personal integrity and conduct. They were a highly trained and disciplined organization of well over four thousand brethren statewide. Even the Academy in Sterner's hometown of Hershey was run much more like a paramilitary basic training camp than the average police academy.

However--and this was the weakness of the State Police--its investigators were slower to generate the more subtle human analysis that could be illuminated by local law enforcement with an intimate knowledge of the community they served. Left to their own devices, state investigators could have labored weeks before identifying the owner of Cat's arrow, which the Sheriff recognized straight away. In any investigation, Sterner well knew, the trick was to balance the two groups to find the truth and bring the guilty to justice.

Sterner thanked Hand for his insights, and Hand showed him to a guest office down the hall with a first-floor window facing a recently harvested cornfield of a neighboring farm. It was hot, stuffy and small, but the window opened just wide enough to ease Sterner's claustrophobia. His host pointed out the copy room, the kitchen, the supply room, the bathroom, the briefing room, the bunk room and the arsenal, which had a steel door and was always locked. Hand gave him a key and had him open it to inspect the rack of standard issue M16 assault rifles, 9mm Glock side arms, pump shotguns and, of course, the ammunition cabinet. There was also a wall of black armor, safety helmets, riot and SWAT gear, should the need arise. Giving a guest investigator access to such ordnance and protection was standard procedure, but Sterner doubted he would ever touch anything in the room. For one thing, he had his own sidearm in the glove compartment of his car. For another, his work had rarely compelled him to use it, and he couldn't imagine this case being different.

———————

After moving his ToughBook and a few other items from the trunk of his car into his new office Sterner went online and checked his e-mail.

"Taylor.benjamin@psp.gov" had responded to his e-mail entitled: "RE: FBI Involvement." It read: "Have we eliminated prank theory? Check local colleges before involving FBI."

Taylor had a point.

Sterner answered the e-mail, acknowledging the suggestion, and added:

"Request requisition for aerial infra-red survey of Rattlesnake Ridge to eliminate prank theory that hut is merely convenient. If not, it is an intentional showcase. Due to rugged terrain, finding the grave without ITIS could take a week. Captain Hand at Doolittle Barracks sent in cadaver dogs but found nothing. —Sterner."

After logging off Sterner looked up a number in the phonebook and called Samaritan College Security. He talked to a Wayne Kendalhart, head of a staff of six security people to patrol the forty-acre campus. Sterner asked him if he was any relation to Deputy Warren Kendalhart. Warren, it turned out, was his cousin. Sterner asked him whether any bells of recognition sounded when he learned of the skeleton in the woods. He said not but invited Sterner to drop by and personally go through their reports on file detailing various pranks and certain troublemakers they were tracking.

He then called Sheriff Guise. Louella reported that there'd been a single car accident involving a drunk driver on a county road south of Murdoch, the next town east of Samaritan, and the Sheriff had been there all morning, and he was then due to testify in court that afternoon. It was a reminder that a decades-old murder was not the only priority for a small town Sheriff.

Louella recommended the Sleep Well Motel out along the interstate east of town, and asked if she could make reservations for him. He said he'd call himself and thanked her. As soon as Sterner got off the phone with the Sleep Well, he heard the fax machine in the copy room humming and found Louella's faxes. The first was handwritten and titled: "Rattlesnake Ridge Lodge Corporation LLC."

"Current Board of Directors: President Lowell Purcells, Vice President Jason Lumley, Secretary Al Martini, Treasurer Arnold Rohrenbach. Other Members: Roy Fries, Emil Winn, David Longenecker, John Hetrick, Newton Wimpleton, Jerzy Pokorny.

"Note: Al has list of original members and every guest hunter for past forty years, but it's a pretty long one."

This is where Sheriff Guise would have come in handy, but since he wasn't available, Sterner opened up the phonebook again and found Al Martini's number. His wife gave Sterner his work number. Martini picked up on the first ring.

"Martini Motors, Al speaking, how can I help you?"

Sterner identified himself and asked if he was the secretary of the Rattlesnake Ridge Lodge Corporation.

"Yes, I sure am," he said.

"What is the Rattlesnake Ridge Lodge Corporation?" Sterner said.

"Technically, it's a tree farm, but that's mostly for tax purposes," Martini said. "There are some healthy oaks on the property, but most of the timber's no good for anything but pulp. The property hasn't been timbered in some years. It's used for hunting, period. Have you made any progress on the case?"

"We're just getting started."

"The Sheriff came to our emergency meeting last night," he said, "and no one has a clue who this gal is, but believe you me, we're all upset as hell about this thing. Not only that, we're missing out on our muzzle-loading season. We're eager to cooperate in any way we can, especially now that we're deputized. Arney and Jase, who are both retired, volunteered to scour the property on their four-by-fours to help look for that grave before the rest of us can join them on the weekend."

Sterner thanked him and then asked him for a list of all the members in the past forty years and a list of all their guests.

"Jesus," Martini said, but agreed, qualifying that it would take time to assemble a list, and some were deceased. Sterner gave him his fax number. Lastly, he asked if he knew anyone who might pull a stunt like this. Martini said he did not.

Sterner copied the list of member names into an e-mail and then added "Theodore Balzac Lamotti" and sent it to Criminal Records to look for priors.

It would be handy when the MATRIX FACTS system was up and running and available to investigators. The system was still in its infancy and direct access in the future was unlikely anyway. The system was a federally funded project to assemble all available information on every citizen in the state onto a central database, everything from real estate ownership and driving records, birthdates and telephone numbers to bank data and credit reports, gun ownership and fingerprints, employment records and marriage and divorce information, all the way down to medical records and magazine subscriptions. The information could be cross-referenced with criminal activity. Because of privacy issues and the Orwellian "Big Brother" implications, the possibility that it could be abused by government officials or burgled by unauthorized hackers, there were less than thirty people currently authorized to access it.

As he finished up his e-mail, Sheriff Guise called him back.

"I suppose you're gonna take me to the woodshed," he said to Sterner.

"I looked pretty stupid in front of my boss yesterday when he found out I didn't know who Cat True was," Sterner said, keeping his anger at bay.

"I apologize about that. Had I known the press was going to jump all over this I certainly would've given you a heads up. I don't know where they're getting their information."

"Now maybe you'll tell me the whole story," Sterner said. "You mentioned you and her father were deputies together."

"What happened was he run off with the Judge's wife. Well, the DA then. Anyway, Davey told me he was thinking about it before he done it. I could've tried to stop him but I didn't. I've felt nothing but guilt about it ever since. Sally told me they were homesteading somewhere up in the Yukon, him and the DA's wife, cut themselves off from everybody in their old life. He just up and abandoned his family. It was an awful thing, a big scandal."

"This was before the Hellcat Case?"

"Oh, my, yes, way before. I think Cat was about eight years old at the time. Hell, every time I look into those sad eyes of hers it just gnaws at me. If she'd had a daddy who was a deputy sheriff, I doubt the rape would've happened, I'll tell you that. And even if it had, what followed would've been very different. Her whole life would've been different. Again, I'm sorry I didn't say nothin'."

"I have to tell you a profiler with the FBI thinks it's possible the roses may have been intended for her."

"Now how is *that* possible? She shot the buck in the state forest and tracked it to the hut. Who could've known she would do something like that?"

"That's what I intend to ask her myself," Sterner said. "Care to come along?"

"I can't today," Sheriff Guise said, "I'm due to testify upstairs in a few minutes. Domestic abuse case that's a real mess. Couple with six kids, both parents serious alcoholics." There was a long pause on the phone but

Sterner could hear the Sheriff breathing heavily, thinking about it. "Maybe my feelings do get the better of me where Cat's concerned. I'm hardly objective. What do the lawyers call it? Maybe I should *recuse* myself. How about I send Warren over to pick you up. He'll take care of you."

"My boss wants me to check with Samaritan College to see if they might register it as a fraternity prank. I talked to a Wayne Kendalhart there. He invited me over."

"That's Warren's cousin. He'd be the man to see."

"It sure is a small town."

"Don't I know it."

After hanging up Sterner started to think about Cat at age eight, wondering what might have gone through her mind when her father just disappeared one day. These thoughts led to Becca. The last call Sterner made was to Emily. Not surprisingly, he got her voicemail.

"Emily. Joe. Listen, I want to apologize for the way I dismissed your concerns for Becca. I want to call a truce until we've ruled out anything physical being wrong with her. I'd like to come with you to the examination to show support. If that's okay, just let me know when and where as soon as possible. Thanks."

Within half an hour, Kendalhart's Explorer pulled into the parking lot at the barracks.

"So you want to question Cat True again," Kendalhart said when Sterner climbed in. "And then campus security at the college, is that right?"

"Yup. That's the itinerary."

"You know what the guys in town do when they see Cat coming?"

"No. What?"

Kendalhart took his hands off the wheel just long enough to place them over his crotch.

Sterner half-grinned and nodded.

"She was after all three of em, you know. They found two additional hypodermics on her when they arrested her."

"I never heard that."

"And they never did find out what she did with it."

"Did with what?"

"You know. Billy's nut. His testicle. The family jewel. She never told anybody what she did with it. The three thousand dollar question. That's what people called it. Two DJs on the radio down in D.C. offered a three thousand dollar reward to anybody who found it. But nobody ever collected. Some say she buried it in the woods in a jar of formaldehyde. Others claimed her mother was some kind of Indian necromancer who used it for a hex to curse her attacker's family. His old man died of a heart attack the next year."

Sterner took a deep breath and shook his head. All part of the Hellcat mystique, he supposed. "So you know where Ms. True lives?"

"Sure."

"Let's head there first."

They headed north through clusters of trees, patch-quilt farmland, pastures and orchards, into town past the Court House, the square, the high school, through more farmland. They were heading down the road toward a place called Mason's Gap parallel to a shallow creek, rolled over a steel cantilever bridge and then took a left onto Hoover Road. About a half mile up the paved road there was another left turn onto an unmarked dirt road that led into deep woods. Not until they were upon it did Sterner spy the log cabin through the brush. It was not so much a dwelling in the woods as a dwelling *of* the woods, its weathered stacked pine logs indistinguishable from the bark of the surrounding trees. Smoke curled out of a black tin stovepipe protruding from a limb-littered, tar shingle roof. They pulled up next to a twenty-year-old Corolla with a bent fender.

"Can't get much more remote than this!" the Deputy offered. "Davey True sure liked his privacy."

"Did you know him?"

"Nope. Only heard stories. He was quite a character, apparently."

"You've been here before?"

"Sheriff's sent me out once or twice when Ol' Sally reported Peeping Toms, but nothing came of it. I think she was just looking for attention."

Sally True came to the door after a few raps. Her eyes were wide with distrust and she looked over the two men carefully but said nothing.

"How do you do?" Sterner said and showed her a card. "I'm Joe Sterner, Pennsylvania State Police. This is Deputy Kendalhart, County Sheriff's Department. We're looking for Cat True. Does she live here?"

"I don't know what you people want with me. You must be wasting an awful lot of taxpayers' money. For what, I don't know."

"I'm sorry, ma'am. Perhaps you misunderstood. We're looking for Catherine True. Does she live here?"

"Of course she lives here. You know that. She's my daughter. And you know very well her name is Catoosa, not Catherine."

"I didn't catch your name."

"You know my name," Sally said looking at him sideways.

Sterner said, "No, ma'am. I'm sorry. We've never met."

"Sally True," Kendalhart said leaning in.

"See? You people can't fool me," she said.

"Is Miss True home or not?" Sterner said. He was getting irritated.

"You know very well where she is."

Sterner sighed. He didn't like losing his temper, but he didn't like evasion, either.

"Is she at work, ma'am?" Kendalhart said.

"Of course she's at work."

"The vet clinic?"

"You know very well where she is. You just mean to harass me."

"Thank you, ma'am," Kendalhart said and turned to Sterner. "I know where it is."

"Just one more thing," Sterner said. "Have you noticed anyone hanging around, maybe following Cat?"

"Only you people. I don't know how much they're paying you, but I wish you'd leave me alone." Sally True closed the door in their faces.

On their way back to the Explorer, Kendalhart said, "Ol' Sally's a bit complicated, if you didn't notice."

"I noticed. Miss True works at a veteran's hospital?"

"Veterinarian. It's a part-time position, I believe," Kendalhart said. "Always has worked there. She's real good with animals, they say."

Sterner grumbled to himself that Kendalhart might have volunteered this information before now. They were halfway down the road when Sterner said, "By the way, I must commend you for preserving the scene the other day. I know the Sheriff gave you grief because it wasn't much of a crime scene, but it turned out to be a big help. That fiber and hair could be useful down the road."

"Oh, sure thing. Well, truth be told, it was more Suzy's idea than mine."

"Suzy?"

"The dispatcher. You probably met her at the Sheriff's Office. The fat girl?"

"Oh, yeah. I know who you mean," Sterner said. "Well, I'll have to thank *her*, then."

"She was on duty Saturday morning when Doc Fries called in. I was speed-trapping the Murdoch pike while the Sheriff was getting his annual physical. *The poke and prod special*, he calls it. Which is why we didn't want to bother him. She called you guys after I high-tailed it up the mountain. If it weren't for those bullet holes in the back of the skull, the Sheriff would've torn me a new one."

"Runs a tight ship, does he?"

"Ship is right. He was in the Navy, you know."

"I did hear that," Sterner said.

———————

As they pulled into the parking lot in a suburban development called Windham Court, a familiar TV news truck was pulling away from a modern two-story house with an addition built onto the side, an unpretentious sign identifying it as Doctor Deitz's Animal Clinic. Ellie Deitz, a twenty-something blond waif wearing a striped caftan, was also the veterinarian's daughter and her receptionist. She mistook Sterner for another annoying reporter before she saw Kendalhart's uniform following him through the door. She pointed them to a back room where Cat, wearing a lab coat, sat calmly feeding a mewing litter of black and white kittens with Pedialyte from an eyedropper.

"Miss True, Joe Sterner," he said. "We met yesterday in the Sheriff's Office."

"Ms. I'm divorced," she said.

"I'm sorry?" he said.

"I'm not."

"I mean, I didn't--realize," he said stammering. "You changed back to your maiden name after the divorce?"

"No, actually, he changed his name to mine," she said in such a deadpan way he couldn't be sure if she was joking. "What do you want?"

"I had a few more questions, if you don't mind," he said.

He opened a notepad but found he was distracted by her handling of the kittens. She was expertly tender but firm like a mother cat, effortlessly removing each from the cardboard box with one hand, drawing the liquid with the other and then squirting the nourishment into its mouth. Their mewing ceased only long enough for the kitten to lap up its meal with a tiny pink tongue on furry lips and jagged teeth. She deposited it back into the box with its rambunctious siblings wrestling on a white cotton towel bed wrapped around a hot water bottle, and then seized the next. Sterner found it both touching and amusing.

"Yes?" she said waiting.

Sterner quickly flipped through his list of questions. "Was last Monday the first morning you were hunting in the state forest this season?"

"No. I've gone out every Monday since archery opened in September. Sometimes Tuesdays and Wednesdays, too."

"Did anyone know you'd be hunting that morning?"

She shrugged. "Everyone here. Some folks at my other job. My mother. Why?"

"You have another job?"

"I work the door weekends at Rosita's Roadhouse." Cat looked over at Deputy Kendalhart. Sterner turned to Kendalhart. He coughed, embarrassed. There was something between them, Sterner realized.

"Out along the interstate," Kendalhart said. "You probably passed it on your way into town. It gets a little rowdy sometimes. We've been called out on occasion."

Sterner frowned. Kendalhart hadn't prepared him for this, either, and Sterner didn't like surprises during interviews. Sterner turned back to Cat. "Did anyone know where you'd be hunting?"

"Sometimes even I don't know. What is this all about?"

"Where do you park that morning?"

"Bend in the road between Greenwood Furnace and Burnside Summit."

"Might anyone have followed you?"

"I saw nobody." She shrugged. "It was dark."

"And what do you drive?"

"Black pick-up. 'Seventy-eight. It's in the parking lot. Why are you asking me all these questions?"

"Sometimes people are involved in something without realizing it," Sterner said. He sighed. "It's the roses. I was wondering if maybe you had an admirer, a stalker, an old flame or an ex-husband."

"You guys really *are* desperate. Look, my ex is in jail for aggravated assault, which is where he belongs. My last lover was a Wisconsin truck driver with a bad back and that was five months ago. There is no way anyone could've predicted I'd find that skeleton."

Sterner thought for a moment and put away his notepad. "All right then."

Another woman's voice piped in. "Excuse me, may I help you?"

Sterner turned to face a stern white-haired woman standing in the doorway in a white lab coat like Cat's, her fists on her hips. "Are these officers harassing you, Cat?"

"No."

"What exactly is your business here?"

"I'm investigating the skeleton found in the woods by Miss True."

"*Ms.* True," she corrected him, "has answered enough questions. I have some lawyer friends in the ACLU who would love to drag you people into court to show just cause for harassing my employee."

"It's okay, Helen," Cat said.

"It is *not* okay." A bee in her bonnet.

"And I could haul you in on obstruction charges, but I hardly see the point, as my business with *Ms.* True is concluded for the moment. We were just leaving." Sterner turned to Cat. "Sorry to bother you."

When they got outside, Kendalhart sighed. "Women, huh? Can't live with em, can't shoot em. Ol' Doc Deitz sure can get her knickers in a twist, can't she?"

"You didn't tell me you knew Ms. True from her second job, deputy," Sterner said. He noted the black pickup with rusty fenders parked nearby. A compound bow was hanging in a gun rack inside the back window.

"You didn't exactly ask me," Kendalhart said.

"Listen, I could've had a trooper ferry me around today. The reason we work with local law enforcement is because you guys know your community better than we do. The more information you can provide my investigation, the faster I can conclude it. It's a waste of my time for you to hold back on me. Do I make myself clear, deputy?"

Kendalhart offered Sterner his best whipped expression, served up with a blue-collar chip on his shoulder. "Crystal, sir. What happened was we got a call last year about a brawl out there one Saturday night and I go check it out. Cat's working the door, which is a kind of bouncer position. She has a reputation for being pretty good at taking care of herself, but she fights dirty, you know? Anyway, these two assholes were going at it and she's on this one guy trying to pull him off, so I get on the other. Next thing I know this asshole's got my neck in an armlock. The other guy runs out the door, so she peels the numbskull off me about the time I throw in the towel. Anyway, we cuffed him and threw his drunk ass into my truck. Disturbing the peace *and* assaulting a law officer. Got him sixty days in County."

"In other words, she saved your ass," Sterner said, amused. They climbed into his Explorer.

"Yeah, something like that," Kendalhart said, "though I'd rather nobody at the office hears--"

"Dispatch to Deputy Kendalhart." It was Louella.

"Kendalhart, go ahead," he said, pressing the hand mike on his collar.

"Warren, we just got a report of a disturbed grave up in Laurel Valley. Are you with Detective Sterner?"

"Yes I am."

"Do you want to take this or should I wait and send the Sheriff?"

Sterner arched his eyebrows with interest and nodded.

"We'll take it," Kendalhart said.

"Meet a Mr. Nathan Rydell at the Crossroads Country Store in Pineville."

"Copy that, on our way, Deputy Kendalhart out."

"Pineville anywhere near Rattlesnake Ridge?" Sterner asked.

"Nowhere near," Kendalhart said. "Rattlesnake Ridge is in the southwest corner of Doolittle County. Pineville and Laurel Valley are in the northwest corner, north of the Turnpike, even. They're both part of Wilder Mountain, but they're a good thirty miles apart."

————————

Pineville was a tiny village of modest two-story homes on quarter-acre lots, with one traffic light at the crossroads to prevent anyone passing through from blinking and missing it. The Crossroads Country Store was the only business for miles. It stood on the northeast corner, a two-story fire trap that dropped out of a time warp from an era before horseless carriages. One had to walk inside to realize the only windows in the place were the ones on either side of the center door on the street face. Except for the post-war fluorescent lighting overhead, the only things that had changed in a century were the shelf products and their prices. In addition to the typical convenience store items, there was a fifty-gallon barrel of pickles, bushels and bushels of every imaginable variety of apples and a wheelbarrow overflowing with peanuts.

Nathan Rydell stood up from a rocking chair across from the cash register to introduce himself as a junior high school substitute teacher in Murdoch. Without solicitation, he offered how he had won a tidy settlement in an automobile accident case that had made him lame but allowed him time to indulge in his passion as an ardent member of the Doolittle County Historical Society, which maintained several neglected cemeteries around the county that would otherwise have returned to the wild. He had routinely stopped at one such half-forgotten plot in Laurel Valley, at the top of a narrow hollow with a single paved road that followed a meandering stream.

It was a dead-end dirt road stopping short at an impassible rock cliff, an abandoned rock quarry and a near-forgotten public dump.

Early inhabitants had lived a clannish life there hunting, trapping and timbering in the latter half of the nineteenth and early twentieth centuries, he said. During the Depression when the paved road was built, they realized they didn't actually have to live in such an isolated area and had long since moved down the mountain and into small villages like Pineville, if not the bustling county seat of Samaritan.

Rydell had of course read in the Samaritan Times about the skeleton and when he discovered the disturbed grave in the old cemetery he'd sped down the mountain to phone the Sheriff's Office from the Crossroads Country Store.

The area was rugged, rocky and heavily-wooded. Ice Age boulders lodged unmovable in the landscape as the North American glacier retreated back into Canada eons ago. Inside the quarter-acre cemetery, bordered by an ankle-high stone fence, maple trees grew unchecked since the cemetery was abandoned in the middle of the previous century, the seeds blown there by neighboring trees that now towered over the lot. The larger trunks inside the fence toppled gravestones and no doubt penetrated rotting caskets with their tentacle-like roots. The whole area was perforated by rat holes, whose inhabitants moved on once their food supply ran out. The site was irreversibly returning to nature despite the valiant efforts of men like Nathan Rydell.

But there was one grave that seemed incongruously untouched by nature's hand. It was the one with the freshly turned earth under a crooked headstone identifying the final resting place for one Abel Nestor, who had died in 1936. As Rydell anxiously led them to his find, Sterner lagged behind to examine the overgrown path through the wrought-iron gate for trace evidence. He found none. It was obvious by the pock-marked dirt surface of the filled-in grave that it had been disturbed before the rain storm the previous Thursday which pre-dated the skeleton discovery story in the press. This was not the work of a copycat.

Rydell told them the little he knew about the cemetery and the four dozen or so graves around them dating back two hundred and fifty years, and then excused himself and withdrew. When he was gone, Trooper Ned Hollings broke ground with the shovel Sterner had brought along. Hollings had led the four troopers who helped search Rattlesnake Ridge for Jane Doe's grave the previous two days and had received the call from Captain

Hand to meet Sterner at his request outside the country store on their way up the valley.

"Okay, I'm taking bets," Trooper Hollings said, spitting into his hands, grabbing hold of the shovel's stem and thrusting the blade into the soil. "Who thinks there's a skeleton at the bottom of this grave?"

"Not me," Kendalhart said.

Trooper Hollings deposited the soil into Sterner's mesh-bottomed pan where he swirled it like a miner panning for gold. "I don't think you'll find any takers on that bet," Sterner said. "You got a first name, Trooper?"

"Ned."

"Understand you were with the Marines."

"Yessir. Two tours in Afghanistan."

"See any action?" Kendalhart asked.

"I saw enough." Hollings said. They knew by his tone not to ask more.

They worked into the evening, with Kendalhart taking over digging duties when Hollings grew weary. Finding any hair and fiber in the overturned earth was like finding the proverbial needle in a haystack. Despite Sterner's painstaking efforts, he found nothing in the soil that betrayed whoever had disturbed the grave. The grave robber had been very careful. At the bottom they found the remnants of a simple, rotted pine coffin without an occupant. There were tattered remnants of clothing--a dark suit, white shirt, high-top black leather shoes--but no bones. Disappointed, they filled in the grave and drove back down the mountain.

As the men gathered at the counter of the Crossroads Country Store to pay for their beverages the white-haired old woman behind the cash register said, "No luck?"

"I'm afraid we can't comment," Kendalhart said. "Sheriff's business."

"I only ask because Abel Nestor was my uncle. I don't like to hear somebody messed with his grave," she said. In a country store in an area like Pineville, there was always plenty of time for gossip, and news from Rydell of the disturbed grave had already traveled far.

"Maybe you could tell us how your uncle died," Sterner said.

"Oh, my lands, died of a fever back in the Depression, as I recall. I must've been about eight or nine years old, but I remember his funeral. Nobody much goes up the hollow, anymore, 'cept the Highways Department to pick up gravel at the quarry up top."

"How tall was your uncle?"

"Average. Maybe five two. Five four."

"Anything else that would distinguish him physically?"

"He was cockeyed. When you talked to him one eye was always looking off. Is that what you mean? Spooked me a might as an urchin knee-high to a rattlesnake."

"Any strangers come in here in the last couple of weeks? Especially somebody younger, in their twenties or thirties?"

"I'm old as the hills. Everybody's younger than me. But strangers?" She thought about it, shook her head. "I don't recall seeing any. We're off the tourist maps."

"What's your name, ma'am?" Sterner said.

"Betty Nagle," she said, shaking Sterner's hand. "Nestor was my maiden name."

Sterner handed her a card with his cell number. "Detective Joe Sterner. Pleased to meet you, Betty. Now if you hear anything about somebody nosing around that cemetery in the last couple of weeks, would you mind calling me and letting me know? But make sure it's solid information, not gossip."

Her eyes lit up. "You bet," she said, delighted to be included in the investigation.

———————

Kendalhart drove Sterner back to town to report to the Sheriff.

"What's the possibility our Jane Doe is Abel Nestor?" the Sheriff said.

"Zero," Sterner said stretching his arms, neck and back as he leaned back in the metal chair facing Guise's desk. "Even if he lived his life as a woman pretending to be a man, there's a big difference between thirty-year-old bones and sixty-year-old bones."

"What's the possibility Jane Doe was hidden in the same grave with Abel Nestor?"

"Unlikely. There should've been trace evidence to suggest that and there wasn't."

"What's the possibility we have someone running around playing games with us?"

"Those odds are pretty good."

The Sheriff sighed. "Yeah, well, I'm starting to develop my own theory. Some prankster picked up a skeleton somewhere, had no idea those were bullet holes in the back of the skull or that he had evidence in a murder. And now he's trying to cover his tracks, leaving us chasing our tails."

"Except Abel Nestor was dug up before news of Jane Doe came out."

"It just don't make no damn sense."

Then the Sheriff asked Kendalhart to give them a few minutes in private. When he left the room, Sheriff Guise pulled a bottle of Scotch and two whiskey glasses from his desk drawer. "He may not seem it, but Ol' Warren's a bit of a prude when it comes to hard liquor. Mind you, the boy's got more problems with women than you can shake a stick at--divorced twice before he was twenty-five, got a kid out of wedlock with a third woman, living with a fourth--but when it comes to booze, he's as pure a puritan as they come. I'm officially off the clock, so I'm allowed," he said pouring them each a double shot.

"I'm still on the clock, but if you won't tell I won't." Normally Sterner would've refused, but he knew drinking with the Sheriff would enhance their rapport, which he needed. Besides, after sifting grave dirt all afternoon out in the cold, he could use a stiff one. They clinked glasses and Sterner took a cautionary sip. It burned his throat but left a warm, numbing and most welcome aftertaste.

"There's something I want to say to you about Cat and Sally, and I'm not quite sure how to say it, exactly," Sheriff Guise said.

"Take a stab," Sterner said.

The Sheriff downed his whiskey in one gulp and poured himself another. "You and I know our place in this world. We are what we do. We define ourselves by our jobs. We read newspapers and magazines and follow the television. We gossip with our neighbors and pay our taxes, go to the movies and share jokes down at the barbershop. We're involved in our communities. And that makes us like ninety-nine percent of the rest of the country. But Cat and Sally are among that minority one percent whose whole reality is limited to what's outside the window. They've got no TV, no stereo, no computers. Maybe a radio, but that's about it. They don't subscribe to newspapers or magazines, follow politics or vote. In short, they could no more function in our world than we could in theirs."

Sterner was intrigued. "What's so different about their world?" Sterner said.

The Sheriff thought about it for a moment. "Let me put it to you this way: If I was to give you a Swiss Army knife and drop you on top of Rattlesnake Ridge and wished you luck, what would you do?"

"Walk down to the road and hitch-hike back to town."

"As would ninety-nine percent of the rest of us. Cat and Sally would put together a shelter, make a fire, forage for food and make themselves at home."

"You mean they're survivalists or something?" Sterner said.

"Well, in a way, but you're missing the bigger picture," Sheriff Guise said. "You could call them anti-social, too, but that's not right, either. They don't fit under any label so easily."

"Ms. True works two jobs," Sterner said. "That implies she functions just fine."

"It's not that she's dysfunctional, but these jobs are both menial and part-time. See, the concept of a career is abstract to her. Ambition is not in her--whatayacallit?--lexicon. She don't define who she is by how she earns a living. She don't care about power or money or fame or the respect of colleagues or even the acceptance of neighbors. She don't fit into anybody's hierarchy. She's sort of wild that way, and you have to respect that. It's not that she's stupid--quite the opposite."

"You mean she's an artist."

"Artists know they're artists. They got art to show for it, don't they? Let's just say she's different and it gets her into trouble."

Sterner drained his glass and set it down empty on the desk. "Sheriff, you surprise me. Here I pegged you for a gruff redneck and it turns out you're a social scientist. If I didn't know better I'd think you were a Democrat."

"I *am* a Democrat, damn you," the Sheriff said picking up the bottle without dropping his poker face. He reached across and was poised to pour Sterner a second round. "One for the road?"

"Best not," Sterner said waving the bottle away. "I've still got work to do. Thank you, though, hits the spot. But why are you telling me all this?"

"Well, I just thought you needed to know. Sometimes Cat comes across as a tough cookie. She thinks she has to act like that but underneath she's a good kid."

"Point taken. You never told me about your meeting with the hunting club."

"Oh, that. Well. Not much to tell, really. They were all real eager to help out any way they could. They tried to pump me for information. They're all angry about this thing and so am I. I'm starting to go back to my original position that this whole thing is a hoax." He looked tired.

"Get some sleep, Sheriff," Sterner said. "I'll keep in touch."

"Do that," he said.

———————

Captain Hand had left for the day by the time Sterner returned to the barracks. He checked his e-mail at the laptop in his office. Taylor told him to report to the Samaritan Airport at 0800 Wednesday a.m. to meet his pilot Jimmy Huang.

There was also an e-mail from the Criminal Records Division with the list of members of the Rattlesnake Ridge Lodge Corporation and prior convictions. One of the members had his license revoked for a DUI a dozen years ago. It had since been reissued. Another had done a stint in County as a teenager for assault. A third was charged but acquitted for vehicular manslaughter back in the 1960's. Nothing relevant, Sterner decided. Theodore Balzac Lamotti came back clean.

An e-mail from Emily's iPhone read, "Thank you. Will let you know. Emily."

He drove to the Sleep Well Motel just off Interstate Route 20 and checked in. It was a desolate row of one-story, thin-walled, no-frills rooms lined up back-to-back in two wings off a canopied entrance port and a two story structure with a simple lobby, front desk and breakfast room downstairs and the proprietor's apartment upstairs, surrounded by black top paved over bulldozed scrub. He took a room in back where the din of traffic noise was only slightly less obnoxious.

The closest restaurant was conveniently across the way--Rosita's Roadhouse--where Cat True worked weekends. All the businesses along the commercial strip between town and the interstate looked different and yet somehow the same as if designed by the same architect and built by the same contractor. Rosita's had a southwestern theme incongruous with the culture of the area, but maybe that was the point. It was a wood-paneled one-story hacienda with a faux hitching post out front between the façade and the parking lot, a large display of barbed wire framed under glass in the entranceway, paintings of cowpokes and Indians in Western landscapes on every paneled wall and wagon wheel chandeliers sporting candelabra bulbs with individual lampshades. The hostess and waitresses wore checkered shirts with bandannas, blue jeans and cowboy boots. As was the custom of such franchises, there was no ceiling per se, just ductwork painted matte black. Their most popular special was barbecued ribs but they also offered a handsome salad bar and served a pretty good sirloin steak and baked potato, and Sterner ordered a nice glass of California merlot. He then returned to his room, showered and fell into bed.

As he lay there waiting for sleep to overtake him, he wondered what it would be like to define yourself by criteria not job-related. Was he like the Sheriff, a confirmed bachelor who had no life outside the job? Was this why his own marriage failed, because he was a cop married to a lawyer, instead of a husband married to a wife? He wondered what it would be like to define your world without newspapers and television and magazines and movies and politics and the so-called outside world, and to think of it instead as simply what was outside your window. It was an eighteenth century conceit, he decided. Pre-Industrial Revolution. Pre-Fourth Estate. The last thing in his mind before drifting off was the view outside his office window at the barracks, the cornfield that had been recently harvested.

———————

6.

TWELVE DAYS BEFORE OPENING DAY

Sterner met the Vietnamese-born pilot Jimmy Huang in the office of the Samaritan Airport precisely at 0800. The entire facility amounted to two corrugated tin hangars for single-engine props, one of which housed an enclosed radio room with a lunch counter heated by a gas stove, the owner/operator working as an air traffic controller, aircraft mechanic and short order cook. Outside was a set of high-octane gas pumps, an orange wind sock and a freshly mowed grass runway.

The chopper's fuel tank had been topped off at Harrisburg International and was ready to fly. The Infrared Thermal Imaging System, or ITIS, was attached to the undercarriage of the fuselage and looked like a bowling ball. It was controlled by the co-pilot (in this case, Sterner) using a video game device with a joy stick and zoom controller.

Sterner had trained on the system the previous summer. There were two screens. One monitored a standard HiDef daylight video camera while the other showed the same HiDef image rendered in fluorescent green from the infrared camera. The two were set to work in tandem. Both had an auto and manual iris adjustment and image stabilization. A time-code generator synchronized date and time and automatically burned it into the image. Both were attached to separate DVRs which could record up to five hours.

The infrared camera registered minute differences in ground temperature. It was used by the Forestry Department to locate smoldering fires. It was used by law enforcement to hunt down suspects or fugitives who were on the run at night, or in hiding around trees or buildings or underneath cover. It was also used by forensic criminologists like Sterner to detect graves that may be hidden beneath a cover of fallen leaves.

It was relatively easy to find a freshly buried body using infrared, a little harder to find one that had been buried for weeks or even months, although the heat emitted from decomposition was still discernible on infrared light. It was hardest of all to find the disturbed earth of an empty grave, but no matter how effectively it may be camouflaged to the naked eye the signature of aerated soil could still be recognized, since it invariably had a different temperature than the surrounding soil.

What was less obvious from the air was the size of any patch of disturbed earth. A groundhog hole or the entrance to a fox den could be easily mistaken for a man-made grave. The solution was in maintaining a constant altitude during the aerial survey, keeping a constant focal length on the zooms and having agents on the ground investigate sites of interest. The rugged nature of the terrain below Rattlesnake Ridge made both these solutions tricky. It took time for the assembled troopers to reach some of the areas of interest.

Sterner had obtained the GPS coordinates of the chicken coop, as well as those of Abel Nestor's grave, from Trooper Hollings, whose SUV, like the cruisers and unlike his own vehicle, were GPS-equipped. When he handed them over to Jimmy on a slip of paper from his pad, the pilot punched them into his flight planner software and within minutes they were in the air. By 0830 they were landing beside the chicken coop, where Sterner huddled with Hollings and his trooper colleagues from the barracks who this morning brought two ATVs on a flatbed for the occasion. In the distance they could hear the occasional crackle from an inline muzzle-loader, thankfully none in their immediate vicinity, due to the cooperation of the Rattlesnake Ridge Lodge Corporation and a game warden named Irvin Groener who was patrolling the adjacent state forest. Still, it was unsettling for the uniforms to hear gunfire all around them. Their blaze orange vests, while clearly identifying them as *State Police*, were after all not bulletproof.

Sterner wanted to cover both sides of Rattlesnake Ridge in the morning and Laurel Valley by the afternoon. He had troopers on the ground on the Doolittle County side. The Burnside County side was a different matter. In any case, he hoped to have enough time for the troopers and the game warden to get to the Burnside County side before the sweep in Laurel Valley after lunch.

What he hadn't counted on was how much time it took to cover just the Doolittle County side of Rattlesnake Ridge, which turned up nothing. When they returned to Samaritan Airport for fuel and lunch, they hadn't even begun to look at the Burnside County side. This presented Sterner with a dilemma: overlook Burnside County, overlook Laurel Valley, or do a less thorough job covering both?

His headache didn't help. He'd ridden in helicopters before, but not for five straight hours. The engine was so loud he and Jimmy had to shout at each other to be heard, though mere inches apart with headsets. As he sucked down a can of Coke and bit into his Lebanon bologna and Velveeta on white bread sandwich, compliments of Jimmy's Pennsylvania Dutch wife, his entire body was aching with exhaustion from the vibration of the propellers. It was mid-November and they had only three hours of daylight left when they got back in the air.

In the end Sterner decided to look at Burnside County, though no evidence of a makeshift grave was found there, either. Jimmy had already logged too many hours of flight time to return the following day, but was enthusiastic about returning Friday or any day thereafter, for the Laurel Valley fly-over. It would be a bad idea to survey past Thanksgiving week because the following Monday was opening day of rifle season when hunters with high-powered rifles would put the troopers too much at risk.

The Sheriff had already gone home when Sterner called to speak to him but Suzy said she'd make sure to give him any message. Sterner then remembered Kendalhart told him it was her idea to use the crime scene tape at the chicken coop, and thanked her for allowing him to retrieve a red hair he believed belonged to the ghoul. Suzy hesitated, then mumbled something about "standard procedure," which gave Sterner the impression she had misinterpreted his compliment. She seemed distressed. It couldn't be easy serving under Louella aboard Sheriff Guise's tight ship.

Sterner found two messages from Betty Nagle, the proprietress of the Crossroads Country Store in Pineville. The first reported that the resident who lived the farthest up Laurel Valley told her a suspicious SUV had passed his way Tuesday night of last week around nine o'clock and returned around midnight. He didn't see the license plate number. He thought they were going up to the dump. It wasn't unusual for someone to illegally dump garbage at night, but it was unusual for them to take that long. The second message was to invite him to meet the congregation of the Laurel Valley Lutheran Church at a supper to welcome their new pastor the Sunday after Thanksgiving. Sterner called her back and thanked her, but said he wasn't sure he could make the supper.

A text message from Emily read, "Dr. Bundens, Monday 9 a.m. Meet here 8:30. And I heard from other parents all about the gun on the playground. Are you insane?"

Sterner didn't have much of an appetite when he left the barracks, but stopped into Rosita's anyway. The hostess, whose name tag identified her as Sharon, remembered him from the previous night and seemed pleased he was back. He tried the New England clam chowder, figuring it would settle his stomach, and washed it down with two pints of Stella Artois on tap. When he got back to his room, he was too tired to shower. He swallowed two aspirin and fell asleep sprawled across the bed, his head at the foot, his feet propped on the headboard, staring at a work of kitschy landscape art, dreaming of fluorescent green landscapes with dark patches showing shallow graves and white skeletons holding bouquets of black roses.

———————

7.

ELEVEN DAYS BEFORE OPENING DAY

Deputy Kendalhart picked Sterner up at the barracks around eleven and drove into Samaritan to the town square and then up Middle Street to the north side of town, making a left onto a street where the Samaritan College campus blended in with businesses and residences. A few of the grand Victorians that had been built by the town elite a century ago now housed the college's fraternities and sororities. Their Greek letters hung off porch awnings and handrails in need of repair and a little paint. They passed an imposing old brick administration building from the 1920s with classical pillars on either side of the entrance at the top of a central staircase, and rolled into a Visitors Parking lot to the side of a large modern brick and glass structure built, according to the cornerstone, in 1975. The Knorr Student Union building housed the campus radio station, the student newspaper, a bowling alley, a concert hall and theater, a snack bar café, a study lounge and campus security.

"Wayne, how ya doing? This is Detective Joe Sterner of the State Police," Kendalhart said to his cousin. Wayne was talking to a student at his metal desk in the tiny office off of the entry. He was a few years older than Warren and had a lot less hair, but there was an unmistakable resemblance between them. Wayne's striking blue eyes widened as his full attention fell on Sterner. He stood up and shook hands.

"Jesus, you guys got here fast," Wayne said, short of breath. "I just hung up the phone to the town police." Sterner noticed the student with him had a frightened expression on his cherubic face and clutched his textbooks tightly to his chest.

"What's up?" Warren said.

"Just happened, like, five minutes ago," Wayne said. "Tell em what you saw, son."

The kid swallowed hard. "I'm walking out the door here to my Poli Sci class across campus at Hill Hall, you know? Crazy motherfucker--this gorilla of a guy--wearing a black ski mask, beans this other guy in the face with a baseball bat, knocked him flat out right in front of me. Then he grabs the guy--who's unconscious, right?--tosses him over his shoulder like a duffel bag, grabs this travel bag the guy had and his baseball bat and walks outside to the parking lot. I followed him and saw him dump everything into the back of this blue van with no windows. He slams the door behind him. The driver's already got the engine running, right? They just drive right out of the lot towards town like nothing was unusual."

"Tell him about the license plate," Wayne said.

"They covered it with, like, a piece of cardboard or something."

"You sure this isn't just some frat house prank?" Warren said to Wayne.

"I don't think so. This sounds like the real deal," Wayne said.

"I swear to God that's exactly what I saw," the kid said.

Kendalhart squeezed his hand mike. "Deputy Kendalhart to Dispatch," he said.

"*Dispatch, go ahead.*" It was Suzy.

Kendalhart turned to the kid. "Would you say the van was light blue or dark blue?"

"Light blue," the boy said. "Like powder blue."

"Need an APB ASAP on a powder blue cargo van last seen driving south on Middle Street in Samaritan," Kendalhart said, then asked the boy, "Late model, or older?"

"Older. Like ten years old or more."

"Older model. Ten years or more," Kendalhart relayed. "Make?" The kid shrugged. "Unknown make, license plate may be covered in cardboard," Kendalhart said. "Three occupants, one may be kidnap victim," Kendalhart said. "Did you copy that, Dispatch?"

"*Copy. Will alert Town and State Police for an All Points Bulletin on a ten-year-old powder blue cargo van, unknown make, possible cardboard over license plate, three occupants.*"

"They could be halfway to Maryland by now," Wayne said looking at his watch.

"The gorilla--white, black, Latino?"

"No idea. Driver had a ski mask on like the other guy."

"Suspects unknown race and age, wanted for questioning in assault and abduction. Could be armed and dangerous."

"*Copy that. Dispatch out.*"

"What did the victim look like?" Sterner said.

"Very, I don't know, distinguished-looking. White guy, dark suit, tie. Kind of average height, except he had black hair and uh--what do you call a mustache that goes all the way back to the temple?" The kid put his books on the desk and drew semi-circles on his cheeks with his index fingers.

"Muttonchops?" Sterner said.

"Right. I thought he might be faculty."

"Nobody like that on the faculty, I can tell you for certain," Wayne said.

"How old?"

"Uhmm. Gee, I don't know. Maybe thirty. Everybody over twenty-five looks alike to me," the kid said and grinned nervously. "Just kidding."

Sterner turned to Wayne. "Do you have grad students here?" Sterner said.

"No. This is strictly a four-year liberal arts school," Wayne said and added, "but we do have students in their thirties, even forties. Nobody with black muttonchops, though. Beards, yes. But no muttonchops. You'd notice that even among a student body of three thousand. Nobody on the staff, either."

"Mister Muttonchops sounds too young to be a student parent, am I right?" Sterner said to the kid.

"Uh, yeah, I'd guess so." the kid said.

"Does Mister Muttonchops ring a bell with you, Warren?" Sterner said. "Anybody in town?"

"Muttonchops? Used to be a pump jockey down at the Exxon but not since Foghat stopped touring. When was that? Early Nineties?"

"Could be somebody's older brother," the kid said. "Maybe visiting somebody?"

"Could be a disguise," Sterner said. "Do you have a theater program here?"

"Sure," Wayne said. "We do theater right down the hall here. Mr. Sederholm runs the program. He's in the English Department."

"Check with him and see if the description rings a bell," Sterner said.

Wayne went through his campus directory to find the number and made the call.

"You think this has something to do with our case?" Kendalhart said.

"You guys working on that skeleton thing?" the kid said a little too excitedly. "That's some gruesome shit."

"Can't say," Kendalhart said.

"Man. I'm a little shook up. Fucking guy knocked that poor dude's teeth right out of his head," the kid said.

"Teeth?" Sterner perked up.

"Yeah, it rolled all bloody onto the floor when he got heaved over the guy's shoulder. Made me want to puke. Probably still sitting down there on the floor. I sure wasn't gonna touch it."

"Show me."

The kid led the law men down the hallway to the double doors facing the center of campus. Dozens of students were walking through contaminating the scene.

Wayne Kendalhart joined them a moment later. "Sederholm says they did *The Importance of Being Earnest* last season and one of the characters wore muttonchops, but they're still in his make-up kit locked in his office."

On the floor in the corner by the door jamb Sterner found a bloody incisor. He made an envelope out of a piece of note paper, scooped it up and stuck it in his pocket.

"What was the assailant wearing?" Sterner said to the kid.

"The Gorilla, you mean? Kind of gray, like, coveralls. Like an airline mechanic or a groundskeeper or janitor. Work gloves. Boots, I think."

"What kind of boots?"

"Work boots. I just saw him for a few seconds."

"Leather gloves? Or cloth?"

"Leather, I guess. I wasn't really paying attention to his clothes."

"Which way was Muttonchops coming?"

"He was coming from outside. The big guy was waiting for him here."

The kid then led them out to the parking lot where the van had been and where they were parked, as well. Sterner noted the wide-open lawn behind the building, with a myriad of sidewalks among the landscaping leading all over campus. Muttonchops could've come from anywhere. He looked for trace evidence but found nothing. The parking lot was gravel, making it impossible to get anything on the tires. It looked like the kidnappers had gotten away clean.

"I guess I'm gonna have to beef up my staff," Wayne said shaking his head.

"What's your name, son?" Sterner said.

"Terry. Terry Meyer," the kid said. "I'm a freshman," as if that meant something.

"Terry, if I put you with a sketch artist, do you think you could help us with a likeness of Muttonchops?"

"Sure, I could try."

Sterner wondered if Muttonchops and the ghoul were one in the same. It could be corroborated if the genetic profiles of the red hair and teeth proved identical. If they matched, the Ghoul might be blackmailing the Killer. The question now was, who was the Ghoul and was he still alive?

———————

Peter was in a panic, beside himself with worry. Like Clay, he had expected to become an instantly rich man by the end of the day, but all his hopes had been dashed when Clay failed to materialize from the maintenance tunnel in the pool house with the cash. Then he heard about the abduction across campus and knew right away Moneybags had changed his mind about paying them. To make matters worse, he couldn't call Moneybags himself for fear his voice would be recognized.

"I'm fuckin' going to the cops, Precious," he told his wife later that evening. "I swear to God, I'm gonna tell em the whole fuckin' story."

"Calm down, honey," she said. "That won't solve anything. Look, let me call the guy, find out what happened."

They drove to the town square and used a payphone in the drug store. She punched in the number and listened as the phone rang at the other end. In the calmest, most casual voice she could manage, she introduced herself to Moneybags. "I'm Mr. O'Leary's associate," she said. "I'm concerned that Mr. O'Leary has not returned from his scheduled appointment."

"Yes," Moneybags said. "Regrettably Mr. O'Leary has been detained."

"If Mr. O'Leary does not return by midnight," she said, "another indiscretion is bound to turn up."

"All the indiscretions, as you put it, have been taken care of."

"I beg to differ, sir," she said, "since one of the indiscretions has been switched with a facsimile."

"I find that very difficult to believe."

"I can assure you, this is indeed the case. If you or your agents were to check the indiscretions carefully you would realize that I am speaking the truth."

"Unfortunately that is no longer possible," Moneybags said.

Precious took a deep breath. "May I remind you that Mr. Fegelman could tie you directly to Mr. O'Leary as well as to your indiscretions?"

"But Mr. Fegelman has passed on and, as I told you, my indiscretions are no longer a matter of concern."

"But a copy of a certain document Mr. Fegelman has written still exists," she said, "and not only will another indiscretion come to light but so will this copy."

"I understood I alone possessed the only copy, as well as the original, both of which by the way have been destroyed."

"The only way you can prevent these matters from being made public is to pay Mr. O'Leary two hundred thousand dollars and send him on his way at the earliest convenience. That would be two hundred thousand, not one hundred thousand, as a penalty for violating the parameters of our arrangement."

"By morning," Moneybags said, "I'll know Mr. O'Leary's real name, and yours is bound to follow, and then there will be no need to pay either of you anything but my last respects." He hung up.

Slowly she returned the phone to its cradle and shook her head at her husband. "So he called your bluff," she said.

Peter ran his fingers through his hair and growled.

Clay woke up naked in the dark with his jaw and mouth in horrific pain. But when he reached up to touch his face, he found his hands weren't working. They were behind his back, tied.

What the fuck happened? He had called Moneybags from the pay phone in Times Square and was told the cash was ready. In his disguise as the Irish rare documents dealer named Mr. O'Leary, modeled after a bartender he knew, Clay had gone to Harrisburg on the train. Peter had picked him up and driven him to Samaritan College. Moneybags was waiting at the bench on the Great Lawn just as he had the last time. Moneybags had handed over the satchel of cash which he remembered inspecting. It was all there. The imaginary Mr. O'Leary had tipped his imaginary hat and wished Moneybags a "G'day," and then-- And then--

Clay couldn't now recall what happened after the payoff. He cried out for assistance but before he could pronounce *HELP,* the naked roots of his missing teeth screamed bloody murder. The raw nerves of his upper jaw were sending urgent alarms when his mouth opened to the dank cold air. He could feel with his tongue that not only were two of his front teeth missing, but the two on either side were loose, as well. His upper lip was swollen, too. He tasted blood. He began to panic because he now realized he was tied to a straight-back chair, unable to move. He started hyperventilating. He grew disoriented, dizzy. He lost his bearings. He felt nauseous. He shivered.

How could Moneybags have double-crossed them? It was in his own best interest to pay them for their silence. Clay screamed for help again in spite of the pain. Wherever he was, he could tell it must be in a small room and it must be carpeted, because something soft was absorbing his screams. Yet he could feel his feet on a hard surface. It smelled like damp dirt and there was a faint urine-like stench of foul chemicals. In the distance was a humming noise like a motor idling. At least that was something to focus on. He wasn't in an isolation chamber deprived of all sensation. As he looked around, he found a red bead of light in the darkness. A red bead of light so tiny and faint he hadn't even noticed it before. But it was something else to focus on now. He decided he would catalogue his current fear for future reference. It was indeed a dramatic situation, and was he not an actor's actor? It was all grist for the mill. Stepping outside of himself calmed him.

After a few interminably long minutes, footsteps above clomped along on a wooden floor. A door squeaked opened. A light bulb supernova ignited over his head, blinding him. Boots trudged heavily down wooden steps. When his eyes adjusted, he caught a brief glimpse of a large man in coveralls and quickly turned away.

"I din' thee you faith. I don't wanna know what you wook wike."

"It's okay, little buddy, I don't care if you see my face or not," the man said. He seemed friendly. "I don't come from here or live around here. You've never seen me before and you'll never see me again."

Clay knew one thing. The man was telling the truth about not being from around there. Clay recognized a flat Midwestern accent when he heard it. Clay dared to open one eye. "Don' hut me, okay? Or the ol' guy'll be up thit queek." Clay examined his shackles, nylon rope like a mountain climber would use. He gazed up at the big man with the strange smile and huge arms casually crossed. The big man's smooth face was deeply suntanned but not handsome. He had a flat nose and a thick neck with short black hair slicked back. He wore a tiny gold ring in a pierced ear, gray coveralls, laced-up brown boots and tan leather work gloves. He was enormous and reminded Clay of a porn actor featured in his extensive DVD collection.

Then Clay appraised the room, a small dirt cellar beneath an old house with crudely milled, unpainted lumber beams above and fieldstone and mortar walls with no windows. On a rough-hewn wooden shelf near a rusty water heater were dusty mason jars filled with string beans and beets. And there, in among the cobwebs, was the red bead of light on a small home video camera, a black cord leading up into a fresh hole in the ceiling. The Clay Show was being televised, he realized. Could it be Moneybags himself watching at the other end?

Perhaps he should approach this situation as an acting exercise. His performance always did improve with an audience. Was he starring in somebody's idea of a reality show? Should he advise them that, as a member of AFTRA and SAG, it was strictly illegal without his express written consent and proper notification to his affiliated unions?

"Wha' didja do to me?" he said.

"Nothing your buddy Doc Fries can't fix for a couple grand, don't worry."

"Who?" Clay said.

"Oh, come now, little buddy, that is just so totally bogus, dude," the big man said. Then he shrugged and produced a baseball bat he'd been leaning on. "Okay, so you want to play dumb? That's okay with me cause we're gonna make a little game of it. See, every time you pitch me a fib I'm gonna knock it right back at ya with my Louisville Slugger here and it'll bite you on your ass like a bad karma boomerang. Now do you really want that, little buddy? I don't think so." The big guy started practice-swinging his baseball bat against Clay's left knee.

"I'm thowwy. I don' know who Duck Freethe ith," Clay said.

The man swung hard at Clay's knee and connected harder. Even before he could feel it he heard the knee cap pop. Then came the pain, an avalanche of agony so beyond horrific Clay's bowels and bladder gave way. He gasped. The room spun.

"Ooops, that was the sound of your professional sports career flying right over the center field wall," the man said. "Hey, you still with me there, little fella?"

When Clay woke up he didn't know where he was. Then a dreadful odor made him jerk backwards. He snapped into unpleasant consciousness. The big man was using a capsule of something horrible smelling to bring him around. On the whole Clay preferred unconsciousness to the jabbing pain in his upper jaw and knee that greeted him back to reality. He shook off his delirium.

"There you are. You were hiding from Daddy," the big man said, eyes twinkling cruelly. He stood up straight and his demeanor grew less friendly. "We were just discussing Doc Fries. Now you know who Doc Fries is, don't you?"

"Fuck. *FUCK!*" Clay said, nausea crawling up into his throat.

"Not Fuck. Fries. Doctor Roy Fries."

Clay looked down and realized his lap was wet. "Fuck me," Clay said and started to gag again from the shock of pain and that horrible odor, but nothing came out of his mouth but saliva. He looked into the lens of the small television camera and was filled with embarrassment. It was every performer's nightmare--losing control while on.

"Maybe later. I never put out on a first date." The big man began to practice-swing on the other knee stretching the bat back over his head like a golfer with a nine iron, stopping just short of the knee, up and down, up and down. Clay could see the impressive muscles bulging through his clothes. The big man was a real scumbag, shit-for-brains musclehead, Clay decided. There was no way out of this situation but to play along, or pretend to.

"Okay. I know Duck Freethe," Clay said.

Musclehead instantly stopped swinging. "Now that wasn't so hard, was it, little buddy? See, here's the thing," Musclehead said setting aside the birch and putting his arm around Clay, all chummy. He whispered in a soft, comforting way. "We figure you're not from New York like the postmark on your envelope indicated. You're not even Irish, since you sort of misplaced your brogue. I'll bet you're just some misguided hometown boy from Samaritan who knows that Doc Fries is sitting on Old Doc Arnold's dental records. Of course it won't make any difference, since the skeleton you stole was a woman who came from somewhere else. Anyway, we took a Polaroid of the real you without your disguise on, while you were napping, and tomorrow morning we're gonna check the Samaritan High School yearbooks about ten years back in the public library. We suspect there's a picture of you in there, am I right?"

"If you don't weleathe me--and I mean *WIGHT FUCKIN' NOW!*--my athothiate ith gonna delivuh anothuh thkeleton to the copth."

Musclehead backed off, straightened, squeezed his nose, sniffed and then wagged his index finger in Clay's face. "See, now, you had a good plan but you made a mistake. You gave us a few days to raise the hundred grand, which in turn gave us a chance to *remove* the bones and grind 'em up into powder. No bones, no graves. Only you didn't bother checking before you showed up for the money, did you, asshole?"

"We have anothuh thkeleton," Clay boasted smugly.

"Bullshit. There were four. You stole one. We took care of the other three."

"We thwitched one. Only you didn' bother checkin' the back of the skullth befoh you gwound 'em up into powduh, did you, athhole?"

Musclehead didn't like lip. He slapped Clay's face hard.

The pain was beyond description. Clay began to cry. When he opened his eyes again, Musclehead was practice-swinging the bat against his other knee again. "Pweathe don' hut me anymoh," he moaned. "Pweathe?"

"I'm only gonna ask you this once," he said. "Before you grody up my boots with your runnin' shits and puke and find yourself in a wheelchair for the rest of your miserable life, just answer me this one question. If you answer truthfully I'll give you some morphine. And believe me, you will love me for that. You will want to blow me for that, because all your pain will drift away like butterflies in a warm summer breeze, I promise. What's your name now, little buddy? Give Daddy a name."

"Cway Whipple," Clay said sobbing, seeing no point in lying.

"Cway?! You mean *Clay?* Whipple? That's a ridiculous name," Musclehead said, turned and shrugged toward the camera for the benefit of the television audience. "So ridiculous it might just be the truth."

"It ith the twuth, I thwear."

"In that case, you've made Daddy a really happy camper," Musclehead said. "Daddy's gonna give you a little taste now as your reward." And then he produced a leather case with a hypodermic in it, drew clear liquid from a small bottle with a thin rubber membrane for a cap and shot it into Clay's thigh. He gently massaged the muscle and gave him a gentle pat on the cheek. "Daddy'll see you again in the morning. Sweet dreams, little buddy."

And it was true what Musclehead had said. Clay loved him for it. All his pain flew away in slow motion like a flock of pigeons around a city park pond in some sentimental movie love story. It was too beautiful for words and Clay forgave him everything before falling into blissful sleep.

8.

TEN DAYS BEFORE OPENING DAY

Sterner's cell woke him. The digital alarm clock on the bedside table read 8:33 a.m. He'd been asleep for slightly more than four hours and awoke disoriented.

"Hello?"

"Detective," the caller said.

"Sheriff." Sterner pinched sleep from the corners of his eyes.

"We've got another skeleton--"

Sterner bolted up to a sitting position. "Come again?"

"--Sitting in one of Roy Fries's dental exam chairs, I shit you not. Damnedest thing I ever saw. No pretty posies this time. Four-eleven Murdoch Street, five blocks east of the square."

Minutes later Sterner arrived at the address. It was a handsome white-washed brick Colonial with black shutters on a quarter-acre lot surrounded by manicured shrubbery and twin hedges accenting the front walk. Huge poplar and birch trees would shade the black-shingled roof in the summertime. Now their bare branches only loomed menacingly overhead under a gray sky. And planted in the front yard near the street was a black pole with a discreet white shingle on which gothic lettering announced *Dr. Roy Fries, DDS*.

To the side of the property, a freshly paved macadam driveway lined with low walls of white-washed brick and featuring recessed lighting led into a small parking area in back, adjacent to the alley. There Sterner parked next to the Sheriff's Explorer, the Medical Examiner's Suburban and Trooper Ned Hollings's SUV. At the bottom of the back porch steps, Hollings and the Sheriff stood over Fries, who sat on the top step sucking on a cigarette like a condemned man, mulling over his predicament with the weight of the world on his shoulders.

"I just can't figure why I'm the target of this campaign," Fries said.

"Roy, are you sure you're telling us everything here?" the Sheriff said. "Because, you know, two of these in a row look like a message of some kind."

"Sheriff, I swear to Christ, I'm completely in the dark here."

Sheriff Guise narrowed his eyes at Fries, then turned toward Sterner and nodded a greeting. Sterner was already adjusting the settings on the camera hanging around his neck when the group turned and moved toward the backdoor. "Roy says he locked up last evening around six. Woman who lives upstairs went to bed around nine, heard nothing. She has a separate entrance there." The Sheriff pointed to a second door on the back porch leading to an ascending covered staircase. "Our perp jimmied the antique lock on the back door here."

Sterner snapped a close-up of the scrapes around the door. They then moved inside through a classic Victorian drawing room that was converted into a patient waiting room with modern plastic chairs, television, magazine rack, water cooler. They made their way through the front hall and foyer to an examination room that looked like it had once been the dining room in the front of the home. It offered patients a nice view of the street through a bay window discreetly veiled from outsiders by sheer curtains. The ME, Doc Johnson, a geriatric gentleman as rotund as the Sheriff, was already at work photographing the scene. His bulk blocked the doorway until his film camera flashed.

"I'm gonna have to replace that chair," Fries grumbled to no one in particular. "Who's gonna want to sit in this one when word leaks out. Know what one of them things cost?"

When Doc Johnson stepped aside, the unobstructed view greeting Sterner made his skin crawl. The skeleton was laid out on the examination chair, which had been articulated back into an almost horizontal position, the bones meticulously arranged to suggest a routine dental check-up, elbows resting on the arms, hand bones arranged as if in the lap, skull supported by the headrest. The only thing missing was the bib. But what gave Sterner the goose bumps was the grin. The concave mirrored examination light on a flexible arm was positioned above, its beam focused directly onto the vicious-looking teeth, making them glow white in the otherwise subdued morning shade. It almost seemed as if the bones might at any moment jump up and bite. Sterner swallowed hard and then snapped several shots, with and without flash.

The physician stepped back to give them room and just shook his head. "I've been Medical Examiner of Doolittle County for thirty-seven years and, I have to say, this is the strangest thing I've ever seen. I may have to retire after this."

"I hate to hear that, Doc," Sheriff Guise said.

"The exam light was on just as you see it when I got in this morning around seven," Fries said. "I called the Sheriff straight away. I didn't touch anything."

"Gunshot wounds?" Sterner said.

"Two small caliber holes in the back of the skull," Doc Johnson said. "No evidence of broken bones. Wormed clean, washed and air-dried, just like your Jane Doe, sounds like." He hadn't seen Jane Doe but knew about her.

"Only this one's male," Sterner said. "Six feet?"

"Six two or three, by my reckoning," Doc Johnson said.

"Maybe they were a couple," Sterner said. "Ring any bells, Sheriff?"

"Couples?" The Sheriff scanned his memory and shook his head. "Must've happened when I was in the service is the only thing I can think of. Are you sure this isn't Abel Nestor we're looking at?"

"Not unless he grew a foot taller in the grave. How about you, Roy? Did you treat any couples twenty, thirty years ago who suddenly went missing or left town and never returned?"

"I wasn't here then so I couldn't say. My practice was in Chambersburg."

"I thought you two went to high school here together," Sterner said. The Sheriff nodded.

"Sheriff and me? Yes, we did," said Fries, "but in those days the town could only support one dentist and that was Old Doc Arnold. I kept after him, if he ever retired I'd buy his business, since all my people are here. He finally took me up on it."

"Then you'd have his records," Sterner said.

"Yes, Fiona and I have been in the basement scouring through them all week in our free time looking for your Jane Doe, but she's just not there."

"Would it be possible to x-ray the teeth here?"

Fries fumbled. "Well, sure," he said nodding at his x-ray machine. "I'm all set up for it. I'll cancel the morning's appointments first thing and we'll get right at it."

"Good. I need to dust for fingerprints first, though."

"Fiona, my hygienist, has a thing about cleanliness. She sprays and wipes everything down real good at the end of every day. Any prints you find will belong to the joker who put that thing here, I can guaran-damn-tee it."

Sterner retrieved his fingerprinting kit from the trunk of his car and dusted the bones from toe to skull. He also dusted the lamp and the chair and the back door. Everything was clean. The ghoul had been very careful.

Fiona hadn't arrived, yet, so Doc Johnson pitched in to help Fries x-ray the teeth when Taylor called Sterner on his cell.

"Congratulations, detective, you've got a match," Taylor said.

"The hair and teeth?" Sterner said.

"The kidnap victim is the ghoul," Taylor said. "Your cold case just turned hot. Get back here, we're taking this public."

"You might want to reconsider, Chief," Sterner said.

"What's up?"

"There's another skeleton."

"You're kidding," Taylor said.

Sterner filled him in.

"E-mail me your pictures," Taylor said. "The Commissioner's taken an interest. He'll want to see everything you have right away."

"I'll upload them ASAP."

"I'm sending you Stuart Flanigan."

"I'll take all the help I can get," Sterner said. Flanigan was the senior investigator on the Baker's Man case the previous summer and Sterner had gotten along well with him, though they hadn't partnered since. He was a good, honest Irishman with a refreshing sense of humor, remarkable after thirty years on the job.

When Sterner got back from the laptop in his car Fries and Doc Johnson were finished with the X-rays. Sterner showed Fries a copy of both sketches of Muttonchops, with and without the mustache, that Terry Meyer had helped put together the night before in Harrisburg. "Do either of these look like anybody you know? Don't think about it. Just give me your first impression."

Fries shook his head at Muttonchops, but looking at the sketch without the mustache, said, "Looks a little like Clay Whipple, but he lives up in New York City."

"I think we're looking for somebody local."

"In that case, I can't say it looks like anybody I know." Fries looked at the Sheriff, who shook his head.

"He may have red hair," Sterner said.

"Why, that definitely sounds like Clay. He's a real carrot-top. Looked like Howdy Doody as a kid, freckles and all." Fries chuckled.

"What does he do in New York?"

"He's an actor."

Bingo. "Tell me about him," Sterner said.

"Kind of a pie-in-the-sky type. Trying to make it big on the Great White Way, you know? By the sound of it, he mostly waits tables."

"How do you know him?"

"He's a patient. Has been all his life. So are his folks."

"But you say he lives in New York?"

"Well, he comes home several times a year, by my understanding."

"How would he know about your chicken coop?"

"I might've mentioned it to him in passing. I talk about my hunting to lots of patients."

"You're talking about John and Clara Whipple's kid," Sheriff Guise said.

"Do you know him, Sheriff?" Sterner said.

"Not hardly. I know his folks. Everybody does. John had the hardware store on Elm Street before the Lowe's and Wal-Mart drove him out of business. Now he works at the Home Depot. I heard the son was an actor, but I haven't seen him in years. Can't say I even remember him, really," Sheriff Guise said, shaking his head.

"He's Muttonchops, Ghoul Number One."

———————

The Whipple home was a modest split-level house on a quarter acre lot in a suburban community of identical properties on the edge of town, built by a real estate developer in the Fifties after the fashion of Levittown and called Blocher Park. John Whipple was at work, his wife said, but invited them inside curious and anxious about whatever they had to say about her only child. The Sheriff had described her well when he called her an anemic bottle blonde who had once been the music teacher in the elementary school until cutbacks eliminated the program. Now she gave private piano lessons on her prized possession, a polished 1948 Spinet, the centerpiece of their living room, a gift from her father on her twelfth birthday.

"Clay's in New York City," Clara declared proudly leading them into her kitchen. From the ceiling hung her vast collection of wicker baskets, which brushed their scalps when they entered to sit at the table. "Can I offer you anything? Coffee? It's already made."

"Yes, I'd love some," Sterner said. "Thank you."

"Sheriff? It's no trouble," Clara said.

"Sure, I missed mine this mornin', too."

"Is Clay alright? Has something happened to him?" Clara fastidiously served them with china cups and saucers reserved for special guests and took the trouble to serve the milk and sugar in a matching china cream pitcher and bowl set on a silver tray.

"We're not sure, ma'am," Sterner said. "Might you have a picture of him we could borrow?"

"Yes, of course. I have several upstairs. He's in some kind of trouble?"

"We just want to ask him some questions. He may know something about the abduction at the college yesterday."

"Well, I don't see how that's possible. He's in New York, as I said."

"Do you know that for certain, ma'am?" Sterner said.

"Well, I don't speak to him every day. He comes back to see us every few months, but usually not for more than a day or two. We pick him up at the Harrisburg Train Station and then drop him off there later. He works nights as a waiter in Times Square."

"He doesn't have a car?" Sterner said.

"No, we offered to give him our old one, but he says it's too expensive to keep a car in New York. So he takes the train, as I said. Did I mention he was an actor? I have a review from *Variety* of his last show here somewhere. Waiting tables is what out-of-work actors do in New York to survive. The competition is fierce, but Clay is very determined."

"Yes, I used to live there. Would you mind calling to see if he could speak to us?"

"Not at all," she said and picked up the phone. After several seconds, she said, "Hi, dear, it's Mom, I'm just calling to see if you're all right. Call me when you get this message." She hung up. "Voice mail on his cell phone. He's probably out on an audition." She found another number in her address book. "I'll call his roommate, Nathan. Nathan Jordan."

Nathan was asleep. He was also an actor, and worked the night shift as a hotel clerk in a midtown hotel. The two roommates didn't see much of each other, but Clay told him he had an overnight out-of-town gig on a drug company industrial in Delaware. She left word to have Clay call her right away when he got back.

"There you are. He's in Delaware," she said smiling.

"Who would pick Clay up at the train station if you or or your husband couldn't?"

"Nobody. That's the thing. I'm the only one who ever picks him up."

"Does he have friends he sees when he comes home?" Sheriff Guise said.

"Why, yes, he has a lot of friends. He was very popular in high school. Of course he hardly ever has time for anyone outside of family when he visits."

"Could you give us names of some of his friends?"

She gave them several names and names of their parents since two of them still lived at home. They then asked her if she or her husband or Clay had any enemies, or if Clay ever said anything negative about an older man or woman who might be wealthy, or had acquired wealth unethically or illegally. She said he never said anything negative about anybody. Clay was a very positive person. Always was.

Clara showed them Clay's room. The walls were decorated with posters. There was a *Top Gun* poster with Tom Cruise and Kelly McGillis, posters from *A Chorus Line* and *Rent,* and a poster of Marilyn Manson from one of his concerts looking shockingly satanic. Sterner found a hairbrush with red strands in it and asked if he could take the hair back to the lab for a comparison. She agreed, but was too polite to ask what he was comparing them to. Before they left she gave them a copy of Clay's headshot, an eight-by-ten-inch black-and-white glossy portrait. It was hardly identical to the Muttonchops composite, but the resemblance was close enough.

"Clay Whipple," Musclehead said in a voice of mock incredulity. "President of the Mask and Wig Club, member of the National Thespians Society, voted *Most Likely to Become Famous.* Congratulations, little buddy. Wow. I'm fuckin' honored. You're a goddamn celebrity. Why, you're everything I wanted to be when I was in high school. Hell, nobody even knew my name when I dropped out my junior year. But you, you were like God's fuckin' gift to the student body. I may have to get your autograph." The big man had stomped down the steps in the blinding light holding up photocopies from pages in Clay's yearbook, the Louisville Slugger under his thick arm. "Lookin' a little narly there, dude."

Clay was groggy and found himself moaning involuntarily. His mouth was dry. His face was numb but the real problem was his left knee.

It ached so badly he had scarcely slept after the drug wore off. The gnawing pain spiked rhythmically with every sluggish heartbeat.

Musclehead grinned at the photocopies. "My, my, my. Here's one of you onstage in a play called *A Christmas Carol*. I had a girlfriend named Carol once. How's that knee?" He kicked it.

Clay winced and groaned.

"Hey, suppose you tell me the name of your girlfriend. I'll give you another dose of morphine, what's say?"

Clay didn't understand. His girlfriend?

"Come on, we know she's local. She has no talent for accents whatsoever, unlike you. Is she in your high school class? Hell, maybe I got her picture right here and don't even know it." Musclehead leafed through the photocopies. "Mary Whitaker? Is that her, little buddy?" He held up the page with Clay's yearbook portrait. The picture next to his was Mary Whitaker. The big man tapped it with his finger.

Clay shook his head. Peter must have enlisted his wife to call Moneybags to ask for Clay's release.

"How about Patricia Schuster? Is that your girlfriend, little buddy?" He held up a picture of Clay in the starring role from "George M." Patty had played George M. Cohan's wife.

Clay shook his head.

"What's her name, little buddy? Give me a name or the batter steps up to the plate and it's your elbow this time. What's it gonna be, eh? The bat or the needle?"

Clay bowed his head and began to cry. He had thought about it. Musclehead was probably going to kill him. Musclehead was going to kill them all. They would all end up in an unmarked grave, two bullet holes in the back of the head, and no one would ever know. Maybe he should say it *was* Mary Whitaker, the quiet girl who sat behind him in home room. He was pretty sure she had had a crush on him. What the hell happened to her, anyway? Probably married some applesauce factory worker and bore a slew of kids.

"What's her name?" When Clay looked up, Musclehead was practice-swinging against his left elbow. "If I don't hear a name out of that fucked-up mouth of yours in the next five seconds...."

Musclehead would never believe him if he named Mary, anyway. She was too convenient. Clay whimpered, moved by his own predicament and thinking how Mary would never know the heroic sacrifice he was making for her. He would hold his own for the sake of Mary's children. He looked over at the red bead of light and into the lens of the camera. At least posterity would bear witness to this selfless act, he thought. Are you there, Moneybags?

Good to his word, Musclehead pounded Clay's left elbow against his side with a powerful thud that nearly toppled him over onto the floor. It strangely hurt less than Clay had expected. The last morphine shot must still be working. That or his whole body was numb from cold and constricted circulation. But it was the idea that his elbow and left arm were broken that upset him. And then there was the pain that would surely come when the drug wore off or when his circulation was restored.

"I'm looking for that name, little buddy," Musclehead said. He set the bat down and presented the needle and the bottle of liquid morphine.

Was it possible to become addicted to morphine after one shot? Clay stared at the needle and realized he coveted that feeling of wings flying in slow motion more than anything else in this world. And yet, was he willing to sacrifice his cousin for it? He looked again at the red bead of light on the camera hidden among the mason jars and steeled himself. *The Clay Whipple Show*. Tears came easily to him. He was an actor's actor, after all. And this, this could be his finest performance.

Clay sobbed. "Cat Twue," he said.

"Cat True? Cat True is one of your partners?" Musclehead said glancing over at the red bead.

Why not? Her name was already out there. Clay nodded.

"Who else? She uses the term *we* way too much for her to be in it alone."

What did they know? "I only know huh. Thee'th the one who called me."

Musclehead looked at the red bead and slowly began to smile. "You're not just saying this to make me happy, are you?"

"I thwayuh," Clay cried.

"The cops said she helped them."

"They don' know thit."

"If little buddy is lying, little buddy will be spending the rest of his miserable life in a wheelchair wearing diapers. Now is little buddy lying? Clay, come on, dude, you can tell me. Is that cunt really your partner or are you just making this up?"

"I thwayuh to God." Clay looked up into the man's face, rolled his eyes back into his head and let out a weak whimper as if relieving himself of a great burden, while underneath he concealed his true thoughts, like the really great actor's actor he knew he was. Zoom in on me, Moneybags!   "I thwayuh on my mothuh'th gwave." He gazed deeply into Musclehead's skeptical eyes with all the dewy-eyed sincerity he had in his sizable arsenal of vulnerable expressions. He seemed to open his very soul confessing to Jesus Christ Himself, while underneath, thought, *FUCK YOU!*

Before returning to Harrisburg, Sterner called the payphone on Terry Meyer's dormitory floor and found him still in his room. When Sterner told him he and the Sheriff wanted to ask more questions, the young man sighed but agreed to meet in a study lounge.

Terry now stared at the headshot and considered it. "Maybe," he said halfheartedly. Then Sterner showed him a photocopy of the headshot with muttonchops drawn in with a felt-tipped pen. He nodded slowly. "Yes, that's the guy. Definitely."

"Good," Sterner said and glanced over at the Sheriff who sat stone-faced. "Now I was wondering if you remembered anything since we talked yesterday that maybe you didn't mention. Something about the gorilla, the van or the driver."

Terry let out a sigh. "I told you everything several times," Terry said.

"Let's focus on the van. You said," referring to his notes, "'it looked like it was ten years old or older.' I want you to close your eyes and picture the van in your mind. What about it made it look old?"

Terry closed his eyes. "Well, it was light blue, like I said, but it had no shine to it. You know, like it needed a wax job."

"It had a dull finish, you mean," the Sheriff said.

"Yes. Exactly," Terry said opening his eyes.

"Was there another color coming through underneath?"

"No, it was all painted pretty evenly," Terry said. His gaze drifted to the ceiling. And then remembered, "Or. As a matter of fact, some of the paint was on the back bumper, I remember, like it had been kind of a sloppy paint job."

Sterner thought a moment then turned to the Sheriff. "If you were going to kidnap somebody in broad daylight, with a veritable certainty that eyewitnesses could identify your getaway vehicle, and you went so far as to cover your license plate with cardboard--"

"Water-based paint," the Sheriff finished the thought.

"And make a quick stop at the nearest--"

The Sheriff stood. "There's a self-service carwash between Racehorse Alley and Somerset Street, by the railroad tracks not three blocks away," the Sheriff said, putting his cap on and snapping up his coat.

Sterner grabbed his jacket and followed him to the door. "Let's hope they haven't thrown out their garbage yet."

———————

The carwash was located discreetly out of view from passing traffic on Somerset Street. There were three ports. Sterner checked the drain of the one furthest from the street and found a faint light blue paint stain.

"Bingo," Sterner said scraping it with a pocket knife and bagging the flakes.

The trash cans had been emptied, but there was a dumpster in the corner of the lot. The Sheriff helped Sterner overturn it onto the macadam. Out tumbled crumpled newspapers and used paper towels, empty soda cans, a near-empty bottle of Windex, discarded fast food and candy wrappers, small plastic containers of ketchup, mustard and mayonnaise, an empty can of engine oil, popsicle sticks, a used condom, a six-pack of empty beer bottles in their original cardboard container, an empty plastic half-gallon bottle of club soda and a shingle of gray cardboard the size of a license plate with folded-over duct tape swatches on three of four corners.

Sheriff Guise knew the owner of the carwash. He was a retired vending machine mechanic who owned and operated several self-serve carwashes in Samaritan and Murdoch. By phone he confirmed that he had routinely transferred trash from the cans to the dumpster himself the previous evening. A garbage hauler had a contract to empty the dumpster twice a week, Tuesday and Saturday mornings, so they were just in time.

Sterner carefully bagged everything from the dumpster and drove it to Harrisburg. His hair sample from the Whipple home got emergency priority status and was rushed through a DNA analyzer at the lab. It showed identical profiles to the other hair sample found in the chicken coop and the tooth found at the college. They all belonged to Clay Whipple. The question now was, where was he? And was he still alive?

———————

Cat was working at the reception desk at Dr. Deitz's Animal Clinic helping Ellie with a filing job when the five o'clock news came on the television in the empty waiting area. When Ellie saw Sterner behind another man speaking at a podium with the state crest displayed on the front, the words *Live: Breaking News* at the bottom of the screen, she seized the remote to turn up the sound and elbowed Cat.

"Hey, isn't that the detective who came to see you?"

"--can confirm that the skeleton of a woman found last weekend in the woods outside of Samaritan is connected to a kidnapping at Samaritan College yesterday through a New York man named Clay Whipple who grew up in the Samaritan area. We are looking at him as a person of interest in the case. Today another skeleton was discovered within the city limits of Samaritan. This second skeleton is that of a man six feet, two inches tall who disappeared between twenty and thirty years ago. We are currently searching our data bases in an effort to identify him. We have not yet been able to identify either Jane Doe, found last weekend, or John Doe, found this morning, and would appeal to the public for any information as to their identities. You can find full descriptions of the skeletal remains at www.psp.gov. We will take questions at this time." Taylor pointed to a reporter.

Cat's expression tightened.

The local news anchor broke into the press conference before the first question was asked, but Ellie quickly switched to a competing channel and found it again.

"--tell us under what circumstances today's skeleton was discovered?"

"I'd rather not go into that, as it may damage our investigation."

"We've received information that the skeleton was in fact found in the dentist's office of a Dr. Roy Fries, the hunter who used the hut where the first skeleton was found. Can you confirm that?"

Taylor glared at Sterner and back at the reporter and bit his lip. "No, I can't," Taylor said.

"Were flowers found with today's skeleton?"

"No, they were not."

"You said Monday we'd have to ask Cat True why she did not contact authorities after discovering the first skeletal remains, Jane Doe, but she has refused to talk to the press. Can you comment on this?"

"Let me state this once again as clearly as I can. Ms. True has no connection to this case other than having discovered the bones ten days ago. In fact, she has proven very helpful in giving authorities a timeline as to when the remains were placed in the woods. She indicated she was reluctant to come forward initially because she was trespassing on the property. I would appeal to the media to make a distinction between the Hellcat case and this one, as investigators have found no connection."

"Thank you," Ellie said, and then turned to Cat and realized she was distressed. "What's wrong? They just cleared you."

"I don't feel so well," Cat said. "I need to go home."

"Okay, sure, take off. I can finish this. See you Monday, girl."

————————

Sally didn't own a television set. Even if she had, broadcast reception was poor at best, and they had no use for a satellite dish even if they could afford one. So when Cat got home and found her mother in the kitchen, making herself a peanut butter and jelly sandwich, she knew there would be no way Sally could've known about the press conference.

"Mom, how tall was Daddy?"

"Why?"

"Because I want to know. How tall was he?"

"He's a big man. Six two. Six three. Why, did you see him?"

"Are you sure he went out west with Linda Helfrick?"

"You saw him, didn't you? He's come back to haunt us, hasn't he?"

"Mom. Listen. I was eight years old. You said Daddy ran off with Linda Helfrick. You said they moved out west. That's what you told me."

"They did."

"How do you know?"

"Vern told me."

"How do you know he was telling you the truth?"

"He wouldn't lie to me."

"Why not? He lied about other things."

"Why are you bringing all this up now? I don't like to talk about that."

"Because today they found a skeleton of a man who was six two, who's been missing for thirty years. And I think it might be my daddy."

Sally was dumbstruck and shook her head. "Can't be," she said finally.

"How do you know if you haven't seen or heard from him in thirty years?"

"Because he came to see me today and said you were making trouble for him. He worries you're being influenced by bad people who want to hurt him. He wants you to stop before we all get into trouble or someone gets hurt. He said he's willing to settle things, but he's not sure he can trust you to do the right thing by him."

"Mother, I swear, you can't tell the difference between a dream and what's real." She headed for her room and closed the door behind her.

Sally grew angry. "I told him I don't know why you make trouble," she said. "You do as you please and I have no control over you. That's what I said."

Cat sighed, dismissed her with a wave and retreated into her room.

———————

Peter and his wife went to a gas station payphone in Murdoch and once again telephoned Moneybags.

"Hello?"

"This is Mister O'Leary's associate. Have you been following the news?"

"I have," the man said.

"Have you reconsidered our offer?"

He sighed, sounded resigned. "Yes. I will comply."

"You will see that Mr. O'Leary is returned safely?"

"Yes. Two hundred thousand dollars was your price, I believe."

"Correct," Precious said.

"I will see to it that Mr. O'Leary is released with the money. Or should I say, Mr. Clay Whipple?"

"There will be no tricks this time, sir, are we clear about that?"

"Perfectly," Moneybags said. "And this prevents the copy of the letter from reaching the authorities, am I right about that?"

"Yes."

"And in fact you will destroy that copy of the letter and I will never hear about it or from you again, am I right about that?"

"Yes."

"Then I believe this concludes our business," the man said and hung up.

Precious hesitated before returning the receiver to its cradle. She then turned to her husband. "We're rich, baby," Precious said. She hugged her disbelieving husband tightly. "Two hundred thousand dollars. And that will be a three-way split, mister."

———————

"*Jesus loves me, this I know*," Musclehead sang, "*for the Bible tells me so. He is weak, but I am strong. Up in heaven, I belong. Yes, Jesus loves me. Yes, Jesus hugs me. Yes, Jesus slugs me. The Bible forecasts snow."*

The big man finished his recital and stood before Clay, leaning on his baseball bat with both hands like a song-and-dance man with a top hat holding a cane. "I'm afraid I have some bad news, little buddy. Are you with me? You look a little out of it, if you don't mind my saying so. We are about to part company, you and me, never to see each other again. I know how sad that must make you feel. I can see how broken up you are about it. Har, har."

Clay tilted his ashen face upward to meet the big man's. He was woozy but a ray of hope sharpened his blurry focus. Moneybags had come to his senses. No doubt Peter had produced the other skeleton to bring him around. It was their insurance policy. Clay wanted to gloat. He looked over at the red bead and nearly smiled. It had all been a test of stamina, patience and acting abilities. He'd shown his mettle. He'd never given up hope--not really. He was an actor's actor with a destiny to fulfill. Someday this experience would be priceless in a sense memory exercise. His parched pale lips curled up slightly into a smile. Grist for the mill.

"But before you go I want you to know something--and I mean this from the bottom of my heart--it's nothing personal."

And then Musclehead pulled back the bat one last time and posed in the classic hitter's stance, checked his footing over an imaginary home plate, wiggled his fanny and the bat in anticipation of the imaginary pitch, winked at Clay and swung mightily for a homer. He caught Clay dead in the forehead. The body, chair and all, flew backwards onto the packed dirt floor where whatever life still remaining in the distressed muscles caused it to spasm for several seconds before surrendering to the inevitable, following out the ghost of its departed occupant.

Cat showered, washing away the odors of the animal clinic, as she did every Friday evening, dressed and made it to Rosita's by 7:30 p.m. Fridays, Saturdays and Sundays were usually busy since Rosita's hired a band those nights to perform on an eight-by-twelve-foot riser ten inches off the floor in a corner of the dining room furthest from the door. The band this evening was Mickey's Gang, a local favorite, and they played mostly new country, with covers of Garth Brooks, Clint Black, Billy Joe Shaver and Steve Earle.

Cat was surprised when Sterner walked through the door.

"Hello," he said and smiled.

She smiled warily back at him and automatically stamped his hand for re-admittance, but said nothing. He was just another customer. But she watched him with curiosity as he greeted the hostess like they were old chums. Sharon led him to a booth in the corner as far away from the stage as you could get. An older man already seated was waving to him.

Roger Dooley had aged since Sterner had last seen him in Washington. He explained he'd recently had a benign lump removed. A strict diet had caused him to shed twenty pounds, but he wasn't back one hundred percent, and had started an ambitious fitness regimen since his operation eleven weeks ago. He was in his late fifties, had short-cropped white hair and dressed in a dark gray suit with a pale green shirt and dark green striped tie. He looked distinguished and spoke like a college professor.

"Joseph, I must thank you for inviting me along on the hunt," Dooley said forty-five minutes later as he picked over the leafy remains of his steak salad. "It's nice to be working again on crimes *in progress*. Everybody at the Bureau these days is obsessed with domestic terrorism. Not much profiling to be done there. Alienated young people eager to make their mark on the world and stage a grand exit."

"I'll take all the help I can get. Thank you for coming."

"Feel free to qualify everything I say. The thing you have to remember about profiling is that it is not an exact science. We delve in probabilities, not absolutes, intuition, not empirical science. Forensic criminalists like yourself sometimes dispute our nebulous analyses with good reason. Profiling is a tool, nothing more. But I've concluded with some certainty that Clay Whipple is probably not the mastermind."

"Really?" said Sterner. "How?"

"According to our resident expert in anatomy, after examining your excellent photographs from the scenes, he confused which phalanges went with which digits." Dooley squeezed the knuckle bones on one hand with the other. "However, the finger bones in the dental chair were laid out perfectly. What I'm wondering is why Ghoul Two didn't lay out the bones at the hut himself. My guess is Ghoul Two has a physical infirmity that made him unable to do it. You say there were no tire tracks in the woods."

"They could've been washed away."

"My bet is Clay hiked in because Ghoul Two could not."

Sterner rolled his eyes. "Or maybe they flipped a coin and Clay lost. Or maybe Clay was familiar with the area and Ghoul Two was not, and there was no reason why both should go." Sterner realized Dooley was right about one thing. He forgot how annoying profilers could be.

"It's only a theory," Dooley shrugged and went back to his salad.

"What about the roses?"

"Still unclear. Could be an actor's flourish, could relate to the identity of Jane Doe or why she was killed, or feelings Ghoul Two has for Jane Doe. Certainly it's significant that the second skeleton did not have roses. Ghoul Two is responding to the kidnapping of his partner, I'd say. Shining that light on the dental work was him screaming for attention. *Look, you guys, you cops, you dentists, you morons, this is what's important, for pity sake, focus on this!* Shows a certain desperation, I think."

"Is he trying to get *our* attention or somebody else's?"

"Both, I should think."

"He doesn't want to give us all the information, does he? He just wants to point us in a particular direction. He wants to tease us. He's an arrogant little bugger."

"Correct. He has a specific agenda. Follow your thought. Meanwhile, the publicity puts pressure on another party. Why?"

"Blackmail," Sterner said.

"I have to say it is shaping up to look like a blackmail plot to me."

"I don't see what else it could be. We're way beyond a practical joke here. Where do you want to start tomorrow?"

"I want to look at the hut. It may help me see things through their eyes."

"I'll see if I can arrange an escort. It's fairly remote."

"I appreciate that." He yawned. "Pardon me. The drive up from Virginia was more taxing than I expected."

"I'll get a check," Sterner said and waved to a nearby waitress.

"I'd stay for the music, but this isn't to my taste. I prefer Puccini."

No sooner had Sterner entered his own room than his cell rang.

"Sterner," he said.

"I just got a call you might be interested in," the Sheriff said.

"Shoot."

"Old Judge Helfrick says he thinks he knows who John and Jane Doe are. He wants to show us something. I don't know whether the old codger is just lonely or getting a little senile or what. Then again it might amount to something, you never know. I owe him a courtesy call at least. You interested?"

"Sure."

"Where are you?"

"Room 27 at the Sleep Well."

"Pick you up in ten minutes."

"I just had dinner with an FBI agent named Roger Dooley who's working the case," Sterner said. They were in the Sheriff's Explorer heading back through town. "He's staying at the Sleep Well. He wants to see the chicken coop at Rattlesnake Ridge tomorrow morning. Any chance Deputy Kendalhart could take him up there?"

"FBI? Are you kidding?" the Sheriff said. "Warren'll be tickled pink to spend the day with a genuine G-man. I'll give him a shout."

"Did this judge give any hint as to who the Does might be over the phone?" Sterner said as they drove.

"Nope," the Sheriff said. "Just said he had something to show us."

"Judge Helfrick presided over the Hellcat case, I believe, and when he was the D.A. it was *his* wife who ran off with Cat's dad, am I right about that?"

"Yup," the Sheriff said.

"Now that's what I call a small town."

"Don't I know it! Linda was his second wife. Met her in Atlantic City. She was a gold digger, that one. Everybody in town could see it but the Judge himself. He was a one hundred and fifty watt bulb in a room full of Christmas lights. But not when it came to women. His first wife was a bitch. Katie died of breast cancer back in the early Seventies. She was the one with the money, one of the Nussbaums. Nussbaum's Apple Sauce? His third wife Louise passed away a few years back after a stroke. Now *she* was a sweetheart. Former grade school teacher. Baked the best oatmeal cookies this side of the Mississip. Old man now lives all by himself up there on Forest Hill Road playing with his model train set in the basement. Whatever you do, don't let him drag you down there to look at his toy trains. We'll be there all night."

In the middle of a twenty-acre lot of oak trees stood a gigantic century-old Victorian with a widow's walk on the roof, an architectural conceit, since it was nowhere near the sea. There was a formal circular drive that led around to the front door. Instead the Sheriff pulled onto a service drive that led behind the house and stopped short of a small construction project in the backyard, where a pile of five-inch PVC pipe was stacked up next to an open ditch that smelled of raw sewage.

A pale, bald, bent old man with large black-rimmed glasses answered the backdoor. He was dressed in a blue blazer and tan chinos with an open-collared pale yellow shirt. He looked like he'd just returned from cocktail hour at the country club.

"Gentlemen, welcome," Judge Helfrick said in a raspy voice, shaking hands after introductions were made. "I apologize for the stench. I'm having some work done on my septic. Come on in."

The judge led them into a natural wood-paneled kitchen with mullioned glass cabinet work from an earlier era. It was a large room with a gigantic wooden table occupying its center beneath twin ceiling fans. A checkbook sat atop a stack of bills to one side with a pad of paper covered with scribbles, an inexpensive Bic pen and several issues of magazines for model train enthusiasts. Also laid out across the table were a dozen worn and mildewed scrap books. One was open and showed several yellowing newspaper clippings. Sterner noted the wall calendar from the Samaritan National Bank was dated 2005. He nodded towards it for the Sheriff's sake.

The Sheriff glanced over. "Time to change your calendar, Judge, don't you think?"

"What? Oh. That was Louise's. I just keep it there because it reminds me of her. Have a seat, gentlemen," the Judge said. "May I offer either of you a beverage? Soda, beer, something manlier?"

They both shook their heads, thanked him and sat down at the kitchen table. The judge sat on the opposite side facing the two lawmen.

"I'll get right to the point, then," the Judge said, turning the scrap book a hundred and eighty degrees and sliding it across the table at them. "My first wife liked to chronicle my illustrious career as a prosecutor in these scrap books. Larry McKim and George Letterer. Ring any bells?"

"Doolittle County Depositors Trust?" the Sheriff said.

"You have a good memory, Vern."

"I was floating in the Gulf of Tonkin at the time, but my mother lost a bundle on them, I remember," the Sheriff said.

The Judge directed his attention at Sterner. "Her and anyone with deposits exceeding forty thousand, the maximum insurance guaranteed by the FDIC in those days. Local man named Harry Rohrer founded the bank after World War II. Expanded to a network of five branches throughout the county. Must've employed a hundred people by about '65 with something like forty million in assets. Did very well for himself for a dumb Dutchman with an eighth grade education. Hired a slick new manager named McKim out of Philadelphia to take over the reins. McKim convinced him he could bring in some big city real estate business. Together with his partner Letterer, they scammed millions through a dozen or more bad loans. The whole thing was a con, with Rohrer later claiming he was too naïve to understand what was going on till it was too late. When it came out Letterer had a criminal record, depositors ran for the hills and the whole enterprise went into the toilet. Bank collapsed like a house of cards.

"I prosecuted all three men for embezzlement in '68. Rohrer was acquitted. He kept a low profile, dabbled in real estate until he passed away a few years back. McKim was convicted and went to prison where he died in '71 or '72 of throat cancer. I won a conviction against Letterer, too, in absentia, because Letterer and his wife disappeared before trial. Some say with a suitcase with two million in cash. As I recall, the FBI lost track of them on a cruise ship to the Bahamas out of New York, December '67."

"We're certain these bones haven't been in the ground that long," Sterner said.

"But I saw the broadcast this afternoon. Letterer was a tall man, six foot two or six three. Here's a picture of him coming out of the court house after his arraignment." The judge wetted his thumb and flipped a few pages in the open scrap book to show them the newspaper photo of Letterer towering over an unidentified woman, probably his wife, a full head shorter. "This second skeleton was a man six foot, two. The first was a woman five foot, four?" He tapped the photo.

"Yessir," the Sheriff said.

"I'm guessing Letterer and his wife ran out of money on the run and came back to the States after a few years, thinking things had cooled down and the coast was clear. Then somebody caught up with them. I were you, detective, I'd check Letterer's dental records in Homesburg Prison down in Philly, because Letterer did an eighteen-month stretch there for fraud about '60, '61."

"Homesburg," Sterner wrote it down in his notepad. "They shut that down some years back."

"I'm sure they've got dental records sitting around somewhere," the Judge said.

"Thanks for the tip, Judge," the Sheriff said. "Might turn out to be something."

The judge nodded and then glanced thoughtfully at Sterner. "Do you have any interest in XO railroads, detective?"

"I'm afraid not."

"Pity. I just finished a new run through the Alps with a replica of an 1835 Adler locomotive." He chuckled proudly. "I have this little fellow slaloming down the Matterhorn who skis right into a gondola that takes him right back up again to the top of the mountain. You've never seen anything like it." His eyes lit up like Becca's, a little scary on an octogenarian.

"Sounds terrific," Sterner said. "Another time, perhaps."

———————

Sterner was dead asleep when he heard a faint knock on his door. He checked the digital alarm clock on his bedside table. It was 1:12 a.m. He switched on the table lamp and jumped into his trousers. When he looked through the peephole he saw Cat True. He made sure he scooped his shirttail into his pants and zipped his fly before cracking the door. Cold air slapped him awake.

"Detective Sterner?" she said. "I need to talk to you." She was upset.

"Can it wait till morning?"

"Please. I think I know who Jane and John Doe are." She was shivering.

He was vaguely aware of an Esplanade SUV driving slowly past, its male occupants looking their way. He wondered how it looked, this woman at his door so late at night. He quickly ushered her inside to a plastic chair at the Formica table by the picture window. The curtains were already drawn. Yes, it was completely improper.

"How did you find me?" Sterner said, retrieving his pad and pen.

"I saw you drive over from Rosita's," Cat said. "I know the night manager here, Benny. He told me your room number. I hope I didn't get him into trouble."

Sterner shrugged. "So," Sterner said and sat across from her on the bed.

Cat swallowed hard. "My father was six two. His name was David Howard True. He was a deputy sheriff here in Doolittle County. The woman he supposedly ran away with was Judge Helfrick's wife Linda, back when he was District Attorney. I don't know much about her--her height or anything--except she was from New Jersey, I think, and was fairly young. Thing is, I never heard from him after they supposedly ran off to the Yukon thirty years ago. It's always bothered me. Do you think it might be them?"

"I don't know, but I'm sure the Sheriff would've said something if he thought so."

"I don't trust Vernon Guise as far as I can throw him, and neither should you."

"Oh? Why is that?" He leaned forward.

"Did he tell you he used to sleep with my mother?"

Sterner straightened wondering if and how that fit into the picture. "No. That he didn't mention."

"I don't know when it started. But not long after Daddy disappeared he started coming around regularly, almost every day. They kept it secret. They swore me to secrecy, too. He told me they were going to get married. He told me he'd adopt me. I was going to be Catherine Guise. But after maybe a year he broke it off. Mom blamed his mother. He lived with her at the time. But then she died a year later. He never came around after that except to, sort of, *visit*. I can't help thinking they might be involved in covering something up. Like murder. There, I said it." She blew bad air out her lungs and relaxed her shoulders, unburdened from decades of suspicion.

Sterner played with his lower lip. "Your father," he said. "Did he ever have any broken bones?"

"Broken bones?" Cat thought about it. "I remember he told me once he broke his arm falling out of a tree as a kid. Then his leg jumping out of a helicopter in Vietnam into elephant grass, whatever that is."

"John Doe had no broken bones."

He watched her transition through six emotions and turn pink. Cat shook her head, threw up her hands and bit her lip. She stood and moved to the door. "I feel like a fool. I'm sorry, sorry I bothered you."

Sterner was moved by her vulnerability. She had shared her deepest, darkest personal suspicions, and he worried he'd been too blunt. He followed to console her. "It's understandable. The dates fit. His height."

"I don't know what's worse," Cat said, hiding her face now in full blush. She forced a smile. "Finding out your daddy was murdered or hearing it confirmed all over again. He left for another woman."

Sterner placed a comforting hand on her shoulder. "For what it's worth," he said, "I grew up in an orphanage. At least you have a mother." He instantly regretted saying it. He'd revealed more about himself than he meant to, more than he had to anyone for a long time. He self-consciously removed his hand and smiled. "I don't know why I said that." He was supposed to be a professional. He was supposed to remain impartial.

"Did the Sheriff ever say anything about her? My mother, I mean."

"I believe he used the term *wacky*."

She shrugged and smiled and shuddered. "She says Daddy sends people to spy on her and follow her around."

"Sounds like paranoid delusion, bipolar disorder. Schizophrenia, they used to call it. Have you thought about getting her some help?"

"How do you do that without becoming part of the conspiracy? Helen, my boss at the animal clinic--you met her--arranged for a social worker to visit last year. But it only convinced her Helen and the social worker were in cahoots with my daddy."

"Hmm."

"You grew up in an orphanage? What was that like?"

He was supposed to keep his distance and remain objective, he told himself. "I was told my folks were killed in an auto accident when I was a baby, but I grew up with about a thousand brothers and sisters."

"That must've been rough."

He shrugged. "They treat you pretty good there, sent me to college in New York."

"Do you go back on holidays?"

He should be showing her out now. But he was enjoying the only real conversation with an attractive woman in many months. "I stopped when I got married, but never returned after the divorce. People I used to know there have families of their own now. As you get older you feel pathetic sitting next to some ten-year-old at dinner who looks at you wondering if he'll ever have a family of his own or wind up taking holiday meals every year sitting next to another pathetic orphan like himself." He chuckled morbidly. "I sound sorry for myself. I don't mean to." He wondered what the hell he was saying. Maybe he wasn't as awake as he thought. He wiped sleep from his eyes.

"Marriage didn't work for you, either, huh?"

Lord but she had beautiful eyes. They so easily held his. "My ex-wife's a corporate lawyer. We're on civil terms, more or less. She had a baby daughter when I met her. Becca's three now, and I'm the only father she's ever known. Her real father is some British millionaire playboy. I'm afraid she's a little confused by it all. I'm not sure I blame her. You?"

"He was a musician. Never home. Not exactly reliable. And he had emotional problems. When we ran out of money and he had to get a real job with the power company, he started pushing me around. Like I was somehow to blame for his failed music career. I walked out. He had his sweet side, though. He could charm the pants off of you. He did me. I admire you to keep in touch with your ex-wife's daughter. Most men wouldn't bother."

"Most would if they knew Becca. She's a very warm-hearted little girl, not to mention pretty and smart and has a great sense of humor."

She brightened. "Tell me a story about her," she said smiling.

This was so wrong. Still he did not care. Sterner thought about it and then said, "When she was just starting to talk I used to dress her. A shirt would get stuck over her head and I'd say, *Where's Becca?* And then her head would pop through and I'd go, *There's Becca.* And she'd smile. We were on the playground on a cold winter day and she had on a new down parka with a rigid hood so that when her head turned the hood stayed in place. I picked her up at one point and she turned to look at me, her face obscured by the hood, and said, *Where's Becca?"* Sterner laughed at the memory.

"You have a nice smile," she said through a nice smile all her own. "You should use it more often."

Sterner grinned shyly, scratched his chin. This was all a mistake. Get her out the door now. Before you make a pass at her and really get into trouble!

"How often do you see her?"

"Not as much as I'd like. Most Sundays."

"And she's finding it tough with the divorce?"

"She's adjusting. But her mother is, shall we say, a formidable presence. She has a nanny who keeps her sane, I think."

"Still, she's lucky to have you."

"I'm lucky to have her." Sterner drifted back to sit on the bed. What was he doing? "You never had kids?"

Cat didn't move. "One. He died."

"I'm sorry."

"Sometimes I think there are too many people in this world anyway. When young men strap bombs to themselves or fly airplanes into buildings, I can't help but think that's Mother Nature's way of telling us we are too many. We're too good at curing diseases and fighting famine, and we're ruining the planet with our sheer numbers."

"You might be right there."

They looked over each other for several awkward seconds, having temporarily run out of topics for conversation.

"Mind if I ask you a personal question?"

"Go ahead."

"You work with animals at the clinic and then you hunt them in the wild. Does that ever bother you?"

"You arrest bad people and help good people, don't you?"

"Sure."

She shrugged. "Same thing. It's my job to help the animals. They're usually somebody's pet. I hunt what I eat. I eat what I kill. I don't eat pets." She smiled.

"And you hold down two jobs. That must be tough."

"My second job is pretty much getting paid to listen to a live band. I'd be hanging out there if I wasn't getting paid." She looked around the room. "Well, I guess I should leave now."

"I guess you should." Sterner walked her to the door and opened it.

"Thanks for making me feel better," she said.

"You're welcome," he said. And then he closed the door, took her in his arms and kissed her tenderly on the lips. It was a warm kiss, moist and smooth, and he tasted mint. He didn't want it to end. She aroused him. There was something in her scent. It wasn't perfume or tobacco or alcohol, though there were traces of those on her clothing. It was her natural body odor. It was intoxicating.

She froze, pulled away and stammered. "I'm not a--not a normal person," she said. "I--I can't do this."

"Neither am I," he said and kissed her again.

But she pulled away this time. "I mean I have a hole inside me. I can't feel anything. I have to get drunk before I can--do *that*!" She was nervous, even panicky.

Do that! echoed in his mind. Sterner stepped back, a bucket of cold water thrown over his heart. What the hell was he doing, anyway?

"I like you," she said. "You're not the usual kind of guy I'm attracted to, but--"

He knew something about that hole. Rape victims were not all that different from orphans in some ways. *I've got one, too*, he thought. *I've always had one. Fill it for me. Please?* He straightened and took hold of her hand. "Don't worry. That won't happen again. I'm sorry."

"I'm sorry, too." She let herself out. "Good night."

He leaned his head against the door after it closed behind her and turned to stone. Immobile, eyes closed for nearly a minute, he savored the remnant scent and tried to remember the last time he tasted a kiss so sweet.

Long before meeting Emily, that was for sure. His ex-wife had been a phenomenal object for his lust, but not a great romantic.

You're not the usual kind of guy I'm attracted to, but--. Did that mean she *was* attracted to him? A kiss like that does not lie. Propriety be damned!

When his eyes opened, he could find no trace evidence that she'd ever been in the room. Were it not for the scribbles in his notepad, he could imagine she had come to him only in a dream.

———————

9.

NINE DAYS BEFORE OPENING DAY

Sterner caught up on lost sleep Saturday morning, the uniformed maid waking him at nine-thirty when she tried to service the room. As he stepped under the shower he began thinking about how to pursue the case in three directions simultaneously. One, if Flanigan got lucky he'd find something in Laurel Valley. That would put Flanigan in charge of excavating the gravesite with Crime Scene. If not, he'd put him with Crime Scene to process the trash at the carwash in hopes of finding a latent fingerprint that could help ID the kidnappers. Two, he'd put Dooley together with the Sheriff's Office to formulate a list of local suspects fitting Dooley's profile of Ghoul Two. And three, if John and Jane Doe turned out to be George Letterer and his wife after checking dental records in Philly he'd go back to Judge Helfrick and re-interview for suspect leads in the murders. He'd familiarize himself with the details in the Doolittle County Depositors Trust scandal. If John Doe was forty when he was killed in the mid-Seventies to mid-Eighties, that might mean he was a Vietnam-era vet. Then again, it might not.

His cell rang as he was toweling off.

"Sterner," he said.

The Sheriff spoke slowly and with deliberation. "I'm looking at the body of a driver in a van accident at a hairpin turn on Burnside Summit Road south of Rattlesnake Ridge. The body is pretty mangled and there's no identification, but the driver sure looks like Clay Whipple to me."

When a kidnap victim turned up dead, it was easy to jump to conclusions. But Sterner was taught that presuppositions interfered with the scientific method and the effective processing of a death scene. He immediately called Harrisburg, dressing with the cell phone crooked on his shoulder.

Outside the sky was gray and the weather turning colder. As Sterner stepped into the chill wind of the motel parking lot he had to forego plans for a sumptuous breakfast and settle for a fast food drive-through along the strip. Speeding to the scene, Sterner pulled up behind Doc Johnson's Suburban. He reduced his speed and followed him, arriving at the scene at the same time as the Medical Examiner.

Burnside Summit Road was a two-lane blacktop that zigzagged over Burnside Mountain a mile north of the Mason Dixon Line and three miles south of the Rattlesnake Ridge property. The road was the southernmost link between Doolittle and Burnside Counties and had been dynamited out of the mountainside during the Depression. It was rarely traveled, since most traffic between the counties still passed on the much older, more direct and faster route ten miles north through the white pines of Greenwood Pass, directly linking Samaritan with Newtonville, Burnside's county seat.

The first sign that he was getting close to the accident scene was a series of road flares around a steep curve three-quarters of the way up the mountain. The Sheriff's Explorer and two State Police cruisers were parked at a pull-off five hundred yards beneath the summit, where the eastern face was at its steepest. It was the next-to-last dogleg of the road and offered the only credible access to the crash site, a manageable descent by foot. Sterner showed his credentials to a trooper directing traffic and peered down into the crash site out his passenger window. He could make out the side of a dark green cargo van standing on its nose in the woods, having smashed into rocks at the base of a thick white pine tree and sheering off its limbs. Instead of parking he drove further up the road to the end of the last dogleg, where a hairpin turn led westbound traffic a hundred and fifty degrees in the opposite direction up and finally over the summit into Burnside County.

It appeared the eastbound van was speeding down the mountain too fast to make the turn or made too wide a turn, sending it through a guardrail and down a hundred and fifty-foot rock cliff. But when Sterner drove up to the turn, he noted that although there were several pairs of tire skid marks rounding the turn, none led off the road and into the shoulder. None led into the abyss where the van had plunged into the rock-face. The only explanation was that either the driver applied his brakes too late or not at all.

Sterner took out his Cyber-shot and started shooting. First the skid marks, then the broken guard rail, which had been weakened from rust and erosion. Sterner shivered when the wind whipped across the ridge from the northeast. The day's temperature was in the low forties down in the valley but the altitude here had to be close to twenty-five hundred feet, sending it to the freezing mark. There were traces of moisture in the gutter on the inside turn. Could there have been ice on the road last night?

On closer inspection, it looked to Sterner like the smashed guard rail had been struck not once but several times in more or less the same place. There were several distinct rust-free scrapes on the distressed metal.

Surveying the edge of the cliff he could see the back of the van, and imagined how Terry Meyer must have seen it driving away from the Knorr Student Union Building for the appointed rinse-off at the carwash along Racehorse Alley.

He watched Sheriff Guise greet Doc Johnson with a handshake and remembered Cat's warning that the Sheriff could not be trusted. Doc Johnson pointed Sterner out to the Sheriff and both men looked up and waved. As Sterner waved back, he wondered whether it was Cat who could not be trusted. He remembered what the Sheriff had said about Cat and the rapes in the Hellcat case. *If she'd had a daddy who was a deputy sheriff, I doubt it would've happened,* he'd said. Had he meant himself? Sterner remembered the picture he'd found on the internet of Cat being escorted by Sheriff's Deputy Guise. What must he have been thinking? *This could've been my adopted daughter!* Sterner got back into his car and drove down to where the others had parked and hiked in.

"Now maybe you'll take a serious look in Burnside County," the Sheriff said by way of a greeting.

"Why's that?" Sterner said.

"That's where he was coming from, isn't it obvious?" the Sheriff said.

"Looks that way," Sterner said, conceding nothing, and then noticed Doc Johnson checking the body. "Careful what you touch, Doc. Crime Scene's on the way." The doc waved showing off his gloved hand. He knew the drill.

Sheriff Guise said escorting him over, "Couple of tourists from Ohio called 9-1-1 about eight a.m."

The van had landed almost perfectly vertical. He noticed chalky scrape marks on the undercarriage where it had apparently hit a rock on the way down. Sterner looked back up at the cliff and noticed the protruding culprit. The van had not arced out very far in its dive from the rocky cliff. Which meant it could not have been traveling at a very high speed when it took the plunge.

"Notice the paint?" the Sheriff said. There was a faint residue of powder blue water-based paint smeared on the back fender behind the right rear tire well where it had not been completely hosed away. "Gotta be your abduction vehicle. Maybe he was trying to make a getaway," the Sheriff said.

Sterner only nodded.

The body was crushed between the driver's seat and the dash, which had collapsed upon impact as the bumper and contents from the engine compartment rose to meet it, squishing the driver like a sardine in a can. The windshield glass had shattered, too, and pebbles of safety glass were all over the clothing. Clay wore the same dark suit that Terry Meyer had described, but without his muttonchops disguise. There was little doubt it was him. What Sterner could make of the driver's gray pallor and contorted expression certainly resembled the head shot they had circulated. The mangled look of horror, however, together with the wide purplish dent in his forehead made it impossible to say for certain. His hair was red, at least. *A real carrot-top*, as Roy Fries had said. Sterner could not see Clay's front teeth without disturbing the body. The lower jaw was embedded into the center of the plastic steering column. It looked both grotesque and odd. No air bag had inflated.

Sterner snapped several shots before observing that whatever had caused the forehead to cave in was nowhere to be seen. It wasn't the steering wheel which was little more than an inch in diameter. It could have been a large limb but when Sterner looked around he could find no credible candidates. There were plenty of limbs but none that fit the bill. And the pine tree bark was almost crumbly to the touch and sappy beneath. There should be pine bark or sap residue on the skin inside the purplish indentation. There was nothing. A baseball bat, on the other hand, would fit perfectly.

Sterner also noticed an absence of blood, not impossible if brain death had been instantaneous following a trauma from a head-on collision. But under these circumstances one would expect a lot of blood from lacerations made by spraying pebbles of shattered windshield glass and pumped out by an adrenalized heart. Instead there was nothing.

Sterner took another dozen shots of the scene and then hiked back up to his car, where he downloaded the file onto his laptop. Finding no wifi signal, he was nevertheless able to successfully e-mail through a cell tower signal to Taylor with a c.c. to Hand, Dooley and Flanigan. About the accident photos he wrote only, "Looks faked," and let the pictures do the talking.

When he got out of his car Sheriff Guise was leaning against the trunk, hands stuffed inside his Carhartt's. Sterner shivered. "Wind sure makes it colder up here," Sterner said.

"Cold enough to freeze the balls off a brass monkey, we used to say in the Navy," he said. "You know what a brass monkey is?"

"Can't say that I do."

"The pallet that held the cannonballs belowdecks. It was made of brass so the iron cannonballs wouldn't rust to it. Only brass shrinks faster than iron when it gets cold, so when it was *really* cold the pallet would shrink and the balls would fall off." The Sheriff grinned. "I'll bet you thought it meant something else." Sterner suspected this wasn't the first time he'd impressed somebody with this cocktail party trivia.

"Learn something new every day," Sterner said.

The Crime Scene unit arrived around one o'clock, at the same time as the State Police accident investigator in his cruiser. The truck was essentially an EMS vehicle adapted for transporting cadavers and human remains and equipped accordingly. Sterner recognized Bobby Giles, the young lab technician who'd processed the red hair, when he stepped out of the driver's seat and approached.

"Just got started on your trash evidence this morning when we got this call," he said defensively. There were seven crime scene labs in the state and a mere thirty technicians thinly spread among them. They were generally overworked and understaffed and under constant pressure to double-check every detail in their work, especially since a scandal in the Allentown lab suggesting sloppy methodology had overturned a number of convictions and given them all a black eye. Only the high regard among prosecutors for the forensic sciences and the glamour generated by the current spate of popular television programs had prevented major bureaucratic upheaval.

"Don't worry," Sterner said, "this takes priority. You know that red hair and teeth you processed?"

"Your kidnap victim, right?" Giles said.

Sterner gestured over his shoulder at the van with his thumb.

"No kidding," Giles said as he peered down at the scene of the accident.

"Need a positive ID ASAP."

"You got it, boss," Giles said.

James Leroy Robinson, a.k.a. Crash, was *the* premiere Pennsylvania State Police accident investigator, and something of a legend. He'd grown up in Camp Hill, joined the Navy in the early Eighties and was stationed in San Diego. When he was discharged, he stayed in California, becoming a claims adjuster for a major insurance carrier. He made his reputation with one of his first cases by single-handedly solving a murder case involving a porn movie producer whose automobile accident had been staged by his wife and her lover. His account of the case, *Fatal Mistakes*, co-written by an <u>L.A. Times</u> reporter, became a bestseller. It was even made into a movie with Wesley Snipes playing Robinson. When his own sister and her husband died in an automobile accident in early 2000, he returned to Harrisburg to take custody of their children and took a job with the State Police. As he emerged from his car, Sterner moved to greet him with a handshake.

"Crash, you're just the man I was hoping to see," Sterner said.

"Don't call me that, man," Robinson said in an intimidating baritone. Not because the nickname angered him. He didn't like it much, but accepted it as part of his celebrity, and knew it was anything but disrespectful. But they were within earshot of the trooper directing traffic. It was unprofessional.

"Sorry. Everybody else does." Sterner didn't know him personally but strictly by reputation.

"What are we looking at, detective?" Robinson said with an air of sober authority. He shivered from the cold, adjusted his porkpie hat and buttoned his collar. He filled every inch of his triple-X sized trench coat and looked nothing whatsoever like Wesley Snipes. The PSP was a predominately white force, traditionally military and very conservative. Robinson took a certain pride in being not only among the few black lawmen among the ranks, but indeed one of its stars.

Sterner lowered his voice and arched his eyebrows. "Far be it for me to prejudice your expert opinion--"

Robinson's eyebrows mirrored Sterner's and he perked up. "Front row seats?" Robinson said.

"Front and center, I'd say," Sterner said.

Robinson rubbed his large tobacco-colored hands together and not just because it was cold. "God, I love my job," he said and broke into a Cheshire cat grin showing off a gold bicuspid. A murder scene that was staged to look like an automobile accident was what men like Robinson lived for and rarely saw. "In my six years on the job I've seen only one other," he said. "A drowning death inside an Eldorado driven backwards into the Delaware River Canal south of Easton. These perps, they're just so stupid it tickles me."

The Harrisburg Crime Scene Unit truck had a portable DNA profile analyzer and Giles was able to process a hair from the driver's head and compare it to the profile he accessed from the crime lab computer on his ToughBook. They were identical. The dead man was Clay Whipple.

Sheriff Guise confessed that he'd touched both doors without gloves, checked the glove compartment and several places on the body for signs of life and identification. So to eliminate his from other prints, the latent print expert, Danny Haywood, needed to fingerprint him. The Sheriff didn't like the idea much but relented.

"I guess I've mucked things up enough here," he said now, wiping the ink from his fingertips with a rag from his SUV. "If you boys have everything under control here, I've got to go tell John and Clara Whipple they just lost their only child and they should forget about a viewing." Cursing under his breath, he added, "And then I'm going home to sleep for thirty-six hours. County doesn't pay me enough to work seven days a week."

"Mind if I ask you something?"

"Go ahead."

Sterner looked hard into the Sheriff's eyes. "David Howard True."

"What about him?"

"You never considered he was John Doe, though my understanding is he disappeared about the same time John Doe went into the ground and nobody's heard from him since."

"Sally hears from him, time to time. He moved up to the Yukon, like I told you."

"How would you characterize your relationship with Mrs. True?"

By his expression it was clear the Sheriff didn't like Sterner's officious tone and ignored him at first. As he continued to clean his fingers, he lowered his voice. "Been raking up the muck, I see. For the record, I wanted to marry Sally after her husband left her but she refused to sue him for the necessary divorce and over time I got tired of waiting. Does that satisfy you?"

The two men squared off as if for a fistfight, each assessing the other in a staring contest. Sterner blinked first.

"Yes. Thank you," he said turning away.

"Anything else you want to know about my private life? Which hand I wipe my ass with? How often I jerk off?"

"No, sir."

"Good. Then I'll be on my way." He turned in a huff and Sterner watched him amble over to his truck. The Sheriff threw the rag under the driver's seat in disgust, climbed in and drove off down the mountain refusing to meet Sterner's eyes.

When Haywood approached Sterner said to him, "Do me a favor, Danny, and run the Sheriff's prints when you get back."

"You serious?" Haywood said. The two had known each other since their days together at the State Police Academy. Still it was the first time anyone had ever asked him to run a set of fingerprints from a fellow law officer.

Sterner shrugged. "Humor me."

"Okay," Haywood said.

"Just between us, though, okay? I owe you one," Sterner said.

"I think it's three or four by now," Haywood winked. "But who's counting?"

Taylor called Sterner to say he'd gotten his e-mail and ask him what his next move was. Sterner told him he'd call a briefing to go over what they had with Dooley and Flanigan that evening. He looked forward to Robinson's report on the accident scene and felt confident that the accident investigator would come to the same conclusion he had, that it was staged. He expected Giles and Haywood to come up with fingerprints either from the van or the trash evidence from the carwash. Taylor told him Homesburg Prison records could not be accessed until Monday at the earliest.

Another call came in as he was wrapping up his conversation with Taylor.

"Hey, Daddy. Are you coming tomorrow?"

"Hey, pookie. It's so good to hear your voice. How are you?"

"Are you coming tomorrow?"

"Well, I'm not sure. Maybe I should talk to Mommy."

Without another word he heard the receiver hand-off. Emily said, "Hey, Joe."

"Hey."

"Are you gonna be around tomorrow?"

"I'm not sure. I'm on a tough case down here in Samaritan. We found a kidnap victim dead this morning and others may follow if we don't put on a full court press."

"You mean that Whipple kid? We saw you on the news yesterday. I taped it so Becca could watch. You looked nervous. When is that egomaniac Taylor ever going to let you answer a question, anyway? He's such a publicity hound. You need to work on your wardrobe, too." It annoyed him that even after the divorce she still tried to dress him her way. "But listen, this might work out. Teddy and I were just talking about driving up to New York to see a Broadway show tonight, maybe do Radio City tomorrow for Becca and drive right home. If we don't do it this weekend we'll be up against the holiday crowds till January. Anyway, we're going to see you Monday morning, right?"

"Yeah, sure, fine. Listen, about the gun on the playground--"

"We'll talk about it Monday."

"Fine." Another argument he could not avoid or win.

Sterner hadn't realized how hungry he was until he got off the phone. He checked his watch. It was 2:30 p.m. He knew Crime Scene would be working through the night if not all the next day. They would have to get a crane to retrieve the van and take it back to Harrisburg on a flatbed. He'd only get in the way. So he wished them all luck and left.

Six miles down the road, at the intersection of Greenwood Furnace Road, Sterner passed an unlikely bar and grill nestled among the trees called Wyman's Tavern, a one-story ranch with a log cabin facade. They had a sign that read: "Hunter's Special: Salisbury Steak $8.99," with a *Stella Artois* neon sign in the window and Deputy Kendalhart's Explorer parked in the parking lot: three good reasons to make a K-turn.

Doolittle County Sheriff's Deputy Warren Kendelhart and Special Agent Roger Dooley of the Federal Bureau of Investigation were at the bar eating buffalo wings and drinking mugs of Budweiser, ignoring a Penn State football game on one of the four TVs and laughing at something the bartender was saying.

"She's got her middle finger wrapped in a splint," the bartender said, "so I ask her what happened and she says, I diddled myself so hard I broke my finger. So I says, I know how to prevent that. And she says, How? And I says, Use my finger." The lawmen laughed.

Sterner threw his arms around their shoulders. "Whatever the government pays you boys, it isn't enough."

"Hey, Joe Sterner, who let you in here?" Dooley said.

"Get you something?" the bartender said. He was a slight young man, with a plaster of Paris cast on his left forearm covered with blue and black felt-tip signatures.

"We're off the clock," Kendalhart said, parroting his boss and sipping his Bud.

"I'm not," Sterner said. "I'll have the Salisbury Steak Special and a pint of Stella." When the bartender moved away, he turned to Kendalhart. "I thought the Sheriff said you were a teetotaler."

"Only the hard stuff."

Dooley lowered his voice. "So did you ID the van driver?"

Sterner nodded. "I e-mailed you." He sat down next to him.

"Hell, I couldn't find a hot spot around here if my life depended on it. Not even a cell signal. But we heard over the radio about the crash. Was it Whipple?"

Sterner nodded.

"What did the scene look like?"

"Front row seats," Sterner said.

Dooley raised his eyebrows and pursed his lips. "Well, well. That's a wrinkle."

"What's that? Some sort of code?" Kendalhart said.

"A staged scene," Dooley said.

Kendalhart nodded thoughtfully.

"Crash Robinson's out there now with Harrisburg Crime Scene," Sterner said.

"*The* Crash Robinson?" Dooley said. "I'd like to meet him."

"He's a little preoccupied at the moment."

"Who's that?" Kendalhart said.

"Ever see that Wesley Snipes movie where he plays an insurance investigator who solves the murder of a porno producer who supposedly drove a Ferrari into his garage at sixty miles an hour? *Fatal Something*?"

"Yeah, it was on HBO last summer."

"Crash is the *real* guy."

"No shit."

The bartender returned with Sterner's Stella. "Food'll be up in a few," he said. "I'll be right back. I gotta change a keg."

"Thanks," Sterner said and took a sip.

"What's he talking about?" Dooley said. "Taps are all full."

"Bartender code for a bathroom break," Kendalhart said and belched.

Dooley nodded thoughtfully.

"Any discoveries on your end?" Sterner said and took a sip of his draft.

"Yeah, coming here for lunch."

Sterner snorted and wiped dribble from his chin with his sleeve.

"You laugh but I'm serious," Dooley said. "Russell, our bartender, says there was a very peculiar fellow in here all by himself a couple of Sundays back, drank three Heinekens, ate about four bowls of peanuts and kept checking his watch."

"Two Sundays ago being the day Whipple placed the bones in the hut."

"Correct."

"And did Russell say what exactly made him peculiar?"

"He watched the entire Redskins game which was tied up with two minutes left on the clock in the fourth quarter when he abruptly left about dark. Such behavior is considered very peculiar here."

"And you're thinking this might be Ghoul Two?"

"Think about it," Dooley said. "They don't want to leave a vehicle on the side of the road that somebody might remember, so Ghoul Two drops Whipple off, comes here for a few frosties and then goes back to pick Whipple up at the appointed hour."

"Get a description?"

"Better than that." Dooley produced a very good caricature on a cocktail napkin. "Russell is a *cartoonist*. He draws caricatures of his customers on napkins and stuffs them in a shoe box under the cash register. Says he's going to exhibit them one day. Who'd'a thunk? Samaritan's own Al Hirschfeld out here in the middle of nowhere!"

"Al who?" Kendalhart said. They ignored him.

"Looks like Michael Moore before he cut his hair. Guy's overweight, huh?" Sterner said.

"Russell thinks three hundred pounds, which fits my theory that he needed somebody else to go into the woods to plant the bones because the hike was too tough for him physically."

"So much for my coin toss theory," Sterner said and looked at the napkin. "Ring any bells with you, Deputy?"

"I know plenty of fat guys, but nobody specific comes to mind."

"I did get your e-mail this morning about this George Letterer character. I'm going to see what the Bureau has on him and the Depositors Trust Bank thing."

"Depositors Trust?" Kendalhart said. "My uncle lost his shirt on that."

"Apparently he was not alone," Sterner said. Russell came back with Sterner's plate. Sterner introduced himself and then said, "You ever get any really big guys in here who somebody might describe as gorillas?"

"Gorillas?" Russell said chewing a plastic straw. "Half the guys we get in here are gorillas. Especially this week. Muzzle-loading season, you know?"

"I know," Sterner said. "How about anybody wearing coveralls, driving around in a cargo van, either powder blue or dark green?"

Russell shrugged. "Sorry."

The Sheriff told John and Clara Whipple who told Peter's mother who told Peter who told his wife. They drove to the BP service station out along the interstate to use the payphone. They could not afford to be careless.

"I'm gonna send the police the Fegelman letter, Precious," Peter said as she picked up the receiver. "That's all there is to it. Fuck him." No, it wasn't *the* Fegelman letter and she knew that. It was a reasonable facsimile written from memory and with Fegelman's forged signature. They'd prepared it just in case.

"Baby, just hold off until I can find out what exactly happened. There's no profit in revenge," she said, pressing the number.

"Hello?"

"Yes, this is Mister O'Leary's associate," she said. "We are very upset to hear Mister O'Leary has been involved in an automobile accident."

"I know nothing about it," he said. "When did this happen?"

"Presumably last night."

"That would explain why he failed to pick up the payment as we arranged."

"Are you telling me you had nothing to do with Mr. O'Leary's accident?"

"Of course not. Look, Mister O'--Clay Whipple is, I believe, his name--left my associates and was to pick up the money here, but he never appeared. I thought maybe he got cold feet and chickened out."

"And neither you nor your associates knew that he was involved in an accident?"

"What accident are you talking about?"

"He was killed in an automobile accident on Burnside Summit Road."

There was a hesitation. "I'm sorry," Moneybags said, "this is the first I heard about it. He was killed, you say? That's awful. I know it gets pretty icy up there on those switchbacks. I can understand why you'd be suspicious, but I assure you, I had nothing to do with it. You have nothing to fear from me, I promise you. I hope this won't interfere with our transaction. If you want your money, I have it for you here. You can pick it up right now yourself. I would welcome a little chat to set things right. You deserve the money. I'll make some tea. I mean to make up for my past."

"No, that would be unacceptable," she said. "We'll call again to make arrangements." She hung up puzzled.

"What?"

"He claims he knows nothing about it."

"Bullshit," Peter said.

"What if he's telling the truth? Baby, we're talking about two hundred thousand dollars. Split not three ways but two. I think we should at least accept the possibility that this really was just an accident like the Sheriff said."

"What did you say we'd have to think about?"

"He said we could come over and pick up the money now if we wanted. He even said he'd welcome a little chat. He said we deserve the money. He offered to serve tea."

"Is he wacko?"

"Or clever."

"He said we could come over right now and pick up the money just like that?"

"That's what he said."

"You think we should?"

She thought about it. "No."

"Me neither. Let me think," Peter said pacing and pounding his forehead with his fist. Finally he stopped dead in his tracks, turned and said, "The water ballet!"

"The what?"

"There's a water ballet at the college swimming pool tonight. I saw a flyer when I was waiting for Clay. Tell him to deliver the money to the door to the maintenance passageway next to the men's locker room a minute after the performance begins. I'll make sure it's ajar. Tell him to throw the money down the stairs. Then he must close the door shut. It will self-lock. I can take it anywhere on campus and nobody without a key will be able to follow. Sound good?"

"Sounds very good."

"Call him back."

Sterner took Dooley off Kendalhart's hands and back to the motel for a nap. All the cold air and cold beer, he explained. Sterner's cell told him he had a message but he didn't check it until he got to the barracks.

"Joe," Flanigan said. "It's Stu. Got a whole lot of nothing up there in Laurel Valley. Groundhog holes and fox dens and beaver vandalism. Tell you one thing, though, I'm getting too old for helicopter duty. For the love of Christ my teeth are still rattling." It ain't age, Sterner thought. "Got your e-mail, meet you at the barracks at six."

He scanned the cocktail napkin and e-mailed it to Taylor with a c.c. to Hand, Flanigan and Dooley, and made hard copies as well.

"Alright, so, here's what we have," Sterner said and turned back to the chalk board, where he underlined the word he'd already written: *EVENTS.* Underneath, *1) JD1 displayed.* He was in the briefing room at the barracks, with Captain Hand, Dooley, Flanigan, Hollings and several other troopers, who occupied chairs with enough of a desk for a clipboard. Everyone was taking notes.

"Sheriff Guise not coming?" Hand said, eyebrows raised.

"He needed rest," Sterner said. "I'll fill him in later." He wouldn't say out loud he no longer trusted him. "Event One. Two weeks ago, Jane Doe is displayed inside a shack in the woods used by a local dentist named Roy Fries for deer hunting. She has two bullet holes in the back of her skull and a bouquet of roses in her lap. She's clean of prints, bullet fragments or any trace evidence to help ID her, her grave location, who dug her up or why. All we know is Jane Doe was killed between the mid-Seventies to late-Eighties and spent the intervening years in the ground.

"Two people are involved in placing her in the hut. We will call them Ghoul One and Ghoul Two." Sterner turned and wrote, *GH-1* and *GH-2*, then circled *GH-1.*

"Ghoul One is a struggling actor living in New York City named Clay Whipple. He grew up here and returns home several times a year for visits with his family and his dentist Roy Fries. The identity of Ghoul Two is unknown." Sterner drew a question mark next to *GH-2.*

"Event Two, thirty miles north, the disturbed grave of one Abel Nestor, buried over seventy years ago, is discovered empty." Sterner turned and wrote, *2)* and then *AN?*

"Trace indicates no one but Nestor was ever buried there. The ghoul who took the bones did so prior to the news of Jane Doe's appearance. Detective Flanigan today concluded that the area surrounding Nestor's grave does not show any additional disturbed graves, either marked or hidden.

"Event Three, Ghoul One, wearing a disguise, is abducted from the Samaritan College student union building in broad daylight." Sterner wrote, *3) GH-1 abducted by.*

"The kidnappers we will call Gorilla One and Gorilla Two, which is how an eyewitness described them." Sterner wrote *GO-1* and *GO-2.*

"Gorillas One and Two use a van painted over with a water-based paint which they wash off at the nearest carwash minutes after the abduction to contradict eyewitness descriptions of the abduction vehicle. It's a carefully planned operation, not a spontaneous act by any means.

"Event Four, that night the bones of John Doe are placed on a dental exam chair at Doctor Fries' office. Again there are two bullet holes in the back of the skull but no roses. The exam light is positioned to illuminate John Doe's teeth. John and Jane Doe were killed at more or less the same time and spent the same years in the ground." Sterner turned and wrote, *4) JD2 appears-GH-2.*

"Today, Event Five, Ghoul One is found dead in the abduction vehicle, staged to look like an accident." Sterner wrote, *5) GH-1* with an *X* through it.

"Do we know that for certain?" Captain Hand said. "Maybe he was trying to escape his captors. Or maybe they released him and the accident was a coincidence."

"The official report won't be finished for a few days. My judgment is, yes, the accident was faked. I don't want to get bogged down here by the details. The point is, just like the kidnapping, there's premeditation. The Gorillas put some thought behind it. That brings me to the next subject, open for discussion," Sterner said and wrote, *SCENARIOS.* "What scenarios explain this chain of events? How does it all fit? I know Roger's theory and I agree with it. But I'd like to hear it from someone with fresh eyes. Stu?"

Flanigan squinted at the chalk board. He was a short, anonymous-looking bloke with thick wavy gray hair, weathered by years of long hours and bad food. But he was still sharp, agile and enthusiastic about the job.

"I'm not sure how the Abel Nestor grave-robbing fits or even *if* it does. But the rest looks like a blackmail plot of some kind."

"Anyone else? Nate?" Sterner said.

"I can see that. A blackmail plot gone awry," Hand said.

"Then we're all on the same page. The Ghouls are blackmailing--let's call him the *Mark*." Sterner wrote, *Ghouls blackmail Mark* on the chalk board and circled *Mark*.

Hollings said, "Why don't we sweat the dentist, dig into his past. He strikes me as the number one candidate for the Mark."

"If his befuddlement is just an act, he's smarter than I give him credit for. I believe he was chosen as the recipient of these bones because of his possession of certain dental records, not because he's the Mark."

"Perhaps it's not so important a point," Dooley said, "but how certain are you that the Does weren't buried with this Nestor fellow?"

"There should've been trace in the soil. But even if they were hermetically sealed in a body bag that wouldn't have contaminated the soil why then take Nestor's remains? That doesn't make sense." Sterner turned back to the chalk board.

"I know," Flanigan said. "The Ghouls switch Nestor with John Doe to fool the Mark. After he knew they took Jane Doe, the Mark would panic and destroy John Doe's bones because he's probably in the same location. But he's fooled by Nestor's bones and thinks the Ghouls have nothing to bargain with. They tell him they have John Doe but he doesn't believe them. *If you don't pay us and/or release Whipple unharmed we'll have John Doe turn up, too.*"

"That makes sense." Sterner wrote, *AN=Insurance.*

"It explains taking Nestor's bones," Hand said, "but why then kill Whipple?"

"Because the Mark doesn't pay," Hollings said. "He's playing hard ball. He doesn't care if John Doe turns up or not," Hand said.

Sterner wrote, *Insurance no good.*

"What if the Mark pays off the Ghouls," Dooley said, "and Ghoul Two gets greedy and *he* kills Whipple?"

Sterner wrote, *GH-2 kills GH-1 for $.* He considered it. "Any other theories?"

"Whipple gives up Ghoul Two before he's killed," Flanigan said. "And that means either there's another dead body out there or there's going to be one very soon."

Sterner wrote, *GH-1 gives up GH-2.*

"The Does disappeared for decades," Dooley said. "Ghoul Two may suffer the same fate. We may never find another body."

"But they could've made Whipple disappear like that, too," Sterner said. "And they didn't. They wanted that to look like an accident. Why?"

"It sends a message," Hand said. "It may look like an accident to everyone else, but Ghoul Two would never buy into that."

"Maybe Whipple doesn't talk but dies under torture," Flanigan said. "Maybe they want Ghoul Two to think it was an accident along with everybody else."

"He may well have been tortured," Sterner said. "We'll have to wait for the autopsy report to know for certain. But it looked to me like he was killed with a single blow to the head. The murder weapon looks to me like the baseball bat that an eyewitness said Gorilla One used to subdue Whipple. Which goes against the theory that Ghoul Two killed him."

"Unless Ghoul Two knew about the bat and wanted it to look that way," Dooley said.

"Point taken," Sterner said. "I haven't erased any theories, you'll notice. But I think we're getting off track here."

"Okay, how about this then?" Dooley said. "If Whipple gives up Ghoul Two, they might kill him just to keep him from blabbing," Dooley said.

"If Ghoul Two is still alive, he must know Whipple is dead. I were him, I'd get the heck out of Dodge. Either that or blow the whistle on the Mark," Hand said.

"But maybe that's what will give him away. Maybe the Mark is trying to smoke him out somehow," Flanigan said.

"Interesting," Sterner said. "A little convoluted, but interesting." He wrote, *Mark smoking out GH-2*.

"Blackmail is one thing, but getting murdered for it is something else," Dooley said. "If I was Ghoul Two, I'd come forward looking for protection. Except the Mark must know Ghoul Two might do that. So why risk scaring Ghoul Two out in the open? Unless he knows Ghoul Two won't come forward for some reason."

"Ghoul Two doesn't want to go to jail," Hollings said.

"Okay," Sterner said, "How about this?" and wrote, *GH-2 complicit?*

"Any other theories?" They were silent. "Okay, it's possible Ghoul Two *will* come forward, but we can't expect that or sit around waiting for it," Sterner said, flipping and catching his chalk like a coin. "Which brings us to our third and final subject for discussion. Where do we go from here?"

"I say, sweat the dentist," Hollings said. "If he's not the Mark, my bet is he knows something."

"We have Ghoul Two's likeness," Dooley said. "I'd say, find him fast and get him off the street for his own good, not to mention, answer all our questions."

"Agreed," Flanigan said. "That is, unless forensics reveals a print on the carwash trash. We don't know anything about Gorillas One or Two. But if we did, I'd say taking those guys off the street should be priority one."

"I concur," Dooley said. "But if forensics can't give us the Gorillas, our best hope of finding them is finding the Mark. My thought is, if this *is* blackmail, then there must be a cash ransom, and unless our Mark has a stash hidden under his mattress, he'd have to withdraw it from a bank account. I can check with the Department of Treasury on Monday to see if any Suspicious Activity Reports were filed by area banks."

"Excellent suggestion," Sterner said. "Of course, banks don't always file SARs when they're supposed to, especially small town banks. I'll ask Sheriff Guise to open a back channel to the local branch managers, see if he can pick up any good old-fashioned gossip off the record."

"Failing that," Dooley said, making a note, "the best way of finding the Mark is finding Ghoul Two."

"Is it me," Flanigan said, "or does it sound like we're talking about comic book characters here?"

Everybody chuckled.

"I wish we were," Sterner said. "Let me mull over individual assignments. Meantime, Roger, why don't you come up here and share with us your insights on the Ghouls."

Dooley took Sterner's place and delivered a dry lecture recounting his initial profile of the Ghoul he'd made for Sterner, then subtracted those qualities he believed could be attributed to Clay Whipple and formulated a rough profile of Ghoul Two.

Flanigan dozed off.

———————

Sterner drove Flanigan and Dooley into town to The Good Samaritan Inn. It was no longer a working hotel, not having hosted overnight guests since the 1960s. The upper floors were converted into offices and apartments. They had to wait twenty minutes for a table. In the lobby, beneath a replica of a crystal chandelier, they sat looking around at the faux colonial décor. Flanigan eyed a remnant of the old inn, framed under glass on the wall. It was a wooden plaque with so many coats of shellac it had the dark orange tinge of Renaissance paintings. On it was posted overnight rates in an ornate scrawl from the days of horses and carriages:

Presidential Suite $8
Pennsylvania Suite $6
Single Rooms/private bath $3
Shared Rooms/shared bath $2
Spring house cot 50 cents
Stables hay loft with blanket 5 cents

"No one turned away," it read at the bottom. It was the closest thing to a museum quality historical artifact one could find in a town without a museum.

"You know, whenever I hear the word *Hellcat* I think of Johnny Carson," Flanigan said out of the blue. "You know his routine about the Hellcat Law?"

"I remember that," Dooley said. "One of his better ongoing bits."

"Know what I'm talking about, Joe?"

"Can't say I do," Sterner said. "Carson was on a little late for me."

"Ah, you younguns need your sleep," Flanigan said. "When the Hellcat Law first came up for debate in the California legislature, Carson picked up on it and did this whole routine in his monologues where he said something like, uh, 'I don't know if you've heard about the new Hellcat Law they're talking about out here, where convicted sex offenders would be released early if they agree to a partial castration.' 'Really?' McMahan would say. 'Yes, it seems lawmakers are trying to come up with a simple catchphrase to streamline all the complicated legal and medical terminology for the inmates.' 'Such as?' McMahan would say. 'Hmm? What?' Carson would say, like he always did, pretending not to hear. McMahan would laugh and repeat, 'Such as?' to set up the joke. 'Well, the latest one they're considering is,' and then he'd drop the punch line of the day, like, 'Split the jelly roll and win parole.' And the drummer would do a rim shot." Flanigan struck an imaginary snare with imaginary drumsticks. "Pa-ching."

"Clip a dime and skip the time," Dooley chuckled. "Ba-ta-bing."

"Prune the honey tree and be set free."

"Lose a clam and go on the lam."

"Treat your lap and beat the rap. They got progressively worse over time until the audience started groaning and booing. And then Carson would say, 'Well, I think it's time we put that joke to bed.' And McMahan would say, 'I think so.' And he'd move on to another topic. But as soon as there was something new in the news, he'd say, 'Have you heard the latest about the Hellcat Law?' And the audience would just crack up, because they knew what was coming."

"My favorite was, Cut a nut to get out of the rut," Dooley said. "Which of course had a double meaning."

"You know, if it weren't for Carson's ridicule, that law might've stood half a chance. It's not a bad idea, really."

"I don't know," Dooley said. "It's a bit medieval for my taste. Like frontal lobotomies for the mentally ill. I believe in *the body sacred*. And I hardly think the Supreme Court would've let it stand."

"Why not? It wasn't mandatory. It was strictly a voluntary program."

"Still," Dooley said shrugging. "Cruel and unusual, and all that."

"Today they could use anti-testosterone drug therapies like they gave that serial killer up in Connecticut a few years back. Remember that guy who sued the state to force them to put him to death?"

Before Dooley could respond, the hostess returned to seat them.

The dining rooms were decorated with faux colonial wallpaper, reproductions of painted rural landscapes, antique vases with artificial flowers, electric candle sconce lights and kitschy pendulum clocks on mantels above non-working fireplaces in what passed for nineteenth century elegance. Their table put them in the middle of the main dining room and as they ate, more and more groups of men in hunting and outdoor apparel surrounded them, the green and autumnal camouflaged shirts and vests and canvas brush pants clashing with the faux antique furnishings and decor.

"Big week for muzzle-loaders," Dooley said as he looked around.

"By the looks of this place, it must be a firing range out there," Flanigan said. "It's a miracle one of the troopers wasn't shot at the search site."

"You'd be surprised," Dooley said. "Hunters don't randomly discharge weapons. No one pulls the trigger unless they have a target in sight."

"Like cops," Sterner said.

"Hopefully like cops," Dooley said.

"I'm sure they wouldn't shoot at all if the deer would just surrender peacefully," Flanigan said. "But seriously, would *you* want to be out in the woods in the middle of a bunch of trigger-happy hunters who've been itching all year to fire those guns?"

"I suppose you have a point," Sterner said. "Every year there always seems to be a story about one hunter who gets shot by another."

"Actually," Dooley said, "I think more hunters are killed falling out of their tree stands than by gun accidents."

"I just don't quite get the appeal of going out into the woods to murder Bambi, myself," Flanigan said.

"How's the chicken?" Dooley said.

"A little dry but otherwise not bad," Flanigan said.

"I take it you've never visited a chicken farm. Ever wonder what kind of life that chicken had, whether it was fed growth hormones, antioxidants, preservatives or God-only-knows-what unnatural chemicals which then wind up in the meat you're eating?"

"No, but thanks for ruining my appetite," Flanigan said, taking another bite of his cordon bleu.

"That chicken," Dooley said, "probably lived its entire life under twenty-four-hour-a-day artificial light surrounded by ten thousand other chickens packed in so tight it was unable to move out of its own excrement. Which is why I only eat free range, myself. The deer in the woods roam free and eat only the natural food the forest provides. Think of deer hunting as shopping in the woods for chemical-free meat."

"Not only that," a hunter at the next table piped in, "but one square mile of forest can support only twenty-two deer, while there are forty-four deer per square mile of forest in Pennsylvania. Which means half the deer population either starves over the winter or invades and destroys farm crops and backyard gardens to survive."

"Okay, okay," Flanigan said, "I'm surrounded. I give up. All I said was, I never saw the appeal, myself."

"And as for that goddamned, unmentionable Walt Disney movie," the hunter continued, "it's a piece of California-pinko-tree-hugging-propaganda crap. These politically correct animal rights knuckleheads ought to start thinking about conservation and preservation instead of misapplying moral concepts reserved for human beings to something so natural it has been going on for ten thousand years. The human race would not have evolved if we were not carnivores, for crying out loud."

"Amen, brother," Flanigan said mock-toasting the guy with his glass of water. He then sipped and widened his eyes, making a face at Sterner and Dooley and whispered, "Did I step into shit or what?"

Sterner chuckled, then lowered his voice and pulled out his notepad. "So. Back to the case."

"Yes," Dooley said leaning in. "Back to the case." He whipped out his own notepad and pen and hung a pair of reading glasses on his nose.

"Finding Ghoul Two. I'm thinking somebody should go to New York and knock on some doors," Sterner said. "Whipple had more connections there than here."

"That would be me," Dooley said. "I've got more connections there than here. I'll pay a visit to my pals in the Federal Building, see what the Bureau might have."

"Also the NYPD bunko squad. They track extortion and blackmail plots going back a hundred years. Cross-reference Whipple's known associates with their records. Start with the roommate, Nathan Jordan. He's also an actor. Here's his number." Sterner showed him his notepad and Dooley copied it down.

"And as for you, Detective I-Hate-Hunters, I've got a list of Whipple's local friends," Sterner said, finding the page in his notepad and sliding it across the table for him to copy. "I want you to pay them a call tomorrow and show them our cartoon guy. Maybe somebody will recognize him. If not, coordinate with the Sheriff's Office Monday. If he's local, somebody knows who he is."

"You got it, partner."

———

After saying their goodnights at the Sleep Well, Sterner walked across the road to Rosita's. He found Cat on her stool at the door. Her eyes widened when she saw him. She smiled. He smiled back.

"Stop over later," he said. "I want to ask you about something."

She nodded. "Okay."

He about-faced and returned to his room. When he stopped to look both ways before crossing, he turned and caught her staring at him through the window of the door. It made him grin.

Outside his room, a dark figure loitered under the awning smoking a cigarette and looking nervous. He was skinny, whoever he was, late-thirties, long dark green leather jacket. He sported a Van Dyke beard and long wild curly hair that made him look like he'd just stuck his finger into an electrical socket. Some alarm went off in Sterner's brain to watch his back. Over his shoulder was an orange Trans Am parked in the far corner of the parking lot, its motor running, the driver watching. Even with the windows closed, he could hear a kick-ass stereo booming an old Blasters rockabilly tune. He was walking into something he did not like.

"Joe Sterner?" the man said.

"Who wants to know?" Sterner said.

The man approached sideways. He was jittery but grinning and Sterner's instincts were to clench his fists and stand ready for a fight. As a student in New York, he'd been mugged once by a junkie with a knife after coming home late at night by subway from a jazz club in the Village to his shabby tenement apartment on West Sixty-First. He was so shocked to watch himself hand over his wallet the experience left an indelible mark. He lost tons of sleep obsessing about it and vowed never again to succumb to such fear, promising himself he'd never again avoid a fight.

But then the man held out his hand. "Artie Samios, DEA. Got a minute?" He was a fast talker but had a sweet smile which softened his intimidating appearance. "I didn't bring a badge. I'm undercover. We're being watched so don't turn around. Shake my hand. Shake my hand like you know me. Like we're old friends. I'll explain inside."

"Sure," Sterner said and shook his hand, game to play along. "Come on in." He turned his room key and opened the door, then let Samios enter first. He didn't want to turn his back on him.

"This won't take long, this'll be quick. I'll be out of here like a flash," Samios said, talking fast, pacing back and forth and casing the room at the same time, unable to relax. "I don't have much time. By the way, you're alone here, right? Kiwi out there thinks you're a traveling salesman and I'm here to sell you crank. Speaking of which, you got maybe twenty or forty bucks you could give me to make it look good? He thinks you're giving me three fifty for a couple grams, but I'll say you led me on to get me to show and then fucked me over."

"Sure, I guess," Sterner said and sat in the chair by the door. He dug into his wallet and handed him a twenty. Samios frowned and motioned for another. Sterner handed over another twenty. Maybe he *was* being mugged. The man stuffed both bills into his pants pocket and grew even more animated, gesticulating wildly, hopped up on God only knows. Probably crank.

"Believe me, this'll be the best forty bucks you ever spent when I tell you what I have to tell you. If I seem a little hyper it's because I had a little too much coffee with dinner, you know, so please excuse me. I'm not normally like this. Anyway *who* am I, you're probably wondering. I'm a drug enforcement agent under deep cover for an imminent bust of Derek

Pensinger and other key members of his Berzerkers Biker Club and their associates for narcotics trafficking, which, when it goes down, will take about thirty-five people all told into custody simultaneously from Richmond to Phillipsburg, New Jersey under federal indictment, probably early next month. Which means I can finally shave off this friggin' beard, cut my hair and go back to wearing a coat and tie just in time for my appearances in several federal courtrooms over the next two years if all goes as planned. That's classified, of course. That information could get me killed. Like tonight. Like by Kiwi out there if word got to him. You follow me? You didn't hear any of this shit from my mouth. I was never here. You've never seen me.

"Okay, *why* am I here? Guy I know, Lenny, part-time truck driver for Nussbaum Foods, takes loads of apples up to Hunts Point in the Bronx when they're stretched a little thin. He's a fulltime meth dealer, hangs out at Blocher's Truckers Paradise where the interstate meets the turnpike, keeps the passing truckers awake on the road--unbeknownst to management, far as we know--all the while thinking he's providing a public service.

"Anyway, I walk into this biker bar outside of Newtonville last night and find Lenny already plastered like wallpaper, so we throw back a few more and I get around to asking what's shaking? Lenny lets slip how the other night he helped out these two *mercs* from South Beach he referred to as the Steroid Twins, and you can't repeat that because he'll know it was me it gets back to him and I'll be a dead man. Anyway, he helped them jack a cargo van for five hundred bucks cash out of the parking lot up there at the Paradise. I asked him what they were up to they needed to jack a cargo van for so much cash. Hell, I knew a guy could sell them a used cargo van for six hundred with no risk of prosecution, know what I mean? He waves his hands no, no, no, I don't get it, he says. They were up here on a freelance *plumbing* job and needed something *untraceable.*

"Now I get paranoid and start checking over *my* shoulder because I think plumbers, wet work, leaks, spooks, CIA--Holy Guacamole, Batman!-- maybe they're after *my* ass, but of course I don't say shit. I don't want to give away the store. Then he volunteers how it's a job in Samaritan and we're over in Burnside County, so I know it's not me they're after, and he mentions one of the Steroid Twins is named Bill, like the two of them had history. Lenny and Bill, I mean. He called him 'my ol' buddy Bill.' I don't think he knows the other guy's name by the sound of it, or didn't want to know, if you follow me. I think they scared him."

"A mercenary named Bill from South Beach," Sterner said and wrote it down in his notepad.

"Right--that you can write down. Nothing else. Lenny belongs to me."

"Where's Lenny from? What's his history?"

Samios waved his hands. "No, no, no. Forget Lenny. This isn't about Lenny. South Beach is in Florida, man. Miami, to be exact. I think he said Bill's straight job was nightclub security, but I'm reading between the lines he freelances as a heavy hitter, which conjured images in *my* head of naked guys hanging in tile showers while Columbian drug lords let him cut off body parts with chain saws. *Totally* freaked me out. Ever see that movie *Scarface*? Not the old black and white one, but the one with Pacino? Anyway, that's all you can write down of what I'm telling you. Nothing else I'm telling you, please. I took a huge risk coming over here tonight. You have *no idea!* But even we at the DEA consider murder-for-hire, which is the vibe I got that these sociopaths are into, a little more serious than methamphetamine trafficking, know what I mean?

"So anyway, I've been following *events*--you know?--on what's been going down over on this side of the mountain: skeletons popping up way too late for Halloween, a kidnapping in broad daylight involving a *cargo van*. Then I hear about the fatal accident over the radio this afternoon involving a *cargo van* and *ca-ching*, call my man who made a few calls and got *your* man, and that's how I got you. This is all hush hush, though, right? I hope I can trust you on this. I'm not hearing any reassurance here. You can't tell anybody anything except you got a tip about a Bill from South Beach. It's my life at stake, you follow me? You understand I was never here. You never met me. If you ever see me again, you don't know me, I don't know you. You pass me in the street--"

"Sure. I get it. Okay." Sterner held up his hand in surrender. He knew undercover cops liked to play it close to the edge and sometimes behaved like drama queens, but this guy was over the top. Coffee, my ass.

"Okay, that's really about it. Bill from South Beach and his buddy. Big guys--probably body-builders--that's what Lenny meant when he called them the Steroid Twins but you can't write that down." He froze for a moment, put his fingers to his temples and shut his eyes, trying to think, then clapped his hands together once and offered double thumbs up. "Right, I think we're done here. Good luck. You're welcome." He pointed his index fingers at Sterner like they were two imaginary six-shooters, fired with both barrels and headed for the door.

"Nothing about who they might be working for?"

Samios froze with his hand on the doorknob, turned and said, "Only that it was a job in Samaritan. A *plumbing* job. I couldn't pursue it or he'd've gotten suspicious, so I let it go. Okay, I'm out of here." He cracked the door, spied outside, then opened it wide and made an ugly face at no one across the room. *"Thanks for wasting my fucking time, asswipe!"* he yelled toward the bathroom, winked at Sterner and slammed the door behind him.

Sterner blinked, suddenly alone and relieved that he was. "That was interesting," he said out loud. He spied out through the curtain and watched Samios strut towards the Trans Am. The driver opened his door and the interior light went on long enough for Sterner to see that the driver was a scary-looking punk in a black leather jacket, early thirties, shaved head with a Celtic tattoo and a pirate earring. He shrugged at Samios.

Samios shrugged back. "Total washout, man," Samios said.

"What?" the driver said.

"Fuckin' beer and gas money," Samios said, waving the twenties, then went around to the passenger door. The driver got out and slammed his fist on the roof of his car. He was pissed.

"Dude, thought you said it was a *score*," he said. Samios shook his head and climbed in. The driver cursed and got back in. A moment later, the engine gunned and they peeled out, laying rubber. As they drove past Samios flipped Sterner the bird.

Bill, from South Beach. The Steroid Twins. Gorillas?

Peter and his wife arrived early, parked in a girl's dorm parking lot across campus and walked together arm-in-arm a quarter mile to the sports complex. They had no trouble getting into the water ballet performance and entered the cavernous pool area with its dank chlorinated air from the lobby. There were only a few dozen spectators in the bleachers already seated, mostly students from the men's swim team, roommates and boyfriends of the participants, and a few parents. Thankfully, there was no one there they recognized from the town, or, more importantly, who might recognize them.

Precious took a seat high in the bleachers built over the locker rooms, the entrances at either end of the pool. The main doors from the lobby were by the women's locker room. Peter headed for the entrance to the men's locker room at the far end of the pool, furthest from the main doors. When no one was looking, he used the pass key he'd copied years before when he worked there to open the adjacent steel door to stairs leading down to the maintenance passageways. He slipped inside, leaving it slightly ajar, and descended to the bottom, turned and found his hiding place beneath the steel staircase, his back to the swimming pool tank wall and its drain and pipe works. He hid in the shadows cast by an overhead bare bulb inside a metal china hat shade dangling from the ceiling and waited.

The overhead steam pipes hissed and moaned and clucked, shuttling heat from the power plant to every building on campus. It was sweltering down there. Within minutes Peter was drenched in sweat, even after taking off his coat and sweater. But his discomfort was made tolerable thinking of the reward soon to be delivered into his patient hands. He occupied his mind calculating how he would spend it all, fully four times his initial share. He began thinking about how to get Precious to spend her money.

Precious, meanwhile, was thinking along similar lines as she sat steadfast at her post high in the bleachers, suspiciously evaluating each and every spectator who entered the event. She didn't know Moneybags, or what even he looked like, but she had no trouble spotting him. He was the only elder attending the event, the only person of any age dragging behind him a handled suitcase with wheels. As instructed, he took a seat nearest the men's locker room at the bottom of the bleachers nearest the deep end of the pool and looked around at the crowd to see if he was being observed. Precious casually turned away to better blend in with the crowd but still kept him in the corner of her eye. He barely glanced at her. Soon he heaved a heavy sigh of resignation and settled in, checking his watch, waiting for the performance to begin.

At eight-thirty-five, more or less as the program promised, the greenish-blue sodium vapors high above them switched off without warning and everyone tensed and grew silent in the darkness for nearly half a minute before the strains of Henry Mancini's "Moon River" faded up and echoed across the acoustically challenged tile floor and steel beamed ceiling from the public address system. Spotlights clamped to iron pipe trees chained along the sides of the Olympic-sized pool soon faded up through a gel of midnight blue and illuminated the water in a magical, theatrical moonlight, transforming the sports arena into a giant aquatic stage. Eight nubile coeds in white bathing caps and one-piece white swimsuits with open backs, who'd slipped into the water when the lights went down, now swam out to start positions in the middle and executed a flawless Esther Williams routine with practiced precision, dog-paddling and backstroking, surface-diving and resurfacing in synch to the subtle strains of honey-voiced Johnny Mathis, barely rippling the glassy water in an elegant, slow-motion Busby Berkeley ballet. The girls swooped apart, then drew together, forming abstract geometric patterns--squares, triangles, rectangles, circles, stars--which appeared for a brief moment only to mutate into something else. The effect was that of a flower budding, blossoming and then wilting in time-lapse photography or suggested the abstract, mirrored patterns in a kaleidoscope, the lights at the pool's edge cross-fading in unnatural colors--scarlet, deep purple, blaze orange, canary yellow--as unpredictably as the routine itself. Their lithe, shining dancer's bodies emerged and submerged from their liquid stage on cue at surprising intervals and with reptilian ease, as if each was born to the aquatic life, unseen gills granting easy access below and above water.

Precious noticed a large man in a gray trench coat enter late and stand just inside the entrance door, keeping to the shadows at the edge of the entrance to the women's locker room. He looked around as if unable to locate his wife while his eyes acclimated to the dim ambient glow reflecting on the audience from the pool. But as the performance continued, she soon realized he had fixed his gaze on Moneybags and did not glance even once at the swimmers. This worried her, but there was little she could do but watch and memorize his profile. She decided he couldn't be local. He had a deep suntan, a diamond stud in his left earlobe and what looked like a Bluetooth cell phone accessory in his ear. She didn't know him but he looked familiar to her, somehow. She tried but couldn't place him. He looked to her at times like a truck driver, an athlete, an actor.

About a minute into the performance, as instructed, Moneybags stood and dragged his suitcase toward the men's locker room. The large man observed this with alarm, spoke inaudibly to no one present and then moved swiftly across the side of the pool between the spectators and swimmers, oblivious to both, and quickly narrowed the distance between himself and Moneybags now at the men's locker room entrance.

From his hidden position beneath the stairs Peter heard the door swing open, the distorted music grow loud and then the suitcase tumbled down the steps and came to rest crookedly on a step just inches from his face. The distorted music grew quiet. The door slammed shut a moment later. And as he would tell Precious later, hearing the sound of that escape bar lock click on the inside of the steel door was, Peter thought, the sweetest sound he'd ever heard. It made him do something he almost never did. He smiled. Unable to contain his excitement, he scurried around and up the steps, snagged the suitcase and fled, nearly forgetting his coat and sweater hanging over a steam pipe valve wheel.

Precious, meanwhile, was in a panic. She stood from her seat trying to see what was going on, finding herself part of a group of like-minded gawkers. They could hear unintelligible shouting echoing across the harsh acoustics of tile and cement and competing with the music on the P.A. system. She hurried down the aisle to the floor and joined other audience members all wondering if they should intervene.

"What do you think you're doing here?" Moneybags said.

"Cocksucker," the large man said, unable to open the locked door. "He dropped it behind a steel door." He kicked it, though it only opened outward.

"I told you I would handle this *my* way," Moneybags was saying.

"I can't," the large man said ignoring Moneybags. "It's locked. You need a key." He kicked the lock in frustration and stepped back to survey the architecture.

The performers in the water, their performance interrupted, found themselves upstaged by the growing ruckus. One by one their concentration evaporated as each paused mid-routine to tread water, squeeze out their noses and stare into the darkness at the escalating commotion and their distracted audience.

"You have no right to intervene," Moneybags said. "This is *my* affair."

"I don't know. It's an unmarked door. I don't know where it leads."

"*Are you listening to me, you sonuvabitch?*"

For the first time the large man addressed Moneybags. "You *fired* us, *remember*? We don't work for you no more!"

The sodium vapors above them pulsed on but only dimly. It would take several minutes for them to come up to full intensity. A security guard marched across the pool house in front of the spectators speaking into a raspy walkie talkie as by now everyone in the room was leering at the two contentious men at the deep end of the pool. Johnny Mathis was unceremoniously silenced mid-chorus.

"Getting fucked up in here. I got campus security on my ass."

"You *see here*, this is my fucking *life* we're talking about. I'll be *ruined*."

"Copy that."

"You *did* kill that boy, *didn't* you, you sonuvabitch?!" Moneybags shouted.

"Fuck off," the large man said, shoving the old man backwards onto the tile floor. He fell hard, his right buttock, hip and shoulder slapping the unforgiving floor. The uniformed security guard now jogged toward the large man to restrain him, but was instead grabbed and swung and tossed bodily into the pool, walkie and all.

The large man then quickly strutted back through the crowd of onlookers, including Precious, who gave him plenty of elbow room. He avoided their eyes and pulled up his collar to obscure his face. He exited where he had entered.

"Hey, come back here, you!" the guard said, looking to Moneybags. *"What was that about killing somebody? Hey, you! Stop right there!"*

Moneybags was on his feet and limping away after the large man. The swimmers swam over to assist the security guard, but he resisted and easily treaded to the ladder. One of them surface-dove to retrieve his soggy walkie from the bottom of the pool, but it was a lost cause.

The swimming coach moved to block Moneybags, but was easily shaken off by the determined old man. He instead retreated to his glass-windowed office and clicked on a microphone plugged into the P.A. system. It fed back in an obnoxious squeal before he could adjust the volume, and announced, *"It's all right, folks. Everything's under control. Campus security and town police are on their way. Everybody stay calm. We'll resume the program momentarily. Swimmers, please return to your starting positions."*

Precious didn't know what to do, so she followed everyone else's lead and returned to her seat. She figured if Moneybags and the large man were both angry and empty-handed, that meant Peter had the money. She waited a good half-hour into the program before slipping out herself. As far as she knew, no other campus security personnel or town police had appeared after the drenched security guard followed Moneybags out the exit door. Idling outside in the street in a no parking zone waited her husband in their SUV. He was still grinning ear to ear.

―――――――

After Samois left Sterner called Dooley on the motel phone.

"Roger. It's Sterner. Listen, I'd like you to see what the Bureau has on a guy named Bill--no last name--from Miami, Florida, a body-builder who works in nightclub security in South Beach. He may freelance as a hit man, a mercenary or an enforcer and may have a partner, also a body-builder. And one of them may use a baseball bat."

"Where'd this come from?" Dooley said.

"A tip, but I can't be specific, so don't ask," Sterner said.

"Does this take precedent over my trip to New York?"

"Nope. This is just your homework assignment. We'll have breakfast tomorrow. Meet in the lobby at eight a.m."

"Sounds good," Dooley said. "I should have something by then. Anything else?"

"As long as you're checking, I wonder if you'd mind running a Theodore Balzac Lamotti."

"You mean the ballet dancer?"

"You've heard of him?"

"Saw him dance in *The Nutcracker* at Kennedy Center last year. How's he connected to the case?"

"Okay, you got me. He just moved in with my ex."

"Say no more. I'll give you all we've got in the a.m."

Sterner then called Flanigan in his room.

"What's up, partner?"

"See what we've got on a drug dealer named Lenny, hangs out at the Truckers Paradise, selling methamphetamine. He sometimes drives a truck for Nussbaum Foods. No last name. Might be connected to a Derek Pensinger and a motorcycle gang called the Berzerkers, with a 'z' not an 's.'"

"You want this now?"

"By tomorrow morning."

"Slave driver."

"Breakfast at eight a.m. We'll meet in the lobby."

"See you then."

Sterner then hung up and checked his e-mail. Taylor had sent him a curt message:

"Expect a visit from an undercover source. Comes highly recommended, but be EXTREMELY careful not to compromise him, given whatever he tells you."

While he was reading this e-mail, another popped up from James Robinson.

"Final report Wednesday, but FYI, to confirm your suspicions, I concur with your findings. Scene is phony as a three-dollar bill. --J.R."

Danny Haywood sent him a quick e-mail, as well. "Vernon Guise has no criminal record beyond two convictions for reckless driving and one for assault prior to service in the Navy, all in Doolittle County."

To Robinson, Sterner wrote: "Send me owner ID info via VIN # ASAP. Thanx."

To Danny, he wrote: "Thanks, buddy. Need kidnap perp ID ASAP. Please help Terry expedite carwash trash after processing van."

He left Taylor for last, c.c.ing Robinson's e-mail, sending along the information he'd given Dooley and Flanigan about Bill and Lenny, and reassuring him Lenny would be treated with great care, so as not to jeopardize the agent's deep cover operation.

Sterner then Googled the *Samaritan Times*, found it online. To his surprise they offered an archive service for subscribers, so he laid down his credit card and for $6.95 accessed the equivalent of public library microfiche archives of the newspaper's daily issues going back to 1946, all right there on his laptop. He searched for "Doolittle County Depositors Trust Bank" and "1967," and found dozens of articles mentioning the company throughout the decade.

The early half of the Sixties featured mild, innocuous and all positive stories about the bank, its employees and its founder Harry Rohrer. Rohrer is seen in a photo announcing the hiring of McKim in August of Sixty-Six under a headline "Local Bank Gets New Management." In May the following year, Letterer is mentioned in connection with several real estate loans around Philadelphia that had defaulted. In June came the revelation that McKim and Letterer both had criminal records, with McKim refusing to resign and denying any wrongdoing. By October, the bank had collapsed, and any depositors with savings in excess of forty thousand dollars were shit out of luck. Indictments were handed out in December. The picture of Letterer emerging from the Court House after his indictment that Judge Helfrick had showed him popped up: Letterer standing next to a woman, presumably his wife, a head shorter.

Sterner accessed the reconstruction of Jane Doe on his computer and put it side-by-side with the picture of Letterer and his wife. It was hardly definitive, but it could be her, he decided.

Letterer's lawyer in the case was Aaron Hemmings, Esq., hired out of Philadelphia from the firm Madden, O'Toole, Jennings. Sterner wrote down the lawyer's name and firm in his notepad. He then Googled the firm name, found Madden, Jennings & Warner, accessed their website, but found no Aaron Hemmings mentioned. Too many years had passed. If there was a match of John Doe's teeth and the dental records of Letterer in Homesburg Prison, he'd send Flanigan to Philly to knock on some doors.

A soft knock came to his own door around one a.m. He'd lost track of time. He logged off, checked himself in the mirror and then the peephole. It was Cat. He took a deep breath, opened the door quickly. She took the cue and entered just as quickly without waiting to be invited. Only after closing the door did Sterner realize she reeked of scotch. He remembered what she'd said about having to get drunk before *doing that* and fought himself as he grew aroused, even as he told himself it was a turn-off.

"I wanted to ask you about a local man named Clay Whipple."

She bumped into the chair as she backed onto the bed. This clearly wasn't the question she'd expected. And she was very intoxicated.

"Who? Well, what about him?"

The way she looked at him he knew she was there for no other reason than to *do that!* But that wasn't why he had asked her to stop by. Or was it? He could've gotten such information from someone else. The truth was he wanted to see her again, smell her again, touch her again. But like this?

"Did you know him?"

"Not personally--er--personally. I'm a little tisbee--uh--tipsy."

"How did you know of him?"

She spoke slowly and slurred, trying to enunciate each word. "I know his dad. He had a picture in his hardware store above the cash register. He was real proud of him. Are you going to fuck me, or what?"

Her bluntness stunned Sterner like a bucket of ice water. He said nothing. Just gave her the cold interrogator's look.

"Okay," was her response, realizing he wasn't, and then acted like she didn't care one way or the other. "I think maybe I screwed up."

Sterner said, "I think it would be improper for us to get involved. I wanted to know what you could tell me about Whipple for background as part of my investigation. People in a small town gossip. I'd be interested in hearing anything you might have heard about him?"

"Ever since they gospelled about me I try not to listen," she pouted, stood, teetered and veered back to the bed to keep from falling over.

"But I'm sure you've heard people mention him, what he was like, who his friends were. Anything would be helpful."

She sat facing him, her hands supporting her on either side. She wobbled. "I think I need to lay down." She fell back onto the bed and let out a heavy sigh.

He approached, stood over her and stared.

"Did you have to pay extra for a room that spins like this?" she said amusing herself, barely able to lift her hand to gesture the spinning motion she was experiencing. "If I don't throw up maybe I could just take a little nap here for a sec. Would that be okay, detective?" And then she rolled away from him, curled into a fetal position and in no time was snoring softly.

"Sure," Sterner said looking down at her with an odd mix of sympathy, amusement and lust before going back to work on the laptop.

_____

10.

EIGHT DAYS BEFORE OPENING DAY

At twelve minutes after eight Sterner's cell phone, still in its charger on the bedside table, woke him. He was flat on his back still fully clothed, his arm around Cat, who, except for the pillow he'd slipped under her head, had not moved from the fetal position she'd been in when she passed out. He retracted his arm to answer.

"Sterner," he said.

"You oversleep, Joe?" Flanigan said. "You never oversleep. Dooley and I are in the lobby waiting for breakfast, remember?"

"Jeez, what time is it?" Sterner looked at the time on his phone. "Oh, boy, sorry, give me ten minutes."

"Take your time. They got free coffee here."

After he hung up, Cat said, "I guess I should go," barely opening her eyes, tasting cotton in her mouth. She drew the palm of her hand to her head and groaned.

"No. Stay. I won't be back for an hour or two."

"Bring coffee," she said and immediately fell back to sleep.

Sterner took a quick shower, dressed self-consciously in the bathroom and quietly slipped out. He found Dooley and Flanigan sitting alone in plastic chairs at one of three cafe tables in the breakfast room off the lobby next to the coffee urn and a tray of pastries.

"Jesus, that's a hilarious story," Dooley was saying. "When you retire, you really ought to write a book. It would make a hell of a movie, too. I can see Jim Carrey or Bill Murray." He tapped Flanigan's coffee cup with his own in a toast.

"Sorry, fellas," Sterner said and poured a cup.

"No problem," Dooley said. "I was just getting a firsthand account of the famous Trailblazer Jack case."

"Who's Trailblazer Jack?" Sterner said.

"Kids these days," Flanigan said to Dooley shaking his head.

"You never heard the story? Stu, you gotta tell Joe."

"Ever heard of Howdy Doody?" Flanigan said.

"Uh, sure. It was a little before my time but I know who you mean. Roy Fries said Clay Whipple looked just like him when he was a kid."

"Hmph. That's interesting. Anyway, used to be this guy named Jack Murphy, had a kid's show Saturday mornings back in the Fifties, early Sixties called *The Trailblazer Jack Show*. A lot like Buffalo Bob Smith, Howdy's ventriloquist, with a frilly buckskin jacket, cheesy sets, live audience of kids, the whole shebang. Jack's sidekick was Silent Woody the Woodchuck, this Vaudeville midget in a woodchuck costume, never said a word, unlike Howdy who never shut up. And Woody's foil was this sweet little brunette named Judy Lipinski--remember her?" Flanigan turned to Dooley, who cooed in shared lust and nodded. "She played Injun Judy. She used to chase Woody around with a tomahawk and all the kids would go crazy. Don't ask me how I remember her name when I can't remember the names of the young guys in Crime Scene I work with every other week, but I remember Injun Judy Lipinski."

"I had a boyhood crush on her, let me tell you," Dooley said.

"Anyway, the last sponsor of *The Trailblazer Jack Show* was the Nussbaum Apple Sauce Company right here in Samaritan, Pennsylvania. And to make a long story short, they finally cancelled Jack because Injun Judy's caricature offended somebody. Ten years later, it's 1975, and Poor Jack's a bloated drunk who can barely fit into his buckskin jacket. Which doesn't stop him from bedding down his grown female fans, mind you. He ekes out a living opening used car lots and shopping malls, always on the hunt for local midgets or kids who can fit into the musty Silent Woody costume which he carries around in the trunk of his Caddy convertible, along with jars of moonshine and other choice hooch he picked up down south on the cheap to resell at his bar in Weehawken."

Dooley laughed. "What a detail!"

"Meanwhile, he's got this crazy fan club led by this knucklehead kid named Calvin Munson, who blames Nussbaum for the cancellation of his favorite show and the fallen star of his great hero. So Calvin, rocket scientist that *he* is, talks his buds into staging a daylight armed robbery of the Samaritan National Bank to take revenge and compensate his hero for poor Jack's years in obscurity, which goes spectacularly wrong, and they of course all get arrested instantly. We were never able to prove Jack was behind it, but we suspected he was. Anyway, I was his arresting officer, my claim to fame, first year on the job as a rookie trooper. I'll tell you the whole story sometime," Flanigan said. "You won't believe it."

"I didn't know you were ever stationed here."

"Doolittle County Barracks. Freshman year. Brings back memories being back here. My aunt introduced me to Joanne that Christmas and I put in for a transfer closer to Philly." He eyed Sterner closely. "Sleep must've done you good, Joe. You almost look human," Flanigan said.

"Could've used more. Up late researching the Depositors Trust thing. Any luck on your end?"

"Nobody in PSP ever heard of a dealer named Lenny. Derek Pensinger, on the other hand, has a long rap sheet of drunk and disorderlies and two rape charges--both dropped--assaults and batteries, possessions of illegal substances, nothing that ever stuck to him long enough to do more than thirty days in Burnside County jail. Apparently he is the founder of the Berzerkers motorcycle gang, whose membership includes several equally charming scumbags with similar records. You want me to head up to this Truckers Paradise and snoop around?"

"We'll go together and then work the caricature."

"Roger got lucky."

"Yeah?" Sterner said and sat down with them sipping his coffee.

Dooley pulled out his notepad. "Two things. The Bureau lost track of this George Letterer character on Grand Bahamas Island in December '67. Never turned up in Europe, according to Interpol. They think he may've gone to South America but nobody knows for sure. Nothing at the Bureau on a Bill from Miami *but* I spoke to a Detective Nancy Rubin at Miami/Dade Homicide last night. The name "Bill" did *not* ring a bell, but the baseball bat *did*. They have an unsolved homicide from two years back in South Beach outside a nightclub called The Eldorado Oasis. Low-level Cuban coke dealer. Crime Scene determined the murder weapon was a baseball bat. They liked one of the club's security guards for it, a Cecil David Beasenbach."

"Jeez! What a name!" Flanigan chimed in, copying down the information in his own notepad.

"But they had nothing they could pin on the guy. No murder weapon was ever found. Far as they know he's been clean ever since. She said if we got anything more to keep them in the loop."

Sterner got out his notepad and copied the name down from Dooley's notepad, "Cecil David Beasenbach. The Eldorado Oasis."

"I e-mailed you his mug and list of priors. He doesn't have much of a rap sheet, but what there is makes him out to be a pretty violent character. Couple of dropped assault charges in Michigan in the late eighties, early nineties. I put his name in an on-line search and found a website for body-building contests in Daytona Beach, Florida. In 1993 he won *Mr. Daytona Beach* when he competed in and lost a *Mr. Florida* contest in Miami that same year. I e-mailed you that, too. That's it."

"Nice work," Sterner said. "Suddenly I'm liking this guy for the Whipple kid."

"Cecil Beasenbach. Imagine being a kid with a name like that!" Flanigan said. "Probably got bullied. You become a body-builder just to defend yourself from the teasing, grow up with a chip on your shoulder."

"My name is *Sue*. How do you *do*?" Dooley said, recalling Johnny Cash.

"And what does a washed-up body-builder do after he grows old?" Sterner said. "Become a mercenary, maybe?"

"Or a personal trainer or a bodyguard or do nightclub security," Dooley said.

"Or muscle for a Cuban coke dealer," Sterner said.

"Or a movie action hero and governor of California," Flanigan said, slapping shut his notepad. "Right. So. Where are you taking us for breakfast, boss? I'm famished."

"Your chicken wasn't enough last night?" Dooley said.

"The helicopter ride and your lecture on chicken farms ruined my appetite, thank you very much. But I'm happy to say it has fully recovered. I'm thinking, pigs in a blanket smothered in butter and maple syrup. Don't suppose they got an I-Hop around."

"No, but I bet we can find something close enough. They're big on pork sausage in this part of the state. All these eighth-generation Germans."

"Not to mention sweetbreads and scrapple," Flanigan said licking his lips.

"What is scrapple again?" Dooley asked.

"Believe me, you don't want to know," Flanigan said.

"I'll drive if you want to finish your coffee, Joe," Dooley said getting up.

"Fair enough," Sterner said, following. "Let's roll."

"Oh, about that other thing? The ballet dancer?" Dooley said.

"Ballet dancer?" Flanigan said.

"New York has him for indecent exposure in '89 and a marijuana possession in '94, both misdemeanors," Dooley said.

Sterner made a note on a new page.

"What ballet dancer?" Flanigan said. "Did I miss something in the briefing?"

"He just moved in with my ex," Sterner explained.

"Guess you checked Criminal Records."

Sterner shrugged. "Clean in Pennsylvania."

Sterner got into the back of Dooley's car but made certain he had a door and window handle that worked. He'd once been trapped in the back of a patrol car in his trooper days and left in the baking summer sun for five minutes while his comrades picked up coffee and donuts. Because the back seats of patrol cars were sometimes used to transport prisoners, there were no door or window handles that allowed him to escape. A panic attack ensued. He couldn't breathe. His heart pounded out of control. He was ready to kick out the window glass before his fellow troopers returned.

They found breakfast at a Pennsylvania Dutch diner called Dot's, just within the town limits of Samaritan, where indeed the menu included pork sausage, apple fritters (dried apple chunks in balls of fried batter), schmeercase (cottage cheese and apple butter), sweetbreads (cow brains) and scrapple (fried pork parts and corn meal). Sterner ordered an extra large black coffee to go when he paid the bill. Flanigan raised an eyebrow but said nothing.

"Addicting, this stuff," Sterner said by way of an explanation.

Back at the Sleep Well, Sterner said he wanted to check his e-mail and told Flanigan to meet him in the lobby at eleven, when they would head up to the Truckers Paradise. Dooley was already packed and checked out, so he hit the road for New York. They wished him luck, shook hands and went their separate ways.

Cat had just gotten out of the shower and was wrapped only in a towel when Sterner let himself into the room.

"Sorry," she said. "Hope you don't mind."

"Not at all. Brought your coffee," he said and held out the paper bag.

"My hero," she said. "Guess I passed out last night."

"Don't worry about it. It happens."

While Cat dressed in the bathroom, Sterner went on-line and checked his e-mail. Robinson sent him the name of the van owner, a Karl Dixon of York, and mentioned the license plate came from a van that had been totaled more than a year ago, probably stolen from a junkyard. Sterner called Dixon and found him at home. He'd indeed had his van stolen at the Truckers Paradise the previous Tuesday while eating at the diner. He was not unhappy to hear he wouldn't be getting it back any time soon, since he expected to be reimbursed for more than it was worth by his insurance company. Sterner then printed out the mug shot Dooley had sent him of Cecil David Beasenbach and a publicity photo of him doing his best Arnold Schwarzenegger pose as "Mr. Daytona Beach 1993."

"Anybody I should know?" Cat said sipping her coffee over his shoulder.

"Do you recognize him?" Sterner said.

Cat shook her head. "Looks mean, though."

"I hope you don't run into him," he said adding, "for your sake."

"Thanks again for letting me shower. I hope I didn't cause any trouble."

He smiled. "It was no trouble at all."

When he opened the door to let her out, a squat, heavyset woman in her mid-twenties holding a clipboard was waiting, about to knock.

"Detective Sterner?" she said.

"Yes?" Sterner noticed a TV van nearby, its side door open, a camera aimed in his direction. Before he could stop her Cat breezed past, oblivious to the camera.

"Oh. Interesting," the woman said when she saw Cat. "Pat Wally, I'm a producer for WHRG-TV News. I was wondering if I could ask you a few questions about your investigation."

"I'm sorry, I'm under strict orders. I can't comment on an ongoing investigation. Please contact Chief of Detectives Benjamin Taylor at State Police Headquarters."

But even as he said the words he could see his grip on both the investigation and his career slipping away as the woman's gaze fixed on Cat, her long, black, very wet hair shining in the morning sunshine as she walked down the sidewalk beneath the awning.

"Miss True," the woman called after her sprinting to catch up, "might I ask *you* a few questions?"

Cat ignored her, turned briefly, saw the camera and flipped it the bird, prompting Pat to gesture cut.

Sterner pulled off the interstate exit at the Truckers Paradise, the entrance point to the Pennsylvania Turnpike. It had a sprawling ten-acre parking lot landscaped with sodium vapor streetlights. At least a dozen rigs and another dozen cab-less trailers were parked there, still with enough space for ten times that number and twice that many cars. At the hub was a

central building housing a car and truck garage, a news stand, a family
restaurant, a gift shop, nap rooms, coin showers and an arcade, in addition
to fuel pumps dispensing diesel and unleaded gasoline of graded octane.
Around the perimeter of the parking lot were other services: a discount
store, a pharmacy, a Laundromat, a car wash, a truck wash, an auto parts
store, two hamburger joints, a fish fry and a roast beef franchise (all with
drive-through), a steak house and an economy motel. In short, the Truckers
Paradise offered anything the average traveler might want, could afford and
legally acquire.

"Something bothering you, Joe?" Flanigan said.

"Naw. Why do you ask?"

"You look worried," Flanigan said.

"What? Me worry?" Sterner said quoting Alfred E. Newman, one of
Flanigan's heroes.

"That coffee you got to-go wasn't for you, was it?" Flanigan said.

"Once a detective, always a detective," Sterner said and confessed, "I
had a guest."

Flanigan slapped his knee and chuckled with glee. "I thought that
might be the case. You looked almost happy this morning."

"Can you keep a secret?" Sterner said.

"Uh-oh. What?"

"Cat True."

The smile dropped from Flanigan's face. He stared at Sterner a
moment and then shook his head. "Ah, Joe," he said quietly. "You really
have a gift for the inappropriate relationship, don't you? Do you really think
that's smart?"

"You're still mad about Annie?"

"My crazy kid sister just used you for an excuse to end her marriage
and fly off to a new life as a ski bunny. But Cat True? Jesus, Joe. She's a
witness. Come on, you know that's against the rules. Not to mention guilty
of felonious assault with a deadly weapon."

"She was a minor. It was expunged."

"Tell that to the world press. What happens if the boss finds out?"

"I have a feeling we'll know soon enough. She was filmed leaving
my room an hour ago by a TV news crew."

Flanigan heaved a sigh. "Jesus."

"When Taylor gets wind he's going to replace me, isn't he?" Sterner
said.

Flanigan was quiet for a moment, thinking. "Probably," he finally said adding, "He may even can your ass. I hope she was worth it."

"The truth?" Sterner said stealing a sideways glance at him. "Nothing happened."

"Bullshit."

"I asked her over looking for background on Clay Whipple. She tottered in too drunk to drive. I let her sleep it off. End of story."

"Like anybody's gonna believe that?" He smiled and patted Sterner's shoulder like a kind-hearted uncle.

Sterner remembered retrieving his camera one afternoon and stealing a shot of Flanigan's sister while she slept naked, the setting sun beaming through the rippling sheer curtains in his apartment and over her porcelain skin on his mattress on the floor. It made a lovely photograph--one of his best--worthy of exhibition. But he doubted Flanigan would be so avuncular if he ever laid eyes upon it. "I guess that puts you first in line to be primary," Sterner said.

"Yeah, thanks a lot," Flanigan said. "Nothing like changing horses midstream on an APE case."

Sterner parked the Crown Victoria near the entrance to the trucker garage.

"Alright. So. This is about where Mr. Karl Dixon of York said he parked his van when it was stolen last Tuesday," Sterner said.

"You want to be good cop or bad cop?" Flanigan said when Sterner turned off the engine.

"Paper, scissors, stone?" Sterner said.

"Loser's the baddie," Flanigan said.

"One, two, three," Sterner said, both men punching the air with their fists in synch, playing the infantile game. Sterner kept his fist clenched but Flanigan opened his hand and then slapped Sterner's fist a beat later.

"You're the baddie, you're the baddie," Flanigan said, scraping one index finger with the other, teasing him more like a ten-year-old than a fifty-something. They both smiled at the ridiculousness of Flanigan's juvenile sense of humor. Before getting out of the car Sterner reached into the glove compartment to retrieve his 9mm semi-automatic in a leather holster and snapped it onto his belt under his leather jacket.

They found a mechanic with long blond locks wearing dirty coveralls and an AC/DC cap. He was wiping the grease off of his hands with a rag and taking a drag from an unfiltered cigarette, leaning against a post outside the truck garage, where inside a loud, distorted boom box was tuned to a classic rock station cranking Mott the Hoople.

"Hey, what's up? You seen Lenny today?" Sterner said to him.

The mechanic looked them up and down and said, "I don't know no Lenny, man."

"We're not here to bust him," Flanigan said flashing his badge. "We just need to ask him some questions. It's real important. Honest."

"We don't have to explain ourselves to this derelict," Sterner told Flanigan.

"Who you calling a *derelict*, dickhead?"

"I wasn't talking to you, pal," Sterner said.

"I said, who you calling a *derelict*?"

"This grease monkey's a waste of time," Sterner said. "He doesn't even know Lenny. I told you he looked like an idiot."

"You gotta give the guy the benefit of the doubt," Flanigan said.

"He's an idiot. He doesn't even know Lenny."

"Who you calling an *idiot*, dickhead?" the mechanic said, flustered. "First, I'm a derelict? Then, I'm an idiot? What the *fuck*--?"

"Look, just ignore him," Flanigan said to the mechanic. "He's about to get fired, anyway. If you don't know Lenny, you don't know him. We appreciate your time." Flanigan shrugged and they turned away.

"I *know* Lenny, okay?" the mechanic said. "I know Lenny."

They turned back to him. "So where might we find him?" Flanigan said.

"The diner," the mechanic said, his thumb pointing to the restaurant in the main building calling itself *Ray's Grill*. "Corner booth. Pirates cap, *okay*?"

"The diner," Flanigan echoed to Sterner. "Corner booth. Pirates cap."

"Let's go say hello," Sterner said. And the two walked away.

"You're welcome. And *you're* an *asshole*," the mechanic said sticking his middle finger out at Sterner. They ignored him.

"I liked that *he's about to get fired* line," Sterner said.

"You liked that?" Flanigan said.

"Had just the right ring of truth to it," Sterner said.

The two policemen entered the diner thirty seconds apart so as not to alarm their suspect. Ray's Grill took up one corner of the main building and had large tinted picture windows set at an angle to eliminate glare and framed in aluminum. Inside were four dozen Formica tables and a checkerboard tile floor. There were about a dozen patrons scattered across the L-shaped counter, another dozen in window booths, mostly truckers sitting alone, with one frantic, middle-aged, white-uniformed waitress in tattered Adidas tending to their coffee cups.

It was obvious to anyone who'd ever walked a dark street at night that the man in the corner booth was up to no good. He was gaunt-cheeked with an emaciated frame and had bad skin, never fully recovering from a serious teenage bout with acne, made worse by red scratch marks all over his face, a telltale sign of long-term methamphetamine abuse. He had long, greasy brown hair and had not shaved in a week. He dressed like a trucker with a plaid work shirt, reversible down vest and a black Pittsburgh Pirates baseball cap, duckbill visor coved, set low over bloodshot eyes. Before him lay a ravaged plate of bacon, eggs, toast, hash browns and the sports pages of the *Harrisburg Tribune*.

Neither had a problem making him and though Lenny watched each of them enter, he was not alarmed, in spite of the fact that Lenny was a perpetually nervous person constantly on the lookout for trouble from every direction. When Lenny reached for his coffee cup, Sterner sat beside him, rudely nudging him toward the window, pinning him in and preventing his escape. Flanigan jumped into the seat across the table. Lenny dribbled coffee onto his chin and wiped it with the back of his sleeve.

"You Lenny?" Sterner said. Lenny took his bearings, counted the walls.

"I think this is Lenny," Flanigan said.

"I do, too. You Lenny?" Sterner said.

"Who are *you* guys?"

Flanigan flashed his badge. "State Police, Lenny. Don't panic. We're not here to bust you for the methamphetamine dealing," he said, "because-- well, we're just not."

"Not today. Maybe tomorrow," Sterner said. "Could we see some identification?"

"Uh, sure," Lenny said, his cap swiveling like a duck between the two of them. He pulled out his wallet and dug out a driver's license nervously scratching his face, unsettled that his cop radar had failed to sound any warning.

Flanigan grabbed it out of his hand. "Yeah, tomorrow maybe, just not today," Flanigan said comparing his picture to his face. "Leonard Gary Kessler. This is the guy, Joe. Let me just write that address down 'cause I got a terrible memory." Flanigan plunged the head tip of a cheap ballpoint advertising a bank chain and flipped open a pad.

Sterner said, "We're here about the stolen van, Lenny. An eyewitness picked your mug out of a photo array as one of three guys who stole a green cargo van in the parking lot here last week," Sterner said, then turned to Flanigan. "What day was it?"

"Tuesday, I think, wasn't it?" Flanigan said.

"No way," Lenny said scratching his cheek.

"No, he's right, it was Tuesday," Sterner said turning back to Lenny.

"Says here you live in Mason's Gap, is that right?" Flanigan said.

"M-m-my home address is Mason's Gap, yeah," Lenny stammered trembling and with a pathetic sort of high-pitched whine plaguing his speech. "But I don't live there since my old lady kicked my ass out last July."

"Aw, that's too bad," Flanigan said.

"I don't care," Sterner said to Flanigan. "Do you care? Where you been living, Lenny?"

"My buddy's place over in Newtonville," Lenny said, his voice cracking, sounding like he was about to cry. "And sometimes here. They got showers and rooms cheap--you know--for the truckers."

"Uh-huh," Sterner said. "Do you know a Derek Pensinger?"

"Uh, no, sir. Never heard of him."

"How about a motorcycle gang called the Berzerkers? Ever hear of them?"

"Mmmm. Nope."

"Look here, Lenny, let's cut to the chase and talk about Cecil and Bill."

"I don't know any Cecil and Bill."

"Were you ever in the service?" Flanigan said. "Because I was in Nam with a guy looked just like you?"

"The service? You mean the military?"

"No, he means the *laundry* service," Sterner said in a show of angry impatience and slapped the table loudly with the palm of his hand to punctuate his irritation. "What do you *think* he means?"

"I've never been in the service. I'm a trucker for Nussbaum Foods."

"First Lieutenant Dick Peale," Flanigan said, lost in the memory of it, smiling. "That was his name. Brave man. Good man. One of the best. God, you look just like him. I remember this one time....Well, I have to explain. We used to bury cases of warm beer about four feet deep in the jungle soil, then set off a Claymore over top, dig it up and it would be ice cold, right? I never knew the physics of it. Something about the concussion drawing the cold up through the ground from deep in the earth--"

Lenny furrowed his brow, trying to follow him, scratching at his chin.

"What? Are you unpatriotic, Lenny? You burn the American flag on weekends or something?" Sterner said loudly in Lenny's ear, then turned to Flanigan growling, "I bet he's a flag-burner. I *hate* flag-burners."

"I'm no flag-burner, mister," Lenny said. "I got a nephew in Baghdad right friggin' now. We're all real proud of him."

"Then why did *you* duck military service?" Sterner poked him hard in the arm.

"Ow! That hurts! I didn't duck nothin'. I just never joined up."

"I think we're straying from the reason we're here, Joe," Flanigan said, then turned to Lenny. "Don't pay any attention to him. He's about to get fired. He's on edge."

"What do you guys *want*?"

Sterner leaned in, lowered his voice and snarled, "Cecil and Bill are in custody for the kidnap/murder of a young man named Clay Whipple. And because you helped them steal the van they used in the commission of said crime, that makes you an accessory to kidnapping and murder, which upon conviction carries a life sentence in this state. *Hello!*" He poked him in the arm again for punctuation.

"Ow!"

"Life without possibility of parole," Flanigan said shrugging.

"Without possibility of parole, Lenny," Sterner said.

"Whoa, whoa, whoa," Lenny said. "You guys are way off. Listen, I remember now. Tuesday, yeah, I ran into these two guys trying to break into their own van. That's what *they* said, anyway. It was *their* van. But they lost their keys or something and could I help? I had a Slim Jim in my car so I popped the door for them. Then I showed 'em how to hot-wire the ignition."

"How did you learn how to hot-wire the ignition?" Sterner said. "You some kind of car thief?"

"I used to be a mechanic. I drive trucks now for Nussbaum Foods. Check their roster. I don't know where you get that stuff about methamphetamine. I'm clean."

Sterner looked at Flanigan with a blank expression, then back at Lenny. They fell mute, incredulous.

Lenny looked at them both. "What?"

"We're not here about the meth-- Did I--?" Sterner turned testily to Flanigan. "*Did* I or *did I not* say that we're *not* here about the methamphetamine?" He snarled this through his teeth loud enough for the other patrons in the diner to turn and stare. Two customers at different tables, sensing trouble, dropped payment for their checks and abruptly exited.

Lenny took off his cap and wiped sweat from his brow on his sleeve. "Sh-sh-sh-sh-sh-sh-sh-sh," Lenny said in a low voice bowing his head. "Come on, guys, give me a break here."

"That's not why we're here, Lenny," Flanigan said calmly. "We made that clear."

"Okay, okay." Lenny patted the air over the table for them to stay calm.

"We're here about *Cecil and Bill*," Sterner said through clenched teeth. "Is this guy *stupid* or what?"

"You gotta give him the benefit of the doubt."

"Why don't we give him his rights, instead? Run him in right now on the accessory-to-murder charge. We got the eyewitness. We got Cecil and Bill in custody. What more do we need?"

"And he did admit it. He confessed."

"I didn't admit--" Lenny said, flustered. "I just helped those guys out is all."

"What was Cecil's last name? I can't remember," Sterner said. "It's easy to remember Bill's but Cecil's is hard to remember. What was it?"

"Bea-sen-bach," Flanigan said enunciating each syllable.

"That's right. Beasenbach."

"You got 'em then," Lenny said laughing nervously. "Good. You know, 'cause I thought they were a little scary myself. They had sort of a bad vibe. They'll tell you, though. I'm an innocent man. Just a victim of circumstance here."

"Cecil David Beasenbach and Bill, uh, Flanigan?"

"No, not Flanigan," Flanigan said. "I'd remember that name." He made a show of looking through his notepad licking his thumb, flicking a page at a time.

"Bill's the other guy," Sterner said. "Lenny's old friend. Cecil's from Florida. Well, Michigan, then Florida."

"Mr. Daytona Beach 1993," Flanigan said to Lenny chuckling in a friendly aside, "if you can believe that one?"

"You have his name in your notes. I saw you write it down. Bill--Taylor? No, that's not right. Bill--Sterner? Christ! And you booked the guy right in front of me. Bill--What's his name, Lenny? Help me out. He said he and you went way back. He said he's known you a real long time."

"He--he said that? Really?" Lenny backpedaled rapidly licking his lips like a lizard, shifting from dumbstruck to a show of vague recognition and surprise. He scratched his cheek again. "Oh. Oh. Oh! You're *kidding*! Oh, well, gosh, is *that* who that was? I didn't even recognize him? I mean, well, he looked familiar but I couldn't place him, you know? He sure bulked up. Yeah, now that you mention it, I think we were on the basketball team together back in senior high," Lenny said. "Wow, so that was Bill Morrison? Gee."

"Morrison. That's it! Jesus Christ! Bill Morrison," Sterner said looking at Flanigan. "Well, it's an easy name to forget."

"Oh, yeah, I have it right here," Flanigan said tapping his notes with the back of his fingers. "Morrison. Bill Morrison. I swear I can't read my own handwriting sometimes. It's a sign of aging. Well, listen, Lenny, I were you, I'd get myself a lawyer, you know, because these charges are pretty serious and they're not just gonna go away. But you'll have nothing to worry about *if* Cecil and Bill corroborate your version of events. They're the ones who're really up shit creek here. I mean, kidnapping and murder. Forget about it. They're toast."

"Oh, okay," Lenny said nodding soberly, eager to cooperate. "Yeah."

"In the meantime, I were you, I'd take a vacation on the other thing, the dealing? It doesn't help your case."

"Right. Right. Well. Okay, thanks. Good advice. I see your point. Will do." Lenny saluted them.

"They didn't say anything to you about who they were working for, did they?"

"Ugh" Lenny rolled his eyes and blew air. "No."

Flanigan leaned in. "They're not exactly cooperating."

"No. You know, to me they were just a couple of guys got locked out of their van, is all I know. And until you jogged my memory I never would've figured that was Bill--"

"Morrison, William Morrison, Billy Morrison," Sterner said aloud to himself. "Why does that name sound familiar?"

"Oh," Lenny said and chuckled covering his mouth, darting looks between them. "Don't tell me you didn't make the connection? Wow.

That's far-out. And you think I'm stupid?" He chuckled again, scratching his upper lip.

"Connection? What connection is that, Lenny?" Flanigan said.

"You know. Bill was the guy got a nut cut off by that bitch," he said. "You know, that Hellcat? That Hellcat thing?"

Flanigan and Sterner looked at each other but said nothing.

"I don't like coincidences, Joe," Flanigan said back in their car. Flanigan was accessing the Criminal Records database on Sterner's laptop, compliments of truck stop's wi fi router.

"I don't like them, either, Stu, but you have to admit they happen sometimes. Remember the Schuster case? The vic's hated brother-in-law working in the same bottling plant as the killer? Just a coincidence."

"She ever talk about it? Hellcat?"

"No," Sterner said, "never came up."

"Maybe you should ask."

Sterner pursed his lips and turned over the engine.

"Here we go. William Morrison the Third. Sexual assault conviction, 1987. Plead guilty, sentenced to time served, no mention of gonad removal by your girlfriend."

Sterner sighed, rolled his eyes and shifted into drive.

"Ah, very interesting. Sexual assault charge, 1990, Newtonville. Guess the surgery didn't slow our boy down any. Charges dropped when victim refused to testify. Reckless driving, 1991. Charges dropped when arresting officer failed to appear. And then, boys and girls, Mr. Morrison either cleaned up his act or took it on the road because that's the last PSP heard about him."

"Five'll getcha ten Dooley'll have more in the Bureau records."

"Or Miami/Dade. I'll send them a quick e-mail." Flanigan tapped at the keyboard. "Where to next, boss?"

Sterner pulled away. "Put out an A.P.B. on Morrison and Beasenbach. We'll pay the Whipples a courtesy call, see if they recognize Ghoul Two."

John Whipple came to the door after the two detectives shuffled up the walkway from the street. He was a small man in stature but stood his ground exuding hardness.

"Can I help you?" he said.

"Mr. John Whipple?" Sterner said.

"Yes."

Sterner and Flanigan flashed their badges. "We apologize for the interruption, sir. I'm Detective Joe Sterner, Detective Stu Flanigan. We're with the State Police. I know this is an awkward time and we very much wanted to convey our condolences, but we're investigating the circumstances surrounding your son's death and need to ask you some questions."

"My wife's in bed. I'd rather not invite you in. If she hears voices she'll think she has to come down and play hostess. That's just how she is. Mind if we talk here?"

"Not at all. I'd like to show you a sketch of a man we believe might be able to give us information about what happened with your son."

"He was killed in an automobile accident, wasn't he? What's to understand?"

"Well, the van he was driving was stolen, for one thing."

"Are you the detective who told the Sheriff Clay was kidnapped from the college wearing a disguise a few days ago?"

"Yes."

"Craziest damn thing I ever heard."

"It may sound crazy but we have proven it beyond any doubt."

Whipple stared at him a moment, then pursed his lips and shook his head. "He was always doing some crazy thing or other."

Sterner pulled out the caricature of Ghoul Two. "Without thinking about it, does this look like someone you know?"

Whipple looked at the caricature, then up and down at both detectives. "It's a damn cartoon. Is this some sort of joke? Because if it is you can stuff it where the sun don't shine."

"It's no joke, sir. My apologies for not explaining. The witness who drew this is a cartoonist. He says it's a good likeness. And I'm afraid it's all we have."

Whipple looked them both over twice, then again at the caricature. "Oh. Yes. That looks just like my nephew Peter. Peter Bream."

Flanigan wrote the name into his notepad. "B-R-E-A-M?"

"That's right," Whipple said.

"I don't believe I saw that name on your wife's list of Clay's friends," Sterner said.

"Not friends. Cousins! He's family."

"We'd like to talk to him. He may have information that could help us in the investigation."

He checked over his shoulder and lowered his voice. "You didn't hear me say this, but my wife and her sister always looked at the world through rose-colored glasses. Both coddled their only sons to their detriment, I'm afraid. My wife always treated Clay like he was a big star. And my sister-in-law told Peter so often what a genius he was, it got so he believed it. Only thing is, nobody else ever did. And that sad fact ruined both their lives, I do believe. Peter lives on the other side of town. One-seventy-five Pickering Street, three houses down from the fire hall."

"One-seventy-five Pickering. Got it," Flanigan said writing it into his notepad.

"One other thing," Sterner said. "Do you know if Clay was familiar with the Laurel Valley area?"

"Laurel Valley?" Whipple said. "No, I don't think so."

"Did any of his friends or relatives ever live in that area or in Pineville?"

"Nope, not that I'm aware."

"Do you know William Morrison the Third?"

"Knew the father. Never the son. I'm just as glad Cat chased all three of those hoodlums out of town. I heard the Sachtler kid straightened out, married a girl in Gettysburg and started a family there. The Van Aiken boy, I heard, got himself killed in a knife fight in New Orleans during Mardi Gras about 1990. He never was no good."

Sterner showed him a picture of Mr. Daytona Beach 1993. "Does this man look familiar? His name's Cecil David Beasenbach."

"Nope, never seen him before. Or heard that name." Inside the telephone rang. "I better get that," Whipple said. "People've been calling all day. You never realize how many friends you have until you" --his voice cracked-- "you lose a child."

Sterner was embarrassed. "Thank you for your time, sir. You've been very helpful. Again, our condolences."

Whipple's chin trembled. He swallowed hard, licked his upper lip, offered a quick nod and then closed the door.

"Knew a guy in Nam once who had a nut shot off," Flanigan said as they approached the front door of the Bream home. "Didn't slow him down any, let me tell you. Had about six kids. You want to play good cop on this one?"

"Let's play this one straight."

"Straight it is," Flanigan said pressing the doorbell.

It was a modest two-story house with a front porch in a modest neighborhood of similar houses. An overweight young man answered the door a minute later wearing green Chinese silk pajamas, a white English terrycloth bathrobe and plastic flip-flops with mismatched socks. Sterner didn't need to pull out the caricature for comparison. This was their man.

"Peter Bream?"

"That's me," Peter said.

Sterner flashed his badge. "State Police. Detective Joe Sterner. This is Detective Stu Flanigan. We were wondering if we could ask you a few questions. Did we catch you at a bad time?"

"No, not at all. This is my standard attire. I was wondering if you guys would want to talk to me. Come on in."

Sterner raised an eyebrow at Flanigan as they followed him inside.

The first thing that caught Sterner's eye was the deer head mounted on the foyer wall, an eight-point buck that greeted any and all guests to the Bream home. He remembered Dooley's e-mail that Ghoul Two might have experience in taxidermy. "Nice work," Sterner said. "Do it yourself?"

"As a matter of fact," Bream said. "I was seventeen. Thought about turning pro for awhile, but those nasty chemicals gave me headaches. His name's Duke."

The second thing Sterner noticed was that the parlor was impeccably put together and decorated with antique bric-a-brac. The walls were pale gray with white trim on the floorboards, bookcases and fireplace, and there was an Oriental rug which looked worn and real, laid over a polished hardwood floor. And though it was new, the couch looked closer in style to furniture from the 1930s, with an easy chair to match. Two floor lamps were vintage deco and there was a small crystal chandelier in the middle of the white stucco ceiling, probably from the same period. The bookshelves on either side of the fireplace showcased mostly nonfiction reference books and works on antiques, computers and the internet, but here and there were several small unglazed white porcelain busts of Greek and Roman figures, like the ones Sterner's boss kept on the bookshelf in his office. There were miniature portraits hanging in oval frames clustered on the back wall flanking an unsigned, early nineteenth century, life-sized oil of a slightly cock-eyed woman who looked French. There was a stack of small antique books on a side table with what looked like an ivory box and a black basalt bowl. On the fireplace mantle was a symmetrical tableau of Sterling silver candlesticks, a collection of silver egg cups, marble obelisks, two intricately painted blue vases and a pair of colorful dinner plates displayed on plate-holders. Above the fireplace was an oval antique mirror with a gilded frame. On the marble coffee table was an ivory handled letter-opener, several antiques magazines, a mahogany pen and pencil set, a crystal candy tray filled with hard mint candies and a Sterling silver business card holder. One would never think looking at the exterior of the house that such visual treats awaited the visitor once inside.

"Your wife did an excellent job decorating," Flanigan said.

"Excuse *me*. I did this room my*self*, thank you. We call it our IRS room. It's technically our storefront but we don't really sell much out of here."

"What do you do for a living, if you don't mind my asking?" Flanigan said.

"Oh, I buy and sell antique smalls over the internet." He gestured around the room. "All this stuff is inventory. I like to display it until I get tired of it. Then I photograph it and auction it off on-line to the highest bidder. If they fail to meet my reserve, I put it in my on-line store." Peter pulled two business cards out of the Sterling silver business card holder and handed them to Sterner and Flanigan. It read: Peter Bream Antiques, Decorative Smalls and Fine Art, and included an e-mail address but no phone number and no street address. "If you see anything you like, it's all for sale, pretty much." He chuckled. "Except Duke. Have a seat."

Sterner took the couch, Flanigan the easy chair. Peter sat on an antique cushion chair opposite them and leaned forward, resting an elbow on one knee. Flanigan picked up the ivory-colored box on the side table and looked it over. It looked just big enough to carry a few ballpoint pens. There was an ink etching of a whale and a whaling ship. "This is pretty interesting. Is it ivory?"

Sterner scanned the titles in the bookcase and found *Gray's Anatomy*.

"Uh, no, whale bone scrimshaw. Early Nineteenth Century. The harpooners would carve them onboard the whaling ships to pass the time, then dip them in ink and wipe them off so the only ink remaining is in the crevices of the etching. It's a hundred and eighty dollars, if you're interested."

Flanigan nodded his head soberly and put the box back on the side table, but perpendicular to how it had been placed. He scanned the room and said, "You actually make a living buying and selling this stuff over the internet? How does that work?"

For much of the ensuing conversation, Peter glared at the scrimshaw box. It irritated him that a guest would not return an object exactly where he found it. Though Flannigan realized Bream's discomfort, he made no effort to appease him.

Bream said, "You know, people are so stupid. They have these live, on-line auctions where they sell lots of multiple nineteenth century Wedgwood or Gouda or Delft earthenware pieces--or parian busts or scrimshaw boxes or tea caddies--for maybe fifty, a hundred bucks, not realizing their true value. They put it on the block for all of one minute during a weekday when most potential buyers are at work. I offer a low bid and if I win I parcel them out--you know, one piece at a time--over several ten-day periods, usually closing on a Sunday night, so rival bidders can duke it out on their day off. These bozos get into bidding wars just for the fun of it, sniping each other to the last second. The last couple of minutes can get really crazy. I've watched the price go up literally ten times without blinking. Don't get me wrong. A lot of stuff I just break even on. But once in a while I'll make five, six hundred dollars on a fifty-dollar investment. And the beauty of it is it's all done on the desktop in my music room. Most days I never even have to change out of my peejays. Like today. The hardest part is dealing with the shipping. I had to turn my basement into a shipping center."

"Sounds like I'm in the wrong business. But it must be kind of lonely," Flanigan said.

"Well, like anything, you have to have the right mentality for it. I do have close, personal relationships with our postman and the UPS guy. And my wife somehow never fails to return home at the end of her shift. On the other hand, I don't have to deal with pain-in-the-ass coworkers and bullying supervisors. Here I'm my own boss. Sure beats nine-to-five."

"The reason we're here--" Sterner said.

"Excuse me, just one second, but I'm really curious," Flanigan said interrupting his partner. "How'd you get into this?"

"Just surfing the web, mostly. About a year ago I found this live auction that offered an eighteenth century Venetian settee valued at twelve grand. God, it was beautiful! The only bid for it was one-fifty, but I thought, 'well, that's too rich for my blood,' so I didn't bother bidding. Well, guess what? It sold for one hundred and fifty dollars and I just went, 'Whoa!' Even among the nimrods around here I could've sold it for at least a couple grand. But out there on the internet you have about a half-billion potential customers."

Sterner took a breath and started to say something but Flanigan broke in.

"But you have to do a lot of research, I'd guess," Flanigan said. When he caught Sterner staring at him, he did a double take and then bit his lip.

"Yeah, but that's the fun part for me. I subscribe to about a dozen magazines and newsletters and buy secondhand books on Amazon which I then sell back when I'm done with them. I work longer hours than I've ever worked on anything, but you end up learning all kinds of cool stuff about history and science, geology, art. I really enjoy it."

"You know, I'm retiring in a couple years," Flanigan said as much to Sterner as Bream, "and I'm always interested in exploring options and expanding my horizons."

Sterner jumped in before the conversation veered too far off-track. "You said you were wondering if we would want to talk to you. What did you mean by that?"

"Because of Clay. Clay Whipple. That's why you're here, right? Clay's my cousin. Was my cousin."

"And why would you think we'd want to talk to you?"

"I'd see him whenever he came to town, a few times a year." Peter shrugged. "I guess I saw him as much or more than anybody besides his folks."

"You don't seem too broken up about his passing, if you don't mind my saying."

"I'm still a little bit in shock, tell you the truth. Anyways, we weren't best friends or nothing. We had similar music tastes, is all. He'd turn me on to some band. I'd turn him on to another. Music's about all we'd ever talk about."

"What kind of music?"

"Death metal, grindcore, thrash, whatever you want to call it. The louder and faster, the better," Peter shrugged. "Probably bands you never heard of. Napalm Death, Morbid Angel, Carcass, Deicide."

Bingo, Sterner thought. "Marilyn Manson? He had a poster in his bedroom."

"Marilyn's a clown. Alice Cooper, two point oh. Clay liked Marilyn as a performer more than anything, being one himself. But musically speaking, I thought Marilyn was over some time ago."

"Ever break one of those expensive plates from your stereo vibration?" Flanigan said grinning.

Peter laughed. "My music room's at the far end of the house, but--*yes*," Peter snorted.

"Ever pick your cousin up at the train station?" Sterner said.

"Ah," Peter said wagging his index finger at him. It had occurred to Peter way too late to do anything about it that he might be remembered at Wyman's Tavern. Even as he sat drinking his Heinekens and devouring bowl after bowl of the addictively salty peanuts, he was composing the current version of events he was now presenting. "Yeah, well, you got me, I guess. His secret mission."

"Secret mission?"

"That's what *he* called it. He phoned me two weekends back, asked me to pick him up in Harrisburg, said I couldn't tell anyone anything. He was on a clandestine mission--top secret--he said. And he paid me fifty bucks, so what the hey? I pick him up at the station, just him with this big black backpack, drop him off along Greenwood Furnace Road, then go for a few brews. At dark, I pick him up, take him back to Harrisburg, then race home in time to catch the end of my auctions. No big deal."

"You didn't find this unusual?" Flanigan said.

"*Very* unusual. But you'd have to know Clay. He had that kind of a sense of humor."

"Sense of humor?"

"There wasn't much he wouldn't do for a practical joke--you know?--spared no expense? Didn't have a wife and mortgage to worry about, that's for sure. He assured me it was nothing illegal. Just a practical joke on his dentist, he said."

"You heard about the skeleton found in the woods?"

"I put two and two together. Believe me, I had no idea he had human bones in that backpack."

"He never told you what was in the backpack?"

"I asked him. He said it was a secret. It was part of the joke."

"Why didn't you call the police when you realized what two and two equaled?" Sterner said.

"I didn't want to get Clay in trouble. For all I knew it *was* just a prank like he said. When I heard it might actually be a murder victim, I just figured Clay picked it up somewhere in New York and hadn't noticed anything unusual or asked any questions. He was kind of half-assed that way. Ignoring the details."

"What happened to the backpack?"

"Took it back onto the New York train with him."

"Did you talk to him since that day?"

"No, not a word."

"Did you know he was abducted from the Samaritan College Student Union Building a few days ago?"

"My mother heard that from my aunt. That's nutty! And what the hell was he doing driving a van on Burnside Summit Road yesterday morning?"

"We think Clay was involved in a blackmail plot and had at least one other partner. Any idea who that might be?"

"*Blackmail?* Clay? You think he was blackmailing Doc Fries? I can't believe that."

"Any ideas about the partner?"

"Couldn't be anybody local, I don't think. Maybe somebody in New York, only thing I can think of."

"Why do you say that?"

"Well, he lives in the big, bad city, for one thing. Lived. And who around here would ever have the balls to blackmail anybody? That kind of stuff you see on *Law and Order*, not in Podunk, USA."

"Are you familiar with Laurel Valley, by any chance?"

"I stopped once or twice at the General Store in Pineville, but no, I'm not all that familiar with that area."

"Do you know if Clay had any friends who lived there?"

"I don't think so," Peter said. "That's a whole different school district. But really, I wouldn't know."

They read Peter his aunt's list of Clay's friends but Peter told them he didn't know too many of them and had seen none of them recently. He'd never heard of William Morrison III. They showed him Beasenbach's picture, but he said he'd never seen him before. Sterner told him they might want to talk to him again and gave him his card, saying not to hesitate to call if Peter could think of anything that might be connected with the case and could help them piece the puzzle together. Peter promised he surely would. Before they left Peter adjusted the placement of the scrimshaw box on the side table and then saw them out, wishing them luck.

After they got into the car Flanigan let out a long, disappointed sigh and said, "That was sure a dead end. For what it's worth, the thought I had was, Ghoul Two either wasn't available to pick Whipple up at the station on his mission to plant the bones, assuming Ghoul Two's local, or couldn't drive him down from New York, assuming he's in New York. Yet obviously Whipple came to town a few days ago by some means and didn't need Bream's help."

"*He* says," Sterner said and started the engine.

"Which makes me think is it possible Ghoul Two has a job or a family life that prevents him from availing himself on Sundays?"

"Interesting thought," Sterner said. "I suppose it wouldn't hurt to check with Amtrak and the rental car companies, see if Whipple ever used a credit card. But waiters usually pay cash when they can from their tip money. Besides, Whipple probably wouldn't have wanted a credit card record of his trips."

"I'll make some calls, anyway," Flanigan said.

"Good idea," Sterner said.

They drove to the end of the street and around the corner in silence until Sterner said, "I don't buy it."

"What?"

"I think Ghoul Two is a local guy. You flew over Laurel Valley. You know what that terrain looks like. Who but a local guy would know about that area?"

"Maybe a hunter from out of state. It's not unusual for out-of-staters to come in to hunt in areas like that."

"Maybe," Sterner said. They drove another two blocks. "I like him."

"Really?"

"I like him for Ghoul Two."

"What did I miss?"

"Not any one thing. The taxidermy. The death metal music. It's an offshoot of heavy metal. The highly organized environment. You pick up how it bugged him that you didn't put that little box back exactly where he had it? Plus, he's got *Gray's Anatomy* on his bookshelf, not your average home reference book. There's a whole detailed section in there on skeletons. A must for first-year med students."

"Not to mention first-year forensic criminologists," Flanigan said with a twinkle in his eye. "Could belong to the wife, though. Could be a nurse."

"Maybe," Sterner said. "He didn't say what she did, did he? I should've asked. He's cool, has that superior attitude. What did his uncle say? Thinks he's a genius."

"Obviously smarter than the average bear," Flanigan said.

"A loner, an outsider in his own community. *Nimrods*, he called his neighbors. His line about people being stupid, that stuff about pain-in-the-ass coworkers and bullying supervisors. I'll bet *he's* a barrel of laughs to work with. Dooley profiled all this. What he said about nobody around here having the balls to conduct blackmail. Nothing about the immorality of it. Or the illegality. They lacked balls, is what he said. I'm telling you, I like him."

"You think all that stuff about the secret mission was just play-acting?"

"I think he was bullshitting us, yes."

Flanigan nodded his head considering the argument. "Maybe the acting talent runs in the family, but that's not enough for a judge to sign a search warrant."

"I know that. But maybe Dooley could check Whipple's phone records, see if the cousins talked to each other more than Bream is claiming. I wonder if he ever worked at Samaritan College," Sterner said.

Sterner made a turn and they drove directly to the campus security office at the Knorr Student Union Building. They went inside but, it being Sunday, the office was closed and all the lights inside were off. A sign on the door read: "In case of emergency, call 911."

Sterner checked his watch. It was 4:12 p.m.

"Jesus, you'd think somebody'd be on duty around here," Flanigan said.

"I guess we'll have to come back tomorrow."

"What the hell is going on down there?" Taylor was saying. They were back at the barracks in Sterner's office, Sterner seated in his desk chair, Flanigan standing over him when the Chief called Sterner on his cell. He looked at Flanigan as he spoke.

"I'm not sure what you mean, sir," Sterner said. Flanigan looked up at the ceiling and pretended to whistle a happy tune.

"What do you mean, what do I mean? I mean, I've been denying loud and long the past seven days that our investigation has nothing to do with the Hellcat case, and now suddenly I get an e-mail from Flanigan that you're putting out an APB on Cat True's castration victim?"

"I wouldn't call him a victim, sir. I'd call him a rapist and a suspect in a kidnapping and murder," Sterner said.

"Yeah, whatever! I don't like coincidences, detective."

"But you have to admit, coincidences sometimes happen. Remember the Schuster case?"

Then I get a call from this TV reporter who says she has Cat True on videotape coming out of your motel room with wet hair at ten-forty-five this morning! Can you explain that? I hope you can because for, what it's worth, I sure couldn't. Please tell me she came to give you information about the case, excused herself to the bathroom, then slipped on a bar of soap and gave herself a swirlie."

Flanigan leaned in to eavesdrop.

"Ms. True is not *involved* in this case in any way, sir," Sterner said. "As you're well aware. She just happened to be the first person to find--"

"She's a witness, detective. And this looks bad. Bureau personnel must be above reproach. If our reputations are less than impeccable, our credibility and the public's trust go right out the window. So the question is, did she or didn't she spend the night in your room?"

Flanigan, listening in, mouthed the word, *Lie.*

Sterner said, "Yes, but nothing happened. She was too intoxicated to drive, so--"

"Impropriety isn't limited to deeds. It's the suggestion of misdeeds, as well. Do you have feelings for this woman?"

Flanigan shook his head *no* at Sterner.

"Yessir, I do."

"Fine. Look, I warned you. So you're off the case. Hand over your notes to Flanigan. I want your butt back here at your desk tomorrow morning, nine a.m. sharp."

"You'll have to make it ten-thirty," Sterner said. "My daughter has a doctor's appointment at nine."

"If you say so. I want a full accounting in writing of your relationship with Ms. True on my desk by noon. And then I want you in my office to go over your investigation in detail for the news briefing. Speak about this to no one. Does Flanigan know about this relationship?"

"Yes, he does, sir."

"Tell him to keep his mouth--" Taylor drew a long breath. *"Oh, never mind. I'll tell him myself."*

"Am I fired, sir?" Sterner asked.

"I can't fire you. I need your testimony next month in Pittsburgh. If the defense attorneys out there find out about this, your credibility in front of the jury will go right out the friggin' window. It'll taint your whole

testimony and could turn the jury in their client's favor. Did that ever occur to you?"

"No, it didn't, sir."

"Yeah, I'll bet it didn't. So you're on desk duty, my friend. Let's leave it at that. Christ, I always knew you were a little dim, but Gawd--"

"Yessir," Sterner said. Would it make any difference if he told his boss he might be in love with her? Of course not.

"Ten-thirty tomorrow morning," Taylor said and hung up.

Sterner looked at Flanigan. "I suspect your next phone call will be the Chief."

"Ah, shit," Flanigan said. His cell rang.

When Flanigan got off the phone with Taylor, Sterner handed over his notepad and went over the details of the case from the beginning of the investigation the previous weekend. Flanigan asked him why he hadn't pursued the Sheriff's suggestion to look in neighboring Burnside County. Sterner responded that he hadn't really had time but encouraged Flanigan to make contact with Sheriff Bucher. Sterner then told him about Sheriff Guise's comments regarding Cat and his affair with her mother. He filled him in on Samios and the DEA agent's mission to nail the Berzerkers and their biker buddies for methamphetamine dealing. And he suggested re-interviewing Judge Helfrick, especially if the Does turned out to be George Letterer and his wife.

Dooley rang Sterner on his cell. He was settled in at a Holiday Inn Express in downtown Manhattan, but hadn't begun to get to work. When Sterner told him about Cat sleeping off a night of drinking in his room Dooley was surprised. Dooley told him he was sorry Sterner had been taken off the investigation, since he thought he had done an excellent job thus far, but understood Taylor's decision. The FBI's standards regarding impropriety were higher than even the PSP's. When Flanigan got on the phone with him, Dooley said he'd look into William Morrison III to see what the Bureau had.

Sterner and Flanigan grabbed drive-through at the Burger King in town and turned in early, shaking hands, both wishing the other luck.

Sterner tried but again could not sleep. He tossed and turned like he had in his own bed. He thought about Cat. Would he ever see her again? Should he? He wanted to ask her about Morrison. He wanted to ask her if she was involved in blackmail, though he was sure she wasn't. He knew he was off the case, but it did not matter to him. He wanted to know. Most of all he did not want to return to Harrisburg to his uncertain fate without looking into those amazing eyes one last time. He shuffled through a number of sexual scenarios, then started rationalizing that if he was going down for sleeping with her, anyway, why not try to make it happen? Around ten o'clock he got out of bed, dressed and walked across the road, telling himself he would only question her and then say goodnight and goodbye. He never got the chance.

"I have to talk to you, detective," Cat said the moment she saw him. "Mom's totally freaked out. When I got home this morning, the Sheriff's truck was parked out front. I raced inside but nobody was home. I started to panic when, through the kitchen window, I spied the Sheriff comforting Mom in his arms in the backyard and ran out to learn what happened. Mom always lets her cat out to prowl after supper, but when he didn't return by bedtime, scratching at the backdoor to be let in, Mom worried he might've gotten into a fight with a wild animal or into the bear trap, or something. Mom's used to me staying out all night, but not Mister Jeepers. He was mauled by some critter in the woods once and she was worried he might contract rabies fighting an infected raccoon. She finally found him strung up by a noose in our smokehouse and gutted like a game animal, his organs and intestines in a bucket beneath. Mom called the Sheriff, and he came over right away and cut the carcass down and put it in a burlap sack for burial."

Sterner took it all in, then said, "When was the last time you saw William Morrison the Third?" he said.

Cat snickered, not making the connection. "Billy Three? Why? What does that have to do with anything? You're kidding me, right?"

Their conversation was interrupted by a jolly party of six middle-aged customers who traipsed through from the parking lot. Sterner stepped aside to let them pass, greeting them with a forced nod and grin. When they were safely out of earshot, he turned to continue the conversation, but another young couple interrupted, exiting past them.

"I just told you somebody murdered Mom's cat and you're asking me about *that?*" Cat said when they were gone. Another car pulled into the lot blinding them with its headlights. Sterner grew impatient and annoyed.

"Come over later. Please? We need to talk."

"Sundays are usually quiet. We close by eleven."

"Fine."

Sterner tried to contain his ulterior motive for questioning her in his room, telling himself he was a professional. He surfed the cable channel offerings, catching up on the news. An hour later, there was a firm knock at the door. He killed the television with the remote and answered. She marched in as if she owned the place and had a bone to pick. She tossed her bag on the bed where she planted herself and folded her arms.

After flicking the lock for privacy, he turned and said, "So. Tell me about Billy Three."

"Did you hear what I said about Mom's cat?"

"I'm sorry. I really am."

"Thank you. You know, when a guy asks me about that stuff, it's usually a sign. It means he's done with me. Wham, bam, so long, ma'am. For your information, I don't remember what I did that night. It's a total blank, okay? I never talk about it because I don't know what I did. It's called 'post traumatic stress amnesia.' Okay?"

"How can I be done with you when I never started?"

"What do you mean?"

He strode over to her. "We did *not* have sex last night."

"You didn't fuck me?"

"No."

"Oh." Cat bit her lip trying to remember, could not. A little disappointed, she said, "Why not?"

"*William Morrison the Third,*" Sterner said impatiently. "When did you see him last?"

"Why?"

"What is it about women that they cannot answer a simple question simply?"

Cat put her hands on her hips and chewed her lip. "Seventeen, eighteen years ago?"

"Are you sure?"

"I think so."

Sterner sat in the chair opposite her. "We think he's working for the man who killed John and Jane Doe. He and his partner, the man in the picture I showed you, Cecil David Beasenbach, probably killed Clay Whipple with a baseball bat sometime Friday or early Saturday morning and staged it to look like an auto accident. But you guess you haven't seen this guy in twenty years?"

"It's the truth."

"Okay, fine, I believe you."

"Thank you."

"Did you know Clay Whipple?"

"I think we had this conversation. I know who he was, sure."

"How did you know him?"

"I used to buy stuff from his dad's hardware store on Elm Street before he went out of business. He had Clay's picture above the cash register."

"Did you know Clay personally?"

"No, never met him."

"How about Peter Bream?"

"I've seen him around town. Nobody I know personally."

"Are you involved now, or have you ever been involved, in blackmail?"

"Of course not."

"Fine."

"Is that it?"

"Yes."

"Good, because I have one for you." She stood.

"Shoot."

"Why are you treating me all of a sudden like I'm a suspect again in your investigation? I'm here to talk about somebody murdering my cat."

"Is that really why you're here?" He moved close to her.

"What do you mean?"

He grabbed her and kissed her mouth hard. She didn't fight him. Instead she wrapped her arms around his neck and pulled him closer. But the sound of broken glass interrupted their prelude to lovemaking before it led anywhere. The picture window behind the curtains shattered as a heavy object hit the fabric and fell to the floor with a heavy thud. The smell of gasoline filled the air as flame from the rag-soaked bottle spread across the carpet towards them setting the floor and curtains ablaze.

They jumped apart and Sterner grabbed the bedspread and threw it over the fire to smother it but a lungful of noxious smoke drove him back, followed shortly thereafter by more flame as the bedspread absorbed the gasoline and fueled the blaze. The room's smoke alarm screeched. The intensity of the heat drove them back behind the bed, the toxic smoke drove them to the floor.

"You have a gun?" Cat said as they retreated.

"My glove compartment," Sterner said. She glared at him.

They crawled to the bathroom where Sterner slammed the door behind them. He grabbed a towel, threw back the plastic shower curtain and then flipped on the cold tap on the tub faucet. After wringing out the towel he said, "Lock the door and put a wet towel under the crack. You'll be safe in the tub."

"What about you?" she said.

He shut the door behind him. Covering his nose and mouth with the towel he tied it off like a bandit in a bad Western and stepped out into the smoke, closing the bathroom door behind him. He moved to the front door, squatted, unlocked it, then threw it open and stuck his head outside. He sensed it coming and jerked backwards, but not fast enough. The baseball bat caught him between the brow and his nose bone, smashing it in spite of his towel bandanna. Had the bat not struck the door jamb at the same time it hit Sterner it likely would have killed him.

Sterner went black, knocked cold, and fell back into the room inches from the flames on the carpet. The big man in the coveralls grabbed his feet and pulled him outside onto the cement, collared him and lifted him up against the wall, then crouched and let him fall over his shoulder. He carried Sterner to the back of the waiting Esplanade and tossed him inside. In the surrounding rooms, sleepy heads began to pop out of doorways, investigating the source of all the commotion.

"Hurry the fuck up, I want the cunt, too, and I don't like witnesses," his partner in the driver's seat said into his mouthpiece. But Cat was already out the door and sprinting down the side of the building towards the office and front desk cradling her bag like a football.

Beasey adjusted his earpiece. "Fuck you, Topper," he said wearily.

"Shit, there she goes, man, c'mon, get moving," Billy said.

Beasey caught sight of her, groaned and slammed the hatch down. "Why can't this ever be easy?" He raced to retrieve his bat and chased after her growling into the face of Sterner's neighbor, an elderly bald man, who quickly shut his door in response. Billy gunned the accelerator and jetted down the parking lot to get around the far wing to the street side of the building. Cat ducked into the breezeway that separated the office and front desk from Sterner's wing, swung open the door to the room housing the ice and vending machines and then kept running, rounding the corner just ahead of the man with the baseball bat.

Beasey turned the corner into the breezeway, saw the swinging door to the ice and vending machines and stopped to investigate.

Benny, the motel manager, a slight Indian man in his late twenties dressed in a short-sleeved white shirt with an open collar and black slacks, had been awakened suddenly from a deep sleep by the squeal of the smoke alarm. Disoriented, he now appeared at the side door to his office carrying a fire extinguisher and hurried past Beasey, crying out hysterically as much to himself as anyone, "Don't panic. The fire department is coming," completely oblivious to the big man in coveralls with his Louisville slugger.

Beasey ran to the front of the building just as Billy pulled up in the Esplanade.

"Lost her," Beasey said. They could hear a distant siren starting up in town two miles away.

"Fuck it," Billy said. "C'mon, get in."

———————

11.

SEVEN DAYS BEFORE OPENING DAY

Sterner woke up cold and naked in the dark. Regaining his wits he realized he was tied to a chair. His hands were numb, the rope cutting off his circulation. He tried to wriggle free but it was futile. His nose was broken but at least it still worked. He began to panic. He was trapped. It was his worst claustrophobic nightmare. He started hyperventilating. At least it wasn't hot in here. Heat exacerbated his panic. There was a damp, moldy, urine-like chemical smell, like somebody had kept feral cats in here. He heard a humming noise nearby. It sounded like a compressor or a small generator. He must be in the middle of nowhere if they needed a generator for electricity. He looked around in the dark, spotted a red bead of light. He surmised what it was.

Time lapsed. He couldn't be sure how much time. A minute. A month. He grew panicked again, reclaimed self-control, then grew panicked again. To offset the claustrophobia, he thought about Becca, how he'd missed seeing her this weekend and would now miss her doctor's appointment. Anger displaced panic. He imagined Emily encouraging her to forget him. Then again, there was no guarantee he would survive the day. Maybe it was not such a bad idea for Becca to forget him, he thought. *The hell.* He grew angry again.

And then there was Cat. Did she survive the fire? Did she suffocate in the bathroom because she made the mistake of trusting him, too? No, this was not his fault. It made him angrier.

He heard something upstairs. Creaks in the floorboards. Giggling. Unintelligible chatter. Then a rhythmic squeaking of springs. Slow, at first. Then faster. Then faster. Panting. Grunting. Howling. Somebody was getting it on. More giggling. Then there was quiet.

He would get through this. Sheer will power would see him through. And if he was wrong and was going to die in this place, as Clay Whipple likely had, so be it. But he wasn't going to give an inch. Fuck 'em.

A light bulb eventually ignited over his head, blinding him. After his eyes adjusted, he looked over and confirmed his suspicions about the red bead. There was a small video camera on a roughly-hewn wooden shelf nearby, nestled between cobweb-covered mason jars of beets and green beans that looked unfit to eat. Looked like an XL-1 with a night vision attachment. Nice. He'd witnessed a PSP SWAT hostage rescue exercise once in total darkness with night vision equipment. A technician accompanying his group recorded it for later review, using the exact same set-up. Very high tech. What did that tell him? It looked like he was in the cellar with a dirt floor, crudely milled beams and floorboards above him, rock and mortar walls and no windows. Must be old as the hills.

Sterner recognized Beasenbach from his leaner Mr. Daytona Beach photo as he lumbered down the steps in gray coveralls with a Louisville Slugger baseball bat tucked casually under his arm pit. Sterner could easily picture him both as Terry Meyer's gorilla and one of Lenny Kessler's steroid twins. He was over six feet tall and maybe three hundred pounds, two-thirds of it in his upper body, with freakish pectorals on a barrel chest, massive biceps and triceps, and grossly overdeveloped deltoid and trapezoid muscles. His deltoids alone must have weighed thirty pounds a piece de-boned on a butcher's scale. There was something odd about his eyes. It took Sterner a moment before he realized what it was. Beasenbach was wearing mascara.

Sterner realized he had a card or two to play. It was a game of control, he knew. If he could control himself, he could control Beasenbach.

"Good morning," the big man said. "So you're the mystery man behind the famous castrating cunt. We thought there was somebody else. We just couldn't figure how a loser like Clay Whipple would ever hook up with Cat Fucking True. They just didn't seem to have anything in common, know what I mean? But then we saw her go to your motel room night after night, and--well, here we are."

The big man swung his bat in front of Sterner's face an inch from his nose.

Sterner did not flinch. If they found out who he really was, the game would be over and he'd be dead.

"Oh," Beasey said grinning. "This is going to be more fun than I could hope. You're not even going to protest your innocence, are you? You're a real hard case."

Sterner said nothing, just stared at him.

"That's okay with me," Beasey said. "I love hard cases. The harder they come, the bigger they fall. We're gonna make a little game of it, ya see. Every time you pitch something to me that's false, it's gonna come back at you like a bad karma boomerang. Now, uh, let's start with your name, little buddy, what do ya say? 'Cause I guess you left your wallet back in your motel room. Give Daddy a name."

He stepped back and began practice-swinging against Sterner's left knee. "If I don't hear a name out of you in the next five seconds, I'm gonna make you a gimp for the rest of your life, what do ya think about that?"

Sterner's eyes narrowed on him unblinkingly with fork-bending concentration.

"Callin' my bluff? Here goes." Beasey pulled back for a mighty swing.

"Beasenbach," Sterner said.

The big man froze. "What did-- what did you say?" the big man said, eyelashes fluttering, bat poised over his head, the power gone from his swing.

"Bea-sen-bach," Sterner said showing no fear.

The big man swallowed. His bat tip drooped to the floor. He thought for a minute and then leaned over it like a cane. "Where you from, Mr. Beasenbach?" he said.

"Michigan," Sterner said.

"Uh-huh?"

"Originally," Sterner said.

"What part?"

"Lansing," Sterner said.

"Yeah?" the big man said considering it uncomfortably. "And you got a first name, Mr. Beasenbach?"

"Cecil."

"Let me guess. Your middle name's Da--?"

"David."

Beasey laughed and wagged his finger at Sterner. "Well, well. You had me going there, I gotta admit. For a second I really thought maybe you were some distant relative or something. But you were just being cute, right? You have me at a disadvantage, sir. You know *my* name, but I don't know *yours*."

He stared, scratched his chin thinking about it.

"So you know my name--so what? That don't mean shit to me. Now we can play all the games you want, but nothing's gonna keep me from hurting you worse than you've *ever* been hurt before. You can scream and cry and plead all you want but nobody's gonna save you. We're out here in the middle of nowhere, little buddy. Nobody knows we're here. I can play with you for days and days and days. Now tell me who you are, little buddy, or--" Beasey tapped Sterner's left knee with the bat and clicked his tongue. He then drew the bat back over his head again and started practice-swinging.

"I'm a bouncer at the Eldorado Oasis in Miami Beach, Florida."

"Nice try, but I quit that job. Your name, little buddy? Tell me or kiss your professional sports career goodbye."

"Mister Daytona Beach, 1993."

"Yeah, yeah, yeah."

"They used to tease me as a kid on the playground because of my name. *Cecil! Cecil plays with dolls! Cecil dresses up in his mommy's nylons! Cecil's a creampuff! Cecil the queer!*" Sterner smacked his lips, taunting him. "*CEEECIL!*"

"You *shut the hell up*," Beasey said, leaning into him, broken nose to broken nose.

"Oh, but they learned to fear me when I got older, though. *You think you're so tough, sister? I'll show you who the creampuff is! The name is* Mister *Beasenbach to you, asshole!* Bodybuilding saved my life. I look back now and I'm grateful, you know what I mean? What did not destroy me made me stronger. And look at me now. Am I not beautiful? More beautiful than any of those clowns on the playground could ever have imagined? I am perfection personified."

"You don't know me. Don't pretend you do."

"I know you," Sterner said staring at him. No fear. He whispered, "I *am* you." Sterner grinned, actually laughing inside. This was fun. If he *was* going to die, he'd do it laughing at his killer. He would give him nightmares. It was the least he could do. *Fuck you!*

Beasey straightened and leaned back onto his heels. He bit his bottom lip in a pout and looked like he might cry. In a high-pitched voice, Beasey said, "Excuse me," holding up an index finger and then headed back upstairs.

A few minutes later the other one came down the steps. Sterner recognized him from the mug shot twenty years ago. Even so, he'd change a lot. For one thing, he'd bulked up, as Lenny observed. Like Beasenbach, his upper body accounted for two-thirds of his weight. He looked like he could bench-press four hundred pounds without breaking a sweat. And he was tanned and wore a diamond stud in his pierced left ear. His hair was considerably thinner, too, but the face was the same. There was no mistaking him. He indeed looked like Beasenbach's steroid twin, but he wore no make-up and his eyes were beadier. He sported a long gray trench coat over a black shirt, black jeans and black combat boots, like some hot shit Terminator wannabe trying to blend in with the public. He approached Sterner sideways, his tiny eyes squinting into slits as he examined Sterner's broken nose from all angles.

"You upset my partner," he whispered softly and close enough that Sterner could smell his bad breath. He oozed malice. "But don't you worry. He'll put himself together. He likes his work too much.

"So. I'm curious. What do you think of the whole baseball bat interrogation strategy? Does it work for you? I prefer chain cutters, myself. Snip off the finger bones one knuckle at a time. That's my idea of persuasion. Baseball bats are clumsy and imprecise. But then we all have our peccadilloes."

Sterner said, "You prefer the castration metaphor. Understandable. As for your boyfriend, it must be true what they say about steroids shrinking the family jewels, making you impotent and emotionally unstable. Turned your buddy Beasenbach into a real *pussy*. But I don't have to tell you that, am I right?" He winked, then spoke into Billy crotch. "So. How's it hangin', Billy Three? What's left of it?"

Billy pinched Sterner's swollen nose hard. "So you've done your homework," Billy said, twisting Sterner's broken nose back and forth with every word. "Very impressive, but it won't change anything. Did Ray tell you about us? Hmmm?"

When he let go, Sterner quaked from searing pain and tears flowed freely down both cheeks. Trickles of new blood dribbled down onto his crusted upper lip.

Billy straightened and sighed. "It's a shame we missed you the other night at the college. That maze of underground maintenance passages between the buildings was a complete surprise to me. Who knew? And I grew up in that shit-hole town, too, as you apparently already know. All of this pain you'll be experiencing could've been avoided if you had just been a little less clever."

He turned to leave, then thought better of it and leaned into Sterner's ear. "You know how she managed to hog-tie me? She crawled into my bed naked and started sucking me off before I even realized I wasn't dreaming. I was eighteen years old, man. It didn't take me long to cum. And I mean that hungry little bitch just licked it up like an ice cream cone in the tropics. Best blow job I ever had from a woman.

"Well, anyway, I probably don't have to tell *you* what a good cocksucker she is, am I right? Then she turned me over and stuck her tongue up my asshole." He wiggled his fanny, shutting his eyes and relishing the memory. "She massaged my ass cheeks, my back, my shoulders, my arms, all the while rimming me, right? You can imagine. I was giddy. Suddenly, before I even knew it, she had me gagged and tied like a rodeo calf. I was just laying there giggling. Who wouldn't be? I thought it was a joke. Little did I know that filthy tongue of hers had on it the cum and shit and blood of the other two guys before me. Think about that next time she French-kisses you." And then he pecked Sterner on the cheek with a kiss. He leaned back to look into Sterner's eyes. "Thought you should know." He sadistically pinched Sterner's nose one last time and went back upstairs.

A few minutes went by. Or maybe it was an hour. Sterner couldn't be sure. His eyes continued to water, but eventually went dry. He could do nothing about his urge to wipe them. He grew thirsty. He grew angry. He grew panicked. He controlled himself.

And then the first one returned, trudging back down the stairs with his baseball bat. He was sniffling. But no longer from tears, though the mascara had clearly run while he was upstairs and been wiped onto his sleeves. Cocaine residue remained around the perimeter of his nostrils, even after dabbing at them with fingers and sleeve. His face was flushed, too. "Looks like my partner made you cry, little buddy. That Topper sure is a heartbreaker, ain't he? Now let's cut to the chase, shall we?" Beasey said. "We want the money, honey. We don't give a fuck about nothin' else, just the money. Give us that cash and we're off you like a rash. Vamoose. Adios, muchachos. We'll leave you and your girlfriend alone to go back to your miserable lives, I promise."

"What money?" Sterner said.

Beasenbach laughed. "*What money!?* You want to play innocent? That's okay with me. I'm talking about that ransom, little buddy. That's *what money!* Remember? It rightfully belongs to us, see, since we had an agreement with our employer. And though he tried to cancel our contract, we did not agree to the terms of that cancellation."

"And what makes you think Cat and I have it?"

"Your buddy Clay ratted out you and your girlfriend before Louie here took his toll," he said, wagging the bat in Sterner's face.

"And you believed him?"

Beasenbach chuckled. "Oh, he was very convincing."

"Being convincing is what actors do for a living."

"No more horseshit. Now I'm going to count to three and if you don't tell me where the money is by three I'm goin' to cripple you for life. It's that simple. Do we understand each other, little buddy?"

He began to practice-swing on Sterner's left knee. "One," he said. "Two."

"Alright, I'll tell you where it is. Better yet, give me a phone, I'll have her bring it to you. She'll deliver it wherever you want."

Beasey froze, let the bat drop, licked his lips. "You see, that's a problem. Because we don't have a telephone here and cell phones don't work, either. No cable, no satellite dish, no internet. I know, it's a real drag. And there's no way we're goin' to transport you somewhere just to make a phone call. That's way too risky. So," he shrugged, "sorry." He screeched a loud obnoxious squeal, sounding like a basketball buzzer signaling the end of a time period.

Before Sterner could get another word in, Beasey slammed the bat into the detective's knee, breaking it. He heard the kneecap pop, the cartilage splinter. He tried to scream but the pain literally took his breath away. The room began to spin. Sterner passed out.

A pungeant odor even more vial than the chemical urine stench came into the room and snapped him back awake. Beasey was reviving him with an ammonia capsule. Sterner's head flopped, uncertain how much time had elapsed. Might have been seconds. Might have been weeks.

"There you are, little buddy! You were hiding from Daddy," Beasey said, placing the foul capsule on a barrel nearby. Sterner saw a hypodermic needle there, too, extracted from a leather traveling case filled with spares. A bag of cotton balls. A bottle of alcohol. A pharmaceutical bottle of clear liquid something-or-other with a rubber cap. "Now tell Daddy where the money is and Daddy'll give you some morphine to take the pain away. Doesn't that sound fun?"

"I hid it," Sterner managed to whisper.

"What? Where? Where did you hide the money?" He leaned in, head to the side, ear to Sterner's mouth.

"I'll take you to it? Or would you rather get it yourself?"

"Just tell Daddy where it is."

Sterner nodded his head that he should come closer. Beasenbach leaned in even closer, but not close enough to be head-butted. "Up Billy's ass," Sterner whispered and managed a smile.

Beasey swung his bat hard into Sterner's left shoulder, breaking the humerus bone, Sterner knew, the momentum tipping him over onto the packed dirt floor, chair and all. Sterner again passed out from the pain.

"*Beasey, get up here now,*" Billy was calling from the top of the cellar steps.

"*I can handle this,*" Beasey said.

"I said *now,*" Billy said. "On the double, soldier. We've got company."

"What the *fuck*--?" Billy said for a greeting, walking out of the clapboard cottage to meet the uninvited guest in his driveway. From the doorway behind Billy stepped Beasey, leaning against the jamb, holding an Uzi SMG casually strapped to his shoulder.

Derek Pensinger pulled up behind the Esplanade and threw his shiny new cherry red Sierra into park, jumping out with open arms, fishing for a buddy hug. Derek, now in his early forties with shaggy dyed-blond hair and graying beard stubble, wore Wayfarer sunglasses, faded black jeans, biker boots and a faded yellow tee under a weathered, black leather motorcycle jacket with the word *Berzerkers* emblazoned across the back amid yellow and red flames. Looking on from the passenger seat was his mascot, his dim-witted younger half-brother Buster, a mullet-haired mute in blue jeans and a filthy army jacket. The young man had suffered brain damage from sniffing glue in his early teens a dozen years ago when he still lived with their alcoholic mother. Derek took him in when their mother drowned in her own vomit a year later.

As was his custom, Derek sucked on a barnburner matchstick, which he now extracted to quip lightheartedly, "Dude, word on the street is you got busted."

"Does it *look* like we got busted? You told us we could have this place as long as we needed it. Well, we still need it, Derek. We paid you good fuckin' money for some privacy, man, so turn your ass right the fuck around right fucking now."

Taken aback, Derek turned up the charm, shined a boyish grin and threw an arm around his old pal's shoulder, one part hipster, one part hillbilly, one part snake oil salesman. "Baby, I hate to tell you this, but I got my guys coming up here in, like," he showed off his vintage Mickey Mouse watch, "ten minutes to cook up product." He threw a thumb over his shoulder at the bed of his pickup where a canvas tarp was covering a cargo of ingredients. "When we heard you got busted, we figured the coast was clear to go back to business as usual."

Billy led him back toward the pickup and brushed his arm aside refusing to be seduced by Derek's charisma. "Who told you we got busted?"

"One of my boys," Derek said, squeezing Billy's arm as if to reassure him he was one of his boys, too.

Billy glared at him and lowered his voice. "Well, I'd say you need to straighten him out, Derek. Look, let me explain something to you, my friend. This is some heavy shit going down here right now that, believe me, you don't want to be a part of--you *or* your boys. This goes way beyond your little shake-and-bake operation. We're delving in the realm of capital crimes here--death penalty shit. You dig me, Derek, man?"

Deflated, Derek eyed Beasey and his Uzi and back-stepped. "Whoa, man, this is so fucked up! I am so sorry. But this puts me in a bit of a bind myself, you know? I got customers waitin'. Where'm I gonna cook up my shit?"

"I don't care, but you can't do it here," Billy barked.

As if on cue, their attention shifted to a Harley engine revving as three approaching vehicles and a motorcycle paraded up the adjacent access road. Beasey came to attention, cocked back the bolt on his SMG and braced himself, ready to spray lead.

"Cocksucker," Billy cursed, bringing his fingertips to his forehead.

"Yo, don't panic. I'll handle this," Derek said waving his arms in the air to draw Beasey's attention. "Just relax, okay?"

The convoy curved through a tunnel carved out of a camouflaging grove of white pine trees to the east. First a Jeep Cherokee, followed by an International Scout, a Harley Fat Boy and an orange Trans Am. They pulled up behind Derek's pickup, killed their engines, laughter and music and got out, bewildered by the situation.

They were a motley bunch, rowdy and tough, always looking for fun and trouble, since the two so often went hand in hand. The Jeep driver, a goon in a sleeveless blue jean jacket named Flake, who sported Wayfarers, a beard and shoulder-length hair, even tossed a six-pack of sixteen-ounce Genesee's on the hood of his Cherokee to jumpstart the party. He eyed Beasey with curiosity. Normally the sight of an Israeli-made 9mm submachine gun held tight to the chest commanded a certain measure of respect. But instead of shriveling, Flake tore off a can, flipped the tab and guzzled it in one gulp. He let out a loud, defiant belch, twisting then compressing the can with his bare hands. He grinned at Beasey as if daring him to put up or shut up.

"Hold on, fellas, everybody's gonna be cool," Derek announced, hoping the idea was contagious. "Everybody's just gonna count to ten and be real cool."

About half of them wore Berzerker jackets. There were nine in all. Had Sterner been able to see them, he would have recognized three. One passenger in the Cherokee wore a reversible down vest and a black Pirates baseball cap. It was Lenny Kessler, the methamphetamine dealer from the Truckers Paradise he'd interviewed the day before. He would have recognized the orange Trans Am, too, and the men in it. The driver wore a Berzerkers jacket, a shaved head with a Celtic tattoo and a pirate earring. His passenger wore a long, dark green leather jacket, a Van Dyke beard and wiry hair. It was Artie Samios.

Eyeing Samios closing his passenger door, Derek went ballistic. "*Kiwi, what the fuck?!*" he snarled, livid at the man with the pirate earring. "Whaja bring him for, man? I told you he is *not cool!* Did I *not* tell you that?"

"He's cool, man. Look, we busted our asses last seventy-two hours buying up old cold meds from every gas station, pharmacy, convenience store and supermarket in three states, man. You know that shit's hard to find since they changed the friggin' formula. We burned up three tanks of gas and two cans of oil, damn near six hundred miles. So come on, Derek! He's cool."

"Nobody's cool unless I say he's cool," Derek said. "You know the rules."

"Alright, alright," Billy said, waving his hands, chuckling his way out of this waking nightmare. "Look, fellas, enough of this who's-cool-who's-not bullshit. Look, there's been a little mix-up, *comprende?* You guys are just gonna have to turn your butts around and cook your shit up someplace else today, okay?"

"Bill, man, we heard you got busted," Lenny said scratching his neck.

"Yeah, well, I don't know where you heard that--"

"Two Smokeys clued me yesterday, man. They knew your names, everything."

Billy bit his lip, paused, shook his head. "Fuckin' Ray," he cursed, judo-chopping air and glared at Derek like it was *his* fault. "Sold us up the fuckin' river, motherfucker."

"Not *my* Ray," Derek said.

"Yes, Derek, *your* Ray."

"They said they booked you themselves. Kidnapping and murder, man. They said I was an accessory for helping you jack that van. Said I'd go away, too, like forever."

"Yeah. Well. Obviously, they lied, shithead."

"They said you even told them we were old friends."

Samios shriveled and took half a step into retreat as if the open car door would protect him from his own ricocheting words.

"They lied, Lenny, okay? Unlike you, Lenny, when cops talk to me I just shrug or shake my head no, you know? You should try it sometime."

"Oh, man," Lenny said scratching his forehead.

"*Oh, man,* is right," Billy said. "Now boys, please, you're gonna have to leave now, okay? You can't cook your shit here today, *okay*?"

It dawned on Lenny. "Holy shit, you're entertaining right now, ain'choo, Bill?" he said suddenly excited. "Can we see the fuck?"

"Yeah. Anybody we know?" Kiwi grinned, eager for a peek.

Billy buried his face in his hands.

"Whoa, whoa, slow down here, brothers," Derek said. "What are you, fucking stupid? This ain't a school trip to the zoo. Look, I made a mistake. Lenny, I gotta talk to you, right? The rest of you, just go home. We'll find another kitchen by tonight. I'll ring you, right? We're all just gonna split and forget we were ever here, understood?"

Billy rubbed his face, closed his eyes and then held up his hand. "Wait, wait, wait! Hold the phone! Everybody just hold on a sec." He chewed his lower lip. "Maybe I'm going about this all wrong." Billy turned to Derek and slowly pointed to Samios without looking directly at him. "Is he cool or is he *not* cool?"

Derek threw his hands in the air. "Are you cool, Patches, or are you *not* cool?"

"I'm cool, man," Samios said shrugging. "Come on, if you don't know I'm cool by now--how long's it been? I mean, come on."

"He's cool," Kiwi said shrugging.

Derek frowned at Kiwi, then turned to Billy and shrugged. "He's cool."

"You're not just saying that because he's already here? You either trust him or you don't. Do you trust him? Because it's your ass at stake, too, Derek. Not just mine."

"He's cool, all right?" Derek said and glared at Kiwi. Kiwi gave him a thumbs up, vouching.

"Okay then, to answer your question, Lenny," Billy turned to Lenny, "yes, we are *entertaining*. Now I'll be honest with you, the guy's a hard case. He's not responding to our inquiries as eagerly as we had hoped. We're getting *nowhere* with him, in fact, and we're getting a little pissed off. If we knew anything about him, we might be able to get him to open up a bit, tell us where the money is he and his girlfriend stole from us. Maybe if I gave you guys a peek, one of you might recognize him. If you can help us, we'll make it worth your while. I'm not saying how much--"

"How much?" Lenny said licking his lips and scratching his neck.

Billy heard snickers, sighed and then chuckled to himself, shaking his head. "Right. Well. If I say I'll reward the guy who recognizes him, you'll all probably recognize him, am I right? But I don't have time for false information. Me and my partner should've vamoosed out of here days ago. Every hour we piss away we risk getting nailed for some pretty heavy shit. So how about this, then? We'll pay each of you to come in, one by one, take a look at the guy on the video monitor. You can see *him* but he can't see *you*. If you know this guy, tell us how you know him. If you don't know him, you still keep the dough, so no reason to lie, right? Everybody with the program?"

"Sure," Lenny said. The others nodded. "But how much?"

"How about," he paused, glanced over at Beasey, "say, two bills. No. Three. Three hundred bucks."

Grunts and guffaws followed.

"Fuck, yes," Lenny said, a response echoed by the others and punctuated by a whistle or two.

"My partner and I can afford to be generous since we're looking at a big pay-out at the end of this thing. Now that payment's up front. To each and every one of you," Billy added. "It not only buys your cooperation, it also buys your silence. The downside is, if the shit hits the fan, you're all accessories, just so you know going in. Nobody's innocent here. Right, do we understand each other? Everybody on board? If not, take a hike now."

They all looked one another over, nodded or shrugged.

"Let's get started, then," Billy said. "Derek, you're up first."

One by one they were each escorted inside for a private viewing. Video village was set up in the living room, using a beat-up Formica kitchen table with five small LCD monitors. The largest one was a yellow-tinted monochromatic set for the camera in the basement on Sterner. The other four smaller screens covered all sides of the house, which is how Billy knew of Derek's approach. They had a VCR hook-up on the basement camera, too, to record interrogations, and a video game remote to control the zoom and recorder. They had furniture blankets crudely tucked into the curtain rods over the windows that kept the room dark and prevented screen glare. An old stuffed, beat, lime-colored sofa from the 1940s that had been there forever, with worn arms and threadbare cushions scarred in cigarette burns, was set up for couch potato viewing. They had an army surplus footlocker for a coffee table, a small shaving mirror on top with cocaine residue on it. There was a half-empty bottle of Jack Daniels, two shot glasses with Rebel flags on them and a small bag of coke with a rolled-up hundred dollar bill for a straw. On the floor was a case of Red Bull and empty bags of beef jerky. The boys were each offered a drink and a toot with their fistful of hundreds, and each partook eagerly of the hospitality.

Without reviving him, Beasey pulled Sterner's chair upright. He grabbed Sterner's hair and held his face to the camera. Billy was able to zoom in tight on Sterner's face with the remote. The light wasn't very good but the camera and the LCD monitor were, and although Sterner's nose was purpled and swollen, with dry and wet blood on his upper lip and darkening eyes, when it was Lenny's turn, he recognized him straight away.

"Fuck a duck! That's one of the Smokeys that rousted me yesterday."

"He's a Smokey?" Billy said, squinting sideways.

"Said he was," Lenny said scratching his eyelid. "I mean, he flashed a badge. He and his partner both did. Or was it just the partner?" Lenny couldn't remember.

"What did he say his name was?"

"Well, uh, truth is, they kind of caught me off-guard. I don't exactly remember."

"What did the badges look like?"

"Well, I'm not sure. Shiny, silver? You know. Badges. You know how they just flash 'em sometimes? I was up all weekend and kind of spacey, you know, havin' my Sunday brunch? Quick movement had a trail on it like old tube TVs. But they *said* they was state police."

"Lenny, you are a horse's ass."

"I'm being straight with you, Bill. They were Smokeys. I'm sure they were."

"Yeah, you were sure we were busted, too, because they said we were. What did his partner look like?"

"Older, small guy in his fifties, Vietnam vet, said I looked like an old army buddy. He was the nice guy. This guy was a prick, called me a flag-burner."

"They ran good cop-bad cop on you?" Billy said, taking him more seriously.

"Uhm, good cop-bad cop. Yeah, yeah, you know, I think they did."

"What did they say to you, exactly?"

"They said they busted you two. They knew your names. The older guy had em written down in his notepad. They said you told em I was an old friend of yours and that my mug got picked out of a photo array by a witness in the parking lot at the Paradise."

"Whoa, whoa, whoa, what witness? There was no witness."

"They didn't say."

"Fuckin' Ray, man. He really fucked us! So help me God, I'm gonna kill that old fuck, I get half a chance.”

“What happened?”

“He fuckin’ canned us after we told him who was extorting him. You believe that shit? What else can you tell me?"

"Umm. No, that was pretty much it. They told me to lay off the meth dealing, that I should lawyer up and, uh--oh, they didn't recognize your name in connection with that Hellcat thing. I kind of ribbed 'em about that."

"They didn't *know* that?"

"No."

"That's weird, since this guy is definitely in bed with Cat True. Yet they knew my name? How is *that* possible?"

"Yeah, they knew both your names. Full names. I mean, they--for a second there they couldn't place your last name," Lenny recalled, back-pedaled, then blinked, "but it came to them."

"Wait a minute. *What?!*"

Lenny swallowed hard and scratched his nose. "I mean, the older guy had it in his notepad but he couldn't find it at first. Then they remembered."

"You didn't help 'em remember, did you, Lenny?"

"No, Bill, c'mon. I'm not *that* stupid!"

"What *did* you tell them?"

"Nothing. I didn't give 'em shit. I fed 'em the line you gave me. You'd locked yourselves out of your van, so I helped you out."

"Alright, well, thanks for the info, Lenny." He squeezed Lenny's fist of cash.

"No problem, Bill. Anytime. This really helps me out, I can't tell you." Lenny got up and stuffed the bills in his pants pocket.

No one else recognized Sterner until it was Kiwi's turn. Kiwi sat down on the sofa and narrowed his eyes at the monitor.

"You know who that looks like? Fuck if it isn't! We need Patches in here. Patches knows him. That looks just like the guy he sold to Saturday night. I never got out of the Trans so I didn't get that good a look at him, myself."

"Where was the sale?"

"The Sleep Well in Samaritan."

"You remember the room number?"

"Naw. You'd have to ask Patches, man. He'd know."

Patches came in, sat down. He was the last one of the group to look at Sterner. He squinted soberly at the monitor, grinned, gulped a shot of Jack, wiped his lip with his sleeve and shook his head. "Don't think I know him," he said with a shrug.

"No?" Billy said and offered him a line of coke.

"Nope."

"Kiwi says you sold him product Saturday night at the Sleep Well Motel."

"This guy?" he said snorting and sniffing, squeezing his nose.

"That's what he said. And the Sleep Well just happens to be where we snatched this guy. Kind of a coincidence, wouldn't you say?"

"He's high. I know the guy he means. It does look a little like him, maybe, but not that much. It's kind of hard to see, though." He squinted and backpedaled. "This guy does seem familiar. I just can't place--" He frowned as he leaned into the screen making a show of trying to remember.

"What was the room number of the guy you sold to?"

"Ummmmmm, nineteen, I think. Yeah, yeah, nineteen."

"You're sure."

"Absolutely."

Billy thought about it out loud. "This guy was in twenty-seven. He could've switched rooms, I suppose, but why would he? Lenny thinks he posed as a state cop. Then again, Lenny's an idiot. He might be working with an older guy in his fifties. Short. Vietnam vet, maybe. Private dick, maybe an ex-cop, maybe a real cop. Sound familiar?"

Patches shrugged and shook his head. "Well, my Saturday night guy's no cop, that's for sure," he said. "I sold to him before. He's a tile salesman. Still, it's kind of-- Can you wake him up so I could see his eyes, maybe? Seems like I talked to him once somewhere, but where?"

Billy put on his earpiece. "Beasey, wake him up."

Beasey broke the ammonia capsule under Sterner's nose. Sterner shot to consciousness. His eyes rolled and fluttered. Beasey held Sterner's head up by his hair so the camera could get a good shot of him. Sterner tried to focus but drifted off.

"This salesman of yours have a name?"

"Guthrie is his name. Jake Guthrie. He's from Dallas or Fort Worth. Has a slow Texas draw. But who is *this* guy? I swear I know that face from somewhere."

"Look, Patches, you're my last hope here. Nobody else knows him. I need to find out who he is fast or I may never break him. I don't break him, I don't get paid, I don't go home happy. Can I ask you to look at him face-to-face, maybe listen to his voice? I can guarantee it won't come back to bite you, if you catch my drift."

"I don't know, man." Patches took a breath and shook his head.

Billy did know. He snap-zoomed out for a full two-shot. "Beasey, we're coming down for a closer look."

"*Copy that*," Beasey said into the camera and let go of Sterner's hair. His head flopped around, Sterner struggling to regain consciousness.

Billy discarded the earpiece and led Patches to the cellar door in the kitchen. Billy politely gestured an "after you" for Patches to proceed ahead of him. "I hope I didn't embarrass you out there in front of the boys. You understand me and my partner are a little wary of strangers, especially since we're behind schedule in our operation."

"No sweat," Patches said grinning and aped Billy's "after you" good manners.

Billy shrugged and led the way downstairs. Patches followed, checking over his shoulder to see if anyone else noticed where they were going. Nobody did. All the boys were busy revving up a party outside.

"I was never a full-fledged Berzerker, either," Billy babbled on. "With Derek, you're either in or you're out. He never completely trusted me. I guess we have that in common." When they got to the bottom, Patches leaned down and drew a snubnose .38 from an ankle holster and held it with both hands to the back of Billy's head. "But I've known half these guys twenty years, ridden and partied hardy all over hell and back, so if Kiwi vouches for you, that's good enough--" When Billy heard the hammer click back, he froze.

"Okay, assholes, down on the ground. Now! No fuckin' around," Samios said in a voice quiet and unrecognizable from his Patches persona, nervous but deadly serious.

"Cocksucker," Billy mumbled raising his hands. "I should've seen this coming."

"Whoa," Beasey said, eying the pistol and slowly reached up. He'd stowed his Uzi and the Louisville Slugger upstairs and was now caught with his pants down.

"Try anything, I'm blowing you both the fuck away. Got me, scumbags?"

"Yessir," Billy said quietly.

"Face down on the ground right now, hands behind your head, fingers locked together. Move it." He shoved Billy forward. They did as they were told, lining up side by side on the earthen floor. "Okay. Nobody moves now, nobody fuckin' dies," Samios said. "Joe. You with me, Joe?"

"Yeah," Sterner said, swimming out of delirium. "Yeah, yes." Sterner snapped to attention and focused on Samios' face and blinked, trying to place him and take stock.

Samios had the .38 in one hand and now nervously pulled a pocketknife from his pants pocket with the other. He opened the blade with his teeth and cut Sterner free.

"If you fire that noisemaker, don't you think it'll attract attention?" Billy said.

"If you're dead, what the fuck do you care, asshole?"

Looking at Samios, Billy had a revelation. "Jesus H. Christ, he's a fuckin' narc!" Billy groaned to Beasey, chuckling at the mediocrity of it all. He rolled his eyes. "And this guy *is* a fuckin' Smokey! Fuck. Me."

"Shut up, faggot," Samios said. "Can you walk, Joe?"

"Not without help," Sterner said, breathing heavily as the pain hit him like a wave now that his circulation was coursing through his veins. "I think my left leg and arm are broken."

"Shit," Samios said. "C'mon, gimme your good arm." He reached over.

"Strip em first," Sterner said. "Gimme that one's coveralls. I'll hold the gun and watch your back." He looked down at Billy. "Hog-tie 'em. Real tight! Tie their mouths shut, if you can."

Billy looked up at Sterner's face. Sterner grinned sadistically. Samios obliged, stripping and hog-tying them with the Sterner's rope.

"Better hurry," Billy managed through his rope gag. "Derek and the boys are gonna get suspicious."

"Shut the fuck up, I said." Samios swatted the back of Billy's head. When Samios was done he pulled out a cell phone and checked for a signal.

"Good luck there, little buddy," Beasey snickered through his gag.

Samios pocketed the cell and grabbed the gun from Sterner offering his arm again. "I want to hear you count out loud to one hundred slowly. And don't even try to get up or I'll blow you both away, so help me."

Billy chuckled. "Yeah, and when we get to a hundred, you're it," he said through his rope gag in a whisper to Beasey, who chuckled.

"Goddammit," Sterner said, his expressions contorting ten different ways as he learned to walk with a broken leg and arm. With Samios supporting him on his right side with his free hand, snubnose in the other, the two slowly made their way upstairs one step at a time, Sterner wincing and grunting painfully every inch of the way.

"I'm not hearing that count," Samios said.

"One," Beasey said.

"Two," they both said in unison. "Three, four, five, six, seven, eight, nine...."

Samios and Sterner were upstairs and headed towards the back door.

"Ten, eleven," Billy and Beasey struggled against their rope shackles. "Twelve, thirteen, fourteen." First Billy, then Beasey, stopped the pointless count and listened to the footfalls across the wooden floorboards above their heads until there was silence. They waited just long enough, then Billy screamed, *"Derek, Derek, Patches is a narc! We're tied up in the cellar, man. Help!"*

"HELP! HELP!" Beasey screamed in a high-pitched voice.

Derek and the Berzerkers were loitering by the Jeep, sipping beers from an ice chest, smoking and goofing around, giddy with their easy score and sharing their plans to spend it when they fell quiet at the sound of muffled screams from the cellar.

"Patches is a fucking narc, Derek, you dickhead! He just pulled a gun on us and took our boy out the back door. C'mon, man, get with the program. You want to give us a little assistance here?"

"HELP! HELP!" Beasey kept screaming in his high-pitched voice.

"You gotta be *shittin' me,*" Derek said, arms flailing in the air. He discarded the matchstick and ran inside.

"Derek, we're in the cellar! Come on, man, come on!"

"HELP! HELP!"

Derek dashed to the monitors. *"No fuckin' way,"* he said when he spied Billy and his partner on the big LCD. To two of his Berzerker buddies in the front doorway, he said, *"Billy's fuckin' tied up in the cellar!"* His buddies scrambled through the cellar door. Then Derek noticed Patches helping Sterner escape down through the garden on another monitor, about to enter a thicket at the edge of the forest. *"Holy shit!"*

"They're escaping out the back door," Billy screamed.

Derek pulled a shiny nickel-plaited .45 automatic he wore in his belt at the crook of his back, cocked it and headed for the back door. He spotted Patches struggling along with Sterner at the thicket forty yards away where an untended garden had gone to seed. He stepped onto the weather-worn floorboards of the small back porch and took aim, arm extended, handgrip twisted banger-style.

The arrow entered his right side, pierced the leather of his jacket and buried deep in his ribs under his arm pit. The razor tip sliced through his right lung and punctured his heart. Derek discharged the automatic in a retort that sounded more like a dynamite explosion than a pistol shot and echoed up and down the hollow. He dropped, fatally stricken, to his knees and then rolled off the porch onto his back, convulsing and coughing blood.

Cat held her release pose, paralyzed with shock by what she had just done, came to her senses, got to her feet and ran off in the opposite direction.

Sterner had felt the round pass over them and Samios had swung around to return fire, only to witness Derek's collapse, an unlikely arrow jutting from his side. Sterner got a good view of the house for the first time, too. It was a modest, derelict two-story cottage that hadn't seen fresh paint in fifty years. It was at least a century old, engulfed on all sides by weeds, vines and briars from the encroaching forest. They simultaneously glimpsed Cat at the edge of the woods to the left when she jumped to her feet from a kneeling position hidden in the overgrown weeds and retreated.

As she withdrew into the trees and brush, Samios said, "Who *the fuck* is that?"

"She's with me." Sterner said, managing a smile.

"My compliments," Samios said and turned his attention back to Derek. "One less asshole to testify against." Then armed Berzerkers came running around the right side of the house and through the backdoor, responding to the gunshot and ready for war. They froze in shock when they discovered their fallen gang leader dying before their eyes.

"Derek!" somebody cried. *"Motherfucker, they fuckin' shot Derek with an arrow, man!"*

"Shit," Samios said. They ducked into the thicket fast.

"Kiwi, get back here," Billy shouted, holding up his own Uzi SMG for emphasis.

Kiwi was halfway down the garden with Derek's .45. "Patches is on *me*, man," Kiwi said, face flushed with rage.

"I said, get the fuck back up here right now, and don't fuckin' argue with me or I'll kill ya where ya stand, motherfucker!" They were all outside by now, standing over Derek's body. Billy cocked his Uzi, meaning business. Kiwi snorted bitter outrage, but turned to join them all the same.

Buster, the dead man's half-brother, sunk to his knees over the body and wailed in grief. Billy flipped on his safety and knelt down to put his arm around him. He touched his forehead against the young man's scalp and closed his eyes as if to say a prayer.

"I am so sorry, Buster," he said. "I am truly so sorry."

Billy then kissed him and stood to look around at the faces he barely knew anymore, biker buds from another century, now old and gone to seed. He considered their quivering lower lips and dewy eyes. He realized their very identity was disintegrating before them. Derek Pensinger was the linchpin that held them all together, through charm, guile, humor and intimidation. Without him, the power vacuum would inevitably splinter them. There was never an heir apparent. The Berzerkers were a cult and with their guru gone, they were all lost in the wilderness.

But Billy also knew an opportunity when he saw one. He would use them before they realized their whole world was forever changed and just move on. All he had to do was say the obvious, and they were his. Articulating mob sentiment was always the key to controlling the mob. *Hitler 101.*

"Okay, here's the skinny, so leather up, Fruit Loops," Billy said, massaging Buster's shoulders as the boy whimpered. "Derek is gone.

There's nothing we can do to bring him back. But we can sure as hell get us some *fuckin' payback*, am I *right*?"

"Fuckin' A," Kiwi said squeezing his nose and sniffing back tears. The others grunted, their blood pressure raised by the flood of emotion, not to mention beer, whiskey and cocaine. They were chomping at the bit, panting like racehorses at the gate awaiting the green flag.

"Time comes we'll throw our brother the proper Viking funeral he always talked about, but for now know this: Patches is a *fuckin' narc*, which means if he gets out of here alive, our gooses are all cooked but good, not just for the meth, but as accessories to kidnapping. He's packin' a thirty-eight snubnose and he brought along a third party with a bow who killed Derek, so nobody's flying off alone after them half-cocked. *Our* guy, who Patches called 'Joe,' has a broken leg and arm, so they're goin' nowhere fast."

"He's a fuckin' pig, too," Lenny said.

"Yes. He. Is. Either of these pigs gets out of here alive, you can kiss your future's goodbye. Now there's three of them against--what?--twelve of us. Those are pretty good odds in our favor, especially considering our firepower. Now let's take a weapons inventory. Who's carrying?" Five of them raised their weapons, which included pistols and a sawed-off double-barrel. "Good. Whoever's not armed, come with me. Beasey and I'll fix you up. We scored a set of eight military-grade, short range wireless comm units and can coordinate operations. We'll run an end around, set up an ambush along the road, then drive them down through the hollow. They have nowhere else out of here. Are you with me, Buster?"

"F-f-fuckin' A," Buster said hoarsely between sniffles. It was the first time some of them had heard him speak in years. He got to his feet flushed, hyperventilating, snorting like a bull seeing red before the charge. For those who knew him as the docile soul he usually was, it broke their hearts.

"Patches is on me, man," Kiwi repeated, shaking his head sadly at Buster.

"Fine, Kiwi, whatever. Jackson, Flake, pick two guys each to go with you near the road. Set up a line for an ambush. Space yourselves a good distance apart and stay out of sight. Make fuckin' sure nobody sees you from the road or gets past you. Anybody spots them, take a shot. Everybody else, converge on the gunfire. Got it?"

Cat caught up with Samios and Sterner down the mountain a quarter mile later as they descended a wooded knob west of the access road. They were both exhausted and stopped to rest against a granite boulder jutting up through the forest floor. The undercover stuck the snubnose in his belt and got out his cell phone to check for a signal.

"I never killed anyone before," Cat said and fell under Sterner's good arm.

"You saved our lives," Sterner said, out of breath as he kissed her forehead.

"Don't fall apart on us now," Samios said.

"I won't," Cat said stiffening.

Samios shrugged. "Hey, if you're not going to do the asshole about to pop your old man, who *are* you gonna do?" he said. "Sweet cheeks, I sure hope you have wheels."

"My truck's a quarter mile down," Cat said.

"DEA agent Samios," Sterner introduced him.

"Call me Artie," Samios said and shook her hand.

"Cat," she said. She locked onto Sterner's sparkling eyes and smiled. Sterner mirrored her rapture.

Samios suddenly did a double take recognizing her. "As in Cat True?" he said.

She nodded.

"Interesting." He looked back and forth between the two of them. "*Very* interesting."

"Where are we, anyway?" said Sterner.

"About eight miles north of Stokeley, Maryland," Cat said.

Samios tried standing on the boulder and holding up his cell high in the air above his head to get a signal, but it did no good. "Correct, though technically we're in Burnside County, Pennsylvania in what they call a *jurisdictional anomaly.* The only access is from the Maryland side of the Mason-Dixon Line. Pennsylvania police are unlikely to leave their state to investigate a forgotten hollow where nobody lives anyway. And Maryland police are unlikely to cross the state line, either. I've been working on Kiwi for months trying to get him to trust me enough to bring me along to their lab. Lucky for you, today was the day he took a chance on me."

"How did *you* get here?" Sterner said to Cat.

"I ran out of the motel room as they were putting you into their truck. I followed with my headlights off, but lost you on the two-lane that parallels the state line. I only spotted the access road at daylight."

"Tell me you guys have reinforcements on the way," Sterner said.

"Sorry," Cat shrugged.

"No time and no cell signal," Samios said and turned to Cat. "I don't suppose you have a CB in your truck."

Cat shook her head.

"I need to find a land line or a cell signal so let's get moving." Sterner took Samios' arm. They started out. Samios froze and whispered, "Get down." Sterner winced and groaned, unprepared, as Samios dropped them to the ground behind the boulder.

Uphill and to the east a hundred yards across a dry ravine they could make out the Cherokee and the Scout with three occupants each creeping down the access road at ten miles per hour. The passengers in the lead vehicle were scanning the leafless trees with binoculars on either side of the road.

"There's something I should mention," Samios said as the convoy passed. Cat and Sterner looked over at him. "The Berzerkers are not just a motorcycle gang that deals meth. They swear an oath of loyalty that rivals the mob. The guy you shot was Derek Pensinger, their leader and founder. I don't have to tell you what that means. These guys will stop at nothing to kill us. And, uh--oh, yeah--I only have five bullets." He rattled his Smith and Wesson.

"Thanks for sharing," Sterner said. "I've got a fractured arm and a pulverized knee, and I don't know how much longer I can go before I'm going to faint. Just thought I should mention *that*."

"As long as everybody's being so honest," Cat said. "I've got only one razor tip left. The other four are practice tips."

Samios pulled a small baggie out of his pants pocket and handed two white pills to Sterner. "First things first. It'll lie to your brain about how tired you are."

Sterner furrowed his brow in disapproval.

"Think of the alternative, man," Samios said and chuckled. "Don't worry. If we get through this I'll arrange a special dispensation from the Pope."

"Maybe later," Sterner said.

Samios offered Cat the pills but she shook her head. He popped them himself and raised his head for another look. As he watched the Cherokee and Scout disappear into the trees below them he turned around and noticed Cat was gone.

"Hey, where'd she go?" Samios whispered.

Sterner turned. He hadn't noticed her leave, either.

"Fuck," Samios said and raised his head to scan the forest. One of the Berzerkers was eighty yards uphill wielding a sawed-off, double-barrel shotgun slowly making his way down the knob right for them. "Bad guy, twelve o'clock." They scrambled to the downhill side of the boulder.

Samios looked at his pistol. "I can't hit a target more than thirty yards out with this thing. If he gets close I can squeeze off maybe one round before he unloads. But that'll bring down everybody else."

"Might get a weapon out of the deal," Sterner whispered.

Samios nodded and drew a finger to his lips. They'd wait for him to come to them.

Billy and Beasey had come prepared. A small arsenal was stowed in the footlocker they were using for a coffee table. They had distributed two Mossberg twelve-gauge pump shotguns with pistol grips, two 9mm M9 Berettas and gave Buster a Ruger .22 automatic. They tried but couldn't extract the arrow from Derek's chest, and the effort upset Buster too much to continue, so they carried the body, arrow and all, down the steps to the cellar. They laid it out in the corner on a blanket, where it could cool in peace. Then Beasey was sent outside to keep an eye on the Esplanade and Derek's truck while Billy organized the drive.

After ten minutes, Billy heard Kiwi report over his comm, "*We found a pickup parked in a grove along the road.*"

"Describe it," Billy said, holed up in the living room, eyes glued to the monitors of his command center fussing over his Uzi.

"*Late Seventies, black, with a lot of rust. Pennsylvania plates.*"

"*Jesus Fuckin' Christ*," Billy said and darted to the doorway to tell Beasey. "How the fuck did she fuckin' follow us here last night?"

"What?" Beasey said.

"*Who?*" Kiwi said.

"Cat Fuckin' True, the castrating cunt herself! She's the one who fuckin' killed Derek." Billy took a deep breath. "Okay, so this is what you do, Kiwi--pop the hood and rip out the distributor, then spread your line equally on either side and wait for 'em to show. And for fucksake, keep your heads down and your mouths shut. Remember, if you hear a shot charge like motherfuckers."

"*That's a ten-four, buddy,*" Kiwi said. "*Hammer down.*"

When the Berzerker failed to appear for his ambush Samios stole a quick look over the top of the boulder. Forty yards up the ravine Cat was standing frozen over the lifeless biker who lay on his back, an arrow sticking obliquely out of his chest.

"Stay here," he said to Sterner, then joined her checking their surroundings for anyone else.

"What gives?" Samios said to her as he relieved the body of the double-barrel, holstering the .38 in his belt. She held up her hand and he realized she was wearing the man's headset and was listening to the radio traffic. She covered the wire mouthpiece mike and whispered, "Know this guy's name?"

"Chumley," Samios whispered. Cat nodded. "Scumbag turned his girlfriend into a punching bag, then bragged how she loved him too much to press charges, worthless piece of shit." He broke the breach and checked the twelve-gauge cartridges. They held standard ball bearing shot for turkey. The wooden gun butt was whittled down to a smooth, curved pistol grip, with the barrels illegally hack-sawed ten inches from the breach. It had less range than the snub-nose, was likely non-lethal beyond ten yards, the copper BB spray having a wide spread, but was more likely to hit any target. More to the point, it was a good scare gun, a noisemaker that could be heard for miles.

She held up her hand again and then said in a low voice, "Check." She took out the earpiece and turned it off, then whispered again. "They disabled my truck and they've taken up positions along the road. The others put a drive on from the house."

Samios rolled his eyes. "We could double-back and steal one of their other vehicles."

Cat shook her head. "They're guarding them. Our only chance is up the mountain."

Samios looked at her a moment, then back toward Sterner.

"I know," she whispered before he could say anything. "It's probably two miles to the summit road. But I don't see any other way out, do you?"

Samios hurried back to Sterner and helped him to his feet. "The good news is, we've got a sawed-off double-barrel and we can monitor their chatter over a radio."

"And the bad news?" Sterner said.

"They've got our escape covered. The only way out is uphill. Think you can manage?"

"Do I have a choice?"

"We're talking maybe two miles to the top."

"Wilder Mountain?"

"Yeah, why?"

"Anywhere near Burnside Summit Road?"

"That's where we'd be heading, yeah. Why?"

"You can get a cell signal up there. Least I got one there on Saturday, on the Doolittle County side."

––––––––––

Samios checked the dead man for spare ammo. He had none. Cat took his belt and shoe laces and made a quick splint for Sterner's leg using a sapling she sawed down with the serrated edge of her knife. She gave Sterner the biker's leather jacket, too, since he had no coat of his own, and was shivering. The size was XXL but a painful fit in the sleeve since Sterner's broken arm was swelling. Cat retrieved the shaft of her arrow. The razor tip head was permanently lodged inside the man's ribcage.

With Cat taking point, bow in hand, arrow poised, they backtracked until they could see the thicket below the garden. It was slow going with Sterner and Samios equally fatigued. Cat then cut left leading them west for two hundred yards, then right, to the north again, and circled up and around the house and driveway toward Burnside Summit Road on a northeast heading.

"Check," Cat said into the earpiece occasionally. And, "Nothin'," she would sometimes add when Chumley was asked what he saw.

The late afternoon sky had gone from partly sunny to overcast, and it wasn't too long before the terrain became confusing. They labored through twisted ravines and around impassible thickets using deer trails where they could. Sterner wasn't paying attention to where they were going. It was all he could do to put one foot ahead of the other and try not to stumble. But Samios began to have reservations about their course, and finally stopped Cat to question her judgment.

"I think you're turned around," Samios said to Cat. "We should be going that way." Samios pointed off to the left.

Cat covered the earpiece and pointed in the direction she was heading.

"How do you know?"

She mouthed "I *know*" with enough conviction that it did not invite question.

"Fine. Excuse *me*," Samios said, admitting he was out of his element.

Twenty paces later they heard a rustling of leaves close by, something moving fast head-on right at them. They froze. Suddenly a doe stormed over a dead trunk with branches upturned like ribs on a dinosaur and skated abruptly to a stop five yards short of Cat, snorting once. Then a second time. A four-point buck drew up behind her, stopping short of the trunk, a shiny red fleshy stake dangling from the white fur beneath his hind quarters. He made no noise as he halted, eyed the situation and cautiously withdrew, melting back into the brush, and was gone. After a long second, the doe snorted a third time and then ran off in a different direction from the buck.

Samios quietly moaned and dropped to his knees clutching his chest, his face pale and contorted. He gasped for air.

Next to him, Sterner stumbled and fell with him to the ground. "Fuck!"

Cat turned, took one look at Samios and gasped.

"I think--I'm having--a heart attack," Samios managed to whisper rolling onto his back.

Sterner forgot about his own pain and quickly unbuttoned the top of Samios' shirt to help him breathe easier. "Take it easy. You're hyperventilating. Calm down. Slow, deep breaths. Look at me," Sterner said and demonstrated slow, deep breathing. Samios mimicked him. "Your body resents your brain getting lied to. Relax. Keep breathing."

"Oh, damn-it-Jesus-fuck, " Samios said cringing from the chest pain. But he did as he was told and slowly calmed, though the color would not return to his ashen face.

"What do we do now?" Cat said kneeling beside them.

Sterner looked around. "I suppose we could hide in the brush, cover ourselves with leaves and let you take the cell to the top of the mountain, but that wouldn't get *us* out of here any quicker. And I don't feel like freezing to death."

"Let me rest a minute. I'll be fine," Samios said.

Cat said, "It's not going to take them long to figure out if we didn't go downhill we're heading up."

"Buy me time," Samios said.

"With what?" Sterner said.

Samios thought a minute. "Derek's pickup--he was bringing ether or acetone or something to cook up the meth with. It's gotta be in his truck bed under the canvas tarp. It'll be flammable as shit, whatever it is," Samios said and pulled out a pack of Marlboro Lights from his jacket pocket. It had a Zippo lighter with a pirate flag wedged under the plastic wrap. He tossed it to Cat. "Use the cigs for fuses or just toss the whole fuckin' lighter in. Come to think of it, nothing gets the attention of the authorities around here like a little wild fire. There's a tower in the state forest eight or ten miles north of here. They won't care where the state line is."

"She'll never be able to get close enough if they're guarding their vehicles," Sterner said.

"I only have to get close enough to use the bow," Cat said. "Remember, moss grows on the north side of the tree. I'll catch up to you."

Sterner looked at her with trepidation, but knew they were low on options.

Cat could read his mind and grabbed the back of his head to draw his mouth up to hers in a fast, sloppy kiss, then abruptly broke off and ran into the woods behind them before he could object.

Sterner was as transparent to Samios as to Cat. "Don't worry," he said. "If she was my woman, I'd have reservations, too. But I think you underestimate her."

———————

12.

HELLCAT

"Chumley, where are you, Chumley?" the voice said.

"Check," Cat said in a low voice.

"Chumley, what's your location, man," the voice said. *"Everybody's down to the road but you."*

Cat hesitated. "Lost," she said jogging through the woods.

"Lost!? How can you be lost? All you had to do was walk downhill, buddy?"

"That ain't Chumley," somebody else said.

"Sounds like a chick," another said.

A few seconds later another voice came on. *"Say it ain't so! I do believe we have Cat True on the line, gentlemen. Meow, meow, pussycat!"*

Cat stopped dead. She had not recognized him before but only realized now who it was, a voice she had not heard in twenty years. It sent chills up and down her spine. The sudden storm surge of memories took her breath away, stiffened her muscles and twisted her stomach. It was all racing back now, that night that stopped time, that night she could never remember. Memories so terrible she had buried them deep in her subconscious, like buried bones in an unmarked grave never to be exhumed. Until now.

———————

As she had done the night before, Cat found the backdoor to the Morrison home unlocked. She entered silently and paused, waiting for her eyes to adjust to the darkness. Adrenaline pumped hot blood through her hardened heart and she had trouble catching her breath.

She told herself she had no choice, really. It was as if she'd been programmed to do this and nothing could prevent it from happening. She was but an instrument of Providence as she understood what Providence was, bringing retribution where retribution was called for upon the individual who had taken innocence forever from her, and how many untold others? Justice would be served.

It would end tonight. It would end *now!*

She waited several minutes. Listening. The father was not in the den. He was likely upstairs. The stairs to the basement were as creaky as she remembered, having cased the house the night before. She kept her feet spread to the outside edges of the steps and used the handrails to take her weight. It was dark down there but for the light switch at the bottom of the stairs and the nightlight in the wall outlet providing just enough glow for her to eventually navigate. It still smelled of sweat, though it was not as hot as it had been the previous night. As before, Billy snoozed away softly in the far corner in his single cot. She checked her hypodermic and set down her tools beside him.

He was sleeping on his side in his briefs, one arm under a pillow, the other under his ribs. He did not fully awaken when she pulled the sheet and blanket ever so slowly away and jabbed the needle into his buttocks, plunging the ketamine through the underpants. When he reacted as if stung by an insect with a wave of his hand she countered his arm with her own. As she had rehearsed it in her mind, she watched herself climb on top of him to subdue him until the drug could take effect. He struggled at first, but the adrenaline pumping through his system was already taking the ketamine to his brain, and in under a minute he was paralyzed and helpless. He called out but the duct tape zipped off the roll and around his head three times before he was even awake enough to understand what was happening. By then, he was hers, hog-tied and rolled onto his back, fully prepped for the procedure.

Cat was surprised she could do these things she had never done before and watched herself as if outside of herself, both audience and participant. It was not real to her but a surreal pornographic horror film rehearsed and played out in her mind so often the actual event seemed a tedious exercise of repetition.

"You took something very precious from me I can never get back," she explained, and then showed him the razor's edge of her hunting knife to his bulging eyes. "So I'm taking something from you you'll never get back." His eyes widened even more.

Of course he tried to struggle, thrusting his pelvis repeatedly to eject her, but just as they had done to her, her weight trapped him. By then the paralyzing drug did its work, and it was safe to turn on the nearby lamplight.

She isolated a testicle, pulled up the skin and sliced into the scrotum with the hunting knife. The genital skin was supple, loose and soft, like tanned deer skin, not like a pig at all. She slit through the second layer, a thin, white protective membrane and squeezed. Out popped the testicle. The blade severed the fleshy tube and tissue in a single swipe. She sprayed the wound with disinfectant and dressed it in gauze and tape. It took less than a minute. There was very little blood. He was helpless to stop her.

"I'll kill you," he had struggled to pronounce over and over, barely audible through the duct tape gag and haze of the drug. But it was not hard to understand him.

When she was done, she leaned down close to his face and said, "If you ever hurt anyone, and I mean *ever* again, I'm coming back for the other one." He wept. She collected her things and was gone, a thief in the night.

"I hear you been a bad boy, Billy Three," she now said.

"Oh, you have no idea, honey! And you know what? I'm just gettin' warmed up! You ARE the girl of my wet dreams!"

Cat flushed with rage, an eruption of raw emotions overtaking all reason. Why hadn't she just slit his throat when she had the chance? Staring off into the past, she instinctively flicked the snap on the sheath of her Ka-Bar at her belt, drew the knife and expertly flipped it over the back of her hand, blade down to blade up and back again. The handle moved easily through her fingers and across the back of her hand like an extension of her arm. She drew it close to her face to admire the glint on its honed edge. As her eyes narrowed to slits, she said quietly through clinched teeth, "I've come for the other one, Billy Boy."

"Oh, it's waitin' for ya, honey. I'm holding it as we speak. Kiwi, Jackson, Flake, why don't you boys get back up here. We need face-time to re-strategize, since our communications have obviously been compromised. Odds are your buddy Chumley has joined our comrade Derek in the Great Biker Beyond. Am I right about that, pussycat?"

"Roger that," Kiwi said.

"Roger Dodger."

"Fuckin' cunt," somebody else said. *"Honey, you ain't never been fucked till you been gangbanged by Berzerkers."*

"Amen to that," another one said.

"Leave a couple guys to guard her truck, Kiwi," Billy said, *"just in case they're foolish enough to turn up down there. Including Buster. Better to keep him away from his brother's body."*

"Roger that."

"What I did to your little gray cat is nothing compared to what I'm going to do to you, pussycat. After I cut off your pretty little head, I'm gonna drop it into my fish tank down in Florida and watch my pet piranha eat your face off. Hell, I'll invite over the whole neighborhood for that show! Those Cubans all miss their cockfights, you know? I may even charge admission. Then when they get done feasting their way through your eyeballs into your sweetbreads, I'm gonna fish you out, saw off the top of your skull, put a hinge on it and fashion my very own customized urinal. And first thing every morning for the rest of my life I'm going to flip up your scalp and piss into your brain pan. Just imagine my golden showers swirling around inside that empty, little head of yours, pussycat."

Silence. Even the bikers were speechless.

"It feels better when you squirm," she said and turned off the headset, stuffing it into her pocket.

———————

Cat maneuvered tree to tree approaching the cottage from the north on the downhill slope. She found a good vantage point fifty yards above and could make out the canvas tarp in the bed of the pick-up. She could see Beasey guarding the pick-up and the Esplanade with his Uzi. Before long the Cherokee returned from the access road with seven men. She watched Beasey and another man with a shaved head go inside the house. Others milled around outside. It wouldn't be long before they started out again, probably in her direction this time. She wasted no time.

She pulled off her buckskin quiver and laid out her remaining arrows on the ground. She had four lead practice tips left. She unzipped her vest, pulled up her sweat shirt and cut into her tee-shirt with the Ka-Bar. She tore off the bottom two inches all the way around her waist, making a strip. She punctured an end of the fabric ribbon with a practice tip and wrapped the remainder around the front of the shaft. Splitting the end with her teeth she tied a tight knot holding the fabric in place. She then pulled out the Zippo, unscrewed the bottom with her fingernail and shook out trickles of lighter fluid, dowsing the fabric. She snapped the nock of the arrow onto her bowstring, took a deep breath, laid the front of the shaft on the rest and then lit up the fabric with the lighter.

With the rag burning on the end of the arrow by the handgrip, there wasn't much time before she had to release. The flame singed the flesh of the knuckles of her left hand and made the arrow impossible to aim with any precision. An ordinary bowman would have had difficulty with the shot. Not Cat. She had instinctively calculated distance, angle and trajectory, factored in the negligible wind speed and direction, air friction, excess weight and added resistance. Fortunately, the target was large. The arrow flew the distance in less than half a second, the flame nearly extinguished by the swift airflow in its speedy trajectory. It struck squarely into the bed of the Sierra, puncturing the canvas tarp where the flame rekindled.

She could do nothing now but grab her remaining arrows and retreat into the woods, hoping for the best. If they noticed the arrow and followed the direction the plastic feather guides pointed, they could easily locate her position and rush her with their guns blazing. But it would have been an uphill charge, and none of them were in any kind of physical condition for the task.

As it turned out, nobody noticed as the flame grew and spread across the canvas tarp. Soon it was a regular little campfire. And as the air inside a glass container of acetone directly beneath it combusted in a pop, rupturing its sides, its contents spilled into the shallow troughs of the truck bed, combusting quickly and cooking the remaining containers.

"Hey," somebody shouted, seeing the smoke and calling others to attention. But before he could utter another sound, smashing glass gave way to a loud *Whoosh!* Container after container shattered in a chain reaction. Before any of them had a chance to react, the bed of the Sierra ignited into a twenty-foot napalm inferno. Someone ran for a fire extinguisher, but before they could retrieve it, the intense heat ignited the gas tank of the pickup, causing the body of the truck to explode, spewing and splattering accelerant in every direction. Small fires dotted the landscape, not only knocking many of the Berzerkers off their feet, but setting them on fire as well.

They screamed curses, patting out the flames on their clothing, dancing in circles, throwing off their jackets or rolling on the ground. The Berzerker with the fire extinguisher now blasted jets of white chemical retardants over two of his brethren before switching his attention to the hood of the Cherokee and the roof of the Esplanade. The Sierra was a lost cause. A white pine tree twenty feet away from the truck at the edge of the woods lit up like a Christmas tree and was burning out of control from the bottom branches to the very top. But there was no wind, and it didn't look like the fire would spread. The house was miraculously untouched.

Samios and Sterner were trying to get to their feet when they heard the truck explosion. Sterner looked back down the hollow but could see nothing through the skeletal tree trunks and branches. He could only make out the distant sound of men shouting and cursing unintelligibly.

"Our cue to get moving," Samios said. He was still pale and messaging his chest. Sterner nodded and the two struggled to their feet, limping away in a synchronous rhythm, each crutching the other.

Billy, Kiwi and Beasey stuck their heads out of the front door to survey the commotion and the view up the mountain. "She's close," Billy said. "Real close. Fan out and fuckin' run her the fuck down. Nobody shoots until you see something then *everybody charges the sound of the gunfire! Do I make myself clear? Ten grand to the motherfucker who disables the bitch! But I want her alive!*"

"Oh, fuck that," Kiwi said.

"Alive," Billy repeated. *"I want my fuckin' money!"*

Beasey sniffed, drew the Uzi, cocked back the bolt and stormed up the hill. The others followed, fanning out on both sides in a wedge formation, their guns drawn safeties off, Kiwi cocking Derek's .45.

Cat easily out-flanked them. She ran hard and fast and quiet, away and around and down to the west side of the house where she knew the terrain best.

She'd studied the house all morning from four directions and had played out various attack scenarios in her head. She knew, for instance, the generator was an aging fifty-five hundred watter, chocked on cement blocks along the west wall. This was where she found her position in the weeds and shot Derek Pensinger. The generator provided a low humming cover noise as it chugged away under an open shed roof nailed haphazardly to the wall. Its roughshod roof was a rotting four-by-eight-foot sheet of unpainted plywood, barely repelling the elements, and supported by two-by-four plank pillars on flagstone pedestals. Not only did the motor conceal her own noise, but it gave her an idea about taking out whoever tried to service it.

She'd considered puncturing the gas tank with a practice arrow to start a fire or, at the very least, drain the tank prematurely before its next scheduled refueling. The plan seemed more viable now. If she was lucky, she might even be able to draw Billy out of the house and cut the head off the snake.

There was no one in sight when she crawled her way through the overgrown grass forty yards from the generator. Now she repeated the steps she'd taken when she started the fire in the truck, laying out her arrows, cutting off a piece of fabric from her tee, dowsing the strip in lighter fluid, then lighting it up. She released on the exposed gas tank, saw it stick and rekindle, then wasted no time gathering her arrows. But when she stood a deafening gunshot rang out behind her.

She turned and found a pot-bellied Berzerker named Luther approaching with a smoking pistol pointed at the sky. He now drew down on her, sticking out his lizard tongue to lick his smirking fat lips.

"Don't fuckin' move, bitch!" he said. Then, "Drop the bow."

She did as she was told, slowly laying down her bow and arrows at her feet.

And then he made his fatal mistake. Gloating over his prize, he turned with pride toward the sound of his buddies charging downhill through the dry leaves above the house. When he looked back at Cat, her right arm was extended towards him and her Ka-Bar was embedded in his chest. The sharp, burning pain brought him to his knees. His expression morphed from smirking pride to surprise to shock to horror. The gun in his hand fell to the ground and he collapsed after it onto his side. As he lay dying, trying to shout and coughing blood instead, his bladder emptied. Death was an ugly thing to watch. Cat decided she had seen enough. She grabbed her bow and remaining arrows and fled downhill into the back garden, where she disappeared into the thicket at the edge of the woods where Sterner and Samios had escaped. Safely out of sight, she briefly checked over her shoulder, and then cut east, crossing through the grove of white pines by the access road. She circled wide counter-clockwise toward the north. In the distance, she could hear the generator sputter, then cough and choke amid angry shouts and curses on the far side of the hollow. The sudden unexpected quiet of nature without machines grinding away was a welcome change. But the cocaine- and testosterone-fueled bikers on a rampage put her in mind of a hornet's nest set ablaze and she was not finished running.

She looked up at the sky. It was getting dark. Night was coming.

———

She stopped long enough to switch on the earpiece and put it back on her ear.

"The house is on fire and she just stabbed Luther!"

"Fuck!"

"My power's down," Billy said. "I've lost electric."

"Where is she? Son of a bitch! Where'd she go?"

"Gotta be downhill."

"Fire extinguisher to the west side of the house now!" Billy said.

"I'm on it."

"We're below the garden but she's nowhere in sight."

"I hope Luther at least winged the bitch before she nailed him."

"She fuckin' shot the generator with an arrow," Billy said. "How the fuck--!"

"I don't see any blood besides Luther's. Shit, I don't think he's gonna make it, man. I don't know what to do. Should I pull the knife out or leave it in? Shit, man. What the fuck do I do?"

"I swear to God, I'm gonna eat her liver by sun-up," Billy said. "Did you hear me, pussycat? Are you still monitoring our traffic? I will never rest before you are mine, mine, mine. So help me, I will hunt you down if it's the last thing I ever do."

"Luther's gone, man. That bitch fuckin' killed Luther. I can't believe it!"

"Three for three. She's so goin' down."

"Derek, Chumley and now Luther! Lady, I'm gonna stick my shotgun up your twat and blow your fuckin' head right off."

"We're gonna carve you up but good, sweet lips. We'll do it with your own fuckin' knife. I'm personally gonna cut off your titties and mount 'em on my handlebars, and then stick your twat around my tailpipe."

"Gonna have us a Hellcat gang bang, boys!"

"Baby, we're gonna fill you so full of cum your nose is gonna run."

"I got a bogie on the bionic ear moving fast east of the house. East and heading north up the mountain, do you copy?"

They knew her position.

"Copy that," Billy said. "Kiwi, Beasey, she's east of the house doing an end around, heading your way. Heads up."

"Kiwi here. Big ten-four."

A burst of automatic weapons fire rang out in the woods ahead of her. She stopped abruptly and listened.

"Got 'em," Beasey said. *"Repeat. Targets are down."*

Sterner and Samios had just crossed a steep gully when Beasenbach fired a burst at them from sixty yards below and behind them. Both went down but only Sterner moved, crawling as fast as he could to distance himself from the Uzi. Samios had less luck. He was hit twice in the back, once in the buttocks and grazed in the head and calf, a round in his chest puncturing a lung. He was coughing crimson blood and fading into unconsciousness, but could still hear what was going on around him. He knew Sterner was trying to crawl away, but of more concern were the gunman's approaching footsteps through the brittle leaves in their wake.

Beasey's boots crunched rhythmically as he approached almost casually up to the crest of the gully on the opposite bank, then descended in a diagonal heading directly towards them, jumping across the dry stream bed and climbing the bank to where Samios lay bleeding. The DEA agent managed only to turn over onto his back. He still had the .38 in his belt but his right hand was useless beneath him and as he struggled to transfer the shotgun to his left hand it proved finally too heavy to aim.

"Jesus loves me, this I know," Beasey sang, *"for the Bible tells me so. He is weak but I am strong. Up in heaven, I belong. Yes, Jesus loves me. Yes, Jesus hugs me. Yes, Jesus slugs me. The Bible forecasts snow."*

Samios waved the muzzle of the sawed-off at Beasey's ankles as the big man walked up toe-to-toe and stood over him. But Samios could get the aim no higher than his assailant's knees before its weight became too great for his waning strength to bear. He lacked even the strength to pull the trigger. He tried to speak but only spit blood.

"Don't get up on my account," Beasey said to him. "Tell you what, I'm going to let you count to one hundred, asshole. And then--oh, why wait?" At pointblank range Beasey emptied his clip into the DEA agent, starting at his knees and spraying him with lead up to his face, which caved under fire into a large hole where his nose and sinus cavity had been, rendering him unrecognizable. Samios convulsed only as long as the SMG fired. When the clip was finished, so was Samios. Smoke and blood oozed out of his riddled clothing and decimated head. His mutilated body offered nothing but a final gurgled sigh.

Cat heard the second burst of submachine gun fire and paused to adjust course.

"Everybody converge on the gunfire," Billy was saying.

"We just ran back downhill to the house, Bill," Lenny said. *"I ain't built for this shit. Where the fuck is Beasey, anyway?"*

"Where are you, Beasey?" Kiwi said. *"These hollows are playing tricks on me. I can't figure out if you're below me or above me."*

"Don't sweat it, fellas," Beasey said. *"Let's just say, you owe me a brewski. I just did your narc for ya."*

"Hot damn. Nice work."

"Good riddance, Patches, you Judas Fuck!"

"What about the other one?"

"He's next."

She took off sprinting, ducking branches and skipping over rocks and logs, stepping on ant hills, damp leaves and moss mounds wherever she could to keep her approach as stealthy as possible. She had two practice tips left and one was snapped onto the nock of the bowstring. As she ran, she reached into the back pocket of her vest for the counterweight and screwed it on the front of her bow, to steady her aim for better long distance shooting.

She came to a bank overlooking a dry stream bed and spotted a dark green blob in the distance. It was the body of Artie Samios fifty yards ahead. Only his perforated green leather jacket made him in any way identifiable on the brown forest floor. Even from this distance, she could see his face was destroyed. Thirty yards beyond Samios, almost out of range, she spotted Beasenbach, staring into a bed of ferns and snapping on a fresh ammo clip.

"There you are, little buddy," Beasey said. "You were hiding from Daddy."

Unarmed, Sterner had crawled as quickly as his broken limbs would allow but now could move only snaillike along the ground, half his body useless, the other pushed to the physical limit. He was winded and spent from his struggle up the mountain and now the adrenal surge was waning as he tried to distance himself from Samios. He was in such paralyzing exhaustion he regretted not taking the pills Samios offered them. The best he could manage was to hide in a bed of ankle-high ferns. But it was not good enough. Samios was dead and he was next.

As Beasenbach drew back the bolt on the Uzi Sterner rolled onto his back to face his fate head-on. Panting hard, he now stared down the big man one last time. Beasey grinned.

"I bet they called you "Little Joey" on the playground. *Little Joey!*"

The arrow missed Beasey's head by inches and struck the ground next to Sterner's feet. The big man whirled instantly and following the arrow's trajectory fired blindly into the forest in a horizontal spray back and forth, up and down, emptying his clip.

Cat knew she'd miss him when she released. It was an eighty-yard shot through dense woods, an impossible distance with a bow. It was a miracle the arrow even cleared the branches and limbs as it arced the gap between them. But the net result had given Sterner a brief reprieve. She hit the ground as soon as Beasenbach started firing and scrambled behind a fat oak trunk where two rounds blasted off bark chips.

Beasey spotted her movement and sprinted in an all-out assault, vaulting Samios' body, sliding down one embankment and charging up the other. As he did he expertly dumped his spent clip and snapped in a replacement, drawing back the bolt, ready to rock and roll.

"Beasey, report. What's going on?" Billy said.

"Bitch just missed me with an arrow," Beasey said, "but I feel ten grand richer already. I can see her moving behind a tree."

"I want her alive," Billy said.

"Fuck you, Topper," Beasey said.

"I want my money!"

Cat drew her last practice arrow but saw Beasey aim again and ducked back behind the tree trunk just in time. A dozen chips blew off the oak trunk as Beasey fired a short burst without slowing his full frontal attack.

Suddenly both barrels exploded from a shotgun behind him and Beasey felt a horizontal rain of low velocity ball bearings bouce off his clothes. He turned and saw Sterner on top of Samios now tossing aside the smoking sawed-off and going for the .38 from the dead agent's belt. Beasey raised his Uzi and took aim closing his left eye.

The lead-tipped practice arrow penetrated the scalp at the occipital bone in the back of his head and had just enough momentum to pop through the big man's right eyeball. Beasey jerked forward and blinked. He was confused, unsure why he was suddenly blinded. He tried aiming with his left eye but found it awkward and unnatural. He could feel an irritating itch in the back of his head but couldn't reach to scratch it. His over-developed biceps and deltoid muscles prevented his thick hands from reaching around that far. He came nowhere near touching the shank of the arrow to extract it. He swung around in circles and began a strange dance, hopping and grunting like--well--like a gorilla.

Sterner took careful aim with both hands and fired the snubnose until it was empty. The short-barreled .38 was a lousy gun for long range shooting but when the target was as big as Beasey at forty yards and the hand that wielded it was as determined as Sterner's it had little problem hitting its mark. Beasey took four of the five rounds in the chest, crumpled to his knees and collapsed forward like a felled tree. He laid there motionless face down and quietly died.

"Beasey, do you copy? Report, soldier! Beasey, do you copy?" Billy said. *"Beasey, do you copy?"* Billy's voice cracked with emotion. *"Beasey, do you copy me, man? Beasey--? Beas--I need a copy, partner."*

Silence. They had heard the shotgun blasts and the .38 crackles and nothing after that. And knew.

"They've gotta be headed for Burnside Summit Road," Kiwi said. *"I'm moving up that way now."*

"Bill, man, I'm real sorry about your bud," Lenny said. *"We're gonna drive around to Burnside Summit Road, too. Shouldn't take more than fifteen minutes, tops."*

"It's gettin' dark out here, man," somebody said. *"We're coming back to my truck for flashlights."*

"I can do you better than that," somebody else said. *"I got night vision on my thirty-aught-six a half-hour away."*

"Now you're talking," Billy said in an unsteady voice. *"Meet Kiwi on Burnside Summit Road. Pick up whoever's still down along the road and take them with you. But send Buster back up here to me."*

Cat stepped on Beasenbach's neck and extracted her arrow from the dead man's head. She took the fully loaded Uzi and found two more clips of ammo stuffed into his pockets, and then retrieved her other arrow from the bed of ferns. Sterner salvaged the cell phone from Samios' pocket, which managed to survive its owner.

"They're moving to head us off on Burnside Summit Road," Cat told Sterner, after removing her earpiece and switching it off.

"Then we have no time to waste. All I need is a cell signal," he said. "Just get me high enough on the mountain for one bar of signal and we'll be okay."

———————

Cat crutched Sterner with difficulty through the rugged terrain uphill in the fading twilight until they came upon a steep, craggy granite cliff face thirty feet straight up that made passage impossible. Sterner tried the cell without success. When they turned to look for a way around they started at the deafening sound of a gunshot. Kiwi had fired into the air behind them and then drew a bead on Cat with Derek's forty-five. Sterner's heart sank.

"This way," Kiwi said waving his gun to his left. "Drop the guns and the bow and toss me the cell." And into his wire mouthpiece he said, "Yeah, I got 'em. We're a hundred and fifty yards below the road. We're comin' in."

Sterner tossed the cell phone at him. He caught it, dropped it, then stomped it under his boot against a rock. Sterner steered Cat where they were told. Kiwi followed five yards behind. He retrieved the Uzi and swung the bow and snubnose off into the woods.

"I'd just as soon do you both right here for what you did to Derek and Luther, so please tempt me," Kiwi said. "But then Billy would miss his money and my boys would miss their fun. And we can't have that, can we?" Cat looked at him over her shoulder. He sneered at her.

Just then they all heard the rotary blades of a fast approaching chopper and simultaneously turned to look up. In no time a white spotlight blinded them as it rounded the cliff face behind them and came to a stationary hover thirty yards above the trees at a forty-five degree angle. A laser targeting spot appeared on the ground at Kiwi's feet and quickly found his forehead. As a former passenger Sterner recognized its outlines immediately. The pilot was Jimmy Huang. A SWAT sniper had the barrel of his M107 .50 caliber rifle trained on Kiwi. A familiar voice boomed over a loudspeaker from a third passenger.

"Pennsylvania State Police. Drop your weapons, or you'll be shot." It was Flanigan.

———————

After the disappearance of one of their own, the Pennsylvania State Police shifted into high gear, Taylor dispatching two additional detectives, the Harrisburg Crime Scene Unit and the regional tactical SWAT team commanded by one Gary Decker, who was also the best sniper they had on the payroll. The Doolittle County State Police Barracks became a command post, the briefing room crowded with anxious state lawmen manning telephones to sift through tips and intelligence, all under the direction of primary case detective Stuart Flanigan.

The forensics team went over Sterner's motel room for clues to his disappearance. They found his wallet, his computer, his clothes, his keys but little else. Cat's fingerprints were found on the doorknobs of the room and bathroom. The two detectives sent to help Flanigan insisted her name be added to the All Points Bulletin already issued on Beasenbach and Morrison, neither of whose prints were found at the scene.

Word leaked to the press Monday around noon that a PSP investigator had disappeared and apparently been kidnapped the night before outside of Samaritan. CNN picked it up and it went to other national cable newscasts quickly, Taylor using the five o'clock newscast Monday to brief the public.

As they watched Taylor field questions on television in the briefing room late that afternoon, a report came in from a fire tower in the Mary Jenison State Forest in Burnside County that smoke had been spotted along the Mason Dixon Line. Since the fire had dissipated after half an hour, the forester on duty concluded that it was probably a trash burn across the state line in Maryland. It was dismissed as irrelevant.

Then came a report to the Burnside County Sheriff's Department in Newtonville that a muzzle-loading hunter in the Mary Jenison State Forest had heard automatic weapons fire somewhere southwest of Burnside Summit Road. Sheriff Lawrence Bucher immediately notified Game Warden Irv Groener and the Doolittle County State Police Barracks, where his call was routed to Detective Stuart Flanigan. Flanigan informed Captain Nathan Hand who dispatched four cruisers to Burnside Summit Road and notified Maryland State Police. Trusting little more than his gut, Flanigan raced to the Samaritan Airport with Decker and his sniper's rifle. At dusk he met Jimmy Huang, who'd been waiting on standby. It was a tight fit since the cockpit was built for two, but none of the three men weighed more than a hundred fifty pounds. The chopper took off within minutes.

Ten minutes out they cleared Burnside Summit and reported several suspicious vehicles parked along the side of the road west and downhill of the crest. Cruisers arrived two minutes later and began rounding up suspects, all of whom were taken into custody and initially charged with hunting without a license and illegal weapons possession, pending more serious charges. Using the Infrared Thermal Imaging System, Flanigan was able to relay the exact GPS coordinates of all the suspects in the woods southwest of Burnside Summit Road, starting with three individuals on an uphill approach, two walking arm-in-arm as if one was injured, the third following with a hot weapon signature that showed it had been recently fired. More cruisers and troopers eventually arrived and descended to take Kiwi into custody. Sterner and Cat were rushed to Samaritan Hospital by EMS.

13.

SIX DAYS BEFORE OPENING DAY

Sterner woke up in an antiseptic room lit by a bedside table lamp. He was wearing nothing but a pale green gown. He had no idea what time it was, but it was dark outside the window. Whatever sedative he was given had long since worn off. His broken left leg was elevated and in traction, covered with a plaster of Paris cast from the bottom of his ankle to the top of his thigh. It ached like hell. They'd given him Tylenol for the soreness, but it was barely adequate. He wondered if they had something better that would lie to his brain.

The doctor told him he would be out of commission for a good six months, physical therapy following the healing process, and additional surgeries could not be ruled out. He was shown the X-rays and the particulars of his injuries were explained to him, technical chatter about patellar subluxations and anterior knee pain. The long and short of it was that the cartilage was all messed up. He'd walk with a limp for maybe a year, and could expect an early arthritic or tendonitis condition in his senior years. As for work, he was on the disabled list until further notice.

His broken left arm was dressed the same as his leg--elevated and covered over with a massive cast from wrist to shoulder. The good news was X-rays had shown the arm fracture to be clean. It was expected to heal normally within six weeks. But now it was no less sore than the leg, the muscle throbbing from the bludgeoning. He felt the splint over his broken nose bone taped to his cheeks. It would forever alter his face, giving him the same fighter's nose that Beasenbach had. Nothing short of plastic surgery would change that, but Sterner wasn't that vain. Who knows? It might even improve his looks.

He wondered how he'd look to the jury in Pittsburgh, entering the courtroom to testify from a wheelchair. Let the defense attorneys just try to impugn the character of a cop who'd been kidnapped and tortured and chased through the woods by introducing an alleged affair with a witness.

Cat.

Where was she? He scanned the room.

He leaned forward a few inches and could see his reflection in the window glass. On top of everything else, he had two black eyes. Opposite the window, Flanigan sat asleep in a chair, feet propped on Sterner's bed, his Oxfords almost in Sterner's ribs. Sterner smiled. But when Flanigan started sawing wood, Sterner shoved the feet off the bed with his good arm, which roused his ex-partner.

"Don't you have a motel room to go to?" Sterner said.

"Just closed my eyes a minute," he said and rubbed his face.

"With snoring like that, how's a guy supposed to heal around here?"

"Sorry, pal."

"Where's Cat?"

"Down the hall. They're keeping her overnight for observation," Flanigan said and turned on a table lamp. "Dehydration, mostly."

"Tell me they collared all the Berzerkers?"

"They collared all the Berzerkers."

"Are you sure? They got em all?"

Flanigan chuckled. "Oh, yeah. Believe you me, hell hath no fury like the DEA with a dead undercover. Samios already gave his people all the evidence they needed to take down the network. The location of the meth lab was just the last piece of the puzzle. They busted about fifty perps this morning across five states. It's all over the news. That and your dramatic rescue. Taylor's in high gear, all full of himself, doing interviews all over the media. You're the big hero."

"I'm lucky to be alive. What about Morrison?"

"MIA. But not for long. Everybody's looking for him--FBI, DEA, PSP, of course, but also Maryland, Virginia, West Virginia--even Florida-- State Police. He so much as surfaces for a breath of fresh air, he'll be in handcuffs faster than you can whistle Dixie."

"Guy's a psycho. As long as he's out there, Cat's in danger."

"Trooper's just outside her room," Flanigan said, and nodded his head at the door. "Yours, too. But if it makes you feel any better...." He produced a brown paper bag and set it on Sterner's lap. With his good hand, Sterner opened it and pulled out a holstered 9mm Glock semi-automatic and a box of shells. "You should never leave a firearm in your glove compartment. Somebody might break in and steal it."

"Looks like somebody did," Sterner said. "Thanks." He put it back in the paper bag and stuffed it into the drawer of his bedside table.

Flanigan dug into his pocket. "Your cell, too, in case you want to call any plastic surgeons." He handed it over.

Sterner chuckled.

"Miss True went over her statement again today, which, let me tell you, is one for the books."

"Ms."

"Huh?"

"Ms. True to you, pal."

"If you say so. Jimenez and Richardson are waiting outside to go over yours again, if you're up to it."

"Sure, bring 'em on. Though if you wouldn't mind, crack the window for me first, huh? I'm a little claustrophobic in here."

"You should see the other rooms. You got the Ritz."

Jimenez and Richardson were colleagues of Flanigan and Sterner. They'd been assigned the investigation of Sterner's kidnapping. Jimenez was a tall, skinny Latino wunderkind in his thirties who'd made his bones working Philly gangs undercover. Richardson was a short, overweight white guy in his late forties who'd come up through the ranks gradually and quietly. Despite their obvious differences, they had very similar personalities, and today, matching ties. Sterner went over the abduction, torture and escape as he had the night before, but was now more lucid and forthcoming with details. Flanigan sat in. He'd already briefed Jimenez and Richardson on their case for background.

"Beasenbach and Morrison thought Cat and I were the blackmailers," Sterner said, "and that we'd collected a ransom that rightfully belonged to them because they had an arrangement with the Mark who had cancelled their contract."

"They didn't kidnap you because you were heading the investigation looking for *them?!*" Jimenez said.

"Nope. They said Whipple claimed Cat was his partner, but they couldn't figure out the link between them until they followed her to my motel room Sunday night and put two and two together."

"Jesus H. Christ, these guys really *were* morons!" Flanigan said.

"They weren't rocket scientists, that's for sure," Sterner said. "I used everything I knew about Beasenbach against him and got under his skin pretty good. Not that it kept the bastard from busting me up. They thought I'd been tipped off by someone named Ray, whoever that is. Anyway, because of his history with Cat, I think Morrison really just wanted to *believe* she was involved. So Whipple's word was good enough for him."

Flanigan pursed his lips and traded looks with Jimenez and Richardson.

"You know that for a fact?" Richardson said.

"Cat was *never* involved. Whipple was covering for his real partners by dropping Cat's name. The press had already put her out there as a suspect, so it wasn't much of a stretch for Whipple to come up with her name or for Morrison to buy into it."

"Wait. I'm confused about something," Flanigan said. "Why would the Mark cancel the contract?"

"I'm not sure. They grabbed Whipple to find out who he and Ghoul Two were, and then John Doe turns up, right? The first ransom was payment to Morrison and Beasenbach. I guess the Mark agreed to release Whipple and give Ghoul Two the second ransom because he knew he was vulnerable. All Ghoul Two had to do was to drop a dime and ID either of the Does or the location of the graves. That must've scared the Mark into paying. But Morrison and Beasenbach didn't want to release Whipple, either because he could identify them or because they already made up their minds they were going to kill him anyway. Or both."

"I can see that," Flanigan said. "The Mark tells them to get lost but they don't like the idea."

"They smell a ransom payment nobody's going to report to the police if they intercept it. Only Ghoul Two outsmarts them."

Flanigan referred to his notes. "A Samaritan College security guard identified Morrison as arguing with an elderly man at the college pool Saturday night, interrupting a water ballet performance, whatever in hell that is. Not much of a description of the elderly man, but before he got away he accused Morrison of--quote--*killing that boy*--end quote."

Sterner closed his eyes to focus on the memory. "Morrison said something to me about the college. Something about just missing me, and there being maintenance passages between the buildings that he knew nothing about. I gathered they tried to intercept the second ransom but failed, because Ghoul Two used those passages to escape with the money. There must be an access point at the pool."

Jimenez and Richardson went over Sterner's story several times, taking copious notes. Afterwards, Flanigan saw them out. When he returned Sterner said to him, "Anything new on John and Jane Doe?"

"After you got snatched, everything on the Does was put on a backburner. But once we got you back last night--safe and, more or less, sound--stuff started trickling in."

"Such as? If you don't mind my asking, since I'm no longer on the case?"

Flanigan offered him a dismissive wave and flipped open his notepad again. "Holmsburg got a hit on John Doe--without question, the fugitive George Letterer. FBI's been notified. Dooley's coming back from New York tomorrow empty-handed. Said he'd stop in to see you on his way to D.C. to spend Thanksgiving with his son, who's a lawyer for the State Department. Anyway, FBI said Letterer's wife, Gale Anne Farrara, was from Norfolk, Virginia. They're searching for her dental records. But I'd say, based on the description, odds are good she's Jane Doe."

"Thank you, Judge Helfrick."

"The Whipple autopsy showed signs of healing in his face and knee injuries prior to expiration, and morphine was evident in his vitals. They're ruling it a homicide."

"Big surprise."

"The ninhydrine test on the gray cardboard turned up nothing, but Crime Scene lifted a latent from a fast food soda cup in your dumpster trash. Only five points, but AFIS confirmed one likely candidate was the late Cecil David Beasenbach."

"May he rot in hell."

"And in the same trash evidence--equally unsurprising--the print of one William Morrison the Third--a fat, juicy eleven-pointer--on a duct tape loop. Crime Scene says no question it was once attached to the stolen license plate of the crashed van. Thank Christ for cheap duct tape glue."

"Remind me to send those Crime Scene guys a bottle of champagne."

"I were you, I'd let all the bubbles out first. It's not like they processed fast enough to do you any good."

"Fine. Flat champagne. Anything more about our Peter Bream?"

"No time."

"Five'll get you ten he has a connection to the college that allowed him access to the maintenance passages. If he is Ghoul Two, maybe Crime Scene can find trace down there to tie him."

"If he *is* Ghoul Two, he was probably pretty careful."

"He was careful when he dropped the bones in our laps. I doubt he ever expected us to look at the ransom drop."

"Good point. I'll get on that first thing tomorrow," Flanigan said, getting up. "By the way, just to give you a head's up, some of the Berzerkers are claiming they were out there trying to rescue you from Morrison, not hunt you."

"Bullshit."

"I know it and you know it, but things could get sticky down the road."

"Okay. Thanks, Stu."

"You got it, partner." He pulled out a felt-tip pen and placed it on the table next to his bed. "In case you want anybody to sign your cast."

"What about you?"

"Already did," Flanigan said, winked and exited. "Get some rest. We'll talk tomorrow."

Sterner checked his leg cast and found: *To the best detective in the force, get well soon, Stuart Flanigan.* And then between *the* and *best* he found an arrowhead pointing upwards to the word *second.*

When Flanigan crossed the visitors' room, unnoticed, he found it crowded with media people. Emily was surrounded and enjoying the spotlight, giving an impromptu interview with several reporters simultaneously. "I'm his ex-wife, actually," she was saying. "But we're still a close-knit family. I'm an attorney, so you'd better not misspell my name." She teasingly shook a finger. "Emily. Emily Harrison Sterner."

Across the room Becca was sleeping curled up on a vinyl couch sucking her thumb, Moira's lap serving as her pillow. Teddy was correcting an indifferent Moira on the subtleties between one ballet position and another, demonstrating in front of her. "*Demi-Plie. Plie. Grand Plie.*"

A geriatric nurse appeared from the corridor. "Visiting hours are now over," the nurse announced to the crowd and pointed to the clock on the wall, which read nine o'clock. There was a general groan. Emily's interviewers immediately started packing up, having lost interest in their subject. "You can come back tomorrow morning after rounds at ten thirty."

"Nurse," Emily said, rushing over, "we're Detective Sterner's family. We've driven down from Harrisburg and have been waiting for hours."

"I'm sorry. Rules are rules." She turned away, but Emily put her hand on her forearm.

"Wait. Please. You see that little girl sleeping over there?" she whispered. The nurse sighed and looked across the room at Becca's cherubic face. "That's Detective Sterner's daughter. I'm sure he'd want to see her. We have to drive home to Harrisburg tonight, and I don't think I can get off work tomorrow to bring her back to see her daddy. This is really our only chance."

"Security is tight. I'll see what I can do."

———————

The reporter on television was standing in the parking lot of the Sleep Well Motel, Sterner's burned-out room over his shoulder, now ribboned off from the general public. He was saying, "A dramatic rescue of a state police detective last evening in south central Pennsylvania. Several men dead, members of the Berzerkers motorcycle gang, as well as a DEA agent working undercover, his name withheld. Authorities say Detective Joseph Sterner is lucky to be alive today after being kidnapped Sunday night, as reported here yesterday, from this motel room behind me outside of Samaritan after it was firebombed, taken to a house across the Mason Dixon Line to Maryland, where authorities say the bikers were operating a methamphetamine lab. Dozens taken into custody across five states yesterday and this morning on weapons and drug charges throughout the I-78, -81, -70 and -20 corridors. Listen to what State Police Chief Benjamin Taylor had to say just hours ago."

They cut to a clip from a news conference, Taylor sermonizing with righteous indignation, "He was abducted, threatened, tortured, bones broken with a baseball bat, and I think it's safe to say he very narrowly averted execution by this gang of drug thugs had our officers not intervened when they did."

The reporter now said, "Also taken into protective custody, her involvement not yet known, the notorious Hellcat, Cat True, a suspect in the Jane and John Doe skeletons case the detective was investigating here since last week. Again, Detective Joseph Sterner in stable condition tonight at Samaritan Hospital until he can be moved to Hershey Medical Center. Details are still sketchy as to why this happened. Police say they are trying to sort it all out. Back to you in the studio."

It amazed Sterner how wrong it all sounded.

"How you doin', detective?" Crash Robinson said from the doorway.

Sterner nearly choked on the gulp of water he was sipping through a straw, set the cup on the table beside his bed and turned off the TV with the remote. "Crash--er--should I call you James?"

"Crash is fine out of earshot of the troopers."

"To what do I owe this pleasure? You know I'm off the case."

"Yeah, yeah. I know all that," he said, flipping his porkpie hat in his hand. "I just wanted to see…do you need anything? Magazines, books, pint of whiskey?"

"I'm good."

"Good, good," Robinson nervously chewed his lip. Something was bugging him. You didn't have to be a detective to figure that much out. "You know, when the Klan used to lynch the brothers down south, they often castrated them," Robinson said, trying to make small talk. "That's why a lot of black folk get nervous hearing all this fascist Hellcat talk. Brings back a lot of bad memories."

Sterner cocked his head.

Robinson looked over his shoulder, pulled up a chair and sat himself in it. "Look, I'm an asshole. You can tell me I'm an asshole to my face, I'll agree with you. I won't take it personally and we'll forget this conversation ever took place."

"I'm listening."

"Okay. Guy I know from my old days on the west coast wants to pay me to use my credentials to smuggle him in to see you. We don't have to debate how unethical that is. He wants to buy the exclusive rights to your story to make a movie."

Sterner rolled his eyes.

"I know, I know. But I figured you had a right to hear his proposal. You don't have to make up your mind right away. He just wanted to plant the seed to let you think about it. He wants you to know he's not insensitive to the abruptness of his offer so soon after your trauma. His words."

Sterner shook his head.

"He's willing to pay you three hundred thousand dollars."

Sterner stopped shaking his head and gave Crash his full attention.

"My advice is to play hard ball and let him double it. He's pretty enthusiastic about the project. At the same time, these guys have a short attention span. Wait too long, they lose interest. Talk to too many journalists, they lose interest. Exclusivity means he wants to control who you talk to. Outside of law enforcement, that is. And if somebody in law enforcement who talks to you talks to a journalist, they lose interest, too. Do you have an agent, yet?"

"Are you kidding?"

"Get one. He says he's already got the green light from the studio."

"This just happened yesterday."

"These guys like to strike while the iron's hot. Gives em bragging rights with their poker buddies. He claims Tom Cruise wants to play you."

Sterner chuckled. "That would make my ex happy. But seriously, I can't talk about an open case. You know that."

"He doesn't want you to talk. Just listen."

"What do you get out of it?"

"Ten grand, if you take the meeting, low five figures if you sign, script consultant, low six figures when the cameras roll, associate producer credit, supposed piece of the action on the back end, maybe millions, but probably not."

Sterner whistled.

"His name's Alex Forney. Say you'll meet him and I'll bring him to Hershey Medical directly from the airport Monday afternoon. They tell me they're moving you there by then. You don't have to make any decision before you talk to him. But talk to him. It's a lot of money. You should think about your future. Tell me you'll meet with him."

"Sure."

"Thank you. One other thing. They're gonna make a movie one way or another. They always do. My advice is to take the money and run and don't look back."

"Is that what you did?"

"That is exactly what I did, my friend. Did you ever see that piece of shit they made out of my case?"

"Sure. I thought Wesley Snipes was great."

"Wesley Snipes *was* great. Who he played, I have no clue. Okay. Now that that's out of the way, cop to cop, glad you're doing well. Heal quickly, comrade." He tagged the leg cast lightly with his hat, got up, replaced the chair where he found it and headed for the door. "Why do I feel like I need a shower?"

"Hey, Crash."

He turned, shoulders slumped.

Sterner held up the felt-tip pen. "Autograph my cast?"

———————

"Hey, Joe," Emily said from the doorway as Robinson passed through.

Sterner looked up and saw his ex-wife and her new boyfriend, and thought what a lovely couple they made. Emily's hands were on Becca's shoulders in front of her completing the picture of a happy family. Becca stared at him and then scrunched her face and let out a strangled shriek, ears instantly streaming down her cheeks when she realized that the black-eyed mummy in traction with the *X* taped over his nose was the only father she ever knew. She turned and buried her face in her mother's designer suit, wailing bitterly.

"It's okay, Pookie," Sterner said and reached out to her.

Becca turned back around, hesitated and then ran to hug him. "Daddy!"

Emily followed her in, with Teddy and Moira in tow.

"Jesus, Joe, they sure did a number on ya," Teddy said. "I hear you gave as good as you got, though."

"Let's not talk about that, Teddy," Emily said. "We're just glad you're back with us, safe and sound."

"Are you gonna die, Daddy?" Becca said, sniffling.

"Don't be silly, Becca," Emily said.

"Not anytime soon, Pookie," Sterner said, cavalierly waving. "This is just temporary. I'll be back to normal in a few weeks, I promise." He stroked her hair and turned to Emily, "Sorry I missed the physical. How did everything go?"

"Fine. She passed with flying colors. We've scheduled the MRI for tomorrow, but they won't know anything until Monday. But let's not talk about that. How are you feeling, really?"

"Really? I've been better."

"The story's all over the news. They're calling you a hero."

"So I gather. Truthfully, I'm just thankful to be alive."

"The reporters are now saying you were with this woman, this Hellcat person. Are you somehow involved with her, Joe? Everybody's speculating. I've been asked but haven't a clue, of course, because you never mentioned her to me."

"It's a long story, but she saved my life out there more than once," Sterner said, but did not elaborate.

"Well," Emily finally said.

"Crash Robinson," Teddy exclaimed when he saw the autograph on Joe's leg cast. "That's the guy Wesley Snipes played in that movie, right?"

"Yeah, that was him you passed on the way in."

"Listen, Joe," Teddy said. "We don't have to discuss details now."

"Teddy, please," Emily said realizing what was coming next.

"What? This may be my only chance. You know the reason I went on sabbatical was to write a screenplay about my experience in the dance world."

"Not now, Teddy," Emily scolded.

"Troupe politics…you would not believe the shit that goes on. Anyways--"

"Teddy!"

"Bottom line, I could write the screenplay for ya. That's all I'm sayin'. Whether we write it together is up to yous."

Cat was asleep in her hospital bed when the orderly came through the door and turned on the light pushing a meal cart. His shadowed hand pulled up the tablecloth covering the lower shelves and pulled something out.

Cat rolled over just in time to see Billy Three standing over her with a ten-inch meat cleaver.

Her reflexes were quick. She rolled backwards onto the floor behind the bed but saw no feet on the opposite side through the struts. No feet and no cart, either. The room was dark. The light was off. Cautiously she stood and realized she was alone in the room.

It had just been a nightmare.

Cat got the nod from the trooper stationed at the door and she entered Sterner's room after a knock.

"Hey, there," he said looking up from People Magazine. Without uttering a word she went over and hugged him. In his arms she began to tremble. "Shhhhh," Sterner said. "It's okay. It's over."

"I can't sleep," she said. "You don't know the awful things they said to me."

"They're all in jail," he said. "They can't hurt you."

"Billy's not. He said he'd hunt me down."

"Everybody is hunting *him*. You're safe here, believe me."

She took a breath. "I told the police everything that happened."

"Don't worry about it," he whispered kissing her forehead. "Don't worry about anything. It's okay." She held him tighter.

"Do you think they'll put me in jail?"

"What for?"

"Killing those men. They put a trooper outside my door."

Sterner chuckled. "He's there to protect you, not to hold you prisoner."

"I'm not under arrest?" she said, pulling away from him in surprise.

"Sweetheart, you rescued a Pennsylvania State Police detective from two murdering kidnappers and a gang of armed meth dealers. They don't arrest you for that. They pin a medal on you and throw you a parade."

_____

14.

FIVE DAYS BEFORE OPENING DAY

The man whose blackmailers called him Moneybags had just been given the results of his X-rays. He was slowly limping down the hospital corridor using a cane with the Lord's Prayer carved into its stem, contemplating his future and mulling over his options. By chance he looked up and spotted Sheriff Guise in the visitors' room holding hands with Sally True. He stopped short and stared, then quickly about-faced and hurried off in the opposite direction. He found another exit at the end of the wing and slipped out unnoticed.

At that moment Chief Taylor arrived, sauntering in with an entourage of press photographers orchestrated by his PR guy, Flanigan and the uniformed Captain Hand in tow. He was all smiles in front of the flashing cameras and onboard video lights, eager to be seen pressing the flesh with the local Sheriff, ever the politician. He explained he wanted to see his detective alone and Sheriff Guise sat back down to wait, checking his watch and making a face.

In Sterner's room, Taylor told him to mend quickly, that the State Police needed more men with cajones like his, blah, blah, blah. Any consideration of Cat True and Sterner's alleged affair was apparently put on the back burner for the time being. As the lawmen merrily signed Sterner's leg cast with the felt-tip pen, Taylor was asked about Cat by a reporter. He would only praise her for helping to rescue his detective, saying nothing more. He quickly steered the questioning away, claiming his thoughts and prayers went out to the family of the late DEA agent Arthur Samios.

Asked what was in store for Sterner, Taylor said they'd be transporting him to Hershey Medical Center as soon as the medical staff gave the okay.

After the members of the press were ushered out of the room by Taylor's PR guy, the phony smiles melted and there was a general sigh of relief.

"Any news on Morrison?" Sterner said.

Flanigan said, "Virginia State Police found an Esplanade with a chemical burn on the roof in a long-term parking lot at Reagan National. It matches Ms. True's description of Morrison's vehicle. It was rented under a phony name. The FBI is processing it. They canvassed the airline counters. Nobody recognized his photo. It's possible he took a shuttle downtown or the Metro most anywhere. If he went to Union Station and paid cash for a train ticket, who'd know? FBI and DC police are working it."

"Don't sweat it, detective," Taylor said, "we'll nail this guy sooner rather than later, I guarantee it. Not something for our hero *du jour* to worry about. Nobody kidnaps a Pennsylvania State Police detective and gets away with it. Am I right, boys?" He turned to Flanigan and Hand fishing for a collective locker room grunt of macho validation, but the men only nodded.

"We've received a trial date in Pittsburgh in three weeks. The ADA on the case didn't expect your testimony to take more than two days at the outside, including cross-examination by the defense. Oh, and Dick, our PR guy, has received several requests for interviews and book deal offers. He'll be in here later to discuss the details."

"I want protection for Ms. True until Morrison's caught," Sterner said. "He swore he'd come after her."

"That would not look too good."

"Keep her under surveillance, then."

Taylor sighed. "Do you have any idea what this 24-hour security detail is costing? It all ends when you're back in Chocolate Town."

Cat was discharged and accompanied detectives Jimenez and Richardson back to the meth lab house to answer their questions about the abduction and escape. They arranged to have her truck picked up, repaired and returned to her home later in the week. Then they presented her with her Strike Eagle compound, retrieved by one of the troopers searching the woods the previous day, and drove her home.

Sally accompanied Cat back to the hospital to visit Sterner. When Cat ushered Sally into Sterner's room, she said, "Mom, this is Joe."

"Yes, we've met," Sterner said. "How are you?"

"Oh, my," Sally said. "You look like you've been in a car wreck."

"I'd be dead if it weren't for your daughter."

"She told me you had a run-in with that Morrison boy."

"That's right," Sterner said. "He's still at large and may be a threat to you both."

"We can take care of ourselves. Vern's being very protective."

"If you see anything suspicious, don't hesitate to call the State Police."

"I see suspicious people every day," she said cheerfully.

"I think Joe means if we see Billy Three, Mom," Cat said and shrugged at Sterner.

"Are you gonna treat her right?" Sally said.

"Pardon me?"

Cat looked at the ceiling and rolled her eyes.

"She said you're her new man. You gonna treat her right?"

"That is my intention."

"Maybe we should go now, Mom."

"She needs a good man. I thought I had one once, but he turned out rotten."

"Mom," Cat said, turning three shades of pink.

"I'm sorry to hear that," Sterner said. "We're not all the same, you know."

Sally huffed.

"I'll see you tomorrow," Cat told him and escorted her mother out. A moment later, she returned, darted across the room and kissed him on the cheek.

"Be careful, okay?"

Cat nodded, smiled, pecked him on the cheek again and left.

———————

In the hospital parking lot, Cat and Sally were approached by a man who flashed a wallet ID and said he was investigating the charge that some of the Berzerkers were claiming they were in the woods looking to help not hunt Sterner and Samios. Cat corrected him. It turned out he was not a cop but a journalist for a Florida tabloid, something she would only discover much later while waiting on line at the grocery store. "Hellcat on a Rampage," screamed the headline, claiming an exclusive interview. She did not buy a copy, but the woman behind her did and asked her for her autograph. She refused.

Cat also refused numerous requests to speak to various journalists and news organizations, some offering large sums of money. She was used to turning down such offers and didn't think twice about it.

———————

"Special Agent Dooley of the Federal Bureau of Investigation, as I live and breathe," Sterner said, looking up from a crossword puzzle.

"How are you feeling, Joseph?" Dooley said. "I must say, you don't look so good."

"Like a broken mop with a hangover," Sterner said, shaking his hand.

"That's the thing about getting older," Dooley said. "Every morning you wake up hung over without benefit of knowing you had a grand time the night before."

"At least you can walk."

"You should've seen me get out of my car just now. After four hours behind the steering wheel, it takes a full minute anymore just to straighten my back. Like one of those time-lapse films on evolution. Monkey to modern man in sixty seconds."

"Care to sign my cast?" Sterner offered the pen.

"I'd be honored." He looked over the other signatures and found a space. "Second best detective, huh? I guess Flanigan didn't want to offend the other signers."

"Apparently. Though I think he was referring to himself," Sterner chuckled. "So you washed out in the Big Apple, I hear."

"Well, not entirely."

"Oh?"

"I should be telling your detective Flanigan this, since he took over the investigation, but I guess it doesn't hurt to fill you in, too."

"Fill me in on what?"

"I checked out Whipple's roommate and some of Whipple's co-workers at the restaurant where he worked and that led nowhere. Whipple's actor friends had nothing. NYPD bunko squad came up with zilch. But then over dinner with a colleague last night, I heard the story of a couple of cold case investigations on an FBI organized crime task force and it got me thinking. Have you ever heard the name Walter Fegelman?"

"Not that I recall? Why?"

"Mr. Fegelman was a longshoreman living a quiet unremarkable life in Baltimore, Maryland--no family and not many friends. He apparently spent much of his free time at the racetrack betting on horses. *And*, it would seem--for at least a couple of decades, anyway--apparently availing himself to freelance hit man-for-hire jobs. About sixteen months ago on his deathbed, he wrote two letters addressed to the Sheriff's Departments of Monmouth County, New Jersey and Rockbridge County, Virginia, detailing murders he'd committed in their jurisdictions, the names of his clients and the exact locations of the victims' graves."

"I never heard anything about this."

"It isn't common knowledge. I hadn't heard anything about it myself. New Jersey and Virginia both have ongoing investigations. But what's interesting is the skulls recovered at the gravesites had one thing in common."

"Let me guess: two low velocity .38 caliber bullet holes."

"It's inconclusive, since it's the standard MO of your garden variety mob hit, though they usually use a .22, maybe a .32, never a .38. The caliber is what makes Mr. Fegelman unique and the fact that the bullets did not exit the forehead suggests low velocity and a specially altered powder charge. Unfortunately, our Mr. Fegelman passed away before he could be interviewed. All we have then are the two letters, two sets of bones and uncorroborated identification of two clients, both mob-affiliated and deceased. It does give one pause, though, does it not?"

"It does indeed. So it's possible a third Fegelman letter arrived at the Doolittle County Sheriff's Department sixteen months ago and was somehow diverted to Ghoul Two and his pal Clay Whipple?"

"That would be my theory."

"So we're looking for somebody in the Sheriff's Department or the Court House with access to the mail."

"That would make sense."

"Call Flanigan right away."

———————

15.

THREE DAYS BEFORE OPENING DAY

"Detective," Sheriff Guise said sticking his head in the door holding a rectangle wrapped in brown paper. Sterner and Flanigan were playing cards.

"Sheriff," Sterner said. "Come on in."

The Sheriff grinned at him, then squinted with concern. "Don't you look just like something the cat dragged in? I do believe I had a pet raccoon once looked just like you around the eyes there. Herbie, we called him. Here I brought you something," he said, turned down the hallway and waved. He handed Sterner the wrapped rectangle as Suzy struggled with an enormous floral arrangement of tulips, carnations and baby's breath cascading over a green porcelain vase, so large she disappeared behind it. The ribbon banner across the front said, "Get Well Soon."

The Thanksgiving holiday had interrupted the investigation. The Sheriff's Office was officially closed Thursday, and investigators took a needed break themselves. It also gave Sterner and Cat a chance to spend time together, albeit limited mostly to his hospital room. They talked about their childhoods, their dreams, their nightmares, their few friends, music, movies, fashion, food. The two were together much of the day. A nurse helped her wheel his bed to the sunny atrium, a two-story greenhouse appendage at the southern end of the hospital building, surrounded by large curving tinted windows and with a terra cotta tile floor. It smelled like a garden, with dozens of plants and floral arrangements left behind by discharged patients. There he was surprised by Becca, who gave him a drawing she had done of Sterner in traction. She didn't scream but smiled sweetly, since she had gotten used to his strange looks and was reassured he would survive. Teddy outdid himself, having roasted a twelve-pound turkey with all the trimmings: gravy, cranberry sauce, dirty mashed potatoes, string beans with shaved almonds, bread rolls and butter. Everyone gorged themselves. Cat and Emily each tried quietly to size up the other much the way Sterner had done with Teddy. To Sterner's relief, Teddy remained stoically mum about their prospective collaboration, no doubt under threat from Emily. Sterner asked him discreetly about the indecent exposure charge and the pot bust. Teddy shrugged the first incident off to a group skinny-dip at a waterfall outside Ithaca, New York while he was visiting a girlfriend who attended Cornell. Only *he* was caught. The pot bust occurred in Prospect Park with a buddy from his old neighborhood he'd run into on a gorgeous spring day by a hothead rookie with a bad attitude. Sterner told Emily about his upcoming visit with the Hollywood producer and the supposed interest of Tom Cruise in playing Sterner's movie role. When Emily stopped laughing, she offered to look over the contract, but Sterner said he had no intention of signing it. Easy money was never easy, he said, and he didn't want to jeopardize his career or damage his reputation. When they left, Emily simply kissed Joe on the cheek and squeezed his hand to say goodbye. After visiting hours ended, the nursing staff had not enforced its rules and Cat stayed until ten o'clock. Sterner realized how comfortable he was talking to her. She seemed so uncomplicated compared to his ex. She made him feel happy, not a feeling he was used to. And then before she left, she gave Sterner one of the best kisses he'd ever experienced. And he had slept soundly for the first night in many weeks.

On Friday morning, inquiries continued. Flanigan interviewed John Whipple again by telephone and obtained all the information needed to solve the case.

"God Almighty," Sterner now said at the sight of the flowers as he fumbled unwrapping his present with just his right hand.

"Here, let me help you with that," the Sheriff said and took it back.

"Whoa," Flanigan said. "Looks like you've got a fan club, Joe."

"Compliments of the Laurel Valley Lutheran Church Auxiliary Club," Sheriff Guise said as he pulled up a chair. "Betty Nagle dropped it off this morning. She said she didn't have time to run it over, so Louella, as is typical, said we'd take care of it."

Flanigan got up to help Suzy put on the tray table at the foot of Sterner's bed as Sterner eyed the simple wood-framed oil painting handed him by the Sheriff, a wooden bowl of apples on a wooden table with Guise's signature signed in the lower right corner, minus his title. It was a little crude, but a fair specimen of good folk art by an untrained talent who nevertheless showed an eye for light and color and dimensionality.

"Very impressive, Sheriff. I really appreciate this. Thank you."

"They don't hang much art around here. Thought it might cheer you up a bit." And then he sneezed, "A-CHOO!" He took out his handkerchief and wiped his nose. "Hockadooner," he exclaimed. "Not to be outdone, Warren got Louella to start up an office collection to get you another arrangement from down the street. Bring that one in, too, wouldja, Suz?" Suzy sighed but complied, and brought in another more modest vase with mums and daffodils and a card, which Flanigan handed to Sterner. Suzy placed it on the window sill.

"Get well soon from the Doolittle County Sheriff's Office," he read. "I very much appreciate all this, Sheriff," Sterner said, admiring the gesture. "Really. Tell Louella and everybody I said thank you very much. I do hope they all come in and sign my cast."

Flannigan handed over the flair pen.

"Oh, sure thing," the Sheriff said, then leaned in and lowered his voice as he wrote his name on Sterner's knee. "By the way, I hope you don't mind my sticking the needle in, but I have to remind you from the get-go I told you about those Berzerkers, that you ought to have a look over in Burnside County."

"Yes, you did, Sheriff, and I didn't listen to you. And I was wrong, I admit it."

The Sheriff grinned, self-satisfied, and nodded his head, gloating. When he backed away from his autograph duties, Sterner noted he'd written, *Vern Guise, Sheriff, Doolittle County.* "I stopped by earlier in the week with Sally True, but I couldn't wait in line all day."

"Yes, I hear you've been spending time with Sally," Sterner said.

"And I hear you've been spending time with Cat," the Sheriff said.

"You two are dating mother and daughter?" Flanigan said.

"Well," said Sterner.

"That's what I call a small town."

Simultaneously Sterner and Guise replied, "Don't we know it."

They cackled until the Sheriff sneezed, "A-CHOO! Hockadooner," he exclaimed, then muttered, "Damned allergies."

"What does that mean, exactly?" Sterner said.

"What? Hockadooner?" He shrugged. "It's Pennsylvania Dutch. Don't think it means anything." He wiped his nose with his handkerchief.

"Oh, I'm forgetting my manners," Sterner said. "Sheriff, this is Detective Stu Flanigan. He's running the John and Jane Doe investigation now."

Flanigan reached over and shook his hand. "We met Monday. Good to see you again, Sheriff."

"And this is, uh, Suzy--?"

"Sheriff, if you'll excuse me," Suzy smiled sheepishly. "Gentlemen, I have to use the Ladies Room."

"Hell's bells, Suzy, you was just *in* the Ladies Room," the Sheriff said without turning to look at her. "What's the matter? You got a nervous stomach or something?"

"It's a feminine problem, Sheriff," Suzy said, rolling her eyes at his male stupidity. "I'm sure you understand," meaning of course she was sure he didn't.

"Oh, Christ Almighty," the Sheriff mumbled shaking his head.

"Don't think you're getting away without signing my cast," Sterner said.

She grinned and was on her way out the door when Sterner interrupted. "Before you go, Suzy," he said, "I wonder if I could just ask you a quick question."

At the door she turned, "I guess, okay," she said, eyes shifting between them.

"Deputy Kendalhart told me it was *your* idea to put up the crime scene tape at the chicken coop where Jane Doe was found. I believe I thanked you for that over the phone when we recovered the hair that tied Whipple to the scene. Do you remember that? And you shrugged it off, saying something to the effect of it being 'standard procedure.' I believe that was the phrase you used, wasn't it? 'Standard procedure?'"

"Yessir," Suzy said smiling, all but saluting.

Sheriff Guise frowned at her.

"What did you mean by that, exactly?"

"It's standard procedure to put up crime scene tape at a crime scene, isn't it?" Suzy shrugged.

"What crime would that have been?" Sterner said.

Suzy was confused. She looked at each of them before answering. Sheriff Guise stared at her. "There were bullet holes in the back of the skull, weren't there?"

"We found bullet holes, yes, but we found them *after* you told Deputy Kendalhart to put the tape up."

Suzy chuckled nervously. "Warren gets confused sometimes. I'm sure he told me--"

"Whipple was your husband's first cousin, isn't that so?" Sterner said.

Suzy began to tremble. She swallowed hard. Sheriff Guise narrowed his eyes at her. This was a set-up, she realized.

"You and your husband attended Whipple's funeral on Tuesday," Flanigan said. "There's no point in denying it. Peter Bream *is* your husband, is he not?"

Suzy held her breath. She could not will herself to move or speak.

To Sheriff Guise Flanigan said, "A forensics team found fingerprints at the Samaritan College swimming pool, inside and outside the locked door to the maintenance passageways that run under campus. Suzy's husband used those passageways as an escape route for a ransom drop Saturday night." He turned back to Suzy. "Your husband used to work in maintenance at the college, didn't he? He's been hired and fired from a lot of interesting jobs. He's worked for, uh," referring to his notes, "Nussbaum Foods, the Jefferson Funeral Home, the Highways Department--which is how he knew about the cemetery in Laurel Valley, since the quarry there is where they go for road gravel--the Samaritan Country Club, Blocher's Truckers Paradise."

"We know about the Fegelman letter, Suzy," Sterner said.

"The what?" Sheriff Guise said.

"Walter Fegelman wrote your department sixteen months ago confessing to the murders-for-hire of George Letterer and his wife, naming the man who hired him, and the location of the victims' graves."

"One of Suzy's responsibilities is to open mail, am I right, Suzy?" Flanigan said. "She intercepted the Fegelman letter and instead of passing it along to you, gave it to her husband who used it for blackmail. She's also responsible for calling us in and leaking the Jane Doe story and Cat's involvement to the press. The more publicity they could get, the more pressure there was on the Mark to pay them. Isn't that right, Mrs. Bream?"

Suzy fainted.

————————

When she was revived, Suzy was read her Miranda rights and taken into custody. She waived her right to legal representation to make a deal in exchange for leniency. She told them the whole story from the beginning, confirming what they had already surmised, how she'd opened the Fegelman letter and recognized its value. She'd smuggled it home in her handbag to show Peter, who concocted a plan to sell it to Ray Blocher, the contractor who'd built Blocher Park and Blocher's Truckers Paradise.

A retired widower, Blocher had put his son Sam in charge of the family businesses, including the Truckers Paradise, a cash bonanza where Ray had had no trouble accumulating plenty of unreported income. Peter himself had worked at the Truckers Paradise, behind the counter at the gift shop when Ray Blocher was still running it on a day-to-day basis. Whenever customers paid with a fifty or hundred dollar bill it was vouchered and collected separately from the rest of the till by Ray himself. Later, Peter knew, the vouchers were simply destroyed by the bookkeeper. Then Peter had a run-in with a nasty customer who complained to Ray and he was fired. Selling the Fegelman letter to Ray Blocher proved not only lucrative but also sweet revenge.

Peter enlisted his cousin Clay into the scheme because he needed a go-between. He was afraid Ray would recognize him or his voice. Clay had never had contact with Blocher and he no longer lived in the area. His acting and make-up skills were also a handy asset in Peter's plan.

Though the cousins were in the same class together at Samaritan High, they shared very little in common but for their love of heavy metal. Each ran with his own clique, Clay on the artistic track, hanging out with the theater and literary crowd, and Peter more down-to-earth, hanging out with the jocks and the shop guys. Clay didn't appreciate sports or understand the appeal of athletic competition, while Peter thought theater was silly and an equal waste of time. But both respected the other's differences and wished the other well after graduation.

Clay attended NYU with a theater major while Peter wasted two years at Shippensburg College, with a declared major in engineering and an undeclared minor in partying. Then, before his junior year, Peter dropped out, keeping his summer job washing dishes at the Samaritan Country Club where Suzy worked as a waitress. Clay graduated but didn't make out much better, waiting tables in Times Square, going on auditions for jobs he never got, and appearing in *avant gardé* theater pieces in the East Village no one came to see. Peter was fired from his dishwashing job for making snide comments to his supervisor, then got a job with the maintenance staff at Samaritan College. He married Suzy, bought a house they couldn't afford, then got fired by the college for borrowing cleaning supplies. He worked a string of odd jobs after that, trying in vain to keep up with the mortgage payments, stress and sleeplessness causing over-eating, adding pounds he would never shed. Neither cousin was very successful, and neither was too happy with his life.

As they grew older, Clay continued to make several trips home a year to get a good meal, do his laundry, borrow money and see his dentist, Dr. Fries, who was a lot cheaper than the dentists in the Big Apple. Their mothers, who always reassured each other it was only a matter of time before the boys found themselves, cheerfully passed along news about one to the other, while the boys only saw each other at holidays--Easter, Christmas and the Fourth of July--when one sister or the other would host the family get-togethers.

Then fortune smiled on Peter and he cast Clay in the role of a lifetime. Clay mailed the only copy they made of the Fegelman letter to Blocher with a note that said a Mr. O'Leary would telephone him on such-and-such a day. To Clay's astonishment, Blocher agreed to pay the sum of fifty thousand dollars cash for the original. Peter picked up Mr. Miles O'Leary, a rare documents dealer from New York, at the Harrisburg Train Station one September morning. It was Clay, of course, already in disguise. They drove to the meeting with Blocher on a park bench on the Great Lawn in the middle of the Samaritan College campus, chosen not accidentally on the Saturday before fall classes began, where an elderly man exchanging a carry bag for a manila envelope would go unnoticed amid a sea of bustling strangers. Everywhere around them families were helping students move into dormitories and frat houses, then touring the campus, making it easy for the two to get lost in the crowd.

After the exchange, Mr. O'Leary moved swiftly to the Student Union Building where he ran first up the stairwell, then down the hall to the far side of the building, then down another stairwell to the basement, where Peter had made sure the steel door to the maintenance tunnels was ajar. Peter had learned about the tunnels when he worked there and had made a copy of the master key which he kept after his dismissal. Prior to Clay's rendezvous with Blocher, Peter had given Clay the complete tour, scouting out the escape route with him to the pool area.

Closing the steel door behind him, Mr. O'Leary made sure he heard the lock click, navigated the corridor lined with steam pipes and electrical conduits, removing his black wig and muttonchops mustache glued to his skin. He met Peter at the door to the pool, where he emerged from the stifling tunnels as his own redheaded self again, a bit winded and dripping with sweat, but none the worse for wear. Peter put the money, the make-up, and Mr. O'Leary's clothes into a large duffel bag while Clay cleaned his face in the men's locker room mirror. Not five minutes after the trade-off, the cousins emerged from the sports complex and got back into Peter's car in the parking lot. They drove directly to the train station, Clay dividing up the cash as they went. By nightfall, Peter was back in Samaritan and Clay was halfway back to the City, both with twenty-five thousand dollars cash.

After selling the Fegelman letter to Blocher, they thought about it and decided they'd short-changed themselves. So the idea was born to blackmail Blocher for the contents of the letter. Their first overture failed, and was met with a gruff rebuke. So they thought about it, and decided to check the truthfulness of the letter first, to see if the remains were really where Fegelman said they were and had not been moved. The Fegelman letter did not identify the victims, only the client, Ray Blocher, and an explicit description of the location of the graves, beside a large boulder in a small wooded area on the Wagnold farm owned by Blocher, who lived nearby. When the two cousins verified the contents by exhuming the skeleton of Jane Doe, ignorant of her identity, they placed the bones in Roy Fries' chicken coop, figuring incorrectly that a record of the teeth would be among Old Doc Arnold's records. Then, before the first skeleton was discovered, Peter exhumed the bones of Abel Nestor and switched them with John Doe's bones, buried deeper in the same grave beneath Jane Doe, for insurance.

As investigators well knew, after the second payoff, Blocher had thugs abduct Clay. Because Blocher might recognize Peter's voice, Suzy had called him to demand Clay's release. When Blocher balked, Peter placed the second skeleton in Roy Fries' dental exam chair, reasoning that if the first teeth were not among Doc Arnold's records, certainly the second set was. Blocher then reconsidered, and agreed to pay them two hundred thousand dollars and release Clay. Only Clay was killed, so they had Blocher drop the payment himself at the college swimming pool later that same day. Suzy had recognized Morrison from the newspaper photos of him from the Hellcat case, but could not place him until she later heard his name in the APB and saw his mug shot.

The only real surprise for investigators was learning that there had been four skeletons, two separate couples, who'd been murdered and buried two different years in two separate graves adjacent to the boulder, or so the Fegelman letter had claimed.

After her confession, Flanigan obtained a warrant and sent the Harrisburg Crime Scene Unit to the grave location Suzy had identified, where they processed the disturbed soil around the large boulder in the wooded area. They also got Suzy's permission to search the Bream home, where they found the ransom money hidden in a crawl space under their house in its original travel bag. They immediately placed Peter Bream under arrest on extortion charges and lying to police investigators.

———————

16.

OPENING DAY

On Monday morning, a day Sterner would not forget for the rest of his life, either in his nightmares or awake, Cat arrived at the hospital early to help him dress. New clothes were provided by the local chapter of the Red Cross. With a borrowed pair of scissors, she cut off a pant leg and sleeve to accommodate his casts. His back was killing him from lying prone too long and he was again given inadequate over-the-counter tablets to ease the pain causing him to rethink his anti-drug stance. A nurse slowly lowered the slings of his traction and issued him new crutches, then made him get out of bed without assistance and ease himself into his new wheelchair. His leg protruded in front of him like a battering ram on an ironclad, but it at least provided a handy shelf on which to park the crutches. He was escorted by the nurse, trooper Ned Hollings and Cat to the Emergency Room exit.

As he filled out his discharge paperwork, a wounded hunter arrived hobbling with an arm around his buddy's shoulder, having accidentally shot himself in the foot with a .243 Winchester. The hunter's ruined boot and sock had been removed and the swollen foot wrapped at the scene in a white cotton towel now drenched with blood, spatter on his pants and his other muddy boot. The hunter was lucky. It was a fairly superficial wound, the high-powered round having missed any bones, but it was a bloody mess and the man was understandably upset about it.

It was shaping up to be that kind of a day. Blood was in the air.

A private EMS vehicle was waiting for Sterner. The driver identified himself and showed them his credentials. The party made introductions all around and shook hands. After the driver and attendant loaded and strapped Sterner into the back, he turned from the steering wheel and boasted, "Should make Hershey Medical within the hour."

"Change of plan," Sterner said. "We're heading to Hoover Road north of town." Sterner's tone left no room for debate.

"Says here Hershey," the guy said and held up a clipboard.

"Hoover Road. Follow that black pick-up." Sterner flashed his badge.

"You're the boss," the driver said with a shrug.

Cat led the caravan, followed by the EMS vehicle and Hollings in his cruiser bringing up the rear. She had talked over Sterner's plan with her mother the night before. Her mother was reluctant. She didn't like strangers in her home, and for all she knew Sterner was nothing but a spy sent to report on her. But Cat assured her he'd be in her bedroom most of the time, unable to move about without help. She told her mother she liked him and he liked her and things might work out between them. Sally still had reservations. Then Cat explained how she had saved his life and was therefore responsible for him. This she accepted.

A half-mile north of town, Sterner got a call on his cell. He checked Caller ID.

"Roger," he said.

"Joseph. Just thought you should know. We got an anonymous tip about Morrison. He's been spotted in a house west of Newtonville. SWAT is there. You can breathe a little easier, I think."

"Thanks for the news. But I think I'll wait for you to tell me he's in custody."

"Count on it. Take care."

"Thanks," Sterner said and punched off.

"Good news?" the attendant said.

"Maybe."

Not far ahead of Sterner's caravan was Flanigan's, with four troopers en route in a cruiser and an unmarked sedan following Doolittle County Sheriff Vernon Guise in his Explorer. They were to make an arrest. The wind was calm and the temperature back up in the fifties, unseasonable for hunting. The does would be hunkered down, reluctant to move. But the rut was in and there was no stopping the bucks from bold and reckless behavior. Distant gunshots were heard crackling across the countryside. They passed two trucks and a compact car, all with antlered, field-gutted bucks tethered to their rooftops. The great annual whitetail deer harvest had commenced throughout the state with the opening day of rifle season.

It occurred to Flanigan that they were after a trophy of their own, and intended to retrieve him in handcuffs before the morning was over.

They arrived at a horse farm on a back road between Mason's Gap and Blocher's Truckers Paradise. The modest three-story stone house stood fifty yards from the road and had to be two hundred years old, with a rear wing added later and covered in white aluminum siding. It was surrounded by a sizable yard, mature oaks and maples providing shade in summer. Beside it, white wooden fences cordoned off horse pastures, corrals and trotting tracks. Beyond them were rolling flatlands of fields, a narrow creek, clusters of trees and the low blue outline of Tunney Mountain in the distance. It was a bucolic setting, complete with white-washed barns and truck sheds, a windmill, even a grand gazebo in the backyard for summer entertaining, surrounded by manicured shrubbery, a persimmon tree, a bird bath. Spruce and white pine trees offered privacy from the road. Altogether a handsome place for a man of means to spend a working retirement.

Sheriff Guise led them to the back door entrance, where they were met by their host, the elderly Ray Blocher, a.k.a. Moneybags, dressed in a cream-colored Irish wool sweater, chinos and work boots. The Sheriff and Blocher were only casually acquainted, never friends, the Sheriff had explained to Flanigan. The Sheriff said Blocher had a reputation as a straight-shooter who drove hard bargains and was tight-fisted with his money. That was all.

"Mornin', Ray," the Sheriff said.

"Sheriff," Blocher said, and held the storm door open for the law men to enter. Blocher then led them with a bit of a limp through the modern kitchen, with its granite counter top and a high-end refrigerator and stove ensemble, into a narrow archway to the older part of the house, where a working stone fireplace warmed the living room with a gentle fire beneath a painting of a show horse from an earlier century. There Blocher introduced them to his coat-and-tie attorney, Rodney McCoy, who got up briefly to glumly shake hands and then settled back into an easy chair, where he remained the rest of the conversation as if chained there. The Sheriff knew McCoy well. His law office was a stone's throw across the street from the Court House.

After introductions, Sheriff Guise got down to business. As with Cat, the Sheriff asked to conduct the interview, and Flanigan had no problem with him doing so, thinking it would be easier for their subject to open up to someone in authority he already knew. Flanigan sat on a sofa and placed a small digital tape recorder with an omni-directional microphone squarely at the center of the coffee table. He dryly identified himself, the troopers standing behind him, the Sheriff, McCoy and Blocher. He gave the location, date, time and read aloud the case number from his notepad, a necessary formality.

"No reason to pussy-foot through the evidence, Ray," Sheriff Guise said. "We got a confession out of the blackmailer. We know about this Fegelman letter. We got forensic findings from two gravesites on the Wagnold farm next door, which you own, and they show trace remains of four bodies. If you got some kind of explanation, we're all ears. But just so we're clear, you're being taken into custody today, no matter what you say."

"May I add for the record," Flanigan piped in, "you have a right to remain silent. Anything you say can and will be held against you in a court of law."

Blocher nodded his head reverently, swallowed hard and lowered himself into a rocking chair. "I understand my rights. I'm willing to waive them," he said, and gently rocked to and fro. "First off, I want to acknowledge my late wife Peg, nothing short of a saint to put up with me all those years, and the Reverend Lance Baker for helping me make my peace today."

"This ain't no awards ceremony, Ray," the Sheriff said, smirking in Flanigan's direction. Flanigan shook his head in disapproval and motioned him to take it easy.

Blocher grimaced, grew still, then stood and began to pace before the fireplace in spite of a limp which obviously pained him. It helped him to talk it out, he said. A cuckoo clock nearby chimed ten times.

———

Dooley checked his watch as he drove along a sparsely traveled, two-lane county road three miles west of Newtonville to a dreary stretch where a dozen rundown clapboard houses clustered on either side of a small protestant church, an anonymous hamlet huddled together against the stark loneliness of the surrounding forest and barren meadows of bleached grass. He steered his unmarked sedan into the church parking lot and pulled up next to two similarly undistinguishable sedans. He stepped out onto the gray gravel with his scuffed black loafers carrying a brown paper bag and carried it up the cement walkway to the side door of the church where he entered. He found the SWAT Commander in the minister's office off the vestibule, wearing a Glock sidearm in a tactical holster strapped to his hip and a hand mic clipped to the collar of his black sweater, the cord coiling over padded shoulders into the walkie-talkie clipped to the belt on his BDUs at the base of his spine. The man was peering out the open window with powerful night vision-enabled binoculars perched on the high window sill, studying the house across the street two doors down.

It was unremarkable, built fast and cheap between world wars, a small, sad, two-story clapboard with rust-colored paint peeling off tarpaper siding, which in places had warped and peeled from rotting ply board underneath, the tar-shingled, concave roof a heavy snowfall away from collapse. Covering its outside walls were creeping vines, sucking the integrity out of the structure like vampires. There was a small cracked cement and crumbly brick front porch with rotting wooden posts supporting a crooked, dilapidated awning. The porch railing was rusted wrought iron and the cement walkway to the street was broken and uneven, its vein-like cracks filled in by weeds like the poor excuse for a yard on either side.

"Found a gas station five miles down," Dooley said and handed the SWAT guy bottled water, then pulled his coffee out.

"We're all set up," the man said, unscrewing the bottled water and taking a sip without even looking at it. "Team One, report," he keyed into his hand mic.

"*Team One,*" a voice whispered. "*In place, ready on your mark.*"

"Team Two, report."

"*Team Two,*" another voice whispered. "*In place and red-eye.*"

"Say the word," he told Dooley.

"Do it."

The Commander took in a deep breath, but instead of exhaling, squeezed the hand mic and said, "OK, send him in."

After Cat backed into her usual spot in front of the cabin next to Sally's parked Toyota, the ambulance backed in close to the front door. The driver and his attendant then helped Sterner climb into his wheelchair and backed it into the cabin breezeway while Hollings, who had parked further away, looked on. He adjusted his trooper hat and scanned the forest perimeter, thumbs hooked in his belt.

"Mom? Mom?" Cat called. "She must be around back," she explained.

Sterner nodded to Hollings. The trooper curtly nodded back and disappeared around the corner of the cabin. With a flick of his thumb he unsnapped it from the holster, but saw no immediate cause to draw his sidearm.

Sterner's cell rang. It was Emily. She was crying.

"Joe. Oh, Joe."

Sterner waved to the attendant to wait a moment. "Emily. What's wrong?"

"We're at the doctor's. The MRIs came back."

"Is it bad?"

"No. I'm sorry. No. Everything's fine. She's normal."

"Well, thank God. Why are you crying then?"

"Becca asked me the same thing. I told her I was just so relieved because I was so worried about her. And she asked me why she thought something was wrong with her. I told her it was because of the shrieking. Do you know what she said?"

"What?"

"She said she was just trying to get me to look at her. She said she wouldn't do it anymore if I asked her not to. Just like that."

"So you asked her not to?"

"I said, 'Honey, please don't shriek like that anymore,' and she said, 'Okay, mommy.'"

Sterner chuckled.

———————

After bruising his hip on the hard tile floor at the college pool a week earlier, Blocher had seen his doctor, he said, claiming to have slipped in the shower. A thorough physical examination was ordered up, including X-rays, which revealed inoperable colon cancer.

"I could just as easily deny your charges and drag this thing through court for years to come, but I don't have any years to come. I'm tired of hiding," he began, addressing Flanigan as if understanding the jurisdiction of the State Police in these matters better than the Sheriff did. "Like Walt, I want to clear the air. I want it all out in the open before I pass on, nothing weighing me down. That's all I really want. The Lord knows my sin is great and there is only one way to free myself." And then he heaved a sigh and his tone shifted. "Ever dine at the Samaritan Inn, sir?" he asked Flanigan.

"Yes," Flanigan said. "Yes, I have."

"Did you happen to notice the plaque from the original inn in the lobby?"

"'No one turned away.'"

"That's the one. 'No one turned away.'" He shook his head. "I was seven years old the first time I saw that, a dirt farmer's son out for Easter

Sunday breakfast after sunrise services." Blocher took a deep breath. "I lost nearly a million in the Depositors Trust collapse, but it wasn't the money. I'd scrimped and saved to put together that war chest as collateral for another three mil in loans to develop what was to be The Travelers Paradise, a Twentieth Century version of the Samaritan Inn. The idea came to me back in the Fifties when they built the Turnpike. Breezewood was nothing but a lifeless crossroads nobody ever heard of in those days. Offer the high-end traveler premium lodgings with a genuine European-style spa and a four-star eatery, the middle-class traveler an affordable motel with a pool and family restaurant, those on a budget a no-frills bed, head, shower and fast food. If they don't like burgers, feed em chicken. If they don't like chicken, feed em fish. If they don't like fish, feed em pancakes. I had all the ducks lined up, all my franchise contracts signed. I paid top dollar for the ideal location and was about to break ground when Depositors Trust pulled the rug out. Knocked me for one hell of a loop. Took me a decade to get back on my feet. By then Breezewood was off and running. I was too slow out of the gate and had to settle for the truckers market. The Truckers Paradise paid out better than I dared hope, but it pales in comparison to what might've been. Back when the start-up could've gone either way, by chance I ran into that son of a bitch. Virginia Beach, Virginia. August 18, 1978."

"Ray, as your attorney," McCoy said, "I advise you to say nothing more."

"Rod, I understand, but I really want to get this off my chest."

"George Letterer, you mean," the Sheriff said.

"Yes, him and that lying bitch of a wife, using phony names, claiming to be Canadian, traveling from Bermuda to visit her dying mother, or so she said. Oh, yes, we had a lovely conversation, me and my wife and son and the two of them. We were checking out as they were waiting to check in. My son made them laugh. He was a young teenager then, clowning around, all giddy and sunburned after our vacation at the beach. They didn't recognize me, but I'd met them at a picnic at Harry Rohrer's place once, acting all snooty, Philadelphia high society lowering themselves to meet and greet us hicks. 'Oh, you're from Pennsylvania,' she said. 'We hear it's beautiful, but we've never been.' Woman or no, I could've knocked that piece of trash across the lobby with one punch, it made me so mad.

"Later, driving north, something in me just snapped. It boiled up inside me black and vile and unstoppable. I can't explain it any better than that. To think that fugitive couple was laughing it up on my dime--all tropical-suntanned and bejeweled and moneyed--after robbing me of my dream and knowing all the other folks they'd hurt--relatives, friends, neighbors--who expected to retire on the savings they stole. Harry Rohrer helped me start my business fifty years ago. These people destroyed him."

"Ray, please, I really don't think--"

"Shut up, Rod. I know what I'm doing here."

"My job is to protect you from yourself, Ray."

"I don't want your protection."

"If you say so," McCoy said. "What am I here for?"

Blocher ignored him and took another deep breath. "Sure, I could've phoned the F.B.I. Had I told Peg, she would've dropped that dime, for sure. Instead I phoned Walt, my old Army buddy. Served with him in Korea. Ran into him at Pimlico one Sunday years before. We both loved the ponies. But Walt had no sense. Gambling was a sickness with him. He was in the hole to a loan shark, so I lent him a few hundred now and then. He always had gambling debts, long as I knew him. Once he was so grateful for a loan he whispered, if I ever needed anything a little unsavory done--like making someone disappear--don't hesitate to call. Of course, I laughed. I didn't take him seriously. Who would?"

"Ray, please--" McCoy said.

"I'm not going to tell you again, Rod. Do I have to fire you to shut you up? What do I have to lose here? I got the ass cancer, crying out loud. I'll be dead in six months, so what the hell difference does it make? Let me make my peace." He collected himself. "So I phoned Walt on the road about the Letterers, the whole thing. He heard how upset I was. Walt didn't hesitate. He flew into action. Delivered the bodies in the trunk of his car the next evening. I couldn't believe it. It shocked me. It really did."

McCoy clicked his tongue, heaved a sigh and slunk even lower into his chair.

"He had their suitcase with twelve grand in it. I wouldn't touch it. I told him to keep it as payment for a job well done."

"And the second couple?" the Sheriff said.

Ray Blocher looked at the Sheriff and hesitated, ran jittery fingers through his thinning hair and gulped. Again he turned to Flanigan. "Taking care of the Letterers was a public service. If the Feebies had gotten hold of em, how much jail time do you think Letterer would've served? Six years? That was McKim's sentence before the SOB chain-smoked himself into an early parole six feet under. And what about her? She was just as much a grifter as he was. She'd've gotten off scot-free, with all our money in some off-shore account waiting for them both when he got out."

"Enough about the Letterers! What about the second couple, Ray?" the Sheriff said again none too politely.

Blocher chewed his lip, reluctant to say more.

———————

As Dooley traded opera glasses for the SWAT Commander's binoculars, a green delivery truck pulled off to the side of the road in front of the house and the young, lanky, gum-chewing driver in a green uniform stepped out wearing earphones connected to what looked like an iPod in his jacket pocket. He carried a small cardboard box under one arm while punching information into a handheld computer. No sooner did he reach the cement walkway than a loud gun shot rang out sounding like a small cannon. He froze in his tracks.

"Who fired?" the Commander said. "Who fired?" He ripped the binoculars from Dooley's hands to scan the house for answers.

"*Not us,*" a voice said. "*Repeat, none of us.*"

Another gun shot rang out equally as loud as the first. The delivery man flinched but otherwise did not move.

"*Hold positions,*" the other voice said. "*Across the street, guy sighting in his deer rifle three doors down in the backyard.*"

"Should I abort?" the delivery guy whispered, frozen in place. He gulped.

A third gun shot rang out. He twitched again, held his breath.

"*Negative. Negative,*" the Commander told him. "*Proceed as instructed.*"

———————

Seeing the antlers mounted on nearly every wall inside the cabin, Sterner told Cat, "You ever run short of money, you could take those up to New York and sell them to the pharmacies in Chinatown. The Chinese grind them up and sell the powder as an aphrodisiac."

"Really?"

Sterner nodded. "Really."

They rolled Sterner into Cat's bedroom and helped him settle in bed. It was a simple room, clean, modestly adorned with stained, grooved pine walls and simple white gauze curtains framing the window. There was a closet, a chest of drawers, a mirror, a bedside table with a lamp and an alarm clock. They showed Cat how the wheelchair folded for storage and put the crutches against the wall so Sterner could reach them easily. They advised him to stay hydrated, keep a bedpan handy and bend out a wire clothes hanger to scratch pesky itches under the casts. They suggested moving a television or radio into the room and finding some good thick books and magazines. The ambulance driver had Cat sign a release form on the clipboard they'd hung off the back of the wheelchair and handed her a copy.

"Very good, then," the driver said finally. "Happy convalescing, sir." He saluted and led the nodding attendant out.

They waited for privacy. When the truck drove away, Cat said, "Are you comfortable?"

"A little warm, maybe."

"Wood stove's on the other side of the wall behind your head." She moved to open the window.

"I get a little claustrophobic sometimes."

"The other rooms aren't any bigger than this one."

"I'm fine. It's nice, really. Any regrets?"

She smiled at him and shook her head.

"Good. Me, neither," he said. "My piece?"

Cat handed him the Glock from her purse along with the box of shells.

"I got a call from Dooley. They think they found Morrison on the other side of Newtonville. We should know soon."

Cat exhaled in relief. "Does that mean you want to change your mind about this?"

"I'm happy if you are."

"Detective, I have you right where I want you," she said smiling.

He grinned back. "Is it too soon to describe my nurse fantasies to you?"

She chuckled and he slipped the Glock under his covers.

"Tell us about the second couple," the Sheriff said again. He was annoyed at being ignored and impatient for Blocher's full confession.

"I didn't know you'd be the one asking me, Sheriff," Blocher said.

"What's that got to do with anything?" the Sheriff said.

"Be a whole lot easier if it was just them."

The Sheriff stuck his thumbs in his belt and stood his ground. "This is my county. If you think you're going to kick me out of the room, it ain't gonna happen. Now you answer me. Who was the other couple?"

"Who were they?" Flanigan coached gently.

"I never wanted to harm that Whipple boy," Blocher continued, but refused to look at the Sheriff, only Flanigan. "I want that stated for the record. I know the Whipples--John and Clara--good people. Hell, I built their house, the one that boy grew up in. I felt awful when John lost his store. I told him if there was anything I could do-- But John's a proud man. I only wanted to find out who was behind the blackmail so I could put a stop to it. It wasn't the money. I had paid them once already. I just had to know who it was. It drove me crazy *not* knowing. Somebody has something over you like that and you don't even know who they are? I just couldn't stand it. But I never wanted any more killing. That was entirely on Smith and his friend, I swear."

"Smith?" the Sheriff said.

"They called themselves Smith and Jones, not that I believed it for a second. I didn't want to know their real names. Derek Pensinger used to work for me--damned good engine mechanic. I co-signed his bank loan so he could open that bike shop of his over in Newtonville. I knew he had connections with some bad people. He put me in touch with Smith. All I knew was, he was from Florida and--well--I was desperate. I wired a ten grand retainer into an off-shore account and they appeared at my door two days later. It was Smith's idea to dig up the bones and hammer them into powder. We dumped the works into Jessup's Creek where it runs between this property and the Wagnold farm down the road. Then they agreed to find out who was doing this to me. They'd take the ransom as payment, they said. That was their deal. I agreed, but when I found out who was blackmailing me, I told them to go home, that I'd handle it. So they got greedy."

"Who was the second couple, then?" the Sheriff said.

Blocher nibbled on his lips and went to the window. He stared out at the view and shook his head.

The delivery guy rang the buzzer at the front door.

Thirty long tense seconds went by, punctuated by another two rifle shots. Then the door swung open and Buster Pensinger looked out with a blank expression.

"Benjamin Pensinger?" the guy said.

After several seconds, Buster said, "They call me Buster."

The delivery guy held up the package and scanned the barcode on the label. The handheld computer beeped. Then he held out the box for Buster.

Buster looked puzzled. He could see his name and address printed out on the label with a return address: "Just Rewards International, Denver, Colorado," with a seven-digit post office box. He stared down at it, giving his visitor a chance to look over his shoulder and into the house.

"I didn't order nothin'," Buster said.

"Probably free promotional shit. Shaving cream, toothpaste, deodorant, aftershave, you know. Fill out a survey, mail it in. I just need to see some ID and get your John Hancock and it's all yours." Another gun shot rang out. The delivery guy flinched. "Jeez, a little nerve-wracking, huh?" he said over his shoulder, forcing an uncomfortable giggle.

"Opening day," Buster said with a shrug.

"No kidding. Look, you can refuse this, you don't want it."

"No, I'll take it! Gimme a second to look for my wallet," Buster said, retreating inside.

———————

Blocher had clammed up, Flanigan realized. He looked tired, stressed. Confession to murder was not an easy task for a young man in good health. It was like giving birth, and Flanigan was the midwife. The perp sometimes buckled under pressure. Blocher was not without a conscience, but ill health was taking its toll. Figuring he was already cast as the good cop, Flanigan said, "Sheriff, maybe it would be better if you *did* step outside for a few minutes and let us talk to Mr. Blocher alone." But the Sheriff would not play the game.

"Hell, no, I won't go outside," the Sheriff said.

"Pride, Sheriff, is the most overlooked of the seven deadly sins," Blocher said.

"Don't you lecture me, you self-righteous, murdering sonuvabitch," the Sheriff shouted.

"It's because I've got blood on my hands I know what I'm talking about."

"Then stop wasting time," the Sheriff said. "Ray, your Redeemer is calling upon you through me to fess up. 'Vomit forth thy sin to be forgiven,' the Good Book says. You done fine so far. We're in the home stretch. Now cross the finish line with me."

"I loved my wife very much, you understand," Blocher said in words spit fast and bitter to taste. "She gave me a son I adored. But she didn't entirely satisfy my appetites. I played around with my bookkeeper. I wasn't her only lover, so when I got her in trouble, I told her to convince the other guy it was his. He married her and things cooled between us, though she continued to work for me. She seemed happy, so I didn't interfere. The daughter was theirs. A year later, not long after the Letterers, she came to me in tears that her husband was having an affair. He was going to run off with *his* girlfriend, abandoning her with our daughter. She told me she wanted them taken out. She knew about the Letterers. I had told her. She knew about Walt. She told me if I didn't do something about her situation, she'd tell Sheriff Hetrick what she knew. I thought about making her disappear instead, but I knew how it would look and that it would come back to me and our daughter would have no mother. On the other hand, the husband and his girlfriend were about to disappear of their own accord anyway. Nobody would mourn their remains after what they were planning. It was easier to go along. So I arranged it with Walt. He didn't like it. I begged him. He finally agreed, but told me we were finished after that. He wanted nothing more to do with me. I couldn't blame him. It was because of the husband's job. Because of who he was."

The Sheriff took a step backwards, struck dumb.

McCoy closed his eyes and shook his head, but refused to interrupt.

Flanigan saw the Sheriff's paralysis, but didn't want to lose the momentum. "Names, Mr. Blocher?" he demanded.

Blocher looked over the family pictures on the fireplace mantel. "Please understand, she's the mother of my child, my only daughter," Blocher said, speaking rapidly now, seeking a small measure of absolution. "I lost Peg to pneumonia two years back. My son is taken care of. He's running the Paradise. He didn't know about those bikers selling drugs. If Sammy knew, he would've tried to stop it, and it might've gotten him hurt or worse. He has a nice family, my grandkids. A little naive but a good-hearted soul, my boy Sammy. A hard-working, God-fearing Christian. I don't know how I'm going to explain this to him." His lower lip quivered.

"Sheriff? You all right?" Flanigan said but received no response. He turned back to Blocher. "It won't be hard to find out from what you've told us already, so why not just give us a name?"

Tears now welled in Blocher's eyes. His voice cracked. "But I have to explain myself first. I never did anything for her, you see--my daughter, I mean. I turned my back on her all her life, even when she got into trouble herself."

"Sonuvabitch," the Sheriff muttered to himself.

"So who was the bookkeeper?" Flanigan said. "Sheriff?"

———————

Hollings found no one in the backyard. There was no one in the woods, either. The trees were skinny, impossible to hide behind. The brush was transparent. The only place left to check was a small stone smokehouse behind a stack of firewood. As he approached he heard a faint, rhythmic squeaking inside. He drew the Glock and then threw open the heavy wooden door, assuming a double-handed firing stance.

———————

The delivery guy waited for Buster trying hard to look bored. He pretended he was listening to an old Three Dog Night song. He hummed along, singing quietly, *"but the loneliest number is the number one,"* a code to his comrades. Had he seen two suspects, he would've sung, *"Two can be as bad as one,"* and hummed the rest.

When Buster returned, the delivery guy glanced at the picture and name on his driver's license, then handed over the computer device to sign the LCD screen with a scratch pen. After Buster scribbled his name, the package was thrust into his hands. The delivery guy offered a small wave, about-faced and headed back to his truck. Buster closed the door. Without looking back, the delivery guy jumped into the driver's seat, started the engine and floored the gas, announcing to all he was, "Clear."

"Execute. Teams one and two, go, go, go, go," the Commander said. As Dooley watched, two five-man SWAT team groups appeared out of nowhere, dressed in black combat attire with the letters "FBI" emblazoned across their chests and backs, balaclavas obscuring their faces, and simultaneously stormed the front and back doors in single file. The lead men held bullet-proof plexiglass shields and Glocks. Their back-ups were armed with pistol-grip Mossberg pump shotguns. Even from their position across the street, they could hear both doors being smashed out of their jambs with tactical entry rams, followed by a lot of angry shouting. They'd given Buster just enough time to open the package, and then charged in hard and fast. Speed, surprise and an overwhelming show of force was the SWAT formula for success.

———————

A red-faced Sheriff Vernon Guise pursed his lips, trembled and shook his head. Flanigan wondered if he was having a heart attack.

"When they told me she was the one blackmailing me, I wanted to pay. It was my way of making it up to her. I even went to see her mother about it. But she didn't know what I was talking about, poor soul. I didn't know how unstable she'd become. I'm sorry, Vern." Blocher turned to the Sheriff. "Truly, I am."

"Sheriff?"

Tears streaming down his cheeks, the Sheriff said, "Sally True."

———————

Hollings had seen plenty of dead bodies before. In Afghanistan he'd seen them nearly every day for a period of six weeks. But what he saw now froze him. The trooper blinked in horror, mouth agape, unable to breathe, paralyzed with disbelief.

The ax swung around behind him and struck him hard between his shoulder blades, severing his spinal cord and snapping his neck, the momentum knocking him bodily into the smokehouse, Glock and all.

Inside the cabin, oblivious to the violence yards away, Sterner interwove the fingers from his good hand with those of Cat's. She bent over him and kissed him tenderly. It became a more passionate kiss until Cat laughed and pulled away. "Hey, my mother's around here somewhere," she said. "This isn't the Sleep Well, you know."

"That's going to be a problem," he said arching his eyebrows.

She blushed and looked out the window. "Let me get you some water."

"Maybe she and Hollings hit it off."

Cat chuckled. "Now that would be interesting."

After stepping out of the room, Sterner craned his neck out the window, but could see only the cab of Cat's parked pick-up, nothing more. He reached under the bed sheet and checked his gun.

Cat was at the kitchen window filling a pitcher with tap water from the sink when she happened to look out and see Billy Three in the backyard kicking Holling's lifeless legs over the jamb of the smokehouse and tossing in his trooper hat after him. Then he shut the door, bloody ax in hand, spit and marched toward the cabin.

She didn't scream. She didn't run to tell Sterner. She simply set down the pitcher, turned off the water and backed away, melting into the shadows.

———————

As they jogged across the street, handguns drawn, Dooley listened to the voice announced on the Commander's hand mic, "*First floor secure, one suspect in custody.*"

A few seconds later, another voice, "*Second floor secure, empty,*" and "*Cellar secure, empty.*" Then, "*Attic secure, empty.*"

"*Target secured.*"

"Damn," the Commander said, losing power in his run and dropping his piece to his side. They were at the front walkway. He turned to Dooley. "He's not there!"

———————

Vernon Guise watched in his rearview mirror as the trooper led the handcuffed man into the back of the State Police cruiser parked behind him. McCoy was speaking rapidly to his client, who nodded wearily. Flanigan stepped into view and blocked it. When he got to the Sheriff's open window, Flanigan reached in and gently laid a hand on his shoulder.

The Sheriff said, "I won't be coming along when you arrest her."

Flanigan nodded. "No problem."

"I'm the one tipped her off that he was gonna leave em high and dry. I as much as sentenced my best friend to death. All the guilt I've felt over the years that I didn't try and stop him!" He shook his head. "And it turns out she had em both killed." He shook his head again. "I kept at her, offering to marry her, you know, if she just proceeded with the goddamned divorce. She always refused. I never could understand why. She claimed he called her now and then to say how sorry he was. She said she thought he might come to his senses and return to her one day. Nobody in a small town ever wants to snoop around a scandal like that. It's impolite. Anyone seriously looking for him would've known she was lying if they'd've just checked up. She knew it. Fear of discovery's probably what drove her so batty."

"You okay to drive, Sheriff?"

He sniffed. "I'll manage."

Flanigan walked back to the cruiser and leaned into the front passenger window to address Blocher in the back through the perforated Plexiglas partition as he was being fastened in a seat harness.

"You didn't pay off your daughter. She wasn't the one blackmailing you. It was a man who used to work for you named Peter Bream and his wife Suzy, who worked in the Sheriff's office."

"But Smith said--"

"William Morrison, the Third," he said.

"What?"

"That's the other thing. You hired the man who raped your daughter."

Blocher took it in, and then leaned his head back and closed his eyes.

Sterner's cell rang. He'd been checking his gun. He slipped it back beneath the bedspread and whipped the cell out of his breast pocket.

"Roger," he said. "Tell me the good news."

"We missed him," Dooley said. He was standing over Buster lying spread eagle on the broken, filthy linoleum floor in the kitchen, hands locked behind his head. Buster secretly grinned while over him stood a SWAT officer guarding him with a shotgun. The SWAT Commander and his men were combing the house for evidence of Morrison's past or current whereabouts but were finding nothing.

"Damn," Sterner said.

"*You back in Hershey already?*"

"No. I'm at Cat True's."

"*Since when?*"

"I know it's a long shot but Morrison may show up."

"*Oh, and you're in any shape to do anything about it?*"

"No, but as long as I'm in Doolittle County, Taylor's got a trooper assigned to protect me. That means Cat and her mother are protected, too."

"And you think that'll fly?"

"Well."

"*OH LU-CY, I'M HO-OME!*" someone said in a bad Desi Arnez impersonation. Billy Three appeared in the bedroom doorway.

"*Who the hell is that?*" Dooley said.

A bloody ax in his hands, an Uzi slung off his shoulder, the sleeves of his coveralls were pushed up to his elbows, his bare forearms and hands drenched with dried blood. He wore a bloody hunting knife on his belt in a leather sheath covered in dried blood. His clothing and face showed smears and spatter. His eyes were bloodshot, wide and wild, his pupils dilated. Seeing Sterner's dumbfounded expression, he let out a loud, maniacal howl of laughter from deep in his belly.

"Joseph? You still there? What's going on?" Dooley said.

Sterner could neither speak nor move.

"Lucy," Billy said towards the kitchen, "ju got a *staynge min* in *ju* bed. Have ju been chitting on me?"

His gaze was not just insanely hopped but truly insane, a glint of blind, murderous roid rage making his manner frenzied and mean, shot full of bloodlust, a textbook case study in cocaine and methamphetamine psychosis. He was high as a kite, but lucid enough to anticipate Sterner's next move.

"Joseph!" Dooley said. Sterner let the phone fall from his hand and slide onto the floor as he reached under the bedspread for the Glock. Billy was across the room in a flash and used the blunt end of the ax head to easily bat the gun out of Sterner's hand. It bounced off the ceiling and landed in the far corner.

Sterner made a play for the Uzi which had swung around after him as Billy followed through on his swing. But Billy quickly backed away and the SMG slipped through Sterner's fingers. Billy swung the Uzi around to his back again and then retrieved Sterner's pistol and stuck it into his belt.

"Oh, *ju gotta* do better than that, *meester*," Billy said. Billy let out another loud belly laugh. *"Bodges?"* he said, *"Bodges?* We don't need no stinkin' *bodges*." And then he clutched the ax firmly in both hands, and Sterner could see his next move would be a very ugly one indeed. Billy grinned sadistically and growled like a rabid bobcat.

Out of the corner of his eye Sterner noticed movement out the window. But when he looked he saw nothing. Until he noticed the compound bow missing from the pick-up's rear window.

Sterner's brain kick-started. "One thing always bothered me," he said with forced calm to Billy who was now raising the ax above his head. "Why kill the Whipple boy? You didn't have to do that to get the ransom."

"Why?" Billy guffawed and indulgently lowered the ax, taken in by the question. *It will not save your ass, Smokey.* "Why not? Kidnapping's a capital crime, too, you know."

"Even so, you might've snagged the cash and high-tailed it back south and nobody would've noticed. Whipple would've kept his mouth shut. But then you killed him, which ratcheted the whole business up to another level. That was an awful big risk. What was your boss thinking?"

"You think that was *his* idea?"

"It wasn't?"

"Smokey, I am self-employed."

"Then why?"

"Hell, I didn't come all the way up here from the sunshine state into this cold-ass keystone dreariness just for the money, honey. I's lookin' fer some ax-*ciones* in me oh-le' home town, *hommes*," he said with giddy delight, anticipating more juicy murder, licking his lips and raising the ax high overhead. "And ax-*ciones* is jist what I'm'a gittin'."

When he took a step forward, the arrow flew through the open window and penetrated Billy's side. He was startled and slow to react, but then moved like lightning. He discarded the ax and swung around the Uzi, instantly firing a long, loud automatic burst through the window, glass shards and ejected shells flying everywhere.

Outside Cat ducked for cover behind her mother's Toyota, pebbles of car window glass raining down over her.

Before the clip emptied, Sterner was rolling out of bed, striding awkwardly across the room like some Frankenstein monster, his left leg and arm rigid as iron encased in plaster of Paris. He swung wide with his club-like arm, catching Billy on the back of his head as he frantically changed clips. Billy backhanded Sterner like he was some annoying pest, but Sterner wasn't going to give him a chance to fire again without a fight. Sterner tackled him, knocking Billy back into the wall, shattering a straight-backed chair and pinning him, until the two slid into a heap on the floor, a flurry of punches and kicks and grunts, each desperate to gain the upper hand. Sterner used his good arm to pummel Billy's face half a dozen times in rapid right hooks, but Billy's head was like a chunk of granite mounted on a thick rubber neck that absorbed the blows like a punching bag. Billy grabbed Sterner's arm cast at the wrist, drew his knees into his own chest, found purchase on Sterner's abdomen and launched him bodily across the room where he crashed into the bed backwards, hitting his head hard against the wall and knocking him unconscious.

Silence.

Seconds passed.

Cat appeared at the window, arrow poised, her back against the outside wall, and stole a quick glance inside. The room was empty except for Sterner motionless on the floor. She did a double take, feared the worst and ran to the front door. Inside at the threshold, a hand reached out and grabbed her by the throat as she passed, slamming her head hard back against the jamb. She saw stars and fell limp.

When she awoke, Billy Three was slapping her face repeatedly in the backyard. Her hands were tied behind her back with sash. He pulled her up by the hair into a kneeling position, and then stepped out of her way, her face positioned to look past him into the smokehouse.

The severed head of Trooper Ned Hollings stared back on the earthen floor inside, the rest of his broken body jammed grotesquely into a twenty-gallon ice tub. Above him, an obese nude woman hung by her neck, her hands tied behind her back like Cat's. As the body swayed slowly back and forth, it rotated around to face them, the dead woman's eyes appearing glazed as she twisted slowly clockwise from a sash cord noose tied off to an overhead beam. A yard-long oval cavity from sternum to groin came into view, between sagging breasts and the top of her thighs, leaving the carcass empty of internal organs. No heart, no lungs, no stomach, no liver, no kidneys, no pancreas, no bladder, no intestines, no uterus, no vagina, no anus, nothing except what glistened wet and red and putrid in the tub beneath the trooper's torso. Like Mister Jeepers, Sally True had been gutted like a deer and strung up like a side of meat ready for the butcher.

Cat had not recognized her instantly. But recognition slowly worked its way into her brain that this was her mother and the horror of it could be read across her stricken face, robbing her of breath.

"Yes, yes," Billy Three was saying as he drank in her expression, relishing the depth of her shock. The arrow in his side had been extracted and he seemed now completely unfazed by the wound. Sterner's punches had marked his face, but he was unperturbed. "I want you to appreciate my little flesh sculpture. Beautiful as it is, *you* are going to be my masterpiece. Twenty years ago you humiliated me in front of the entire world. It killed my old man and turned my own mother against me. My best friends betrayed me. My neighbors shunned me. But in all that time that has passed, I've wondered just one thing, and today you're gonna help me answer the question. Is there really more than one way to skin a cat?"

One hand held her by the hair, while the other showed her his hunting knife, covered, she now knew, with her mother's blood. He held it close to her face and laughed, the realization of a long festering revenge fantasy about to come true, an echo of her own all those years ago.

Cat grew enraged as he guffawed. Her face reddened and she uttered an other-worldly growl deep in her stomach which twisted around and up into her throat, turning into an animal howl of agony and volcanic violence.

He didn't wait for it to climax and dragged her by the hair in the direction of the compost pile. "Where shall we display our work of art?"

She put her feet under her and tripped him, wriggling free, and ran. But the sash cord tying her hands dragged on the ground and all Billy Three had to do was jump on it to stop her. The rein tightened, jolting her wrists back, nearly wrenching her arms from their sockets. She shrieked, crying out from pain and futility and dropped to her knees, her shoulder muscles screaming.

"Oh, you're riled up now, aren't you, pussycat?" he said, jerking her back towards him. She fell onto her back, then rolled to her side and got to her feet to spit into his face.

"Cat fight," he called out and laughed again, assuming a boxer's stance. "You're gonna take some softening up, I see. I'm down with that."

He swung at her face. Her arms shackled behind her, she ducked, kicking him between the legs. He doubled over. She kicked him again, this time in the face, and ran.

Staggering, he shook off the blow and then dove for the rope, but it slipped through his fingers. He jumped to his feet and sprinted hard after her as she vaulted the compost pile, just missing the bear trap, and jumped feet first into a tree trunk at the edge of the woods, using her momentum to spring back, surprising him by launching head and shoulders into his chest as he chased after, knocking him back, flat onto the ground. His foot had missed the bear trap by inches without even noticing. Cat rolled off him and onto her side and saw that his head was poised near the trigger.

"Meow, meow," he chuckled at her efforts, enjoying himself, and rocked forward to a sitting position without gleaning his situation.

Cat jumped to her feet and leapt and landed, one foot on his chest, the other on his neck forcing the back of his head down onto the pressure plate. The jagged steel jaws sprang into the air, clamping shut like the mouth of a shark. He wriggled and screamed and grabbed hold of the jaws desperate to pull the trap apart. He was succeeding, too, but Cat then stomped his throat, this time crushing his esophagus and larynx and quickly backed away. He let go of the jaws, and tried to get up, rolling over onto all fours, the chain leashing him like a vicious rabid dog. He crawled toward the rock where the chain was staked and pushed it aside to free himself. She kicked him hard in the ribs where she shot him with the arrow. He grabbed for her ankle, missed, strangled, gagged, clutched at the claws again. She kicked him again in the rib wound. He fell onto his back again to face her but was losing consciousness. She stomped his throat again. The jagged steel teeth tore open the flesh over his jugular. Blood trickled as he twisted. He choked, convulsed.

Sterner awoke drowsily later that night and took his bearings in the subdued lamplight of a familiar room, but unable to move. He was back at Samaritan Hospital. His old casts with the autographs were gone, obliterated. Fresh new ones replaced them. His left leg was back in traction. He had a fresh gauze bandage around his head. His nose was healing, the swelling down, but he had reddened bruises on his chin and cheeks and a split lip where Billy had landed solid punches.

Cat looked down on him, smiling. She was wearing an identical head bandage and hospital gown.

He smiled back until the pain in his head overwhelmed him, his sedative all but worn off.

"Oh. My. God." He struggled, bringing his free hand to his head, bandages over blistered knuckles.

"Matching concussions," she smiled, pointing to her own head bandage.

"They told me you killed him."

"I don't remember."

"And Hollings?"

She nodded.

"And...." It wasn't a question.

Cat didn't respond, just smiled wanly, sad, and laid her head on his chest. He reached over and placed his hand on her scalp and gently stroked her hair above the bandage.

Behind her, Sterner noticed a familiar geriatric nurse standing next to Flanigan and Dooley. She stepped forward and took hold of Cat's shoulder. "We really need to get you back into bed, dear," she said softly. Cat smiled, sighed and straightened to look into his eyes, the nurse adding, "We're just next door, detective."

Cat smiled, nodded, bit her lip and sniffed back a tear.

"It's okay. I'm not going anywhere," he said.

She nodded, dabbed her cheek with a wrist bearing an ID bracelet. "I love you," she whispered. She took his hold of his good hand and interlaced her fingers with his.

"I love you, too," he whispered back, and squeezed.

She kissed him on the lips, smiled again, nodded to the nurse and headed for the door. "Good night," she said from the doorway.

"Good night," he answered.

Flanigan and Dooley stepped forward when they were gone.

"She really okay?" Sterner said.

"They tell me she's fine. Amnesia isn't unusual with a concussion. She may never remember what happened. Considering what that maniac did to the mother that may not be such a bad thing. She was found catatonic, sitting at the kitchen table when the first responders arrived."

Sterner considered this, then took a deep breath. "Get a confession out of Blocher?"

Flanigan patted his arm cast. "And then some. I'll brief you in the morning when you're feeling better, but for all intents and purposes, I'd say you can rest assured this case is *closed*." He nodded reassuringly, if not quite convinced himself and traded looks with Dooley. A loose end lingered and Sterner could read it in their expression.

"What?"

Dooley hesitated, pursed his lips, shook his head. "It's nothing important. It's--okay, it's Mr. Morrison's missing testicle."

Sterner furrowed his brow. "She partially castrated him when he was eighteen," Sterner shrugged. "You knew that, right?"

Again, Flanigan traded looks with Dooley.

"She finished the job," Flanigan said.

"Postmortem," Dooley added.

"Are you serious?"

"As a heart attack," Flanigan said.

Sterner thought about it, then shrugged again. "Fuck em. He *did* kill her mother."

"She was my mother, I'd've done worse than that."

"It's just that Crime Scene went over the entire property with a fine tooth comb, and we can't find it," Dooley said.

"We were wondering if you had some ideas."

"The three thousand dollar question," Sterner mused.

"Huh?"

"Somebody offered a reward twenty years ago to anyone who found Billy's severed testicle. Nobody ever collected. I really don't know. Sorry, fellas."

"She can't remember, either," Dooley offered.

"I don't suppose it really matters. Just one of those things that'll bug the shit out of me in the middle of the night."

"She could've thrown it in the woods and some critter or bird carried it off. Or maybe she flushed it down the toilet. C'mon. Who cares?"

Flanigan shrugged. "Well. Get some sleep."

"Thanks, Stu. Thanks, Roger."

"You got it, partner."

"Sleep well, Joseph."

After they left, Sterner focused his mind on ignoring his aches and pains without calling for more drugs and eventually fell back asleep. Hours later he awoke suddenly with a disturbing answer to Flanigan's riddle. Words Cat had spoken in his motel room now echoed inside his head, words of little meaning then. He wondered would it change his feelings for her. Would it change any plans they might make together? What did it mean? Would he love her any less?

I hunt what I eat, she had said. *I eat what I kill.*

And coming soon:

JURY JACKER

A Joe Sterner Mystery